Praise for #1 *New York Times* bestselling author

NORA ROBERTS

"Her stories have fueled the dreams
of twenty-five million readers."
—*Entertainment Weekly*

"A superb author...Ms. Roberts is an enormously gifted
writer whose incredible range and intensity
guarantee the very best of reading."
—*Rave Reviews*

"Roberts's style has a fresh, contemporary snap."
—*Kirkus Reviews*

"Nora Roberts is among the best."
—*The Washington Post Book World*

"When Roberts puts her expert fingers on the pulse
of romance, legions of fans feel the heartbeat."
—*Publishers Weekly*

"With clear-eyed, concise vision and a sure pen, Roberts
nails her characters and settings with awesome precision,
drawing readers into a vividly rendered world of family-
centered warmth and unquestionable magic."
—*Library Journal*

Dear Reader,

It can be argued that there are no second chances in show business, but as these two classic stories by bestselling author Nora Roberts prove, second chances can and do exist, both in Hollywood and in love.

In *Once More with Feeling*, it's been five years since composer Brandon Carstairs left Raven Williams without a word. Now he wants the talented singer back—but only to work with him on a project. Despite the pain he caused in her life, they have a history of making beautiful music together, and when passions reignite, Raven is certain they can finally find a tune that will stand the test of time.

In *Dual Image*, Ariel Kirkwood is a thriving actress playing the role of a lifetime, and Booth DeWitt is the man she's falling in love with. But the sexy screenwriter is doing everything in his power to fight his feelings for the captivating starlet—even though all he really wants is to be with her.

We hope these two stories will serve as a reminder that while sometimes we take a chance on love and lose, love can come around again, and that's when we need to grab hold and never let go.

The Editors

Silhouette Books

NORA ROBERTS

Play It Again

Silhouette Books

Published by Silhouette Books

America's Publisher of Contemporary Romance

SILHOUETTE BOOKS

PLAY IT AGAIN

ISBN-13: 978-0-373-28181-7

Recycling programs for this product may not exist in your area.

Copyright © 2014 by Harlequin Books S.A.

The publisher acknowledges the copyright holder of the individual works as follows:

ONCE MORE WITH FEELING
Copyright © 1983 by Nora Roberts

DUAL IMAGE
Copyright © 1985 by Nora Roberts

This edition published by arrangement with Harlequin Books S.A.

For questions and comments about the quality of this book, please contact us at CustomerService@Harlequin.com.

Visit Silhouette Books at www.Harlequin.com

Printed in U.S.A.

CONTENTS

ONCE MORE
WITH FEELING

To Ran,
for all the songs yet unwritten,
for all the songs yet unsung.

Chapter 1

He stood out of view as he watched her. His first thought was how little she had changed in five years. Time, it seemed, hadn't rushed or dragged but had merely hung suspended.

Raven Williams was a small, slender woman who moved quickly, with a thin, underlying nervousness that was unaccountably appealing. She was tanned deep gold from the California sun, but at twenty-five her skin was as smooth and dewy soft as a child's. She pampered it when she remembered and ignored it when she forgot. It never seemed to make any difference. Her long hair was thick and straight and true black. She wore it simply, parted in the center. The ends brushed her hips and it swirled and floated as she walked.

Her face was pixielike, with its cheekbones well-defined and the chin slightly pointed. Her mouth smiled easily, but her eyes reflected her emotions. They were smoky gray and round. Whatever Raven felt would be reflected there. She had an overwhelming need to love and be loved. Her own need was one of the reasons for her tremendous success. The other was her voice—the rich, dark, velvet voice that had catapulted her to fame.

Raven always felt a little strange in a recording studio: insulated, sealed off from the rest of the world by the glass and the soundproofing. It had been more than six years since she had cut her first record, but she was still never completely comfortable in a studio. Raven was made for the stage, for the live audience that pumped the blood and heat into the music. She considered the studio too tame, too mechanical. When she worked in the studio, as she did now, she thought of it exclusively as a job. And she worked hard.

The recording session was going well. Raven listened to a playback with a single-mindedness that blocked out her surroundings. There was only the music. It was good, she decided, but it could be better. She'd missed something in the last song, left something out. Without knowing precisely what it was, Raven was certain she could find it. She signaled the engineers to stop the playback.

"Marc?"

A sandy-haired man with the solid frame of a lightweight wrestler entered the booth. "Problem?" he said simply, touching her shoulder.

"The last number, it's a little…" Raven searched for the word. "Empty," she decided at length. "What do you think?" She respected Marc Ridgely as a musician and depended on him as a friend. He was a man of few words who had a passion for old westerns and

Jordan almonds. He was also one of the finest guitarists in the country.

Marc reached up to stroke his beard, a gesture, Raven had always thought, that took the place of several sentences. "Do it again," he advised. "The instrumental's fine."

She laughed, producing a sound as warm and rich as her singing voice. "Cruel but true," she murmured, slipping the headset back on. She went back to the microphone. "Another vocal on 'Love and Lose,' please," she instructed the engineers. "I have it on the best authority that it's the singer, not the musicians." She saw Marc grin before she turned to the mike. Then the music washed over her.

Raven closed her eyes and poured herself into the song. It was a slow, aching ballad suited to the smoky depths of her voice. The lyrics were hers, ones she had written long before. It had only been recently that she had felt strong enough to sing them publicly. There was only the music in her head now, an arrangement of notes she herself had produced. And as she added her voice, she knew that what had been missing before had been her emotions. She had restricted them on the other recordings, afraid to risk them. Now she let them out. Her voice flowed with them.

An ache passed through her, a shadow of a pain buried for years. She sang as though the words would bring her relief. The hurt was there, still with her when the song was finished.

For a moment there was silence, but Raven was too dazed to note the admiration of her colleagues. She pulled off the headset, suddenly sharply conscious of its weight.

"Okay?" Marc entered the booth and slipped his arm around her. He felt her tremble lightly.

"Yes." Raven pressed her fingers to her temple a moment and gave a surprised laugh. "Yes, of course. I got a bit wrapped up in that one."

He tilted her face to his, and in a rare show of public affection for a shy man, kissed her. "You were fantastic."

Her eyes warmed, and the tears that had threatened were banished. "I needed that."

"The kiss or the compliment?"

"Both." She laughed and tossed her hair behind her back. "Stars need constant admiration, you know."

"Where's the star?" a backup vocalist wanted to know.

Raven tried for a haughty look as she glanced over. "You," she said ominously, "can be replaced." The vocalist grinned in return, too used to Raven's lack of pretentions to be intimidated.

"Who'd carry you through the session?"

Raven turned to Marc. "Take that one out and shoot him," she requested mildly, then looked up at the booth. "That's a wrap," she called out before her eyes locked on the man now standing in full view behind the glass.

The blood drained from her face. The remnants of emotion from the song surged back in full force. She nearly swayed from the power of it. "Brandon." It was a thought to be spoken aloud but only in a whisper. It was a dream she thought had finally run its course. Then his eyes were on hers, and Raven knew it was real. He'd come back.

Years of performing had taught her to act. It was always an effort for her to slip a mask into place, but by the time Brand Carstairs had come down from the booth, Raven wore a professionally untroubled face. She'd deal with the storm inside later.

"Brandon, it's wonderful to see you again." She held out both hands and tilted her face up to his for the expected, meaningless kiss of strangers who happen to be in the same business.

Her composure startled him. He'd seen her pale, seen the shock in her eyes. Now she wore a façade she'd never had before. It was slick, bright and practiced. Brand realized he'd been wrong; she *had* changed.

"Raven." He kissed her lightly and took both her hands. "You're more beautiful than anyone has a right to be." There was the lightest touch of brogue in his speech, a mist of Ireland over the more formal British. Raven allowed herself a moment to look at him, really look at him.

He was tall and now, as always, seemed a bit too thin. His hair was as dark as her own but waved where hers was needle straight. It was thick and full over his ears and down to the collar of his shirt. His face hadn't changed; it was still the same face that drove girls and women to scream and swoon at his concerts. It was rawboned and tanned, more intriguing than handsome, as the features were not altogether even. There was something of the dreamer there, from his mother's Irish half. Perhaps that was what drew women to him, though they were just as fascinated by the occasional British reserve. And the eyes. Even now Raven felt the pull of his large, heavy-lidded aquamarine eyes. They were unsettling eyes for as easygoing a man as Brand Carstairs. The blue and green seemed constantly at odds. But it was the charm he wore so easily that tilted the scales,

Raven realized. Charm and blatant sex appeal were an irresistible combination.

"You haven't changed, have you, Brandon?" The question was quiet, the first and only sign of Raven's distress.

"Funny." He smiled, not the quick, flashing grin he was capable of, but a slow, considering smile. "I thought the same of you when I first saw you. I don't suppose it's true of either of us."

"No." God, how she wished he would release her hands. "What brings you to L.A., Brandon?"

"Business, love," he answered carelessly, though his eyes were taking in every inch of her face. "And, of course, the chance to see you again."

"Of course." Her voice was coldly polite, and the smile never reached her eyes.

The sarcasm surprised him. The Raven he remembered hadn't known the meaning of the word. She saw his brow lift into consideration. "I do want to see you, Raven," Brand told her with his sudden, disarming sincerity. "Very much. Can we have dinner?"

Her pulse had accelerated at his change of tone. Just reflex, just an old habit, she told herself and struggled to keep her hands passive in his. "I'm sorry, Brandon," she answered with perfect calm. "I'm booked." Her eyes slipped past him in search of Marc, whose head was bent over his guitar as he jammed with another musician. Raven could have sworn with frustration. Brand followed the direction of her gaze. Briefly his eyes narrowed.

"Tomorrow, then," he said. His tone was still light and casual. "I want to talk to you." He smiled as to an old friend. "I'll just drop by the house awhile."

"Brandon," Raven began and tugged on her hands.

"You still have Julie, don't you?" Brand smiled and held on to her hands, unaware of—or ignoring—her resistance.

"Yes, I..."

"I'd like to see her again. I'll come by around four. I know the way." He grinned, then kissed her again, a quick, friendly brushing of lips before he released her hands, turned and walked away.

"Yes," she murmured to herself. "You know the way."

An hour later Raven drove through the electric gates that led to her house. The one thing she hadn't allowed Julie or her agent to thrust on her was a chauffeur. Raven enjoyed driving, having control of the low, sleek foreign car and indulging from time to time in an excess of speed. She claimed it cleared her head. It obviously hadn't done the job, she thought as she pulled up in front of the house with a short, peevish squeal of the brakes. Distracted, she left her purse sitting on the seat beside her as she sprang from the car and jogged up the three stone steps that led to the front door. It was locked. Her frustration only mounted when she was forced to go back and rip the keys from the ignition.

Slamming into the house, Raven went directly to the music room. She flung herself down on the silk-covered Victorian sofa and stared straight ahead without seeing anything. A gleaming mahogany grand piano dominated the room. It was played often and at odd hours. There were Tiffany lamps and Persian rugs and a dime-store flowerpot with a struggling African violet. An old, scarred music cabinet was filled to overflowing. Sheet music spilled onto the floor. A priceless Fabergé box sat next to the brass unicorn she had found in a thrift shop and had fallen in love with. One wall was crowded with awards: Grammys, gold and platinum records, plaques and statues and the keys to a few cities. On another was the framed sheet music from the first song she had written and a breathtaking Picasso. The sofa on which she sat had a bad spring.

It was a strange hodgepodge of cultures and tastes and uniquely Raven's own. She would have thought *eclectic* a pretentious word. She had allowed Julie her exacting taste everywhere else in the house, but here she had expressed herself. Raven needed the room the same way she needed to drive her own car. It kept her sane and helped her remember exactly who Raven Williams was. But the room, like the drive, hadn't calmed her nerves. She walked to the piano.

She pounded out Mozart fiercely. Like her eyes, her music reflected her moods. Now it was tormented, volatile. Even when she'd finished, anger seemed to hover in the air.

"Well, I see you're home." Julie's voice, mild and unruffled, came from the doorway. Julie walked into the room as she had walked into Raven's life: poised and confident. When Raven had met her nearly six years before, Julie had been rich and bored, a party-goer born into old money. Their relationship had given them both something of importance: friendship and a dual dependence. Julie handled the myriad details attached to Raven's career. Raven gave Julie a purpose that the glittery world of wealth had lacked.

"Didn't the recording go well?" Julie was tall and

blond, with an elegant body and that exquisitely casual California chic.

Raven lifted her head, and the smile fled from Julie's face. It had been a long time since she'd seen that helpless, ravaged look. "What happened?"

Raven let out a long breath. "He's back."

"Where did you see him?" There was no need for Julie to ask for names. In all the years of their association only two things had had the power to put that look on Raven's face. One of them was a man.

"At the studio." Raven combed her fingers through her hair. "He was up in the booth. I don't know how long he'd been there before I saw him."

Julie pursed her lightly tinted lips. "I wonder what Brand Carstairs is doing in California."

"I don't know." Raven shook her head. "He said business. Maybe he's going to tour again." In an effort to release the tension, she rubbed her hand over the back of her neck. "He's coming here tomorrow."

Julie's brows rose. "I see."

"Don't turn secretary on me, Julie," Raven pleaded. She shut her eyes. "Help me."

"Do you want to see him?" The question was practical. Julie, Raven knew, was practical. She was organized, logical and a stickler for details—all the things Raven wasn't. They needed each other.

"No," Raven began almost fiercely. "Yes…" She swore then and pressed both hands to her temples. "I don't know." Now her tone was quiet and weary. "You know what he's like, Julie. Oh, God, I thought it was over. I thought it was finished!"

With something like a moan, she jumped from the stool to pace around the room. She didn't look like a star in jeans and a simple linen blouse. Her closet held everything from bib overalls to sables. The sables were for the performer; the overalls were for her.

"I'd buried all the hurts. I was so sure." Her voice was low and a little desperate. It was still impossible for her to believe that she had remained this vulnerable after five years. She had only to see him again, and she felt it once more. "I knew sooner or later that I'd run into him somewhere." She ran her fingers through her hair as she roamed the room. "I think I'd always pictured it would be in Europe—London—probably at a party or a benefit. I'd have expected him there; maybe that would have been easier. But today I just looked up and there he was. It all came back. I didn't have any time to stop it. I'd been singing that damn song that I'd written right after he'd left." Raven laughed and shook her head. "Isn't that wild?" She took a deep breath and repeated softly, wonderingly, "Isn't that wild?"

The room was silent for nearly a full minute before Julie spoke. "What are you going to do?"

"Do?" Raven spun back to her. Her hair flew out to follow the sudden movement. "I'm not going to *do* anything. I'm not a child looking for happily-ever-after anymore." Her eyes were still dark with emotion, but her voice had grown gradually steadier. "I was barely twenty when I met Brandon, and I was blindly in love with his talent. He was kind to me at a time when I badly needed kindness. I was overwhelmed by him and with my own success."

She lifted a hand to her hair and carefully pushed it behind her shoulders. "I couldn't cope with what he wanted from me. I wasn't ready for a physical relationship." She walked to the brass unicorn and ran a fingertip down its withers. "So he left," she said softly. "And I was hurt. All I could see—maybe all I wanted to see—was that he didn't understand, didn't care enough to want to know why I said no. But that was unrealistic." She turned to Julie then with a frustrated sigh. "Why don't you say something?"

"You're doing fine without me."

"All right, then." Raven thrust her hands in her pockets and stalked to the window. "One of the things I've learned is that if you don't want to get hurt, you don't get too close. You're the only person I've never applied that rule to, and you're the only one who hasn't let me down." She took a deep breath.

"I was infatuated with Brandon years ago. Perhaps it was a kind of love, but a girl's love, easily brushed aside. It was a shock seeing him today, especially right after I finished that song. The coincidence was…" Raven pushed the feelings away and turned back from the window. "Brandon will come over tomorrow, and he'll say whatever it is that he has to say, then he'll go. That'll be the end of it."

Julie studied Raven's face. "Will it?"

"Oh, yes." Raven smiled. She was a bit weary after the emotional outburst but more confident. She had regained her control. "I like my life just as it is, Julie. He's not going to change it. No one is, not this time."

Chapter 2

Raven had dressed carefully, telling herself it was because of the fittings she had scheduled and the luncheon meeting with her agent. She knew it was a lie, but the smart, sophisticated clothes made her feel confident. Who could feel vulnerable dressed in a St. Laurent?

Her coat was white silk and full cut with batwing sleeves that made it seem almost like a cape. She wore it over matching pants with an orchid cowlneck blouse and a thick, gold belt. With the flat-brimmed hat and the carefully selected earrings, she felt invulnerable. You've come a long way, she had thought as she had studied herself in the bedroom mirror.

Now, standing in Wayne Metcalf's elaborate fitting room, she thought the same thing again—about both of them. Wayne and Raven had started the rise to fame together, she scratching out a living singing in seamy clubs and smoky piano bars and he waiting tables and sketching designs no one had the time to look at. But Raven had looked and admired and remembered.

Wayne had just begun to eke out a living in his trade when plans had begun for Raven's first concert tour. The first professional decision she made without advice was the choice of her costume designer. She had never regretted it. Like Julie, Wayne was a friend close enough to know something about Raven's early personal life. And like Julie, he was fiercely, unquestionably loyal.

Raven wandered around the room, a much plusher room, she mused, than the first offices of Metcalf Designs. There'd been no carpet on that floor, no signed lithographs on laquered walls, no panoramic view of Beverly Hills. It had been a cramped, airless little room above a Greek restaurant. Raven could still remember the strange, heavy aromas that would seep through the walls. She could still hear the exotic music that had vibrated through the bare wood floor.

Raven's star had not risen with that first concert tour, it had rocketed. The initial taste of fame had been so heady and so quick, she had hardly had the time to savor it all: tours, rehearsals, hotel rooms, reporters, mobs of fans, unbelievable amounts of money and impossible demands. She had loved it, although the traveling had sometimes left her weak and disoriented and the fans could be as frightening as they were wonderful. Still she had loved it.

Wayne, deluged with offers after the publicity of that first tour, had soon moved out of the one-room office above the *moussaka* and *souvlaki*. He'd been Raven's designer for six years, and although he now had a large staff and a huge workload, he still saw to every detail of her designs himself.

While she waited for him, Raven wandered to the bar and poured herself a ginger ale. Through all the years of luncheon meetings, elegant brunches and recording sessions, she had never taken more than an occasional drink. In this respect, at least, she would control her life.

The past, she mused, was never very far away, at least not while she still had to worry about her mother. Raven shut her eyes and wished that she could shut off her thoughts as easily. How long had it been that she had lived with that constant anxiety? She could never remember a life without it. She had been very young when she had first discovered that her mother wasn't like other mothers. Even as a little girl, she had hated the oddly sweet smell of the liquor on her mother's breath that no mints could disguise, and she had dreaded the flushed face, the first slurred, affectionate, then angry tones that had drawn mocking stares or sympathetic glances from friends and neighbors.

Raven pressed her fingers against her brow. So many years. So much waste. And now her mother had disappeared again. Where was she? In what sordid hotel room had she holed herself up in to drink away what was left of her life? Raven made a determined effort to push her mother out of her mind, but the terrible images, the frightful scenes, played on in her mind.

It's my life! I have to get on with it, Raven told herself, but she could feel the bitter taste of sorrow and guilt rise in her throat. She started when the door across swung open and Wayne walked in.

He leaned against the knob. "Beautiful!" he said admiringly, surveying her. "Did you wear that for me?"

She made a sound that was somewhere between a laugh and a sob as she moved across the room to hug him. "Of course. Bless you!"

"If you were going to dress up for me, you might at least have worn something of mine," he complained but returned the embrace. He was tall, a thin reed of a man who had to bend over to give her the quick kiss. Not yet thirty, he had a scholarly attractive face with hair and eyes the same rich shade of brown. A small white scar marred his left eyebrow and gave him, he preferred to think, a rakish profile.

"Jealous?" Raven grinned and drew away from him. "I thought you were too big for that."

"You're never too big for that." He released her, then made his way across to the bar. "Well, at least take off your hat and coat."

Raven obliged, tossing them aside with a carelessness that made Wayne wince. He gazed at her for a long moment as he poured out a Perrier. She grinned again and did a slow model's turn. "How am I holding up?" she demanded.

"I should have seduced you when you were eighteen." He sighed and drank the sparkling water. "Then I wouldn't be constantly regretting that you slipped through my fingers."

She came back for her ginger ale. "You had your chance, fella."

"I was too exhausted in those days." He lifted his scarred brow in a practiced gesture that always amused her. "I get more rest now."

"Too late," she told him and touched her glass to his. "And you're much too busy with the model-of-the-week contest."

"I only date all those skinny girls for the publicity."
He reached for a cigarette and lit it elegantly. "I'm basically a very retiring man."

"The brilliance of the pun I could make is terrifying, but I'll pass."

"Wise," he concluded, then blew out a delicate trail of smoke. "I hear Brand Carstairs is in town."

Raven's smile fled, then returned. "He never could keep a low profile."

"Are you okay?"

She shrugged her shoulders. "A minute ago I was beautiful, now you have to ask if I'm okay?"

"Raven." Wayne laid a hand on top of hers. "You folded up when he left. I was there, remember?"

"Of course I remember." The teasing note left her voice. "You were very good to me, Wayne. I don't think I would have made it without you and Julie."

"That's not what I'm talking about, Raven. I want to know how you feel now." He turned her hand over and laced his fingers through hers. "I could renew my offer to go try to break all his bones, if you like."

Touched and amused, she laughed. "I'm sure you're a real killer, Wayne, but it isn't necessary." The straightening of her shoulders was unconscious, a gesture of pride that made Wayne smile. "I'm not going to fold this time."

"Are you still in love with him?"

She hadn't expected such a direct question. Dropping her gaze, she took a moment to answer. "A better question is, Did I ever love him?"

"We both already know the answer to that one," Wayne countered. He took her hand when she would have turned away. "We've been friends a long time. What happens to you matters to me."

"Nothing's going to happen to me." Her eyes were back on his, and she smiled. "Absolutely nothing. Brandon is the past. Who knows better than I that you can't run away from the past, and who knows better how to cope with it?" She squeezed his hand. "Come on, show me the costumes that are going to make me look sensational."

After a quick, final glance at her face, Wayne walked over to a gleaming Chippendale table and pushed the button on an intercom. "Bring in Ms. Williams's designs."

Raven had approved the sketches, of course, and the fabrics, but still the completed designs took her by surprise. They had been created for the spotlights. She knew she'd sparkle on stage. It felt odd wearing blood red and silver sequins in Wayne's brightly lit, elegant room with mirrors tossing her image back at her from all angles. But then, she remembered, it was an odd business.

Raven stared at the woman in the mirrors and listened with half an ear to Wayne's mumbling as he tucked and adjusted. Her mind could not help but wander. Six years before, she'd been a terrified kid with an album shooting off the top of the charts and a whirlwind concert tour to face. It had all happened so fast: the typical overnight success—not counting the years she had struggled in smoke-choked dives. Still, she'd been young to make a name for herself and determined to prove she wasn't a one-shot fluke. The romance with Brand Carstairs, while she had still been fresh, hot news, hadn't hurt her career. For a brief time it had made her the crown princess of popular music. For more than six months their faces appeared on every magazine cover, dominating the newsstands. They'd laughed about it, Raven remembered, laughed at the silly, predictable headlines: "Raven and Brand Plan Love Nest"; "Williams and Carstairs Make Their Own Music."

Brand had complained about his billing. They had ignored the constant flare and flash of cameras because they had been happy and saw little else but each other. Then, when he had gone, the pictures and headlines had continued for a long time—the cold, cruel words that flashed the intimacies of private hurts for the public eye. Raven no longer looked at them.

Over the months and years, she had grown from the crown princess to a respected performer and celebrity in her own right. That's what's important, she reminded herself. Her career, her life. She'd learned about priorities the hard way.

Raven slipped into the glistening black jumpsuit and found it fit like a second skin. Even her quiet breathing sent sequins flashing. Light streaked out from it at the slightest movement. It was, she decided after a critical survey, blisteringly sexy.

"I'd better not gain a quarter of an ounce before the tour," she remarked, turning to view her slim, sleek profile. Thoughtfully, she gathered her hair in her hand and tossed it behind her back. "Wayne…" He was kneeling at her feet, adjusting the hem. His answer was a grunt. "Wayne, I don't know if I have the nerve to wear this thing."

"This thing," he said mildly as he rose to pluck at the sleeve, "is fantastic."

"No artistic snub intended," she returned and smiled

as he stepped back to survey her up and down in his concentrated, professional gaze. "But it's a bit…" She glanced at herself again. "Basic, isn't it?"

"You've got a nice little body, Raven." Wayne examined his creation from the rear. "Not all my clients could wear this without a bit of help here and there. Okay, take it off. It's perfect just as it is."

"I always feel like I've been to the doctor when I've finished here," she commented as she slipped back into her white slacks and orchid blouse. "Who knows more about our bodies' secrets than our dressmakers?"

"Who else knows more about *your* secrets, darling?" he corrected absently as he made notes on each one of the costumes. "Women tend to get chatty when they're half-dressed."

"Oh, what lovely gossip do you know?" Fastening her belt, Raven walked to him, then leaned companionably on his shoulder. "Tell me something wonderfully indiscreet and shocking, Wayne."

"Babs Curtin has a new lover," he murmured, still intent on his notes.

"I said shocking," Raven complained. "Not predictable."

"I've sworn an oath of secrecy, written in dressmaker's chalk."

"I'm very disappointed in you." Raven left his side to fetch her coat and hat. "I was certain you had feet of clay."

"Lauren Chase just signed to do the lead in *Fantasy*."

Raven stopped on her way to the door and whirled. "What?" She dashed back across the room and yanked the notebook from Wayne's hand.

"Somehow I thought that would get your attention," Wayne observed dryly.

"When? Oh, Wayne," she went on before he could answer. "I'd give several years of my young life for a chance to write that score. Lauren Chase...oh, yes, she's so right for it. Who's doing the score, Wayne?" Raven gripped his shoulders and closed her eyes. "Go ahead, tell me, I can take it."

"She doesn't know. You're cutting off the circulation, Raven," he added, disengaging her hands.

"Doesn't know!" she groaned, crushing the hat down on her head in a way that made Wayne swear and adjust it himself. "That's worse, a thousand times worse! Some faceless, nameless songwriter who couldn't possibly know what's right for that fabulous screenplay is even now sitting at a piano making unforgivable mistakes."

"There's always the remote possibility that whoever's writing it has talent," he suggested and earned a lethal glare.

"Whose side are you on?" she demanded and flung the coat around her shoulders.

He grinned, grabbed her cheeks and gave her a re-sounding kiss. "Go home and stomp your feet, darling. You'll feel better."

She struggled not to smile. "I'm going next door and buy a Florence DeMille," she threatened him with the name of a leading competitor.

"I'll forgive you that statement," Wayne said with a hefty sigh. "Because along with my feet of clay I've a heart of gold."

She laughed and left him with her rack of costumes and his notebook.

* * *

The house was quiet when Raven returned. The faint scent of lemon oil and pine told her that the house had just been cleaned. As a matter of habit, she peeked into her music room and was satisfied that nothing there had been disturbed. She liked her disorganization just as it was. With the idle thought of making coffee, Raven wandered toward the kitchen.

She had bought the house for its size and rambling openness. It was the antithesis of the small, claustrophobic rooms she had grown up in. And it smelled clean, she decided. Not antiseptic; she would have hated that, but there was no lingering scent of stale cigarettes, no sickly sweet odor of yesterday's bottle. It was her house, as her life was hers. She'd bought them both with her voice.

Raven twirled once around the room, pleased with herself for no specific reason. I'm happy, she thought, just happy to be alive.

Grabbing a rose from a china vase, she began to sing as she walked down the hall. It was the sight of Julie's long, narrow bare feet propped up on the desk in the library that stopped her.

Raven hesitated, seeing Julie was on the phone, but was quickly gestured inside.

"I'm sorry, Mr. Cummings, but Ms. Williams has a strict policy against endorsements. Yes, I'm sure it's a marvelous product." Julie lifted her eyes from her pink-tinted toenails and met Raven's amused grin. She rolled her eyes to the ceiling, and Raven settled cross-legged in an overstuffed leather chair. The library, with its warm, mahogany paneling and stately furnishings, was Julie's domain. And, Raven thought, snuggling down more comfortably, it suited her.

"Of course, I'll see she gets your offer, but I warn you, Ms. Williams takes a firm stand on this." With one last exasperated glance at the ceiling, Julie hung up. "If you didn't insist on being nice to everybody who calls you, I could have thought of a few different words for that one," Julie snapped.

"Trouble?" Raven asked, sniffing her rose and smiling.

"Get smart and I'll tell them you'll be thrilled to endorse his Earth Bubble Shampoo." She laced her fingers behind her head as she made the threat.

"Mercy," Raven pleaded, then kicked off her elegant, orchid-toned shoes. "You look tired," she said, watching Julie stretch her back muscles. "Been busy?"

"Just last-minute nonsense to clear things for the tour." A shrug dismissed the complications she had handled. "I never did ask you how the recording went. It's finished, isn't it?"

"Yeah." Raven took a deep breath and twirled her rose by the stem. "It went perfectly. I haven't been happier with a session since the first one. Something just clicked."

"You worked hard enough on the material," Julie remarked, thinking of the endless nights Raven had spent writing and arranging.

"Sometimes I still can't believe it." She spoke softly, the words hardly more than thoughts. "I listen to a playback, and it's all there, the strings, the brass, the rhythm and backups, and I can't believe it's me. I've been so incredibly lucky."

"Talented," Julie corrected.

"Lots of people have talent," Raven reminded her. "But they're not sitting here. They're still in some dreary piano bar, waiting. Without luck, they're never going to be anywhere else."

"There are also things like drive, perseverance, guts." Raven's persistent lack of self-confidence infuriated Julie. She'd been with her almost from the beginning of Raven's start in California six years before. She'd seen the struggles and the disappointments. She knew about the fears, insecurities and work behind the glamour. There was nothing about Raven Williams that Julie didn't know.

The phone interrupted her thoughts on a lecture on self-worth. "It's your private line," she said as she pressed the button. "Hello." Raven tensed but relaxed when she saw Julie smile. "Hi, Henderson. Yes, she's right here, hold on. Your illustrious agent," Julie stated as she rose. She slipped her feet back into her sandals. Raven got up from her chair just as the doorbell chimed.

"I guess that's Brandon." With admirable ease, she flopped into the chair that Julie had just vacated. "Would you tell him I'll be along in a minute?"

"Sure." Julie turned and left as Raven's voice followed her down the hall.

"I left it where? In your office? Henderson, I don't know why I ever bother carrying a purse."

Julie smiled. Raven had a penchant for losing things: her purse, her shoes, her passport. Vital or trivial, it simply didn't matter. Music and people filled Raven's thoughts, and material objects were easily forgotten.

"Hello, Brand," Julie said as she opened the front door. "Nice to see you again." Her eyes were cool, and her mouth formed no smile.

"Hello, Julie."

There was warmth in his greeting. She sensed it and

ignored it. "Come in," she invited. "Raven's expecting you; she'll be right out."

"It's good to be here again. I've missed this place."

"Have you?" Her tone was sharp.

His grin turned into a look of appraisal. Julie was a long-stemmed woman with a sleek cap of honey-blond hair and direct brown eyes. She was closer to Brand's age than Raven's and was the sort of woman he was usually attracted to: smart, sophisticated and coolly sexy. Yet, there could never have been anything between them but friendship. She was too fiercely devoted to Raven. Her loyalty, he saw, was unchanged.

"Five years is a long time, Julie."

"I'm not sure it's long enough," she countered. Old resentments came simmering back to the surface. "You hurt her."

"Yes, I know." His gaze didn't falter at the confession, and there was no plea for understanding in his eyes. The lack of it touched off respect in Julie, but she dismissed it. She shook her head as she looked at him.

"So," she said softly, "you've come back."

"I've come back," he agreed, then smiled. "Did you think I wouldn't?"

"She didn't," Julie retorted, annoyed with herself for warming to him. "That's what matters."

"Julie, Henderson's sending over my purse." Raven came down the hall toward them in her quick, nervous stride. "I told him not to bother; I don't think there's anything in it but a comb and an expired credit card. Hello, Brandon." She offered her hands as she had at the recording studio, but now she felt more able to accept his touch.

She hadn't bothered to put her shoes back on or to

repaint her mouth. Her smile was freer, more as he remembered it. "Raven." Brand brought her hands to his
lips. Instantly she stiffened, and Brand released her.
"Can we talk in the music room?" His smile was easy,
friendly. "I was always comfortable in there."

"Of course." She turned toward the doorway. "Would
you like something to drink?"

"I'd have some tea." He gave Julie his quick, charming grin. "You always made a good cup of tea."

"I'll bring it in." Without responding to the grin,
Julie moved down the hall toward the kitchen. Brand
followed Raven into the music room.

He touched her shoulder before she could cross to
the sofa. It was a gesture that asked her to wait. Turning
her head, Raven saw that he was giving the room one
of his long, detailed studies. She had seen that look on
his face before. It was a curious aspect of what seemed
like a casual nature. There was an intensity about him
at times that recalled the tough London street kid who'd
once fought his way to the top of his profession. The
key to his talent seemed to be in his natural gift for observation. He saw everything, remembered everything.
Then he translated it into lyric and melody.

The fingers on her shoulder caressed once, almost
absently, and brought back a flood of memories. Raven
would have moved away, but he dropped the hand and
turned to her. She had never been able to resist his eyes.

"I remember every detail of this room. I've pictured
it from time to time when I couldn't do anything but
think of you." He lifted his hand again to brush the back
of it against her cheek.

"Don't." She shook her head and stepped away.

"It's difficult not to touch you, Raven. Especially

here. Do you remember the long evenings we spent here? The quiet afternoons?"

He was moving her—with just his voice, just the steady spell of his eyes. "It was a long time ago, Brandon."

"It doesn't seem so long ago at the moment. It could be yesterday; you look the same."

"I'm not," she told him with a slight shake of her head. He saw her eyes darken before she turned away. "If I had known this was why you wanted to see me, I wouldn't have let you come. It's over, Brandon. It's been over for a long time."

"Is it?" Raven hadn't realized he was so close behind her. He turned her in his arms and caught her. "Show me, then," he demanded. "Just once."

The moment his mouth touched hers, she was thrown back in time. It was all there—the heat, the need, the loving. His lips were so soft, so warm; hers parted with only the slightest pressure. She knew how he would taste, how he would smell. Her memory was sharper than she had thought. Nothing was forgotten.

He tangled his fingers in the thickness of her hair, tilting her head further back as he deepened the kiss. He wanted to luxuriate in her flavor, in her scent, in her soft, yielding response. Her hands were trapped between their bodies, and she curled her fingers into the sweater he wore. The need, the longing, seemed much too fresh to have been dormant for five years. Brand held her close but without urgency. There was a quiet kind of certainty in the way he explored her mouth. Raven responded, giving, accepting, remembering. But when she felt the pleasure drifting toward passion, she resisted. When she struggled, he loosened his hold but didn't release her. Raven stared up at him with a look he well remembered but had never been able to completely decipher.

"It doesn't seem it's altogether finished after all," he murmured.

"You never did play fair, did you?" Raven pushed out of his arms, furious and shaken. "Let me tell you something, Brandon. I won't fall at your feet this time. You hurt me before, but I don't bruise so easily now. I have no intention of letting you back into my life."

"I think you will," he corrected easily. "But perhaps not in the way you mean." He paused and caught her hair with his fingers. "I can apologize for kissing you, Raven, if you'd like me to lie."

"Don't bother. You've always been good at romance. I rather enjoyed it." She sat down on the sofa and smiled brightly up at him.

He lifted a brow. It was hardly the response he had expected. He drew out a cigarette and lit it. "You seem to have grown up in my absence."

"Being an adult has its advantages," Raven observed. The kiss had stirred more than she cared to admit, even to herself.

"I always found your naiveté charming."

"It's difficult to remain naive, however charming, in this business." She leaned back against the cushion, relaxing deliberately. "I'm not wide-eyed and twenty anymore, Brandon."

"Tough and jaded are you, Raven?"

"Tough enough," she returned. "You gave me my first lesson!"

He took a deep drag on his cigarette, then considered the glowing tip of it. "Maybe I did," he murmured. "Maybe you needed it."

"Maybe you'd like me to thank you," she tossed back, and he looked over at her again.

"Perhaps." He walked over, then dropped down beside her on the sofa. His laugh was sudden and unexpected. "Good God, Raven, you've never had this bloody spring fixed."

The tension in her neck fled as she laughed with him. "I like it that way." She tossed her hair behind her back. "It's more personal."

"To say nothing of uncomfortable."

"I never sit on that spot," she told him.

"You leave it for unsuspecting guests, I imagine." He shifted away from the defective spring.

"That's right. I like people to feel at home."

Julie brought in a tea tray and found them sitting companionably on the sofa. Her quick, practiced glance found no tension on Raven's face. Satisfied, she left them again.

"How've you been, Brandon? Busy, I imagine." Raven crossed her legs under her and leaned over to pour the tea. It was a move Brandon had seen many times. Almost savagely, he crushed out his cigarette.

"Busy enough." He understated the five albums he had released since she'd last seen him and the three grueling concert tours. There'd been more than twenty songs with his name on the copyright in the past year.

"You've been living in London?"

"Mostly." His brow lifted, and she caught the gesture as she handed him his tea.

"I read the trades," she said mildly. "Don't we all?"

"I saw your television special last month." He sipped

his tea and relaxed against the back of the sofa. His eyes were on her, and she thought them a bit more green than blue now. "You were marvelous."

"Last month?" She frowned at him, puzzled. "It wasn't aired in England, was it?"

"I was in New York. Did you write all the songs for the album you finished up yesterday?"

"All but two." Shrugging, she took up her own china cup. "Marc wrote 'Right Now' and 'Coming Back.' He's got the touch."

"Yes." Brand eyed her steadily. "Does he have you, too?" Raven's head whipped around. "I read the trades," he said mildly.

"That comes under a more personal heading." Her eyes were dark with anger.

"More bluntly stated, none of my business?" he asked, sipping again.

"You were always bright, Brandon."

"Thanks, love." He set down his cup. "But my question was professional. I need to know if you have any entanglements at the moment."

"Entanglements are usually personal. Ask me about my dancing lessons."

"Later, perhaps. Raven, I need your undivided devotion for the next three months." His smile was engaging. Raven fought his charm.

"Well," she said and set her cup beside his. "That's bluntly stated."

"No indecent proposal at the moment," he assured her. Settling back in the hook of the sofa's arm, he sought her eyes. "I'm doing the score for *Fantasy*. I need a partner."

Chapter 3

To say she was surprised would have been a ridiculous understatement. Brand watched her eyes widen. He thought they were the color of peat smoke. She didn't move but simply stared at him, her hands resting lightly on her knees. Her thoughts had been flung in a thousand different directions, and she was trying to sit calmly and bring them back to order.

Fantasy. The book that had captured America's heart. A novel that had been on the bestseller list for more than fifty weeks. The sale of its paperback rights had broken all records. The film rights had been purchased as well, and Carol Mason, the author, had written the screenplay herself. It was to be a musical; *the* musical of the nineties. Speculation had been buzzing for months on both coasts as to who would write the score. It would be the coup of the decade, the chance of a lifetime. The plot was a dream, and the reigning box-office queen had the lead. And the music... Raven already had half-formed songs in her head. Carefully she reached back and poured more tea. Things like this don't just fall in your lap, she reminded herself. Perhaps he means something entirely different.

"You're going to score *Fantasy*," she said at length, cautiously. Her eyes met his again. His were clear, confident, a little puzzled. "I just heard that Lauren Chase had been signed. Everywhere I go, people are wondering who's going to play Tessa, who's going to play Joe."

"Jack Ladd," Brand supplied, and the puzzlement in Raven's eyes changed to pure pleasure.

"Perfect!" She reached over to take his hands. "You're going to have a tremendous hit. I'm very happy for you."

And she was. He could see as well as hear the absolute sincerity. It was typical of her to gain genuine pleasure from someone else's good fortune, just as it was typical of her to suffer for someone else's misfortune. Raven's feelings ran deep, and he knew she'd never been afraid to show emotion. Her unaffectedness had always been a great part of her appeal. For the moment, she had forgotten to be cautious with Brand. She smiled at him as she held his hands.

"So that's why you're in California," she said. "Have you already started?"

"No." He seemed to consider something for a moment, then his fingers interlaced with hers. Her hands were narrow-boned and slender, with palms as soft as a child's. "Raven, I meant what I said. I need a partner. I need you."

She started to remove her hands from his, but he

tightened his fingers. "I've never known you to need anyone, Brandon," she said, not quite succeeding in making her tone light. "Least of all me."

His grip tightened quickly, causing Raven's eyes to widen at the unexpected pain. Just as quickly, he released her. "This is business, Raven."

She lifted a brow at the temper in his voice. "Business is usually handled through my agent," she said. "You remember Henderson."

He gave her a long, steady look. "I remember everything." He saw the flash of hurt in her eyes, swiftly controlled. "Raven," his tone was gentler now. "I'm sorry."

She shrugged and gave her attention back to her tea. "Old wounds, Brandon. It does seem to me that if there was a legitimate offer, Henderson would have gotten wind of it."

"There's been an offer," Brand told her. "I asked him to let me speak to you first."

"Oh?" Her hair had drifted down, curtaining her face, and she flipped it behind her back. "Why?"

"Because I thought that if you knew we'd be working together, you'd turn it down."

"Yes," she agreed. "You're right."

"And that," he said without missing a beat, "would be incredibly soft-headed. Henderson knows that as well as I do."

"Oh, does he?" Raven rose, furious. "Isn't it marvelous the way people determine my life? Did you two decide I was too feeble-brained to make this decision on my own?"

"Not exactly." Brand's voice was cool. "We did agree that left to yourself, you have a tendency to be emotional rather than sensible."

"Terrific. Do I get a leash and collar for Christmas?"

"Don't be an idiot," Brand advised.

"Oh, so now I'm an idiot?" Raven turned away to pace the room. She had the same quicksilver temper he remembered. She was all motion, all energy. "I don't know how I've managed all this time without your pretty compliments, Brandon." She whirled back to him. "Why in the world would you want an emotional idiot as a collaborator?"

"Because," Brandon said and rose, "you're a hell of a writer. Now shut up."

"Of course," she said, seating herself on the piano bench. "Since you asked so nicely."

Deliberately he took out another cigarette, lit it and blew out a stream of smoke, all the while his eyes resting on her face. "This is an important project, Raven," he said. "Let's not blow it. Because we were once very close, I wanted to talk to you face-to-face, not through a mediator, not through a bloody telephone wire. Can you understand that?"

She waited a long moment before answering. "Maybe."

Brand smiled and moved over to her. "We'll add stubborn to those adjectives later, but I don't want you mad again."

"Then let me ask you something before you say anything I'll have to get mad about." Raven tilted her head and studied his face. "First, why do you want a collaborator on this? Why share the glory?"

"It's also a matter of sharing the work, love. Fifteen songs."

She nodded. "All right, number two, then. Why me, Brandon? Why not someone who's scored a musical before?"

He answered her by walking around her and slipping down on the piano bench beside her. Without speaking, he began to play. The notes flooded the room like ghosts. "Remember this?" he murmured, glancing over and into her eyes.

Raven didn't have to answer. She rose and walked away. It was too difficult to sit beside him at the same piano where they had composed the song he now played. She remembered how they had laughed, how warm his eyes had been, how safe she had felt in his arms. It was the first and only song they had written and recorded together.

Even after he had stopped playing, she continued to prowl the room. "What does 'Clouds and Rain' have to do with anything?" she demanded. He had touched a chord in her; he heard it in the tone of her voice. He felt a pang of guilt at having intentionally peeled away a layer of her defense.

"There's a Grammy over there and a gold record, thanks to that two minutes and forty-three seconds, Raven. We work well together."

She turned back to look at him. "We did once."

"We will again." Brand stood and came to her but this time made no move to touch her. "Raven, you know how important this could be to your career. And you must realize what you'd be bringing to the project. *Fantasy* needs your special talents."

She wanted it. She could hardly believe that something she wanted so badly was being offered to her. But how would it be to work with him again, to be in constant close contact? Would she be able to deal with it? Would she be sacrificing her personal sanity for professional gain? *But I don't love him anymore,* she reminded herself. Raven caught her bottom lip between her teeth in a gesture of indecision. Brand saw it.

"Raven, think of the music."

"I am," she admitted. "I'm also thinking of you—of us." She gave him a clear, candid look. "I'm not sure it would be healthy for me."

"I can't promise not to touch you." He was annoyed, and his voice reflected it in its crisp, concise tone. "But I can promise not to push myself on you. Is that good enough?"

Raven evaded the question. "If I agreed, when would we start? I've a tour coming up."

"I know, in two weeks. You'll be finished in six, so we could start the first week in May."

"I see." Her mouth turned up a bit as she combed her fingers through her hair. "You've looked into this thoroughly."

"I told you, it's business."

"All right, Brandon," she said, conceding his point. "Where would we work? Not here," she said quickly. There was a sudden pressure in her chest. "I won't work with you here."

"No, I thought not. I have a place," he continued when Raven remained silent. "It's in Cornwall."

"Cornwall?" Raven repeated. "Why Cornwall?"

"Because it's quiet and isolated, and no one, especially the press, knows I have it. They'll be all over us when they hear we're working together, especially on this project. It's too hot an item."

"Couldn't we just rent a small cave on the coast somewhere?"

He laughed and caught her hair in his hand. "You

know how poor the acoustics are in a cave. Cornwall's incredible in the spring, Raven. Come with me."

She lifted a hand to his chest to push back, not certain if she was about to agree or decline. He could still draw too much from her too effortlessly. She needed to think, she decided; a few days to put it all in perspective.

"Raven."

She turned to see Julie in the doorway. "Yes?"

"There's a call for you."

Vaguely annoyed, Raven frowned at her. "Can't it wait, Julie? I…"

"It's on your private line."

Brand felt her stiffen and looked down curiously. Her eyes were completely blank.

"I see." Her voice was calm, but he detected the faintest of tremors.

"Raven?" Without thinking, he took her by the shoulders and turned her to face him. "What is it?"

"Nothing." She drew out of his arms. There was something remote about her now, something distant that puzzled him. "Have some more tea," she invited and smiled, but her eyes remained blank. "I'll be back in a minute."

She was gone for more than ten, and Brand had begun to pace restlessly through the room. Raven was definitely no longer the malleable young girl she had been five years before; he knew that. He wasn't at all certain she would agree to work with him. He wanted her—for the project and yes, for himself. Holding her, tasting her again, had stirred up much more than memories. She fascinated him and always had. Even when she had been so young, there had been an air of secrecy about her. There still was. It was as if she kept certain parts of herself locked in a closet out of reach. She had held him off five years before in more than a physical sense. It had frustrated him then and continued to frustrate him.

But he was older, too. He'd made mistakes with her before and had no intention of repeating them. Brand knew what he wanted and was determined to get it. Sitting back at the piano, he began to play the song he had written with Raven. He remembered her voice, warm and sultry, in his ear. He was nearly at the end when he sensed her presence.

Glancing up, Brand saw her standing in the doorway. Her eyes were unusually dark and intense. Then he realized it was because she was pale, and the contrast accentuated the gray of her irises. Had the song disturbed her that much? He stopped immediately and rose to go to her.

"Raven…"

"I've decided to do it," she interrupted. Her hands were folded neatly in front of her, her eyes direct.

"Good." He took her hands and found them chilled. "Are you all right?"

"Yes, of course." She removed her hands from his, but her gaze never faltered. "I suppose Henderson will fill me in on all the details."

Something about her calm disturbed him. It was as if she'd set part of herself aside. "Let's have dinner, Raven." The urge to be with her, to pierce her armor, was almost overwhelming. "I'll take you to the Bistro; you always liked it there."

"Not tonight, Brandon, I…have some things to do."

"Tomorrow," he insisted, knowing he was pushing

but unable to prevent himself. She looked suddenly weary.

"Yes, all right, tomorrow." She gave him a tired smile. "I'm sorry, but I'll have to ask you to leave now, Brandon. I didn't realize how late it was."

"All right." Bending toward her, he gently kissed her. It was an instinctive gesture, one that demanded no response. He felt the need to warm her, protect her. "Seven tomorrow," he told her. "I'm at the Bel-Air; you only have to call me."

Raven waited until she heard the front door shut behind her. She pressed the heel of her hand to her brow and let the tide of emotions rush through her. There were no tears, but a blinding headache raged behind her eyes. She felt Julie's hand on her shoulder.

"They found her?" Julie asked, concerned. Automatically she began kneading the tension from Raven's shoulders.

"Yes, they found her." She let out a long, deep breath. "She's coming back."

Chapter 4

The sanitarium was white and clean. The architect, a good one, had conceived a restful building without medical overtones. The uninformed might have mistaken it for an exclusive hotel snuggled in California's scenic Ojai. It was a proud, elegantly fashioned building with several magnificent views of the countryside. Raven detested it.

Inside, the floors were thickly carpeted, and conversation was always low-key. Raven hated the controlled silence, the padded quiet. The staff members wore street clothes and only small, discreet badges to identify themselves, and they were among the best trained in the country, just as the Fieldmore Clinic was the best detoxification center on the west coast. Raven had made certain of its reputation before she had brought her mother there for the first time over five years before.

Raven waited in Justin Karter's paneled, book-lined, tasteful office. It received its southern exposure through a wide, thick-paned window. The morning sunlight beamed in on a thriving collection of leafy green plants. Raven wondered idly why her own plants seemed always to put up only a halfhearted struggle for life, one they usually lost. Perhaps she should ask Dr. Karter what his secret was. She laughed a little and rubbed her fingers on the nagging headache between her brows.

How she hated these visits and the leathery, glossy smell of his office. She was cold and cupped her elbows, hugging her arms across her midriff. Raven was always cold in the Fieldmore Clinic, from the moment she walked through the stately white double doors until long after she walked out again. It was a penetrating cold that went straight to the bone. Turning away from the window, she paced nervously around the room. When she heard the door open, she stopped and turned around slowly.

Karter entered, a small, youthful man with a corn-colored beard and healthy pink cheeks. He had an earnest face, accentuated by tortoise-rimmed glasses and a faint smattering of freckles. Under other circumstances, Raven would have liked his face, even warmed to it.

"Ms. Williams." He held out a hand and took hers in a quick, professional grip. It was cold, he realized, and as fragile as he remembered. Her hair was pinned up at the nape of her neck, and she looked young and pale in the dark tailored suit. This woman was far different from the vibrant, laughing entertainer he had watched on television a few weeks before.

"Hello, Dr. Karter."

It always amazed him that the rich, full-toned voice

belonged to such a small, delicate-looking woman. He had thought the same years before when she had been hardly more than a child. He was an ardent fan but had never asked her to sign any of the albums in his collection. It would, he knew, embarrass them both.

"Please sit down, Ms. Williams. Could I get you some coffee?"

"No, please." She swallowed. Her throat was always dry when she spoke to him. "I'd like to see my mother first."

"There are a few things I'd like to discuss with you."

He watched her moisten her lips, the only sign of agitation. "After I've seen her."

"All right." Karter took her by the arm and led her from the room. They walked across the quiet, carpeted hallway to the elevators. "Ms. Williams," he began. He would have liked to have called her Raven. He thought of her as Raven, just as the rest of the world did. But he could never quite break through the film of reserve she slipped on in his presence. It was, Karter knew, because he knew her secrets. She trusted him to keep them but was never comfortable with him. She turned to him now, her great, gray eyes direct and expressionless.

"Yes, Doctor?" Only once had Raven ever broken down in his presence, and she had promised herself she would never do so again. She would not be destroyed by her mother's illness, and she would not make a public display of herself.

"I don't want you to be shocked by your mother's appearance." They stepped into the elevator together, and he kept his hand on her arm. "She had made a great deal of progress during her last stay here, but she left prematurely, as you know. Over the past three months, her condition has…deteriorated."

"Please," Raven said wearily, "don't be delicate. I know where she was found and how. You'll dry her out again, and in a couple of months she'll leave and it'll start all over. It never changes."

"Alcoholics fight a continuing battle."

"Don't tell me about alcoholics," she shot back. The reserve cracked, and the emotion poured through. "Don't preach to me about battles." She stopped herself, then, shaking her head, pressed her fingers to the concentrated source of her headache. "I know all about alcoholics," she said more calmly. "I haven't your dedication or your optimism."

"You keep bringing her back," he reminded Raven softly.

"She's my mother." The elevator doors slid open, and Raven walked through them.

Her skin grew colder as they moved down the hallway. There were doors on either side, but she refused to think of the people beyond them. The hospital flavor was stronger here. Raven thought she could smell the antiseptic, the hovering medicinal odor that always made a hint of nausea roll in her stomach. When Karter stopped in front of a door and reached for a knob, Raven laid a hand on top of his.

"I'll see her alone, please."

He sensed her rigid control. Her eyes were calm, but he had seen the quick flash of panic in them. Her fingers didn't tremble on his hand but were stiff and icy. "All right. But only a few minutes. There are complications we need to discuss." He took his hand from the knob. "I'll wait for you here."

Raven nodded and twisted the knob herself. She took a moment, struggling to gather every ounce of strength, then walked inside.

The woman lay in a hospital bed on good linen sheets, dozing lightly. There was a tube feeding liquid into her through a needle in her arm. The drapes were drawn, and the room was in shadows. It was a comfortable room painted in soft blue with an ivory carpet and a few good paintings. With her fingers dug into the leather bag she carried, Raven approached the bed.

Raven's first thought was that her mother had lost weight. There were hollows in her cheeks, and her skin had the familiar unhealthy yellow cast. Her dark hair was cropped short and streaked liberally with gray. It had been lovely hair, Raven remembered, glossy and full. Her face was gaunt, with deathly circles under the eyes and a mouth that seemed dry and pulled in. The helplessness stabbed at Raven, and for a minute she closed her eyes against it. She let them fall while she looked down on the sleeping woman. Without a sound, without moving, the woman in bed opened her eyes. They were dark and gray like her daughter's.

"Mama." Raven let the tears roll freely. "Why?"

By the time Raven got to her front door, she was exhausted. She wanted bed and oblivion. The headache was still with her, but the pain had turned into a dull, sickening throb. Closing the door behind her, she leaned back on it, trying to summon the strength to walk up the stairs.

"Raven?"

She opened her eyes and watched Julie come down the hall toward her. Seeing Raven so pale and beaten,

Julie slipped an arm around her shoulders. Her concern took the form of a scolding. "You should have let me go with you. I should never have let you go alone." She was already guiding Raven up the stairs.

"My mother, my problem," Raven said tiredly.

"That's the only selfish part of you," Julie said in a low, furious voice as they entered Raven's bedroom. "I'm supposed to be your friend. You'd never let me go through something like this alone."

"Please, don't be angry with me." Raven swayed on her feet as Julie stripped off the dark suit jacket. "It's something I feel is my responsibility, just mine. I've felt that way for too long to change now."

"I am angry with you." Julie's voice was tight as she slipped the matching skirt down over Raven's hips. "This is the only thing you do that makes me genuinely angry with you. I can't stand it when you do this to yourself." She looked back at the pale, tired face. "Have you eaten?" Raven shook her head as she stepped out of the skirt. "And you won't," she concluded, brushing Raven's fumbling hands away from the buttons of the white lawn blouse. She undid them herself, then pushed the material from Raven's shoulders. Raven stood, unresisting.

"I'm having dinner with Brandon," Raven murmured, going willingly as Julie guided her toward the bed.

"I'll call him and cancel. I can bring you up something later. You need to sleep."

"No." Raven slipped between the crisp, cool sheets. "I want to go. I need to go," she corrected as she shut her eyes. "I need to get out; I don't want to think for a while. I'll rest now. He won't be here until seven."

Julie walked over to pull the shades. Even before the room was darkened, Raven was asleep.

It was some minutes past seven when Julie opened the door to Brandon. He wore a stone-colored suit with a navy shirt open at the throat. He looked casually elegant, Julie thought. The nosegay of violets was charming rather than silly in his hands. He lifted a brow at the clinging black sheath she wore.

"Hello, Julie. You look terrific." He plucked one of the violets out of the nosegay and handed it to her. "Going out?"

Julie accepted the flower. "In a little while," she answered. "Raven should be down in a minute. Brand…" Hesitating, Julie shook her head, then turned to lead him into the music room. "I'll fix you a drink. Bourbon, isn't it? Neat."

Brand caught her arm. "That isn't what you were going to say."

She took a deep breath. "No." For a moment longer she hesitated, then began, fixing him with her dark brown eyes. "Raven's very important to me. There aren't many like her, especially in this town. She's genuine, and though she thinks she has, she hasn't really developed any hard edges yet. I wouldn't like to see her hurt, especially right now. No, I won't answer any questions," she said, anticipating him. "It's Raven's story, not mine. But I'm going to tell you this: She needs a light touch and a great deal of patience. You'd better have them both."

"How much do you know about what happened between us five years ago, Julie?" Brandon asked.

"I know what Raven told me."

"One day you ought to ask me how I felt and why I left."

"And would you tell me?"

"Yes," he returned without hesitation. "I would."

"I'm sorry!" Raven came dashing down the stairs in a filmy flutter of white. "I hate to be late." Her hair settled in silky confusion over the shoulders of the thin voile dress as she stopped at the foot of the stairs. "I couldn't seem to find my shoes."

There was a becoming blush of color on her cheeks, and her eyes were bright and full of laughter. It passed through Brand's mind quickly, and then was discarded, that she looked a little too bright, a little too vibrant.

"Beautiful as ever." He handed her the flowers. "I've never minded waiting for you."

"Ah, the golden Irish tongue," she murmured as she buried her face in the violets. "I've missed it." Raven held the flowers up to her nose while her eyes laughed at him over them. "And I believe I'll let you spoil me tonight, Brandon. I'm in a mood to be pampered."

He took her free hand in his. "Where do you want to go?"

"Anywhere. Everywhere." She tossed her head. "But dinner first. I'm starving."

"All right, I'll buy you a cheeseburger."

"Some things do stay the same," she commented before she turned to Julie. "You have fun, and don't worry about me." She paused a moment, then smiled and kissed her cheek. "I promise I won't lose my key. And say hello to…" She hesitated as she walked toward the door with Brandon. "Who is it tonight?"

"Lorenzo," Julie answered, watching them. "The shoe baron."

"Oh, yes." Raven laughed as they walked into the cool, early spring air. "Amazing." She tucked her arm through Brandon's. "Julie's always having some millionaire fall in love with her. It's a gift."

"Shoe baron?" Brand questioned as he opened the car door for Raven.

"*Mmm.* Italian. He wears beautiful designer suits and looks as though he should be stamped on the head of a coin."

Brand slid in beside her and in an old reflex gesture brushed the hair that lay on her shoulder behind her back. "Serious?"

Raven tried not to be moved by the touch of his fingers. "No more serious than the oil tycoon or the perfume magnate." The leathery smell of the upholstery reminded her abruptly of Karter's office. Quickly she pushed away the sensation. "What are you going to feed me, Brandon?" she asked brightly—too brightly. "I warn you, I'm starving."

He circled her throat with his hand so that she had no choice but to meet his eyes directly. "Are you going to tell me what's wrong?"

He'd always seen too much too quickly, she thought. It was one of the qualities that had made him an exceptional songwriter.

Raven placed her hand on top of his. "No questions, Brandon, not now."

She felt his hesitation. Then he turned his hand over and gripped hers. Slowly, overriding her initial resistance, he brought her palm to his lips. "Not now," he agreed, watching her eyes. "I can still move you," he murmured and smiled as though the knowledge pleased him. "I can feel it."

Raven felt the tremors racing up her arms. "Yes." She drew her hand from his but kept her eyes steady. "You can still move me. But things aren't the same anymore."

He grinned, a quick flash of white teeth, then started the engine. "No, things aren't the same anymore."

As he pulled away, she had the uncomfortable impression that they had said the same words but meant two different things.

Dinner was quiet and intimate and perfect. They ate in a tiny old inn they had once discovered by chance. Here, Brand knew, there would be no interruptions for autographs, no greetings and drinks from old acquaintances. Here there would be just the two of them, a man and a woman amidst candlelight, wine, fine food, and an intimate atmosphere.

As the evening wore on, Raven's smile became more spontaneous, less desperate, and the unhappiness he had seen deep in her eyes before now faded. Though he noticed the transition, Brand made no comment.

"I feel like I haven't eaten in a week," Raven managed between bites of the tender roast beef that was the house speciality.

"Want some of mine?" Brand offered his plate.

Raven scooped up a bit of baked potato; her eyes seemed to laugh at him. "We'll have them wrap it up so I can take it home. I want to leave room for dessert. Did you see that pastry tray?"

"I suppose I could roll you to Cornwall," Brand considered, adding some burgundy to his glass.

Raven laughed, a throaty sound that appealed and aroused. "I'll be a bag of bones by the time we go to Cornwall," she claimed. "You know what those whirlwind tours can do." She shook her head as he offered her more wine.

"One-night stands from San Francisco to New York." Brand lifted his glass as Raven gave him a quizzing look. "I spoke to Henderson." He twirled a strand of her hair around his finger so absently, Raven was certain he was unaware of the gesture. She made no complaint. "If it's agreeable with you, I'll meet you in New York at the end of the tour. We'll fly to England from there."

"All right." She took a deep breath, having finally reached her fill of the roast beef. "You'd better set it up with Julie. I haven't any memory for dates and times. Are you staying in the States until then?"

"I'm doing a couple of weeks in Vegas." He brushed his fingers across her cheek, and when she would have resisted, he laid his hand companionably over hers. "I haven't played there in quite a while. I don't suppose it's changed."

She laughed and shook her head. "No. I played there, oh, about six months ago, I guess. Julie won a bundle at the baccarat table. I was a victim of the slots."

"I read the reviews. Were you as sensational as they said?" He smiled at her while one finger played with the thin gold bracelet at her wrist.

"Oh, I was much more sensational than they said," she assured him.

"I'd like to have seen you." His finger drifted lazily to her pulse. He felt it jump at his touch. "It's been much too long since I've heard you sing."

"You heard me just the other day in the studio," she pointed out. She took her hand from his to reach for her wine. He easily took her other one. "Brandon," she began, half-amused.

"I've heard you over the radio as well," he continued, "but it's not the same as watching you come alive at a concert. Or," he smiled as his voice took on that soft, intimate note she remembered, "listening to you when you sing just for me."

His tone was as smooth as the burgundy she drank. Knowing how easily he could cloud her brain, she vowed to keep their conversation light. "Do you know what I want right now?" She lowered her own voice as she leaned toward him, but he recognized the laughter in her eyes.

"Dessert," he answered.

"You know me so well, Brandon." She smiled.

She wanted to go dancing. By mutual consent, when they left the restaurant they avoided the popular, trendy spots in town and found a crowded, smoky hole-in-the-wall club with a good band, much like the dozens they had both played in at the beginnings of their respective careers. They thought they wouldn't be recognized there. For almost twenty minutes they were right.

"Excuse me, aren't you Brand Carstairs?" The toothy young blonde stared up at Brand in admiration. Then she glanced at Raven. "And Raven Williams."

"Bob Muldroon," Brand returned in a passable Texas drawl. "And my wife Sheila. Say howdy, Sheila," he instructed as he held her close and swayed on the postage-sized dance floor.

"Howdy," Raven said obligingly.

"Oh, Mr. Carstairs." She giggled and thrust out a cocktail napkin and a pencil. "Please, I'm Debbie. Could you write, 'To my good friend Debbie'?"

"Sure." Brand gave her one of his charming smiles

and told Raven to turn around. He scrawled quickly, using her back for support.

"And you, too, Raven," Debbie asked when he'd finished. "On the other side."

It was typical of her fans to treat her informally. They thought of her as Raven. Her spontaneous warmth made it difficult for anyone to approach her with the awe normally reserved for superstars. Raven wrote on her side of the napkin when Brand offered his back. When she had finished, she noted that Debbie's eyes were wide and fixed on Brand. The pulse in her throat was jumping like a jackhammer. Raven knew what fantasies were dancing in the girl's mind.

"Here you are, Debbie." She touched her hand to bring the girl back to reality.

"Oh." Debbie took the napkin, looked at it blankly a moment, then smiled up at Brand. "Thanks." She looked at Raven, then ran a hand through her hair as if she had just realized what she had done. "Thanks a lot."

"You're welcome." Brand smiled but began to edge Raven toward the door.

It was too much to expect that the incident had gone unnoticed or that no one else would recognize them. For the next fifteen minutes they were wedged between the crowd and the door, signing autographs and dealing with a barrage of questions. Brand made certain they weren't separated from each other as he slowly maneuvered a path through the crowd.

They were jostled and shoved a bit but he judged the crowd to be fairly civilized. It was still early by L.A. standards, and there hadn't been too much drinking yet. Still he wanted her out. This type of situation was notoriously explosive; the mood could change abruptly.

One overenthusiastic fan and it could all be different. And ugly. Raven signed and signed some more while an occasional hand reached out to touch her hair. Brand felt a small wave of relief as he finally drew her out into the fresh air. Only a few followed them out of the club, and they were able to make their way to Brand's car with just a smattering of extra autographs.

"Damn it. I'm sorry." He leaned across her to lock her door. "I should have known better than to have taken you there."

Raven took a long breath, combing her hair back from her face with her fingers as she turned to him. "Don't be silly; I wanted to go. Besides, the people were nice."

"They aren't always," he muttered as the car merged with Los Angeles traffic.

"No." She leaned back, letting her body relax. "But I've been pretty lucky. Things have only gotten out of hand once or twice. It's the hype, I suppose, and it's to be expected that fans sometimes forget we're flesh and blood."

"So they try to take little chunks of us home with them."

"That," Raven said dryly, "can be a problem. I remember seeing a film clip of a concert you gave, oh, seven or eight years ago." She leaned her elbow on the back of the seat now and cupped her cheek in her palm. "A London concert where the fans broke through the security. They seemed to swallow you whole. It must have been dreadful."

"They loved me enough to give me a couple of broken ribs."

"Oh, Brandon." She sat up straight now, shocked. "That's terrible. I never knew that."

He smiled and moved his shoulders. "We played it down. It did rather spoil my taste for live concerts for a while. I got over it." He turned, heading toward the hills. "Security's tighter these days."

"I don't know if I'd be able to face an audience after something like that."

"Where else would you get the adrenaline?" he countered. "We need it, don't we? That instant gratification of applause." He laughed and pulled her over beside him. "Why else do we do it, Raven? Why else are there countless others out there scrambling to make it? Why did you start up the road, Raven?"

"To escape," she answered before she had time to think. She sighed and relaxed against his shoulder when he didn't demand an explanation. "Music was always something I could hold on to. It was constant, dependable. I needed something that was wholly mine." She turned her head a bit to study his profile. "Why did you?"

"For most of the same reasons, I suppose. I had something to say, and I wanted people to remember I said it."

She laughed. "And you were so radical at the start of your career. Such pounding, demanding songs. You were music's bad boy for some time."

"I've mellowed," he told her.

"'Fire Hot' didn't sound mellow to me," she commented. "Wasn't that the lead cut on your last album?"

He grinned, glancing down at her briefly. "I have to keep my hand in."

"It was number one on the charts for ten consecutive weeks," she pointed out. "That isn't bad for mellow."

"That's right," he agreed as if he'd just remembered. "It knocked off a little number of yours, didn't it? It was kind of a sweet little arrangement, as I recall. Maybe a bit heavy on the strings, but…"

She gave him an enthusiastic punch on the arm.

"Raven," Brand complained mildly. "You shouldn't distract me when I'm driving."

"That sweet little arrangement went platinum."

"I said it was sweet," he reminded her. "And the lyrics weren't bad. A bit sentimental, maybe, but…"

"I like sentimental lyrics," she told him, giving him another jab on the arm. "Not every song has to be a blistering social commentary."

"Of course not," he agreed reasonably. "There's always room for cute little ditties."

"Cute little ditties," Raven repeated, hardly aware that they had fallen back into one of their oldest habits by debating each other's work. "Just because I don't go in for showboating or lyrical trickery," she began. But when he swung off to the side of the road, she narrowed her eyes at him. "What are you doing?"

"Pulling over before you punch me again." He grinned and flicked a finger down her nose. "Showboating?"

"Showboating," she repeated. "What else do you call that guitar and piano duel at the end of 'Fire Hot'?"

"A classy way to fade out a song," he returned, and though she agreed with him, Raven made a sound of derision.

"I don't need the gadgetry. My songs are…"

"Overly sentimental."

She lifted a haughty brow. "If you feel my music is overly sentimental and cute, how do you imagine we'll work together?"

"Perfectly," he told her. "We'll balance each other, Raven, just as we always did."

"We're going to have terrible fights," she predicted.

"Yes, I imagine we will."

"And," she added, failing to suppress a smile, "you won't always win."

"Good. Then the fights won't be boring." He pulled her to him, and when she resisted, he cradled her head on his shoulder again. "Look," he ordered, pointing out the window, "why is it cities always look better at night from above?"

Raven looked down on the glittering Los Angeles skyline. "I suppose it's the mystique. It makes you wonder what's going on and you can't see how fast it's moving. Up here it's quiet." She felt his lips brush her temple. "Brandon." She drew away, but he stopped her.

"Don't pull away from me, Raven." It was a low, murmured request that shot heat up her spine. "Don't pull away from me."

His head lowered slowly, and his lips nibbled at hers, hardly touching, but the hand at the back of her neck was firm. He kept her facing him while he changed the angle of the kiss. His lips were persuasive, seductive. He kissed the soft, dewy skin of her cheeks, the fragile, closed eyelids, the scented hair at her temple. She could feel herself floating toward him as she always had, losing herself to him.

Her lips parted so that when his returned, he found them inviting him to explore. The kiss deepened, but slowly, as if he savored the taste of her on his tongue.

Her hand slid up his chest until she held him and their bodies touched. He murmured something, then pressed his mouth against the curve of her neck. Her scent rose and enveloped him.

She moaned when he took her breast, a sound of both hunger and protest. His mouth came back to hers, plundering now as he responded to the need he felt flowing from her. She was unresisting, as open and warm as a shaft of sunlight. Her body was yearning toward him, melting irresistibly. She thought his hand burned through the thin fabric of her dress and set fire to her naked skin. It had been so long, she thought dizzily, so long since she had felt anything this intensely, needed anything this desperately. Her whole being tuned itself to him.

"Raven." His mouth was against her ear, her throat, the hollow of her cheek. "Oh, God, I want you." The kiss was urgent now, his hands no longer gentle. "So long," he said, echoing her earlier thought. "It's been so long. Come back with me. Let me take you back with me to the hotel. Stay with me tonight."

Passion flooded her senses. His tongue trailed over her warmed skin until he came again to her mouth. Then he took possession. The heat was building, strangling the breath in her throat, suffocating her. There was a fierce tug of war between fear and desire. She began to struggle.

"No." She took deep gulps of air. "Don't."

Brand took her by the shoulders and with one quick jerk had her face turned back up to his. "Why?" he demanded roughly. "You want me, I can feel it."

"No." She shook her head, and her hands trembled as she pushed at his chest. "I don't. I can't." Raven tried to deepen her breathing to steady it. "You're hurting me, Brandon. Please let me go."

Slowly he relaxed his fingers, then released her. "The same old story," he murmured. Turning away from her, he carefully drew out a cigarette and lit it. "You still give until I'm halfway mad, then pull away from me." He took a long, deep drag. "I should have been better prepared for it."

"You're not fair. I didn't start this; I never wanted…"

"You wanted," he tossed back furiously. "Damn it, Raven, you wanted. I've had enough women to know when I'm holding one who wants me."

She stiffened against the ache that was speeding through her. "You're better off with one of your many women, Brandon. I told you I wouldn't fall at your feet this time, and I meant it. If we can have a professional relationship, fine." She swallowed and straightened the hair his fingers had so recently caressed. "If you can't work with things on that level, then you'd best find another partner."

"I have the one I want." He tossed his cigarette through the open window. "We'll play it your way for a while, Raven. We're both professionals, and we both know what this musical's going to do for our careers." He started the engine. "I'll take you home."

Chapter 5

Raven hated to be late for a party, but there was no help for it. Her schedule was drum tight. If it hadn't been important that she be there, to rub elbows with Lauren Chase and a few other principals from the cast and crew of *Fantasy,* she'd have bowed out. There were only two days left before the start of her tour.

The truth was, Raven had forgotten about the party. Rehearsals had run over, then she had found herself driving into Beverly Hills to window shop. She hadn't wanted to buy anything but had simply wanted to do something mindless. For weeks there had been nothing but demand after demand, and she could look forward only to more of the same in the weeks to come. She would steal a few hours. She didn't want to think about her mother and the clean white sanitarium or song lists and cues or her confusion over Brand as she browsed through the treasures at Neiman Marcus and Gucci. She looked at everything and bought nothing.

Arriving home, she was met by a huge handwritten note from Julie tacked on her bedroom door.

> Party at Steve Jarett's. I know—you forgot. IMPORTANT! Get your glad rags together, babe, and go. Out with Lorenzo for dinner, we'll see you there. J.

Raven swore briefly, rebelled, then capitulated before she stalked to the closet to choose an outfit. An hour later she was cruising fast through the Hollywood Hills. It was important that she be there.

Steve Jarett was directing *Fantasy.* He was, at the moment, the silver screen's boy wonder, having just directed three major successes in a row. Raven wanted *Fantasy* to be his fourth as much as he did.

The party would be crowded, she mused, and looked wistfully at the open, star-studded sky. And noisy. Abruptly she laughed at herself. Since when did a noisy, crowded party become a trial by fire? There had been a time when she had enjoyed them. And there was no denying that the people who haunted these parties were fascinating and full of incredible stories. Raven could still be intrigued. It was just that... She sighed, allowing herself to admit the real reason she had dragged her feet. Brandon would be there. He was bound to be.

Would he bring a date? she wondered. Why wouldn't he? She answered herself shortly, downshifting as she took a curve. Unless he decided to wait and take his pick from the women there. Raven sighed again, seeing the blaze of lights that told her she was approaching Jarett's house. It was ridiculous to allow herself to get tied up in knots over something that had ended years before.

Her headlights caught the dull gleam of sturdy iron gates, and she slowed. The guard took her name, checked his list, then admitted her. She could hear the music before she was halfway up the curving, palm-lined drive.

There was a white-jacketed teenager waiting to hand her out of the Lamborghini. He was probably a struggling actor or an aspiring screenwriter or cinematographer, Raven thought as she smiled at him.

"Hi, I'm late. Do you think I can slip in without anybody noticing?"

"I don't think so, Ms. Williams, not looking like that."

Raven lifted her brows, surprised that he had recognized her so quickly in the dim light. But even if he had missed the face and hair, she realized, he would never have mistaken the voice.

"That's a compliment, isn't it?" she asked.

"Yes, ma'am," he said so warmly that she laughed.

"Well, I'm going to do my best, anyway. I don't like entrances unless they're on stage." She studied the sprawling, white brick mansion. "There must be a side door."

"Around to the left." He pointed. "There's a set of glass doors that lead into the library. Go through there and turn left. You should be able to slip in without being noticed."

"Thanks." She went to take a bill out of her purse, discovered she had left it in the car and leaned in the window to retrieve it. After a moment's search, she found a twenty and handed it to him.

"Thank *you!* Raven," he enthused as she turned away.

Then he called to her, "Ms. Williams?" Raven turned back with a half smile. "Would you sign it for me?"

She tossed back her hair. "The bill?"

"Yeah."

She laughed and shook her head. "A fat lot of good it would do you then. Here." She dug into her bag again and came up with a slip of paper. One side was scrawled on, a list of groceries Julie had given her a few weeks before, but the other side was blank. "What's your name?" she demanded.

"Sam, Sam Rheinhart."

"Here, Sam Rheinhart," she said. Dashing off a quick line on the paper, she gave him the autograph. He stared after her, the twenty in one hand and the grocery list in the other, as she rushed off.

Raven found the glass doors without trouble. Though they were closed, the sounds of the party came clearly through. There were groups of people out back listening to a very loud rock band and drifting around by the pool. She stayed in the shadows. She wore an ankle-length skirt and a dolman-sleeve pullover in a dark plum color with silver metallic threads running through which captured the moonlight. Entering through the library, she gave herself a moment to adjust to the darkness before groping her way to the door.

There was no one in the hall immediately outside. Pleased with herself, Raven stepped out and gravitated slowly toward the focus of noise.

"Why, Raven!" It was Carly Devers, a tiny blond fluff of an actress with a little-girl voice and a rapier sharp talent. Though they generally moved in different circles, Raven liked her. "I didn't know you were here."

"Hi, Carly." They exchanged obligatory brushes of

the cheek. "Congratulations are in order, aren't they? I heard you were being signed as second lead in *Fantasy.*"

"It's still in the working stage, but it looks like it. It's a gem of a part, and of course, working with Steve is *the* thing to do these days." As she spoke, she gave Raven a piercing look with her baby blue eyes. "You look fabulous," she said. Raven knew she meant it. "And of course, congratulations are in order for you as well, aren't they?"

"Yes, I'm excited about doing the score."

Carly tilted her head, and a smile spread over her face. "I was thinking more about Brand Carstairs than the score, darling." Raven's smile faded instantly. "Oops." Carly's smile only widened. "Still tender." There was no malice in her amusement. She linked her arm with Raven's. "I'd keep your little collaboration very tight this time around, Raven. I'm tempted to make a play for him myself, and I guarantee I'm not alone."

"What happened to Dirk Wagner?" Raven reminded herself to play it light as they drew closer to the laughter and murmurs of the party.

"Old news, darling, do try to keep up." Carly laughed, a tinkling bell of a sound that Raven could not help but respond to. "Still, I don't make it a habit to tread on someone else's territory."

"No signs posted, Carly," Raven said carelessly.

"Hmm." Carly tossed back a lock of silver-blond hair. A waiter passed by with a tray of glasses, and she neatly plucked off two. "I've heard he's a marvelous lover," she commented, her eyes bright and direct on Raven's.

Raven returned the look equably and accepted the offered champagne. "Have you? But then, I imagine that's old news, too."

"Touché," Carly murmured into her glass.

"Is Brandon here?" she asked, trying to prove to herself and her companion that the conversation meant nothing.

"Here and there," Carly said ambiguously. "I haven't decided whether he's been trying to avoid the flocks of females that crawl around him or if he's seeking them out. He doesn't give away much, does he?"

Raven uttered a noncommittal sound and shrugged. It was time, she decided, to change the subject. "Have you seen Steve? I suppose I should fight my way through and say hello."

It was a typical enough party, Raven decided. Clothes ranged from Rive Gauche to Salvation Army. There was a steady drum beat from the band by the pool underlying the talk and laughter. The doors to the terrace were open wide, letting out the clouds of smoke and allowing the warm night air to circulate freely. The expansive lawns were ablaze with colored lights. Raven was more interested in the people but gave the room itself a quick survey.

It was decorated stunningly in white—walls, furniture, rugs—with a few vivid green accents slashed here and there. Raven decided it was gorgeous and that she couldn't have lived in it in a million years. She'd never be able to put her feet up on the elegant, free-form glass coffee table. She went back to the people.

Her eyes sought out Julie with her handsome Italian millionaire. She spotted Wayne with one of his bone-thin models hanging on his arm. Raven decided that the rumors that he would design the costumes for *Fantasy* must be true. There were others Raven recognized: producers, two major stars whom she had watched countless times in darkened theaters, a choreographer she knew only by face and reputation, a screenwriter she had met before socially and several others whom she knew casually or not at all. She and Carly were both drawn into the vortex of the party.

There were dozens of greetings to exchange, along with hand-kissing and cheek-brushing, before Raven could begin to inch her way back toward the edges. She was always more comfortable with one or two people at a time than with a crowd, unless she was onstage. At a touch on her arm, she turned and found herself facing her host.

"Well, hello." Raven smiled, appreciating the chance for a tête-à-tête.

"Hi. I was afraid you weren't going to make it."

Raven realized she shouldn't have been surprised that he had noticed her absence in the crowds of people. Steve Jarett noticed everything. He was a small, slight man with a pale, intense face and dark beard who looked ten years younger than his thirty-seven years. He was considered a perfectionist, often a pain when shooting, but the maker of beautiful films. He had a reputation for patience—enough to cause him to shoot a scene over and over and over again until he got precisely what he wanted. Five years before, he had stunned the industry with a low-budget sleeper that had become the unchallenged hit of the year. His first film had received an Oscar and had opened all the doors that had previously been firmly shut in his face. Steve Jarett held the keys now and knew exactly which ones to use.

He held both of her hands and studied her face. It was he who had insisted on Brand Carstairs as the writer of the original score for *Fantasy* and he who had approved the choice of Raven Williams as collaborator. *Fantasy* was his first musical, and he wasn't going to make any mistakes.

"Lauren's here," he said at length. "Have you met her?"

"No, I'd like to."

"I'd like you to get a real feel for her. I've copies of all of her films and records. You might study them before you begin work on the score."

Raven's brow rose. "I don't think I've missed any of her movies, but I'll watch them again. She is the core of the story."

He beamed suddenly, unexpectedly. "Exactly. And you know Jack Ladd."

"Yes, we've worked together before. You couldn't have picked a better Joe."

"I'm making him work off ten pounds," Jarett said, plucking a canape from a tray. "He has some very unflattering things to say about me at the moment."

"But he's taking off the ten pounds," Raven observed.

Jarett grinned. "Ounce by ounce. We go to the same gym. I keep reminding him Joe's a struggling writer, not a fulfilled hedonist."

Raven gave a low, gurgling laugh and popped a bite of cheese into her mouth. "Overweight or not, you're assembling a remarkable team. I don't know how you managed to wrangle Larry Keaston into choreographing. He's been retired for five years."

"Bribes and perseverance," Jarett said easily, glancing over to where the trim, white-haired former dancer lounged in a pearl-colored armchair. "I'm talking him into doing a cameo." He grinned at Raven again. "He's pretending dignified reluctance, but he's dying to get in front of the cameras again."

"If you can even get him to do a time step on film, you'll have the biggest coup of the decade," Raven observed and shook her head. And he'd do it, she thought. He has the touch.

"He's a big fan of yours," Jarett remarked and watched Raven's eyes widen.

"Of mine? You're joking."

"I am not." He gave Raven a curious look. "He wants to meet you."

Raven stared at Jarett, then again at Larry Keaston. Such things never ceased to amaze her. How many times, as a child, had she watched his movies on fuzzy black and white TV sets in cramped rooms while she had waited for her mother to come home? "You don't have to ask me twice," she told Jarett. She linked her arm in his.

Time passed quickly as Raven began enjoying herself. She talked at length with Larry Keaston and discovered her girlhood idol to be personable and witty. He spoke in a string of expletives delivered in his posh Boston accent. Though she spoke briefly with Jack Ladd, she had yet to meet Lauren Chase when she spotted Wayne drinking quietly in a corner.

"All alone?" she asked as she joined him.

"Observing the masses, my dear," he told her, sipping lightly from his whiskey and soda. "It's amazing how intelligent people will insist on clothing themselves in inappropriate costumes. Observe Lela Marring," he suggested, tilting his head toward a towering brunette in a narrow, pink minidress. "I have no idea why a woman would care to wear a place mat in public."

Raven suppressed a giggle. "She has very nice legs."

"Yes, all five feet of them." He swerved his line of vision. "Then, of course, there's Marshall Peters, who's trying to start a new trend. Chest hair and red satin."

Raven followed the direction of his gaze and this time did giggle. "Not everyone has your savoir-faire, Wayne."

"Of course not," he agreed readily and took out one of his imported cigarettes. "But surely, taste."

"I like the way you've dressed your latest protégée," Raven commented, nodding toward the thin model speaking to a current hot property in the television series game. The model was draped in cobwebby black and gold filigree lace. "I swear, Wayne, she can't be more than eighteen. What do you find to talk about?"

He gave Raven one of his long, sarcastic looks. "Are you being droll, darling?"

She laughed in spite of herself. "Not intentionally."

He gave her a pat on the cheek and lifted his glass again. "I notice Julie has her latest conquest with her, a Latin type with cheekbones."

"Shoes," Raven said vaguely, letting her eyes drift around the room. They rested in disbelief on a girl dressed in skin-tight leather pants and a spangled sweatshirt who wore heart-shaped glasses over heavily kohl-darkened eyes. Knowing Wayne would be horrified, she started to call his attention to her when she spotted Brand across the room.

His eyes were already on hers. Raven realized with a jolt that he had been watching her for some time. It had been at just such a party that they had first met, with noise and laughter and music all around them. Their eyes had found each other's then also.

It had been Raven's first Hollywood party, and she had been unashamedly overwhelmed. There had been people there whom she had known only as voices over the radio or faces on the screen. She had come alone then, too, but in that case it had been a mistake. She hadn't yet learned how to dodge and twist.

She remembered she had been cornered by an actor, though oddly she couldn't recall his name or his face. She hadn't had the experience to deal with him and was slowly being backed against the wall when her eyes had met Brand's. Raven remembered how he had been watching her then, too, rather lazily, a half smile on his mouth. He must have seen the desperation in her eyes, because his smile had widened before he had started to weave his way through the crowd toward her. With perfect aplomb, Brand had slid between Raven and the actor, then had draped his arm over her shoulders.

"Miss me?" he had asked, and he had kissed her lightly before she could respond. "There're some people outside who want to meet you." He had shot the actor an apologetic glance. "Excuse us."

Before another word could be exchanged, he had propelled Raven through the groups of people and out to a terrace. She could still remember the scent of orange blossoms that had drifted from an orchard nearby and the silver sprinkle of moonlight on the flagstone.

Of course Raven had recognized him and had been flustered. She had managed to regain her poise by the time they were alone in the shadows on the terrace. She had brushed a hand through her hair and smiled at him. "Thanks."

"You're welcome." It had been the first time he had studied her in his direct, quiet fashion. She could still remember the sensation of gentle intrusion. "You're not quite what I expected."

"No?" Raven hadn't known exactly how to take that.

"No." He'd smiled at her. "Would you like to go get some coffee?"

"Yes." The agreement had sprung from her lips before she had given it a moment's thought.

"Good. Let's go." Brand had held out his hand. After a brief hesitation, Raven had put hers into it. It had been as simple as that.

"Raven...Raven."

She was tossed back into the present by the sound of Wayne's voice and his hand on her arm.

"Yes...what?" Blandly Raven looked up at him.

"Your thoughts are written all over your face," he murmured. "Not a wise move in a room full of curious people." Taking a fresh glass of champagne from a tray, he handed it to her. "Drink up."

She was grateful for something to do with her hands and took the glass. "I was just thinking," she said inadequately, then made a sound of frustration at Wayne's dry look. "So," she tried another tactic, "it seems we'll be working on the same project."

"Old home week?" he said with a crooked grin.

She shot him a direct look. "We're professionals," she stated, aware that they both knew whom she was speaking of.

"And friends?" he asked, touching a finger to her cheek.

Raven inclined her head. "We might be; I'm a friendly sort of person."

"Hmm." Wayne glanced over her shoulder and watched Brand approach. "At least he knows how to dress," he murmured, approving of Brand's casual but perfectly cut slate-colored slacks and jacket. "But are you sure Cornwall's necessary? Couldn't you try Sausalito?"

Raven laughed. "Is there anything you don't know?"

"I certainly hope not. Hello, Brand, nice to see you again."

Raven turned, smiling easily. The jolt of the memory had passed. "Hello, Brandon."

"Raven." His eyes stayed on her face. "You haven't met Lauren Chase."

With an effort Raven shifted her eyes from his. "No." She smiled and looked at the woman at his side.

Lauren Chase was a slender wisp of a woman with a thick mane of dark, chestnut hair and sea-green eyes. There was something ethereal about her. Perhaps, Raven thought, it was that pale, almost translucent skin or the way she had of walking as though her feet barely touched the ground. She had a strong mouth that folded itself in at the corners and a long, slender neck that she adorned with gold chains. Raven knew she was well into her thirties and decided she looked it. This was a woman who needn't rely on dewy youth for her beauty.

She had been married twice. The first divorce had become an explosive affair that had received a great deal of ugly press. Her second marriage was now seven years old and had produced two children. Raven recalled there was little written about Lauren Chase's current personal life. Obviously, she had learned to guard her privacy.

"Brand tells me you're going to put the heart in the music." Lauren's voice was full and rich.

"That's quite a responsibility." Raven shot Brand a

glance. "Generally Brand considers my lyrics on the sentimental side; often I consider him a cynic."

"Good." Lauren smiled. "Then we should have a score with some meat in it. Steve's given me final word on my own numbers."

Raven lifted a brow. She wasn't altogether certain if this had been a warning or a passing remark. "Then I suppose we should keep you up to date on our progress," she said agreeably.

"By mail and phone," Lauren said, slanting a glance at Brand, "since you're traipsing off halfway around the world to write."

"Artistic temperament," Brand said easily.

"No question, he has it," Raven assured her.

"You should know, I suppose." Lauren lifted a shoulder. Abruptly she fixed Raven with a sharp, straight look. "I want a lot out of this score. This is the one I've been waiting for." It was both a challenge and a demand.

Raven met the look with a slow nod. Lauren Chase was, she decided, the perfect Tessa. "You'll get it."

Lauren touched her upper lip with the tip of her tongue and smiled again. "Yes, I do believe I will at that. Well," she said, turning to Wayne and linking her arm through his, "why don't you get me a drink and tell me about the fabulous costumes you're going to design for me?"

Raven watched them move away. "That," she murmured, toying with the stem of her glass, "is a woman who knows what she wants."

"And she wants an Oscar," Brand remarked. Raven's eyes came back to his. "You'll remember she's been nominated three times and edged out three times. She's determined it isn't going to happen again." He smiled then, fingering the dangling amethyst Raven wore at her ear. "Wouldn't you like to bag one yourself?"

"That's funny, I'd forgotten we could." She let the thought play in her mind. "It sounds good, but we'd better get the thing written before we dream up an acceptance speech."

"How're rehearsals going?"

"Good. Very good." She sipped absently at her champagne. "The band's tight. You leave for Vegas soon, don't you?"

"Yes. Did you come alone?"

She glanced back at him, confused for a moment. "Here? Why, yes. I was late because I'd forgotten about it altogether, but Julie left me a note. Did she introduce you to Lorenzo?"

"No, we haven't crossed paths tonight." As she had begun to search the crowd for Julie, Brand took her chin to bring her eyes back to his. "Will you let me take you home?"

Her expression shifted from startled to wary. "I have my car, Brandon."

"That isn't an answer."

Raven felt herself being drawn in and struggled. "It wouldn't be a good idea."

"Wouldn't it?" She sensed the sarcasm before he smiled, bent down and kissed her. It was a light touch—a tease, a promise or a challenge? "You could be right." He touched her earring again and set it swinging. "I'll see you in a few weeks," he said with a friendly grin, then turned and merged back into the crowd.

Raven stared after him, hardly realizing she had touched her lips with her tongue to seek his taste.

Chapter 6

The theater was dark and quiet. The sound of Raven's footsteps echoed, amplified by the excellent acoustics. Very soon the quiet would be shattered by stagehands, grips, electricians, all the many backstage people who would put together the essential and hardly noticed details of the show. Voices would bounce, mingling with hammering and other sounds of wood and metal. The noise would have a hollow, empty tone, almost like her footsteps. But it was an important sound, an appealing sound, which Raven had always enjoyed.

But she enjoyed the quiet, too and often found herself roaming an empty theater long before she was needed for rehearsals, hours before the fans started to line up outside the main doors. The press would be there then, with their everlasting, eternal questions. And Raven wasn't feeling too chummy with the press at the moment. Already she'd seen a half dozen different stories about herself and Brandon—speculation about their pending collaboration on *Fantasy* and rehashes of their former relationship. Old pictures had been dredged up and reprinted. Old questions were being asked again. Each time it was like bumping the same bruise.

Twice a week she put through a call to the Fieldmore Clinic and held almost identical conversations with Karter. Twice a week he transferred her to her mother's room. Though she knew it was foolish, Raven began to believe all the promises again, all the tearful vows. She began to hope. Without the demands of the tour to keep her occupied and exhausted, she knew she would have been an emotional wreck. Not for the first time in her life, she blessed her luck and her voice.

Mounting the stage, Raven turned to face an imaginary audience. The rows of seats seemed to roll back like a sea. But she knew how to navigate it, had known from the first moment of her first concert. She was an innate performer, just as her voice was natural and untrained. The hesitation, the uncertainty she felt now, had to do with the woman, not the singer. The song had hovered in her mind, but she still paused and considered before bringing it into play. Memories, she felt, could be dangerous things. But she needed to prove something to herself, so she sang. Her voice lifted, drifting to the far corners of the theater; her only accompaniment was her imagination.

> Through the clouds and the rain
> You were there,
> And the sun came through to find us.

Oversentimental? She hadn't thought so when the words had been written. Now Raven sang what she hadn't sung in years. Two minutes and forty-three seconds that bound her and Brand together. Whenever it had played on the radio, she had switched it off, and never, though the requests had been many, had she ever incorporated it in an album or in a concert. She sang it now as a kind of test, remembering the drifting, almost aching harmony of her own low tones combined with Brand's clean, cool voice. She needed to be able to face the memory of working with him if she was to face the reality of doing so. The tour had reached its halfway point. There were only two weeks remaining.

It didn't hurt the way she had been afraid it would; there was no sharp slap across the face. There was more of a warm ache, almost pleasant, somehow sexual. She remembered the last time she had been in Brand's arms in the quiet car in the hills above L.A.

"I've never heard you sing that."

Caught off-guard, Raven swung around to stage right, her hand flying in quick panic to her throat. "Oh, Marc!" On a laugh, she let out a long breath. "You scared the wits out of me. I didn't know anyone was here."

"I didn't want you to stop. I've only heard the cut you and Carstairs made of that." He came forward now out of the shadows, and she saw he had an acoustic guitar slung over his shoulder. It was typical; she rarely saw him without an instrument in his hands or close by. "I've always thought it was too bad you never used it again; it's one of your best. But I guess you didn't want to sing it with anyone else."

Raven looked at him with genuine surprise. Of

course, that had been the essential reason, but she hadn't realized it herself until that moment. "No, I guess I didn't." She smiled at him. "I guess I still don't. Did you come here to practice?"

"I called your room. Julie said you'd probably be here." He walked to her, and since there were no chairs, he sat on the floor. Raven sat with him. She crossed her legs in the dun-colored trousers and let her hair fall over the soft shoulders of her topaz angora sweater. She was relaxed with him, ready to talk or jam like any musician.

Raven smiled at Marc as he went through a quick, complicated lick. "I'm glad you came by. Sometimes I have to get the feel of the theater before a performance. They all begin to run together at this part of a tour." Raven closed her eyes and tilted her head, shaking her hair back. "Where are we, Kansas City? God, I hate the thought of getting back on that airplane. Shuttle here, shuttle there. It always hits me like this at the halfway point. In a couple of days I'll have my second wind."

Marc let her ramble while he played quick, quiet runs on the guitar. He watched her hands as they lay still on her knees. They were very narrow, and although they were tanned golden brown, they remained fragile. There was a light tracing of blue vein just under the skin. The nails were not long but well-shaped and painted in some clear, hardening polish with a blush of pink. There were no rings. Because they were motionless, he knew she was relaxed. Whatever nerves he had sensed when he had first spoken to her were stilled now.

"It's been going well, I think," she continued. "The Glass House is a terrific warm-up act, and the band's tight, even though we lost Kelly. The new bass is good, don't you think?"

"Knows his stuff," Marc said briefly. Raven grinned and reached over to tug his beard.

"So do you," she said. "Let me try."

Agreeably Marc slipped the strap over his head, then handed Raven his guitar. She was a better-than-average player, although she took a great deal of ribbing from the musicians in her troupe whenever she attempted the guitar. Periodically she threatened them with a bogus plan to incorporate her semiskillful playing into the act.

Still she liked to make music with the six strings. It soothed her. There was something intimate about holding an instrument close, feeling its vibrations against your own body. After hitting the same wrong note twice, Raven sighed, then wrinkled her nose at Marc's grin.

"I'm out of practice," she claimed, handing him back his Gibson.

"Good excuse."

"It's probably out of tune."

He ran quickly up and down the scales. "Nope."

"You might be kind and lie." She changed position, putting her feet flat on the floor and lacing her hands over her knees. "It's a good thing you're a musician. You'd have made a lousy politician."

"Too much traveling," he said as his fingers began to move again. He liked the sound of her laughter as it echoed around the empty theater.

"Oh, you're right! How can anyone remain sane going from city to city day after day? And music's such a stable business, too."

"Sturdy as a crap table."

"You've a gift for analogy," she told him, watching the skill of his fingers on the strings. "I love to watch you play," she continued. "It's so effortless. When Brandon was first teaching me, I…" but the words trailed off. Marc glanced up at her face, but his fingers never faltered. "I—it was difficult," she went on, wondering what had made her bring up the matter, "because he was left-handed, and naturally his guitar was, too. He bought me one of my own, but watching him, I had to learn backwards." She laughed, pleased with the memory. Absently she lifted a hand to toy with the thick, dangling staff of her earring. "Maybe that's why I play the way I do. I'm always having to twist it around in my head before it can get to my fingers."

She lapsed into silence while Marc continued to play. It was soothing and somehow intimate with the two of them alone in the huge, empty theater. But his music didn't sound lonely as it echoed. She began to sing with it quietly, as though they were at home, seated on a rug with the walls close and comforting around them.

It was true that the tour had tired her and that the midway point had her feeling drained. But the interlude here was lifting her, though in a different way than the audience would lift her that night. This wasn't the quick, dizzying high that shot endurance back into her for the time she was on stage and in the lights. This was a steadying hand, like a good night's sleep or a home-cooked meal. She smiled at Marc when the song was over and said again, "I'm glad you came."

He looked at her, and for once his hands were silent on the strings. "How long have I been with you, Raven?"

She thought back to when Marc had first become a semiregular part of her troupe. "Four—four and a half—years."

"Five this summer," he corrected. "It was in August, and you were rehearsing for your second tour. You had on baggy white pants and a T-shirt with a rainbow on it. You were barefoot. You had a lost look in your eyes. Carstairs had gone back to England about a month before."

Raven stared at him. She had never heard him make such a long speech. "Isn't it strange that you would remember what I was wearing? It doesn't sound very impressive."

"I remember because I fell in love with you on the spot."

"Oh, Marc." She searched for something to say and found nothing. Instead, she reached up and took his hand. She knew he meant exactly what he said.

"Once or twice I've come close to asking you to live with me."

Raven let out a quick breath. "Why didn't you?"

"Because it would have hurt you to have said no and it would have hurt me to hear it." He laid the guitar across his lap and leaning over it, kissed her.

"I didn't know," she murmured, pressing both of his hands to her cheeks. "I should have. I'm sorry."

"You've never gotten him out of your head, Raven. It's damn frustrating competing with a memory." Marc squeezed her hands a moment, then released them. "It's also safe. I knew you'd never make a commitment to me, so I could avoid making one to you." He shrugged his well-muscled shoulders. "I think it always scared me that you were the kind of woman who would make a man give everything because you asked for nothing."

Her brows drew together. "Am I?"

"You need someone who can stand up to you. I'd

never have been able to. I'd never have been able to say no or shout at you or make crazy love. Life's nothing without things like that, and we'd have ended up hurting each other."

She tilted her head and studied him. "Why are you telling me all this now?"

"Because I realized when I watched you singing that I'll always love you but I'll never have you. And if I did, I'd lose something very special." He reached across to touch her hair. "A fantasy that warms you on cold nights and makes you feel young again when you're old. Sometimes might-have-beens can be very precious."

Raven didn't know whether to smile or to cry. "I haven't hurt you?"

"No," he said so simply she knew he spoke the truth. "You've made me feel good. Have I made you uncomfortable?"

"No." She smiled at him. "You've made me feel good."

He grinned, then rose and held out a hand to her. "Let's go get some coffee."

Brand changed into jeans in his dressing room. It was after two in the morning, but he was wide-awake, still riding on energy left over from his last show. He'd go out, he decided, and put some of it to use at the blackjack table. He could grab Eddie or one of the other guys from the band and cruise the casinos.

There'd be women. Brand knew there'd be a throng of them waiting for him when he left the privacy of his dressing room. He could take his pick. But he didn't want a woman. He wanted a drink and some cards and some action; anything to use up the adrenaline speeding through his system.

He reached for his shirt, and the mirror reflected his naked torso. It was tight and lean, teetering on being thin, but there were surprising cords of muscles in the arms and shoulders. He'd had to use them often when he'd been a boy on the London streets. He always wondered if it had been the piano lessons his mother had insisted on that had saved him from being another victim of the streets. Music had opened up something for him. He hadn't been able to get enough, learn enough. It had been like food, and he had been starving.

At fifteen Brand had started his own band. He was tough and cocky and talked his way into cheap little dives. There had been women even then; not just girls, but women attracted by his youthful sexuality and arrogant confidence. But they'd only been part of the adventure. He had never given up, though the living had been lean in the beer-soaked taverns. He had pulled his way up and made a local reputation for himself; both his music and his personality were strong.

It had taken time. He had been twenty when he had cut his first record, and it had gone nowhere. Brand had recognized that its failure had been due to a combination of poor quality recording, mismanagement and his own see-if-I-care attitude. He had taken a few steps back, found a savvy manager, worked hard on arrangements and talked himself into another recording session.

Two years later he had bought his family a house in the London suburbs, pushed his younger brother into a university and set off on his first American tour.

Now, at thirty, there were times he felt he'd never been off the merry-go-round. Half his life had been given over to his career and its demands. He was tired of wandering. Brand wanted something to focus his life, something to center it. He knew he couldn't give up music, but it wasn't enough by itself anymore. His family wasn't enough, and neither was the money or the applause.

He knew what he wanted. He had known five years before, but there were times he didn't feel as sure of himself as he had when he had been a fifteen-year-old punk talking his way past the back door of a third-rate nightclub. A capacity crowd had just paid thirty dollars a head to hear him, and he knew he could afford to take every cent he made on that two-week gig and throw it away on one roll of the dice. He had an urge to do it. He was restless, reckless, running on the same nerves he had felt the night he'd taken Raven home from their dinner date. He'd only seen her once after that—at Steve Jarett's house. Almost immediately afterward he had flown to Las Vegas to begin polishing his act.

It was catching up with him now—the tension, the anger, the needs. Not for the first time, Brand wondered whether his unreasonable need for her would end if he could have her once, just once. With quick, impatient movements, he thrust the tail of his shirt into the waist of his jeans. He knew better, but there were times he wished it could be. He left the dressing room looking for company.

For an hour Brand sat at the blackjack table. He lost a little, won a little, then lost it again. His mind wasn't on the cards. He had thought the noise, the bright lights, the rich smell of gambling was what he had wanted. There was a thin, intense woman beside him with a huge chunk of diamond on her finger and sapphires around her neck. She drank and lost at the same steady rhythm. Across the table was a young couple he pegged as honeymooners. The gold band on the girl's finger looked brilliantly new and untested. They were giddy with winning what Brand figured was about thirty dollars. There was something touching in their pleasure and in the soft, exchanged looks. All around them came the endless chinkity-chink of the slots.

Brand found himself as restless as he had been an hour before in his dressing room. A half-empty glass of bourbon sat at his elbow, but he left it as he rose. He didn't want the casino, and he felt an enormous surge of envy for the man who had his woman and thirty dollars worth of chips.

When he entered his suite, it was dark and silent, a sharp contrast to the world he had just left. Brand didn't bother hitting the switches as he made his way into the bedroom. Taking out a cigarette, he sat on the bed before lighting it. The flame made a sharp hiss and a brief flare. He sat with the silence, but the adrenaline still pumped. Finally he switched on the small bedside lamp and picked up the phone.

Raven was deep in sleep, but the ringing of the phone shot panic through her before she was fully awake. Her heart pounded in her throat before the mists could clear. She'd grown up with calls coming in the middle of the night. She forgot where she was and fumbled for the phone with a sense of dread and anticipation.

"Yes…hello."

"Raven, I know I woke you. I'm sorry."

She tried to shake away the fog. "Brandon? Is something wrong? Are you all right?"

"Yes, I'm fine. Just unbelievably inconsiderate."

Relaxing, Raven sank back on the pillows and tried to orient herself. "You're in Vegas, aren't you?" The dim light told her it was nearing dawn. He was two hours behind her. Or was it three? She couldn't for the life of her remember what time zone she was in.

"Yes, I'm in Vegas through next week."

"How's the show going?"

It was typical of her, he mused, not to demand to know why the hell he had called her in the middle of the night. She would simply accept that he needed to talk. He drew on the cigarette and wished he could touch her. "Better than my luck at the tables."

She laughed, comfortably sleepy. The connection was clean and sharp; he didn't sound hundreds of miles away. "Is it still blackjack?"

"I'm consistent," he murmured. "How's Kansas?"

"Where?" He laughed, pleasing her. "The audience was fantastic," she continued, letting her mind wander back to the show. "Has been straight along. That's the only thing that keeps you going on a tour like this. Will you be there in time for the show in New York? I'd love you to hear the warm-up act."

"I'll be there." He lay back on the bed as some of the superfluous energy started to drain. "Cornwall is sounding more and more appealing."

"You sound tired."

"I wasn't; I am now. Raven…"

She waited, but he didn't speak. "Yes?"

"I missed you. I needed to hear your voice. Tell me what you're looking at," he demanded, "what you see right now."

"It's dawn," she told him. "Or nearly. I can't see any buildings, just the sky. It's more mauve than gray and the light's very soft and thin." She smiled; it had been a long time since she had seen a day begin. "It's really lovely, Brandon. I'd forgotten."

"Will you be able to sleep again?" He had closed his eyes; the fatigue was taking over.

"Yes, but I'd rather go for a walk, though I don't think Julie would appreciate it if I asked her to come along."

Brand pried off his shoes, using the toe of one foot, then the other. "Go back to sleep, and we'll walk on the cliffs one morning in Cornwall. I shouldn't have woken you."

"No, I'm glad you did." She could hear the change; the voice that had been sharp and alert was now heavy. "Get some rest, Brandon. I'll look for you in New York."

"All right. Good night, Raven."

He was asleep almost before he hung up. Fifteen hundred miles away, Raven laid her cheek on the pillow and watched the morning come.

Chapter 7

Raven tried to be still while her hair was being twisted and knotted and groomed. Her dressing room was banked with flowers; they had been arriving steadily for more than two hours. And it was crowded with people. A tiny little man with sharp, black eyes touched up her blusher. Behind her, occasionally muttering in French, was the nimble-fingered woman who did her hair. Wayne was there, having business of his own here in New York. He'd told Raven that he'd come to see his designs in action and was even now in deep discussion with her dresser. Julie opened the door to another flower delivery.

"Have I packed everything? You know, I should have told Brandon to give me an extra day in town for shopping. There're probably a dozen things I need." Raven turned in her seat and heard the swift French oath as her partially knotted hair flew from the woman's fingers. "Sorry, Marie. Julie, did I pack a coat? I might need one." Slipping the card from the latest arrangement of flowers, she found it was from a successful television producer with whom she'd worked on her last TV special. "They're from Max.... There's a party tonight. Why don't you go?" She handed the card to Julie and allowed her lip liner to be straightened by the finicky makeup artist.

"Yes, you packed a coat, your suede, which you could need this early in the spring. And several sweaters," Julie said distractedly, checking her list. "And maybe I will."

"I can't believe this is it, the last show. It's been a good tour, hasn't it, Julie?" Raven turned her head and winced at the sharp tug on her hair.

"I can't remember you ever getting a better response or deserving one more...."

"And we're all glad it's over," Raven finished for her.

"I'm going to sleep for a week." Julie found space for the flowers, then continued to check off things in her notebook. "Not everyone has your constant flow of energy."

"I love playing New York," she said, tucking up her legs to the despair of her hairdresser.

"You must hold still!"

"Marie, if I hold still much longer, I'm going to explode." Raven smiled at the makeup artist as he fussed around her face. "You always know just what to do. It looks perfect; I feel beautiful."

Recognizing the signal, Julie began nudging people from the room. Eventually they went, and soon only Julie and Wayne were left. The room quieted considerably; now the walls hummed gently with the vibrations of the warm-up act. Raven let out a deep sigh.

"I'll be so glad to have my face and body and hair back," she said and sprawled in the chair. "You should have seen what he made me put all over my face this morning."

"What was it?" Wayne asked absently as he smoothed the hem of one of her costumes.

"Green," she told him and shuddered.

He laughed and turned to Julie. "What are you going to do when this one takes off to the moors?"

"Cruise the Greek Islands and recuperate." She pushed absently at the small of her back. "I've already booked passage on the ninth. These tours are brutal."

"Listen to her." Raven sniffed and peered at herself critically in the glass. "She's the one who's held the whip and chair for four weeks. He certainly makes me look exotic, doesn't he?" She wrinkled her nose and spoiled the effect.

"Into costume," Julie commanded.

"See? Orders, orders." Obediently Raven rose.

"Here." Wayne lifted the red and silver dress from the hanger. "Since I nudged your dresser along, I'll be your minion."

"Oh, good, thanks." She stepped out of her robe and into the dress. "You know, Wayne," she continued as he zipped her up, "you were right about the black number. It gets a tremendous response. I never know if they're applauding me or the costume after that set."

"Have I ever let you down?" he demanded as he tucked a pleat.

"No." She turned her head to smile at him over her shoulder. "Never. Will you miss me?"

"Tragically." He kissed her ear.

There was a brief, brisk knock at the door. "Ten minutes, Ms. Williams."

She took a long breath. "Are you going to go out front?"

"I'll stay back with Julie." He glanced over at her, lifting a brow in question.

"Yes, thanks. Here, Raven, don't forget these wonderfully gaudy earrings." She watched Raven fasten one. "Really, Wayne, they're enough to make me shudder, but they're fabulous with that dress."

"Naturally."

She laughed, shaking her head. "The man's ego," she said to Raven, "never ceases to amaze me."

"As long as it doesn't outdistance the talent," he put in suavely.

"New York audiences are tough." Raven spoke quickly, her voice jumping suddenly with nerves and excitement. "They scare me to death."

"I thought you said you loved playing New York." Wayne took out a cigarette and offered one to Julie.

"I do, especially at the end of a tour. It keeps you sharp. They're really going to know if I'm not giving them everything. How do I look?"

"The dress is sensational," Wayne decided. "You'll do."

"Some help you are."

"Let's go," Julie urged. "You'll miss your cue."

"I never miss my cue." Raven fussed with the second earring, stalling. He'd said he'd be here, she told herself. *Why isn't he?* He could have gotten the time mixed up, or he could be caught in traffic. Or he could simply have forgotten that he'd promised to be here for the show.

The quick knock came again. "Five minutes, Ms. Williams."

"Raven." Julie's voice was a warning.

"Yes, yes, all right." She turned and gave them both a flippant smile. "Tell me I'm wonderful when it's over, even if I wasn't. I want to end the tour feeling marvelous."

Then she was dashing for the door and hurrying down the hall where the sounds of the warm-up band were no longer gentle; now they shook the walls.

"Ms. Williams, Ms. Williams! Raven!"

She turned, breaking the concentration she'd been building and looked at the harried stage manager. He thrust a white rose into her hand.

"Just came back for you."

Raven took the bud and lifted it, wanting to fill herself with the scent. She needed no note or message to tell her it was from Brand. For a moment she simply dreamed over it.

"Raven." The warm-up act had finished; the transition to her own band would take place on the darkened stage quickly. "You're going to miss your cue."

"No, I'm not." She gave the worried stage manager a kiss, forgetful of her carefully applied lipstick. Twirling the rose between her fingers, she took it with her. They were introducing her as she reached the wings.

Big build-up; don't let the audience cool down. They were already cheering for her. *Thirty seconds; take a breath.* Her band hit her introduction. Music crashed through the cheers. *One, two, three!*

She ran out, diving into a wave of applause.

The first set was hot and fast, staged to keep the audience up and wanting more. She seemed to be a ball of flame with hundreds of colored lights flashing around her. Raven knew how to play to them, play with them, and she pumped all her energy into a routine she had done virtually every night for four weeks. Enthusiasm and verve kept it fresh. It was hot under the lights, but she didn't notice. She was wrapping herself in the audience, in the music. The costume sizzled and sparked. Her voice smoked.

It was a demanding forty minutes, and when she rushed offstage during an instrumental break, she had less than three minutes in which to change costumes. Now she was in white, a brief, shimmering top covered with bugle beads matched with thin harem pants. The pace would slow a bit, giving the audience time to catch their breath. The balance was in ballads, the slow trembling ones she did best. The lighting was muted, soft and moody.

It was during a break between songs, when she traditionally talked to the audience, that someone in the audience spotted Brand in their midst. Soon more people knew, and while Raven went on unaware of the disturbance, the crowd soon became vocal. Shielding her eyes, she could just make out the center of the commotion. Then she saw him. It seemed they wanted him up on stage.

Raven was a good judge of moods and knew the value of showmanship. If she didn't invite Brand on stage, she'd lose the crowd. They had already taken the choice out of her hands.

"Brandon." Raven spoke softly into the mike, but her voice carried. Though she couldn't see his eyes with the spotlight in her own, she knew he was looking at her. "If you come up and sing," she told him, lightly, "we

might get you a refund on your ticket." She knew he'd
grin at that. There was an excited rush of applause and
cheers as he rose and came to the stage.

He was all in black: trim, well-cut slacks and a casual
polo sweater. The contrast was striking as he stood beside her. It might have been planned. Smiling at her, he
spoke softly, out of the range of the microphone. "I'm
sorry, Raven, I should have gone backstage. I wanted
to watch you from out front."

She tilted her head. It was, she discovered, more
wonderful to see him than she had imagined. "You're
the one being put to work. What would you like to do?"

Before he could answer, the demands sprang from
the crowd. Once the idea formed, it was shouted over
and over with growing enthusiasm. Raven's smile faded.
"Clouds and Rain."

Brand took her wrist and lifted the rose she held.
"You remember the words, don't you?"

It was a challenge. A stagehand rushed out with a
hand mike for Brand.

"My band doesn't know it," she began.

"I know it." Marc shifted his guitar and watched
them. The crowd was still shouting when he gave the
opening chords. "We'll follow you."

Brand kept his hand on Raven's wrist and lifted his
own mike.

Raven knew how it needed to be sung: face-to-face,
eye to eye. It was a caress of a song, meant for lovers.
The audience was silent now. Their harmony was close,
intricate. Raven had once thought it must be like making love. Their voices flowed into each other. And she
forgot the audience, forgot the stage and for a moment
forgot the five years.

There was more intimacy in singing with him than she had ever allowed in any other aspect of their relationship. Here she could not resist him. When he sang to her, it was as if he told her there wasn't anyone else, had never been anyone else. It was more moving than a kiss, more sexual than a touch.

When they finished, their voices hung a moment, locked together. Brand saw her lips tremble before he brought her close and took them.

They might have been on an island rather than on stage, spotlighted for thousands. She didn't hear the tumultuous applause, the cheers, the shouting of their names. Her arms went around him, one hand holding the mike, the other the rose. Cameras flashed like fireworks, but she was trapped in a velvet darkness. She lost all sense of time; her lips might have moved on his for hours or days or only seconds. But when he drew her away, she felt a keener sense of loss than any she had ever known before. Brand saw the confusion in her eyes, the dazed desire, and smiled.

"You're better than you ever were, Raven." He kissed her hand. "Too bad about those sentimental numbers you keep sticking into the act."

Her brows rose. "Try to boost your flagging career by letting you sing with me, and you insult me." Her balance was returning as they took a couple of elaborate bows, hands linked.

"Let's see if you can carry the rest on your own, love. I've warmed them back up for you." He kissed her again, but lightly now, on the cheek, before he waved to the audience and strolled offstage left.

Raven grinned at his back, then turned to her audience. "Too bad he never made it, isn't it?"

* * *

Raven should have been wrung dry after the two hours were over. But she wasn't. She'd given them three encores, and though they clamored for more, Brand caught her hand as she hesitated in the wings.

"They'll keep you out there all night, Raven." He could feel the speed of her pulse under his fingers. Because he knew how draining two hours onstage could be, he urged her back down the hall toward her dressing room.

There were crowds of people jammed in together in the hallway, congratulating her, touching her. Now and then a reporter managed to elbow through to shoot out a question. She answered, and Brandon tossed off remarks with quick charm while steering her determinedly toward her dressing room. Once inside, he locked the door.

"I think they liked me," she said gravely, then laughed and spun away from him. "I feel so good!" Her eyes lit on the bucket of ice that cradled a bottle. "Champagne?"

"I thought you'd need to console yourself after a flop like that." Brand moved over and drew out the bottle. "You'll have to open the door soon and see people. Do try to put on a cheerful front, love."

"I'll do my best." The cork popped, and the white froth fizzed a bit over the mouth of the bottle.

Brand poured two glasses to the rim and handed her one. "I meant it, Raven." He touched his glass to hers. "You were never better."

Raven smiled, bringing the glass to her lips. Again, he felt the painful thrust of desire. Carefully Brand took the glass from her, then set both it and his own down again. "There's something I didn't finish out there tonight."

She was unprepared. Even though he drew her close slowly and took his time bringing his mouth to hers, Raven wasn't ready. It was a long, deep, kiss that mingled with the champagne. His mouth was warm on hers, seeking. His hands ran over her hips, snugly encased in the thin black jumpsuit, but she could sense he was under very tight control.

His tongue made a thorough, lengthy journey through the moist recesses of her mouth, and she responded in kind. But he wanted her to do more than give; he wanted her to want more. And she did, feeling the pull of need, the flash of passion. She could feel the texture of his long, clever fingers through the sheer material of her costume, then flesh to flesh as he brought them up to caress the back of her neck.

Her head was swimming with a myriad of sensations: excitement and power still clinging from her performance; the heady, heavy scent of mixed flowers which crowded the air; the firm press of his body against her; and desire, more complex, more insistent than she had been prepared for.

"Brandon," she murmured against his lips. She wanted him, wanted him desperately, and was afraid.

Brand drew her away, then carefully studied her face. Her eyes were like thin glass over her emotions. "You're beautiful, Raven, one of the most beautiful women I know."

She was unsteady and tried to find her balance without clinging to him. She stepped back, resting her hand on the table that held their glasses. "One of the most?" she challenged, lifting her champagne.

"I know a lot of women." He grinned as he lifted his own glass. "Why don't you take that stuff off your face so I can see you?"

"Do you know how long I had to sit still while he troweled this stuff on?" Moving to the dressing table, she scooped up a generous glob of cold cream. Her blood was beginning to settle. "It's supposed to make me glamorous and alluring." She slathered it on.

"You make me nervous when you're glamorous, and you'd be alluring in a paper sack."

She lifted her eyes to his in the mirror. His expression was surprisingly serious. "I think that was a compliment." She smeared the white cream generously over her face and grinned. "Am I alluring now?"

Brand grinned back, then slowly let his eyes roam down her back to focus on her snugly clad bottom. "Raven, don't fish. The answer is obvious."

She began to tissue off the cream and with it the stage makeup. "Brandon. It was good to sing with you again." After removing the last of the cream from her face, Raven toyed with the stem of her champagne glass. "I always felt very special when I sang with you. I still do." He watched her chew for a moment on her bottom lip as if she was unsure about what she should say. "I imagine they'll play up that duet in the papers. They'll probably make something else out of it, especially— especially with the way we ended it."

"I like the way we ended it." Brand came over and laid his hands on her shoulders. "It should always be ended that way." He kissed the back of her neck while his eyes smiled into hers in the glass. "Are you worried about the press, Raven?"

"No, of course not. But, Brandon…"

"Do you know," he interrupted, brushing the hair away from her neck with the back of his hand, "no one else calls me that but my mother. Strange." He bent, nuzzling his lips into the sensitive curve of her neck. "You affect me in an entirely different way."

"Brandon…"

"When I was a boy," he continued, moving his lips up to her ear, "and she called me Brandon, I knew that was it. Whatever crime I'd committed had been found out. Justice was about to strike."

"I imagine you committed quite a few crimes." She forced herself to speak lightly. When she would have moved away, he turned her around to face him.

"Too many to count." He leaned to her, but instead of the kiss she expected and prepared for, he caught her bottom lip between his teeth. She clutched at his shirt as she struggled for breath and balance. Their eyes were open and on each other's, but his face dimmed, then faded, as passion clouded her vision.

Brand released her, then gave her a quick kiss on the nose. Raven ran a hand through her hair, trying to steady herself. He was tossing her back and forth too swiftly, too easily.

"Do you want to change before we let anyone in?" he asked. When she could focus again, Raven saw he was drinking champagne and watching her. There was an odd look on his face, as if, she thought, he were a boxer checking for weaknesses, looking for openings.

"I—yes." Raven brought herself back. "Yes, I think I would, but…" She glanced around the dressing room. "I don't know what I did with my clothes."

He laughed, and the look was gone from his face. Relieved, Raven laughed with him. They began to search through the flowers and sparkling costumes for her jeans and tennis shoes.

Chapter 8

It was late when they arrived at the airport. Raven was still riding on post-performance energy and chattered about everything that came into her head. She looked up at a half-moon as she and Brand transferred from limo to plane. The private jet wasn't what she had been expecting, and studying the comfortably lush interior of the main cabin helped to allay the fatigue of yet one more flight.

It was carpeted with a thick, pewter-colored shag and contained deep, leather chairs and a wide, plush sofa. There was a padded bar at one end and a doorway at the other which she discovered led into a tidy galley. "You didn't have this before," she commented as she poked her head into another room and found the bath, complete with tub.

"I bought it about three years ago." Brand sprawled

on the sofa and watched her as she explored. She looked different than she had a short time before. Her face was naked now, and he found he preferred it that way. Makeup seemed to needlessly gloss over her natural beauty. She wore faded jeans and sneakers, which she immediately pried off her feet. An oversize yellow sweater left her shapeless. It made him want to run his hands under it and find her. "Do you still hate to fly?"

Raven gave him a rueful grin. "Yes. You'd think after all this time I'd have gotten over it, but…" She continued to roam the cabin, not yet able to settle. If she had to, Raven felt she could give the entire performance again. She had enough energy.

"Strap in," Brand suggested, smiling at the quick, nervous gestures. "We'll get started, then you won't even know you're in the air."

"You don't know how many times I've heard that one." Still she did as he said and waited calmly enough while he told the pilot they were ready. In a few minutes they were airborne, and she was able to unstrap and roam again.

"I know the feeling," Brand commented, watching her. She turned in silent question. "It's as though you still have one last burst of energy to get rid of. It's the way I felt that night in Vegas when I called and woke you up."

She caught back her hair with both hands. "I feel I should jog for a few miles. It might settle me down."

"How about some coffee?"

"Yes." She wandered over to a porthole and pressed her nose against it. It was black as pitch outside the glass. "Yes, coffee would be nice, then you can tell me what marvelous ideas you have forming for the score. You've probably got dozens of them."

"A few." She heard the clatter of cups. "I imagine you've some of your own."

"A few," she said, and he chuckled. Turning away from the dark window, she saw him leaning against the opening between the galley and the main cabin. "How soon do you think we'll start to fight?"

"Soon enough. Let's wait at least until we're settled into the house. Is Julie going back to L.A., or have you tied up all your loose ends there?"

A shadow visited her face. Raven thought of the one brief visit she had paid to her mother since the start of the tour. They had had a day's layover in Chicago, and she had used the spare time to make the impossible flight to the coast and back. There had been the inevitable interview with Karter and a brief, emotional visit with her mother. Raven had been relieved to see that the cast had gone from her mother's skin and that there was more flesh to her face. There had been apologies and promises and tears, just as there always were, Raven thought wearily. And as she always did, she had begun to believe them again.

"I never seem to completely tie up the loose ends," she murmured.

"Will you tell me what's wrong?"

She shook her head. She couldn't bear to dwell on unhappiness now. "No, nothing, nothing really." The kettle sang out, and she smiled. "Your cue," she told him.

He studied her for a moment while the kettle spit peevishly behind him. Then, turning, he went back into the galley to fix the coffee. "Black?" he asked, and she gave an absent assent.

Sitting on the sofa, Raven let her head fall back while the energy began to subside. It was almost as if she could feel it draining. Brand recognized the signs as soon as he came back into the room. He set down her mug of coffee, then sipped thoughtfully from his own as he watched her. Sensing him, Raven slowly opened her eyes. There was silence for a moment; her body and her mind were growing lethargic.

"What are you doing?" she murmured.

"Remembering."

Her lids shuttered down, concealing her eyes and their expression. "Don't."

He drank again, letting his eyes continue their slow, measured journey over her. "It's a bit much to ask me not to remember, Raven, isn't it?" It was a question that expected no answer, and she gave it none. But her lids fluttered up again.

He didn't have her full trust, nor did he believe he had ever had it. That was the root of their problems. He studied her while he stood and drank his coffee. There was high, natural color in her cheeks, and her eyes were dark and sleepy. She sat, as was her habit, with her legs crossed under her and her hands on her knees. In contrast to the relaxed position, her fingers moved restlessly.

"I still want you. You know that, don't you?"

Again Raven left his question unanswered, but he saw the pulse in her throat begin to thump. When she spoke, her voice was calm. "We're going to work together, Brandon. It's best not to complicate things."

He laughed, not in mockery but in genuine amusement. She watched his eyes lose their brooding intensity and light. "By all means, let's keep things simple." After draining his coffee, he walked over and sat beside her. In a smooth, practiced move, he drew her against his side. "Relax," he told her, annoyed when she resisted. "Give me some credit. I know how tired you are. When are you going to trust me, Raven?"

She tilted her head until she could see him. Her look was long and eloquent before she settled into the crook of his shoulder and let out a long sigh. Like a child, she fell asleep quickly, and like that of a child, the sleep was deep. For a long moment he stayed as he was, Raven curled against his side. Then he laid her down on the sofa, watching as her hair drifted about her.

Rising, Brand switched off the lights. In the dark he settled into one of the deep cabin chairs and lit a cigarette. Time passed as he sat gazing out at a sprinkle of stars and listening to Raven's soft, steady breathing. Unable to resist, he rose, and moving to her, lay down beside her. She stirred when he brushed the hair from her cheek, but only to snuggle closer to him. Over the raw yearning came a curiously sweet satisfaction. He wrapped his arm around her, felt her sigh, then slept.

It was Brand who awoke first. As was his habit, his mind and body came together quickly. He lay still and allowed his eyes to grow accustomed to the darkness. Beside him, curled against his chest, Raven slept on.

He could make out the curve of her face, the pixie sharp features, the rain straight fall of hair. Her leg was bent at the knee and had slipped between his. She was soft and warm and tempting. Brand knew he had experience enough to arouse her into submission before she was fully awake. She would be drowsy and disoriented.

The hazy gray of early dawn came upon them as he watched her. He could make out her lashes now, a long sweep of black that seemed to weigh her lids down. He wanted her, but not that way. Not the first time. Asleep, she sighed and moved against him. Desire rippled along his skin. Carefully Brand shifted away from her and rose.

In the kitchen he began to make coffee. A glance at his watch and a little arithmetic told him they'd be landing soon. He thought rather enthusiastically about breakfast. The drive from the airport to his house would take some time. He remembered an inn along the way where they could get a good meal and coffee better than the instant he was making.

Hearing Raven stir, he came to the doorway and watched her wake up. She moaned, rolled over and unsuccessfully tried to bury her face. Her hand reached out for a pillow that wasn't there, then slowly, on a disgusted sigh, she opened her eyes. Brand watched the stages as her eyes roamed the room. First came disinterest, then confusion, then sleepy understanding.

"Good morning," he ventured, and she shifted her eyes to him without moving her head. He was grinning at her, and his greeting was undeniably cheerful. She had a wary respect for cheerful risers.

"Coffee," she managed and shut her eyes again.

"In a minute." The kettle was beginning to hiss behind him. "How'd you sleep?"

Dragging her hands through her hair, she made a courageous attempt to sit up. The light was still gray but now brighter, and she pressed her fingers against her eyes for a moment. "I don't know yet," she mumbled from behind her hands. "Ask me later."

The whistle blew, and as Brand disappeared back into the galley, Raven brought her knees up to her chest and buried her face against them. She could hear him talking to her, making bright, meaningless conversation, but her mind wasn't yet receptive. She made no attempt to listen or to answer.

"Here, love." As Raven cautiously raised her head, Brand held out a steaming mug. "Have a bit, then you'll feel better." She accepted with murmured thanks. He sat down beside her. "I've a brother who wakes up ready to bite someone's—anyone's—head off. It's metabolism, I suppose."

Raven made a noncommittal sound and began to take tentative sips. It was hot and strong. For some moments there was silence as he drank his own cream-cooled coffee and watched her. When her cup was half empty, she looked over and managed a rueful smile.

"I'm sorry, Brandon. I'm simply not at my best in the morning. Especially early in the morning." She tilted her head so that she could see his watch, made a brave stab at mathematics, then gave up. "I don't suppose it matters what time it actually is," she decided, going back to the coffee. "It'll take me days to adjust to the change, anyway."

"A good meal will set you up," he told her, lazily sipping at his own coffee. "I read somewhere where drinking yeast and jogging cures jet lag, but I'll take my chances with breakfast."

"Yeast?" Raven grimaced into her mug, then drained it. "I think sleep's a better cure, piles of it." The mists were clearing, and she shook back her hair. "I guess we'll be landing soon, won't we?"

"Less than an hour, I'd say."

"Good. The less time I spend awake on a plane, the less time I have to think about being on one. I slept like a rock." With another sigh, Raven stretched her back, letting her shoulders lift and fall with the movement. "I made poor company." Her system was starting to hum again, though on slow speed.

"You were tired." Over the rim of his cup he watched the subtle movements of her body beneath the oversize sweater.

"I turned off like a tap," she admitted. "It happens that way sometimes after a concert." She lifted one shoulder in a quick shrug. "But I suppose we'll both be better today for the rest. Where did you sleep?"

"With you."

Raven closed her mouth on a yawn, swallowed and stared at him. "What?"

"I said I slept with you, here on the couch." Brand made a general gesture with his hand. "You like to snuggle."

She could see he was enjoying her dismayed shock. His eyes were deep blue with amusement as he lifted his cup again. "You had no right..." Raven began.

"I always fancied being the first man you slept with," he told her before draining his cup. "Want some more coffee?"

Raven's face flooded with color; her eyes turned dark and opaque. She sprang up, but Brand managed to pluck the cup from her hand before she could hurl it across the room. For a moment she stood, breathing hard, watching him while he gave her his calm, measuring stare.

"Don't flatter yourself," she tossed out. "You don't know how many men I've slept with."

Very precisely, he set down both coffee cups, then

looked back up at her. "You're as innocent as the day you were born, Raven. You've barely been touched by a man, much less been made love to."

Her temper flared like a rocket. "You don't know anything about who I've been with in the last five years, Brandon." She struggled to keep from shouting, to keep her voice as calm and controlled as his. "It's none of your business how many men I've slept with."

He lifted a brow, watching her thoughtfully. "Innocence isn't something to be ashamed of, Raven."

"I'm not…" She stopped, balling her fists. "You had no right to—" She swallowed and shook her head as fury and embarrassment raced through her. "—While I was asleep," she finished.

"Do what while you were asleep?" Brandon demanded, lazing back on the sofa. "Ravish you?" His humor shimmered over the old-fashioned word and made her feel ridiculous. "I don't think you'd have slept through it, Raven."

Her voice shook with emotion. "Don't laugh at me, Brandon."

"Then don't be such a fool." He reached over to the table beside him for a cigarette, then tapped the end of it against the surface without lighting it. His eyes were fixed on hers and no longer amused. "I could have had you if I'd wanted to, make no mistake about it."

"You have colossal nerve, Brandon. Please remember that you're not privy to my sex life and that you wouldn't have had me because I don't want you. I choose my own lovers."

She hadn't realized he could move so fast. The indolent slouch on the sofa was gone in a flash. He reached up, seizing her wrist, and in one swift move had yanked her down on her back, trapping her body with his. Her gasp of surprise was swallowed as his weight pressed down on her.

Never, in all the time they had spent together past and present, had Raven seen him so angry. An iron taste of fear rose in her throat. She could only shake her head, too terrified to struggle, too stunned to move. She had never suspected he possessed the capacity for violence she now read clearly on his face. This was far different from the cold rage she had seen before and which she knew how to deal with. His fingers bit into her wrist while his other hand came to circle her throat.

"How far do you think I'll push?" he demanded. His voice was harsh and deep with the hint of Ireland more pronounced. Her breathing was short and shallow with fear. Lying completely still, she made no answer. "Don't throw your imaginary string of lovers in my face, or, by God, you'll have a real one quickly enough whether you want me or not." His fingers tightened slightly around her throat. "When the time comes, I won't need to get you drunk on champagne or on exhaustion to have you lie with me. I could have you now, this minute, and after five minutes of struggle you'd be more than willing." His voice lowered, trembling along her skin. "I know how to play you, Raven, and don't you forget it."

His face was very close to hers. Their breathing mixed, both swift and strained, the only sound coming from the hum of the plane's engines. The fear in her eyes leaped out, finally penetrating his fury. Swearing, Brand pushed himself from her and rose. Her eyes stayed on his as she waited for what he would do next. He stared at her, then turned sharply away, moving over to a porthole.

Raven lay where she was, not realizing she was massaging the wrist that throbbed from his fingers. She watched him drag a hand through his hair.

"I slept with you last night because I wanted to be close to you." He took another long, cleansing breath. "It was nothing more than that. I never touched you. It was an innocent and rather sweet way to spend the night." He curled his fingers into a fist, remembering the frantic flutter of her pulse under his hand when he had circled it around her throat. It gave him no pleasure to know he had frightened her. "It never occurred to me that it would offend you like this. I apologize."

Raven covered her eyes with her hand as the tears began. She swallowed sobs, not wanting to give way to them. Guilt and shame washed over her as fear drained. Her reaction to Brand's simple, affectionate gesture had been to slap his face. It had been embarrassment, she knew, but more, her own suppressed longing for him that had pushed her to react with anger and spiteful words. She'd tried to provoke him and had succeeded. But more, she knew now she had hurt him. Rising from the sofa, she attempted to make amends.

Though she walked over to stand behind him, Raven didn't touch him. She couldn't bear the thought that he might stiffen away from her.

"Brandon, I'm so sorry." She dug her teeth into her bottom lip to keep her voice steady. "That was stupid of me, and worse, unkind. I'm terribly ashamed of the way I acted. I wanted to make you angry; I was embarrassed, I suppose, and…" The words trailed off as she searched for some way to describe the way she had felt. Even now something inside her warmed and stirred at the knowledge that she had lain beside him, sharing the intimacy of sleep.

Raven heard him swear softly, then he rubbed a hand over the back of his neck. "I baited you."

"You're awfully good at it," she said, trying to make light of what had passed between them. "Much better than I am. I can't think about what I'm saying when I'm angry."

"Obviously, neither can I. Look, Raven," Brand began and turned. Her eyes were huge, swimming with restrained tears. He broke off what he had been about to say and moved to the table for his cigarettes. After lighting one, he turned back to her. "I'm sorry I lost my temper. It's something I don't do often because it's a nasty one. And you've got a good aim with a punch, Raven, and it reminded me of the last time we were together five years ago."

She felt her stomach tighten in defense. "I don't think either of us should dwell on that."

"No." He nodded slowly. His eyes were calm again and considering. Raven knew he was poking into her brain. "Not at the moment, in any case. We should get on with today." He smiled, and she felt each individual muscle in her body relax. "It seems we couldn't wait until we settled in before having a fight."

"No." She answered his smile. "But then I've always been impatient." Moving to him, Raven rose on her toes and pressed her lips tightly to his. "I'm really sorry, Brandon."

"You've already apologized."

"Yes, well, just remember the next time, it'll be your turn to grovel."

Brand tugged on her hair. "I'll make some more coffee. We should have time for one more cup before we have to strap in."

When he had gone into the galley, Raven stood where she was a moment. The last time, she thought, five years ago.

She remembered it perfectly: each word, each hurt. And she remembered that the balance of the fault then had also been hers. They'd been alone; he'd wanted her. She had wanted him. Then everything had gone wrong. Raven remembered how she had shouted at him, near hysteria. He'd been patient, then his patience had snapped, though not in the way it had today. Then, she remembered, he'd been cold, horribly, horribly cold. Comparing the two reactions, Raven realized she preferred the heat and violence to the icy disdain.

Raven could bring the scene back with ease. They'd been close, and the desire had risen to warm her. Then it was furnace hot and she was smothering, then shouting at him not to touch her. She'd told him she couldn't bear for him to touch her. Brand had taken her at her word and left her. Raven could easily remember the despair, the regret and confusion—and the love for him outweighing all else.

But when she had gone to find him the next morning, he had already checked out of his hotel. He had left California, left her, without a word. And there'd been no word from him in five years. No word, she mused, but for the stories in every magazine, in every newspaper. No word but for the whispered comments at parties and in restaurants whenever she would walk in. No word but for the constant questions, the endless speculation in print as to why they were no longer an item—why Brand Carstairs had begun to collect women like trophies.

So she had forced him out of her mind. Her work, her talent and her music had been used to fill the holes he had left in her life. She'd steadied herself and built a life with herself in control again. That was for the best, she had decided. Sharing the reins was dangerous. And, she mused, glancing toward the galley, it would still be dangerous. *He* would still be dangerous.

Quickly Raven shook her head. Brandon was right, she told herself. It was time to concentrate on today. They had work to do, a score to write. Taking a deep breath, she walked to the galley to help him with the coffee.

Chapter 9

Raven fell instantly in love with the primitive countryside of Cornwall. She could accept this as the setting for Arthur's Camelot. It was easy to imagine the clash of swords and the glint of armor, the thundering gallop of swift horses.

Spring was beginning to touch the moors, the green blooms just now emerging. Here and there was the faintest touch of pink from wild blossoms. A fine, constant drizzling mist added to the romance. There were houses, cottages really, with gardens beginning to thrive. Lawns were a tender, thin green, and she spotted the sassy yellow of daffodils and the sleepy blue of wood hyacinths. Brand drove south toward the coast and cliffs and Land's End.

They had eaten a country breakfast of brown eggs, thick bacon and oat cakes and had set off again in the little car Brand had arranged to have waiting for them at the airport.

"What's your house like, Brandon?" Raven asked as she rummaged through her purse in search of something to use to secure her hair. "You've never told me anything about it."

He glanced at her bent head. "I'll let you decide for yourself when you see it. It won't be long now."

Raven found two rubber bands of differing sizes and colors. "Are you being mysterious, or is this your way of avoiding telling me the roof leaks."

"It might," Brand considered. "Though I don't recall being dripped on. The Pengalleys would see to it; they're quite efficient about that sort of thing."

"Pengalleys?" Raven began to braid her hair.

"Caretakers," he told her. "They've a cottage a mile or so off from the house. They kept an eye on the place, and she does a bit of housekeeping when I'm in residence. He does the repairs."

"Pengalley," she murmured, rolling the name over on her tongue.

"Cornishmen, tried and true," Brand remarked absently.

"I know!" Raven turned to him with a sudden smile. "She's short and a bit stout, not fat, just solidly built, with dark hair pulled back and a staunch, rather disapproving face. He's thinner and going gray, and he tipples a bit from a flask when he thinks she's not looking."

Brand quirked a brow and shot her another brief glance. "Very clever. Just how did you manage it?"

"It had to be," Raven shrugged as she secured one braid and started on the next, "if any gothic novel

I've ever read had a dab of truth in it. Are there any neighbors?"

"No one close by. That's one of the reasons I bought it."

"Antisocial?" she asked, smiling at him.

"Survival instinct," Brand corrected. "Sometimes I have to get away from it or go mad. Then I can go back and slip into harness again and enjoy it. It's like recharging." He felt her considering look and grinned. "I told you I'd mellowed."

"Yes," she said slowly, "you did." Still watching him, Raven twisted the rubber band around the tip of the second braid. "Yet you've still managed to put out quite a bit. All the albums, the double one last year; all but five of the songs were yours exclusively. And the songs you wrote for Cal Ripley—they were the best cuts on his album."

"Did you think so?" he asked.

"You know they were," she said, letting the rubber band snap into place.

"Praise is good for the ego, love."

"You've had your share now." She tossed both braids behind her back. "What I was getting at was that for someone who's so mellow, you're astonishingly productive."

"I do a lot of my writing here," Brand explained. "Or at my place in Ireland. More here, actually, because I've family across the channel, so there's visiting to be done if I'm there."

Raven gave him a curious look. "I thought you still lived in London."

"Primarily, but if I've serious work or simply need to be alone, I come here. I've family in London as well."

"Yes." Raven looked away again out into the misty landscape. "I suppose large families have disadvantages."

Something in her tone made him glance over again, but her face was averted. He said nothing, knowing from experience that any discussion of Raven's family was taboo. Occasionally in the past, he had probed, but she had always evaded him. He knew that she had been an only child and had left home at seventeen. Out of curiosity, Brand had questioned Julie. Julie knew all there was to know about Raven, he was certain, but she had told him nothing. It was yet another mystery about Raven which alternately frustrated and attracted Brand. Now he put the questions in the back of his mind and continued smoothly.

"Well, we won't be troubled by family or neighbors. Mrs. Pengalley righteously disapproves of show people, and will keep a healthy distance."

"Show people?" Raven repeated and turning back to him, grinned. "Have you been having orgies again, Brand?"

"Not for at least three months," he assured her and swung onto a back road. "I told you I'd mellowed. But she knows about actors and actresses, you see, because as Mr. Pengalley tells me, she makes it her business to read everything she can get her hands on about them. And as for musicians, *rock* musicians, well…" He let the sentence trail off meaningfully, and Raven giggled.

"She'll think the worst, I imagine," she said cheerfully.

"The worst?" Brand cocked a brow at her.

"That you and I are carrying on a hot, illicit love affair."

"Is that the worst? It sounds rather appealing to me."

Raven colored and looked down at her hands. "You know what I meant."

Brand took her hand, kissing it lightly. "I know what you meant." The laugh in his voice eased her embarrassment. "Will it trouble you to be labeled a fallen woman?"

"I've been labeled a fallen woman for years," she returned with a smile, "every time I pick up a magazine. Do you know how many affairs I've had with people I've never even spoken to?"

"Celebrities are required to have overactive libidos," he murmured. "It's part of the job."

"Your press does yours credit," she observed dryly.

Brand nodded gravely. "I've always thought so. I heard about a pool going around London last year. They were betting on how many women I'd have in a three-month period. The British," he explained, "will bet on anything."

Raven allowed the silence to hang for a moment. "What number did you take?"

"Twenty-seven," he told her, then grinned. "I thought it best to be conservative."

She laughed, enjoying him. He would have done it, too, she reflected. There was enough of the cocky street kid left in him. "I don't think I'd better ask you if you won."

"I wish you wouldn't," he said as the car began to climb up a macadam drive.

Raven saw the house. It was three stories high, formed of sober, Cornish stone with shutters of deep, weathered green and a series of stout chimneys on the roof. She could just make out thin puffs of smoke before they merged with the lead-colored sky.

"Oh, Brandon, how like you," she cried, enchanted. "How like you to find something like this."

She was out of the car before he could answer. It was then that she discovered the house had its back to the sea. There were no rear doors, she learned as she dashed quickly to the retaining wall on the left side. The cliff sheared off too close to the back of the house to make one practical. Instead, there were doors on the sides, set deep in Cornish stone.

Raven could look down from the safety of a waist-high wall and watch the water foam and lash out at jagged clumps of rock far below. The view sent a thrill of terror and delight through her. The sea roared below, a smashing fury of sound. Raven stood, heedless of the chill drizzle, and tried to take it all in.

"It's fabulous. Fabulous!" Turning, she lifted her face, studying the house again. Against the stone, in a great tangle of vines, grew wild roses and honeysuckles. They were greening, not yet ready to bloom, but she could already imagine their fragrance. A rock garden had been added, and among the tender green shoots was an occasional flash of color.

"You might find the inside fabulous, too," Brand ventured, laughing when she turned her wet face to him. "And dry."

"Oh, Brandon, don't be so unromantic." She turned a slow circle until she faced the house again. "It's like something out of *Wuthering Heights*."

He took her hand. "Unromantic or not, mate, I want a bath, a hot one, and my tea."

"That does have a nice sound to it," she admitted

but hung back as he pulled her to the door. She thought the cliffs wonderfully jagged and fierce. "Will we have scones? I developed a taste for them when I toured England a couple years ago. Scones and clotted cream— why does that have to sound so dreadful?"

"You'll have to take that up with Mrs. Pengalley," Brand began as he placed his hand on the knob. It opened before he could apply any pressure.

Mrs. Pengalley looked much as Raven had jokingly described her. She was indeed a sturdily built woman with dark hair sternly disciplined into a sensible bun. She had dark, sober eyes that passed briefly over Raven, took in the braids and damp clothing, then rested on Brandon without a flicker of expression.

"Good morning, Mr. Carstairs, you made good time," she said in a soft, Cornish burr.

"Hullo, Mrs. Pengalley, it's good to see you again. This is Ms. Williams, who'll be staying with me."

"Her room's ready, sir. Good morning, Miss Williams."

"Good morning, Mrs. Pengalley," said Raven, a trifle daunted. This, she was sure, was what was meant by "a formidable woman." "I hope I haven't put you to too much trouble."

"There's been little to do." Mrs. Pengalley's dark eyes shifted to Brand again. "There be fires laid, and the pantry's stocked, as you instructed. I've done you a casserole for tonight. You've only to heat it when you've a mind to eat. Mr. Pengalley laid in a good supply of wood; the nights're cool, and it's been damp. He'll be bringing your bags in now. We heard you drive up."

"Thanks." Brand glanced over, seeing that Raven was already wandering around the room. "We're both in need of a hot bath and some tea, then we should do well enough. Is there anything you want in particular, Raven?"

She glanced back over at the sound of her name but hadn't been attentive to the conversation. "I'm sorry. What?"

He smiled at her. "Is there anything you'd like before Mrs. Pengalley sees to tea?"

"No." Raven smiled at the housekeeper. "I'm sure everything's lovely."

Mrs. Pengalley inclined her head, her body bending not an inch. "I'll make your tea, then." As she swept from the room, Raven shot Brand a telling glance. He grinned and stretched his back.

"You continually amaze me, Brandon," she murmured, then went back to her study of the room.

It was, Raven knew, the room in which they would be doing most of their work over the next weeks. A grand piano, an old one which, she discovered on a quick testing run, had magnificent tone, was set near a pair of narrow windows. Occasional rag rugs dotted the oak-planked floor. The drapes were cream-colored lace and obviously handworked. Two comfortable sofas, both biscuit-colored, and a few Chippendale tables completed the furniture.

A fire crackled in the large stone fireplace. Raven moved closer to examine the pictures on the mantel.

At a glance, she could tell she was looking at Brand's family. There was a teenage boy in a black leather jacket whose features were the same as Brand's though his dark hair was a bit longer and was as straight as Raven's. He wore the same cocky grin as his brother. A woman was next; Raven thought her about twenty-five and astonishingly pretty with fair hair and slanted green eyes and a true English rose complexion. For all the difference in coloring, however, the resemblance to Brand was strong enough for Raven to recognize his sister. She was in another picture along with a blond man and two boys. Both boys had dark hair and the Carstairs mischief gleaming in their eyes. Raven decided Brand's sister had her hands full.

Raven studied the picture of Brand's parents for some time. The tall, thin frame had been passed down from his father, but it seemed only one of the children had inherited his fair, English looks. Raven judged it to be an old snapshot—twenty, perhaps twenty-five, years old. It had been painstakingly staged, with the man and woman dead center, standing straight in their Sunday best. The woman was dark and lovely. The man looked a bit self-conscious and ill at ease having to pose, but the woman beamed into the camera. Her eyes bespoke mischief and her mouth a hint of the cockiness so easily recognized in her children.

There were more pictures: family groups and candid shots, with Brand in several of them. The Carstairses were very much a family. Raven felt a small stir of envy. Shaking it off, she turned back to Brand and smiled.

"This is quite a group." She flicked her fingers behind her toward the mantel. "You're the oldest, aren't you? I think I read that somewhere. The resemblance is remarkable."

"Sweeney genes from my mother's side," Brand told her, looking beyond her shoulder at the crowded grouping of frames. "The only one they slipped up on a bit was Alison." He ran a hand through his damp hair and came to stand beside her. "Let me take you upstairs, love, and get you settled in. The grand tour can wait until we're dry." He slipped an arm around her. "I'm glad you're here, Raven. I've never seen you with things that are mine before. And hotel rooms, no matter how luxurious, are never home."

Later, lounging in a steaming tub, Raven thought over Brand's statement. It was part of the business of being an entertainer to spend a great many nights in hotel rooms, albeit luxury suites, in their positions, but they were hotel rooms nonetheless. Home was a place for between concerts and guest appearances, and to her, it had become increasingly important over the years. It seemed the higher she rose, the more she needed a solid base. She realized it was the same with Brand.

They'd both been on the road for several weeks. He was home now, and somehow Raven knew already that she, too, would be at home there. For all its age and size, there was something comforting in the house. Perhaps, Raven mused as she lazily soaped a leg, it's the age and size. Continuity was important to her, as she felt she'd had little of it in her life, and space was important for the same reason.

Raven had felt an instant affinity for the house. She liked the muffled roar of the sea outside her window and the breathtaking view. She liked the old-fashioned porcelain tub with the curved legs and the oval, mahogany-framed mirror over the tiny pedestal sink.

Rising from the tub, she lifted a towel from the heated bar. When she had dried herself, she wrapped a thick, buff-colored towel around her before letting down her hair. The two braids fell from where she had pinned them atop of her head. Absently, as she wandered back into the bedroom, she began to undo them.

Her luggage still sat beside an old brass chest, but she didn't give much thought to unpacking. Instead she walked to the window seat set in the south wall and knelt on the padded cushion.

Below her the sea hurled itself onto the rocks, tossed up by the wind. There was a sucking, drawing sound before it crashed back onto the shingles and cliffs. Like the sky, they were gray, except for where the waves crested in stiff, white caps. The rain drizzled still, with small drops hitting her window to trail lazily downward. Placing her arms on the wide sill, Raven rested her chin on them and lost herself in dreamy contemplation of the scene below.

"Raven."

She heard Brand's call and the knock and answered both absently. "Yes, come in."

"I thought you might be ready to go downstairs," he said.

"In a minute. What a spectacular view this is! Come look. Does your room face the sea like this? I think I could sit here watching it forever."

"It has its points," he agreed and came over to stand behind her. He tucked his hands into his pockets. "I didn't know you had such a fondness for the sea."

"Yes, always, but I've never had a room where I felt right on top of it before. I'm going to like hearing it at night." She smiled over her shoulder at him. "Is your house in Ireland on the coast, too?"

"No, it's more of a farm, actually. I'd like to take you there." He ran his fingers through her hair, finding it thick and soft and still faintly damp. "It's a green, weepy country, and as appealing as this one, in a different way."

"That's your favorite, isn't it?" Raven smiled up at him. "Even though you live in London and come here to do work, it's the place in Ireland that's special."

He returned the smile. "If it wasn't that there'd have been Sweeneys and Hardestys everywhere we looked, I'd have taken you there. My mother's family," he explained, "are very friendly people. If the score goes well, perhaps we can take a bit of a vacation there when we're done."

Raven hesitated. "Yes…I'd like that."

"Good." The smile turned into a grin. "And I like your dress."

Puzzled, Raven followed his lowered glance. Stunned, she gripped the towel at her breasts and scrambled to her feet. "I didn't realize…I'd forgotten." She could feel the color heating her cheeks. "Brandon, you might have said something."

"I just did," he pointed out. His eyes skimmed down to her thighs.

"Very funny," Raven retorted and found herself smiling. "Now, why don't you clear out and let me change?"

"Must you? Pity." He hooked his hand over the towel where it met between her breasts. The back of his fingers brushed the swell of her bosom. "I was just thinking I liked your outfit." Without touching her in any other way, he brought his mouth down to hers.

"You smell good," he murmured, then traced just the inside of her mouth with his tongue. "Rain's still in your hair."

A roaring louder than the sea began in her brain. Instinctually she was kissing him back, meeting his tongue with hers, stepping closer and rising on her toes. Though her response was quick and giving, he kept the kiss light. She sensed the hunger and the strength under tight control.

Under the towel, his finger swept over her nipple, finding it taut with desire. Raven felt a strong, unfamiliar ache between her thighs. She moaned with it as each muscle in her body went lax. He lifted his face and waited until her eyes opened.

"Shall I make love to you, Raven?"

She stared at him, aching with the churn of rising needs. He was putting the decision in her hands. She should have been grateful, relieved, yet at that moment she found she would have preferred it if he had simply swept her away. For an instant she wanted no choice, no voice, but only to be taken.

"You'll have to be sure," he told her quietly. Lifting her chin with his finger, he smiled. His eyes were a calm blue-green. "I've no intention of making it easy for you."

He dropped his hand. "I'll wait for you downstairs, though I still think it's a pity you have to change. You're very attractive in a towel."

"Brandon," she said when he was at the door. He turned, lifting a brow in acknowledgment. "What if I'd said yes?" Raven grinned, feeling a bit more steady with the distance between them. "Wouldn't that have been a bit awkward with Mrs. Pengalley still downstairs?"

Leaning against the door, he said lazily, "Raven, if you'd said yes, I wouldn't give a damn if Mrs. Pengalley and half the country were downstairs." He shut the door carefully behind him.

Chapter 10

Both Raven and Brand were anxious to begin. They started the day after their arrival and soon fell into an easy, workable routine. Brand rose early and was usually finishing up a good-sized breakfast by the time Raven dragged herself downstairs. When she was fortified with coffee, they started their morning stretch, working until noon and Mrs. Pengalley's arrival. While the housekeeper brought in the day's marketing and saw to whatever domestic chores needed to be seen to, Brand and Raven would take long walks.

The days were balmy, scented with sea spray and spring. The land was rugged, even harsh, with patches of poor ground covered with heather not yet in bloom. The pounding surf beat against towering granite cliffs. Hardy birds built their nests in the crags. Their cries could be heard over the crash of the waves. Standing high, Raven could see down to the village with its neat rows of cottages and white church spire.

They'd work again in the afternoon with the fire sizzling in the grate at their backs. After dinner they went over the day's work. By the end of the week they had a loosely based outline for the score and the completed title song.

They didn't work without snags. Both Raven and Brand felt too strongly about music for any collaboration to run smoothly. But the arguments seemed to stimulate both of them; and the final product was the better for them. They were a good team.

They remained friends. Brand made no further attempt to become Raven's lover. From time to time Raven would catch him staring intently at her. Then she would feel the pull, as sensual as a touch, as tempting as a kiss. The lack of pressure confused her and drew her more effectively than his advances could have. Advances could be refused, avoided. She knew he was waiting for her decision. Underneath the casualness, the jokes and professional disagreements, the air throbbed with tension.

The afternoon was long and a bit dreary. A steady downpour of rain kept Raven and Brand from walking the cliffs. Their music floated through the house, echoing in corners here and there and drifting to forgotten attics. They'd built the fire high with Mr. Pengalley's store of wood to chase away the dampness that seemed to seep through the windows. A tray of tea and biscuits that they had both forgotten rested on one of the Chippendale tables. Their argument was reaching its second stage.

"We've got to bring up the tempo," Raven insisted. "It just doesn't work this way."

"It's a mood piece, Raven."

"Not a funeral dirge. It drags this way, Brandon. People are going to be nodding off before she finishes singing it."

"Nobody falls asleep while Lauren Chase is singing," Brand countered. "This number is pure sex, Raven, and she'll sell it."

"Yes, she will," Raven agreed, "but not at this tempo." She shifted on the piano bench so that she faced him more directly. "All right, Joe's fallen asleep at the typewriter in the middle of the chapter he's writing. He's already believing himself a little mad because of the vivid dreams he's having about his character Tessa. She seems too real, and he's fallen in love with her even though he knows she's a product of his own imagination, a character in a novel he's writing, a fantasy. And now, in the middle of the day, he's dreaming about her again, and this time she promises to come to him that night."

"I know the plot, Raven," Brand said dryly.

Though she narrowed her eyes, Raven checked her temper. She thought she detected some fatigue in his voice. Once or twice she'd been awakened in the middle of the night by his playing. "'Nightfall' is hot, Brandon. You're right about it being pure sex, and your lyrics are fabulous. But it still needs to move."

"It moves." He took a last drag on his cigarette before crushing it out. "Chase knows how to hang on to a note."

Raven made a quick sound of frustration. Unfortunately he was usually right about such things. His instincts were phenomenal. This time, however, she was certain that her own instincts—as a songwriter and as a woman—were keener. She knew the way the song had to be sung to reap the full effect. The moment she had read Brand's lyrics, she had known what was needed. The song had flowed, completed, through her head.

"I know she can hang on to a note, and she can handle choreography. She'll be able to do both and still do the song at the right tempo. Let me show you." She began to play the opening bars. Brand shrugged and rose from the bench.

Raven moved the tempo to *andante* and sang to her own accompaniment. Her voice wrapped itself around the music. Brand moved to the window to watch the rain. It was the song of a temptress, full of implicit, wild promises.

Raven's voice flowed over the range of notes, then heated when it was least expected until Brand felt a tight knot of desire in the pit of his stomach. There was something not quite earthy in the melody she had created. The quicker tempo made a sharp contrast, much more effective than the pace Brand had wanted. She ended abruptly in a raspy whisper without any fade-out. She tossed her hair, then shot him a look over her shoulder.

"Well?" There was a half smile on her face.

He had his back to her and kept his hands tucked into his pockets. "You have to be right now and again, I suppose."

Raven laughed, spinning around on the bench until she faced the room. "You've a way with compliments, Brandon. It sets my heart fluttering."

"She doesn't have your range," he murmured. Then, making an impatient movement, he wandered over to the teapot. "I don't think she'll get as much out of the low scale as you do."

"Mmm." Raven shrugged as she watched him pour out a cup of tea. "She's got tremendous style, though; she'll milk every ounce out of it." He set the tea down again without touching it and roamed to the fire. As she watched him, a worried frown creased Raven's brow. "Brandon, what's wrong?"

He threw another log on the already roaring fire. "Nothing, just restless."

"This rain's depressing." She rose to go to the window. "I've never minded it. Sometimes I like a dreary, sleepy day. I can be lazy without feeling guilty. Maybe that's what you should do, Brandon, be lazy today. You've got that marvelous chessboard in the library. Why don't you teach me to play?" She lifted her hands to his shoulders and feeling the tension, began to knead absently. "Of course, that might be hard work. Julie gave up playing backgammon with me. She says I haven't any knack for strategy."

Raven broke off when Brand turned abruptly around and removed her hands from his shoulders. Without speaking, he walked away from her. He went to the liquor cabinet and drew out a bottle of bourbon. Raven watched as he poured three fingers into a glass and drank it down.

"I don't think I've the patience for games this afternoon," he told her as he poured a second drink.

"All right, Brandon," she said. "No games." She walked over to stand in front of him, keeping her eyes direct. "Why are you angry with me? Certainly not because of the song."

The look held for several long moments while the

fire popped and sizzled in the grate. Raven heard a log fall as the one beneath it gave way.

"Perhaps it's time you and I talked," Brandon said as he idly swirled the remaining liquor in the glass. "It's dangerous to leave things hanging for five years; you never know when they're going to fall."

Raven felt a ripple of disquiet but nodded. "You may be right."

Brand gave her a quick smile. "Should we be civilized and sit down or take a few free swings standing up?"

She shrugged. "I don't think there's any need to be civilized. Civilized fighting never clears the air."

"All right," he began but was interrupted by the peal of the bell. Setting down his glass, Brand shot her a last look, then went to answer.

Alone, Raven tried to control her jitters. There was a storm brewing, she knew, and it wasn't outside the windows. Brand was itching for a fight, and though the reason was unclear to her, Raven found herself very willing to oblige him. The tension between them had been glossed over in the name of music and peace. Now, despite her nerves, she was looking forward to shattering the calm. Hearing his returning footsteps, she walked back to the tea tray and picked up her cup.

"Package for you." Brand gestured with it as he came through the doorway. "From Henderson."

"I wonder what he could be sending me," she murmured, already ripping off the heavy packing tape. "Oh, of course." She tossed the wrappings carelessly aside and studied the album jacket. "They're sample jackets for the album I'm releasing this summer." Without glancing at him, Raven handed Brand one of the covers, then turned to another to read the liner notes.

For the next few minutes Brand studied the cover picture without speaking. Again, a background of white, Raven sitting in her habitual cross-legged fashion. She was looking full into the camera with only a tease of a smile on her lips. Her eyes were very gray and very direct. Over her shoulders and down to her knees, her hair spilled—a sharp contrast against the soft-focused white of the background. The arrangement appeared to be haphazard but had been cleverly posed nonetheless. She appeared to be nude, and the effect was fairly erotic.

"Did you approve this picture?"

"Hmm?" Raven pushed back her hair as she continued to read. "Oh, yes, I looked over the proofs before I left on tour. I'm still not completely sure about this song order, but I suppose it's a bit late to change it now."

"I always felt Henderson was above packaging you this way."

"Packaging me what way?" she asked absently.

"As a virgin offering to the masses." He handed her the cover.

"Brandon, really…how ridiculous."

"I don't think so," he said. "I think it's an uncannily apt description: virgin white, soft focus, and you sitting naked in the middle of it all."

"I'm not naked," she retorted indignantly. "I don't do nudes."

"The potential buyer isn't supposed to know that, though, is he?" Brand leaned against the piano and watched her through narrowed eyes.

"It's provocative, certainly. It's meant to be." Raven frowned down at the cover again. "There's nothing wrong with that. I'm not a child to be dressed up in Mary Janes and a pink pinafore, Brandon. This is business. There's nothing extreme about this cover. And I'm more modestly covered than I would be on a public beach."

"But not more decently," he said coldly. "There's a difference."

Color flooded her face, now a mixture of annoyance and embarrassment. "It's not indecent. I've never posed for an indecent picture. Karl Straighter is one of the finest photographers in the business. He doesn't shoot indecent pictures."

"One man's art is another's porn, I suppose."

Her eyes widened as she lowered the jackets to the piano bench. "That's a disgusting thing to say," she whispered. "You're being deliberately horrible."

"I'm simply giving you my opinion," he corrected, lifting a brow. "You don't have to like it."

"I don't need your opinion. I don't need your approval."

"No," he said and crushed out his cigarette. "You bloody well don't, do you? But you're going to have it in any case." He caught her by the arm when she would have turned away. The power of the grip contrasted the cool tone and frosty eyes.

"Let go of me," Raven demanded, putting her hand on top of his and trying unsuccessfully to pry it from her arm.

"When I'm finished."

"You have finished." Her voice was abruptly calm, and she stopped her frantic attempts to free herself. Instead she faced him squarely, emotion burning in her eyes. "I don't have to listen to you when you go out of your way to insult me, Brandon. I won't listen to you. You can prevent me from leaving because you're stronger than I am, but you can't make me listen." She swallowed but managed to keep her voice steady. "I run my own life. You're entitled to your opinion, certainly, but you're not entitled to hurt me with it. I don't want to talk to you now; I just want you to let me go."

He was silent for so long, Raven thought he would refuse. Then, slowly, he loosened his grip until she could slip her arm from his fingers. Without a word she turned and left the room.

Perhaps it was the strain of her argument with Brand or the lash of rain against the windows or the sudden fury of thunder and lightning. The dream formed out of a vague montage of childhood remembrances that left her with impressions rather than vivid pictures. Thoughts and images floated and receded against the darkness of sleep. There were rolling sensations of fear, guilt, despair, one lapping over the other while she moaned and twisted beneath the sheets, trying to force herself awake. But she was trapped, caught fast in the world just below consciousness. Then the thunder seemed to explode inside her head, and the flash of lightning split the room with a swift, white flash. Screaming, Raven sat up in bed.

The room was pitch dark again when Brand rushed in; he found his way to the bed by following the sounds of Raven's wild weeping. "Raven. Here, love." Even as he reached her, she threw herself into his arms and clung. She was trembling hard, and her skin was icy. Brand pulled the quilt up over her back and cuddled her. "Don't cry, love, you're safe here." He patted and stroked as he would for a child frightened of a storm. "It'll soon be over."

"Hold me." She pressed her face into his bare shoulder. "Please, just hold me." Her breathing was quick, burning her throat as she struggled for air. "Oh, Brandon, such an awful dream."

He rocked her and laid a light kiss on her temple. "What was it about?" The telling, he recalled from childhood, usually banished the fear.

"She'd left me alone again," Raven murmured, shuddering so that he drew her closer in response. The words came out as jumbled as her thoughts, as tumbled as the dream. "How I hated being alone in that room. The only light was from the building next door—one of those red neon lights that blinks on and off, on and off, so that the dark was never still. And so much noise out on the street, even with the windows closed. Too hot…too hot to sleep," she murmured into his shoulder. "I watched the light and waited for her to come back. She was drunk again." She whimpered, her fingers opening and closing against his chest. "And she'd brought a man with her. I put the pillow over my head so I wouldn't hear."

Raven paused to steady her breath. It was dark and quiet in Brand's arms. Outside, the storm rose in high fury.

"She fell down the steps and broke her arm, so we moved, but it was always the same. Dingy little rooms, airless rooms that smelled always of gin no matter how you scrubbed. Thin walls, walls that might as well not have existed for the privacy they gave you. But she always promised that this time, this time it'd be different. She'd get a job, and I'd go to school…but always one day I'd come home and there'd be a man and a bottle."

She wasn't clinging any longer but simply leaning against him as if all passion were spent. Lightning flared again, but she remained still.

"Raven." Brand eased her gently away and tilted her face to his. Tears were still streaming from her eyes, but her breathing was steadier. He could barely make out the shape of her face in the dark. "Where was your father?"

He could see the shine of her eyes as she stared at him. She made a soft, quiet sound as one waking. He knew the words had slipped from her while she had been vulnerable and unaware. Now she was aware, but it was too late for defenses. The sigh she made was an empty, weary sound.

"I don't know who he was." Slowly she drew out of Brand's arms and rose from the bed. "She didn't, either. You see, there were so many."

Brand said nothing but reached into the pocket of the jeans he had hastily dragged on and found a pack of matches. Striking one, he lit the bedside candle. The light wavered and flickered, hardly more than a pulse beat in the dark. "How long," he asked and shook out the match, "did you live like that?"

Raven dragged both hands through her hair, then hugged herself. She knew she'd already said too much for evasions. "I don't remember a time she didn't drink, but when I was very young, five or six, she still had some control over it. She used to sing in clubs. She had big dreams and an average voice, but she was very lovely…once."

Pausing, Raven pressed her fingers against her eyes and wiped away tears. "By the time I was eight, she was…her problem was unmanageable. And there were always men. She needed men as much as she needed to drink. Some of them were better than others. One of them took me to the zoo a couple of times...."

She trailed off and turned away. Brand watched the candlelight flicker over the thin material of her nightgown.

"She got steadily worse. I think part of it was from the frustration of having her voice go. Of course, she abused it dreadfully with smoking and drinking, but the more it deteriorated, the more she smoked and drank. She ruined her voice and ruined her health and ruined any chance she had of making something of herself. Sometimes I hated her. Sometimes I know she hated herself."

A sob escaped, but Raven pushed it back and began to wander the room. The movement seemed to make it easier, and the words tumbled out quicker, pressing for release. "She'd cry and cling to me and beg me not to hate her. She'd promise the moon, and more often than not, I'd believe her. 'This time'—that was one of her favorite beginnings. It still is." Raven let out a shaky sigh. "She loved me when she wasn't drinking and forgot me completely when she was. It was like living with two different women, and neither one of them was easy. When she was sober, she expected an average mother-and-daughter relationship. Had I done my homework? Why was I five minutes late getting home from school? When she was drunk, I was supposed to keep the hell out of her way. I remember once, when I was twelve, she went three months and sixteen days without a drink. Then I came home from school and found her passed out on the bed. She'd had an audition that afternoon for a gig at this two-bit club. Later she told me she'd

just wanted one drink to calm her nerves. Just one..."
Raven shivered and hugged herself tighter. "It's cold,"
she murmured.

Brand rose and stooped in front of the fire. He added
kindling and logs to the bed of coals in the grate. Raven
walked to the window to watch the fury of the storm
over the sea. Lightning still flashed sporadically, but
the violence of the thunder and the rain were dying.

"There were so many other times. She was working
as a cocktail waitress in this little piano bar in Houston. I was sixteen then. I always came by on payday so
I could make certain she didn't spend the money before I bought food. She'd been pretty good then. She'd
been working about six weeks straight and had an affair going with the manager. He was one of the better ones. I used to play around at the piano if the place
was empty. One of my mother's lovers had been a musician; he'd taught me the basics and said I had a good
ear. Mama liked hearing me play." Her voice had quieted. Brand watched her trail a finger down the dark
pane of window glass.

"Ben, the manager, asked me if I wanted to play during the lunch hour. He said I could sing, too, as long
as I kept it soft and didn't talk to the customers. So I
started." Raven sighed and ran a hand over her brow.
Behind her came the pop and crackle of flame. "We left
Houston for Oklahoma City. I lied about my age and
got a job singing in a club. It was one of Mama's worst
periods. There were times I was afraid to leave her
alone, but she wasn't working then, and..." She broke
off with a sound of frustration and rubbed at an ache
in her temple. She wanted to stop, wanted to block it
all out, but she knew she had come too far. Pressing her

brow against the glass, she waited until her thoughts came back into order.

"We needed the money, so I had to risk leaving her at night. I suppose we exchanged roles for a time," she murmured. "The thing I learned young, but consistently forgot, was that an alcoholic finds money for a bottle. Always, no matter what. One night during my second set she wove her way into the club. Wayne was working there and caught onto the situation quickly. He managed to quiet her down before it got too ugly. Later he helped me get her home and into bed. He was wonderful: no lectures, no pity, no advice. Just support."

Raven turned away from the window again and wandered to the fire. "But she came back again, twice more, and they let me go. There were other towns, other clubs, but it was the same then and hardly matters now. Just before I turned eighteen I left her." Her voice trembled a bit, and she took a moment to steady it. "I came home from work one night, and she was passed out at the kitchen table with one of those half-gallon jugs of wine. I knew if I didn't get away from her I'd go crazy. So I put her to bed, packed a bag, left her all the money I could spare and walked out. Just like that." She covered her face with her hands a moment, pressing her fingers into her eyes. "It was like being able to breathe for the first time in my life."

Raven roamed back to the kitchen. She could see the vague ghost of her own reflection. Studying it, listening to the steady but more peaceful drum of rain, she continued. "I worked my way to L.A., and Henderson saw me. He pushed me. I'm not certain what my ambition was before I signed with him. Just to survive, I think. One day and then the next. Then there were contracts and recording sessions and the whole crazy circus. Doors started opening. Some of them were trap doors, I've always thought." She gave a quick, wondering laugh. "God, it was marvelous and scary and I don't believe I could ever go through those first few months again. Anyway, Henderson got me publicity, and the first hit single got me more. And then I got a call from a hospital in Memphis."

Raven turned and began to pace. The light silk of her nightgown clung, then swirled, with her movements. "I had to go, of course. She was in pretty bad shape. Her latest lover had beaten her and stolen what little money she had. She cried. Oh, God, all the same promises. She was sorry; she loved me. Never again, never again. I was the only decent thing she'd ever done in her life." The tears were beginning to flow again, but this time Raven made no attempt to stop them. "As soon as she could travel, I brought her back with me. Julie had found a sanitarium in Ojai and a very earnest young doctor. Justin Randolf Karter. Isn't that a marvelous name, Brandon?" Bitterness spilled out with the tears. "A marvelous name, a remarkable man. He took me into his tasteful, leather-bound office and explained the treatment my mother would receive."

Whirling, Raven faced Brand, her shoulders heaving with sobs. "I didn't want to know! I just wanted him to do it. He told me not to set my hopes too high, and I told him I hadn't any hopes at all. He must have found me cynical, because he suggested several good organizations I could speak to. He reminded me that alcoholism is a disease and that my mother was a victim. I said the hell she was; *I* was the victim!" Raven forced the words out as she hugged herself tightly. "*I* was the victim; *I* had had to live with her and deal with her lies and her sickness and her men. It was so safe, so easy, for him to be sanctimonious and understanding behind that tidy white coat. And I *hated* her." The sobs came in short, quick jerks as she balled her hands and pressed them against her eyes. "And I loved her." Her breath trembled in and out as everything she had pent up over the weeks of her mother's latest treatment poured through her. "I still love her," she whispered.

Weary, nearly spent, she turned to the fire, resting her palms on the mantel. "Dr. Karter let me shout at him, then he sat with me when I broke down. I went home, and they started her treatment. Two days later I met you."

Raven didn't hear him move, didn't know he stood behind her, until she felt his hands on her shoulders. Without speaking she turned and went into his arms. Brand held her, feeling the light tremors while he stared down at the licking, greedy flames. Outside, the storm had become only a patter of rain against the windows.

"Raven, if you had told me, I might have been able to make things easier for you."

She shook her head, then buried her face against his chest. "No, I didn't want it to touch that part of my life. I just wasn't strong enough." Taking a deep breath, she pulled back far enough to look in his eyes. "I was afraid that if you knew you wouldn't want anything to do with me."

"Raven." There was hurt as well as censure in his voice.

"I know it was wrong, Brandon, even stupid, but you have to understand: everything seemed to be happening to me at once. I needed time. I needed to sort out how I was going to live my life, how I was going to deal with my career, my mother, everything." Her hands gripped his arms as she willed him to see through her eyes. "I was nobody one day and being mobbed by fans the next. My picture was everywhere. I heard myself every time I turned on the radio. You know what that's like."

Brand brushed her hair from her cheek. "Yes, I know what that's like." As he spoke, he could feel her relax with a little shudder.

"Before I could take a breath, Mama walked back into my life. Part of me hated her, but instead of realizing that it was a normal reaction and dealing with it, I felt an unreasonable guilt. And I was ashamed. No," she shook her head, anticipating him, "there's no use telling me I had no need to be. That's an intellectual statement, a practical statement; it has nothing to do with emotion. I don't expect you to understand that part of it. You've never had to deal with it. She's my mother. It isn't possible to completely separate myself from that, even knowing that the responsibility for her problem isn't mine." Raven gave him one last, long look before turning away. "And on top of everything that was happening to me, I fell in love with you." The flames danced and snapped as she watched. "I loved you," she murmured so quietly he strained to hear, "but I couldn't be your lover."

Brand stared at her back, started to reach for her, then dropped his hands to his sides. "Why?"

Only her head turned as she looked over her shoulder at him. Her face was in shadows. "Because then I would be like her," she whispered, then turned away again.

"You don't really believe that, Raven." Brand took her shoulders, but she shook her head, not answering.

Firmly he turned her to face him, making a slow, thorough study of her. "Do you make a habit of condemning children for their parents' mistakes?"

"No, but I..."

"You don't have the right to do it to yourself."

She shut her eyes on a sigh. "I know, I know that, but..."

"There're no buts on this one, Raven." His fingers tightened until she opened her eyes again. "You know who you are."

There was only the sound of the sea and the rain and fire. "I wanted you," she managed in a trembling voice, "when you held me, touched me. You were the first man I'd ever wanted." She swallowed, and again he felt the shudder course through her. "Then I'd remember all those cramped little rooms, all those men with my mother...." She broke off and would have turned away again if his hands hadn't held her still.

Brand removed his hands from her arms, then slowly, his eyes still on hers, he used them to frame her face. "Sleeping with a stranger is different from making love with someone you care for."

Raven moistened her lips. "Yes, I know that, but..."

"Do you?" The question stopped her. She could do no more than let out a shaky breath. "Let me show you, Raven."

Her eyes were trapped by his. She knew he would release her if she so much as shook her head. Fear was tiny pinpoints along her skin. Need was a growing warmth in her blood. She lifted her hands to his wrists. "Yes."

Again Brand gently brushed the hair away from her cheeks. When her face was framed by his hands alone, he lowered his head and kissed her eyes closed. He could feel her trembling in his arms. Her hands still held his wrists, and her fingers tightened when he brought his mouth to hers. His was patient, waiting until her lips softened and parted.

The kisses grew deeper, but slowly, now moister until she swayed against him. His fingers caressed, his mouth roamed. Firelight flickered over them in reds and golds, casting its own shadows. Raven could feel the heat from it through the silk she wore, but it was the glow inside of her which built and flamed hot.

Brand lowered his hands to her shoulders, gently massaging as he teased her lower lip with his teeth. Raven felt the gown slip down over her breasts, then cling briefly to her hips before it drifted to the floor. She started to protest, but he deepened the kiss. The thought spiraled away. Down the curve of her back, over the slight flare of her hips, he ran his hands. Then he picked her up in his arms. With her mind spinning, she sank into the mattress. When Brand joined her, the touch of his naked body against hers jolted her, bringing on a fresh surge of doubts and fears.

"Brandon, please, I..." The words were muffled, then died inside his mouth.

Easily, his hands caressed her, stroking without hurry. Somewhere in the back of her mind she knew he held himself under tight control. But her mind had relaxed, and her limbs were heavy. His mouth wandered to her throat, tasting, giving pleasure, arousing by slow, irresistible degrees. He worked her nipple with his thumb, and she moaned and moved against him. Brand allowed his mouth to journey downward, laying light, feathering kisses over the curve of her breast. Lightly, very lightly, he ran his tongue over the tip. Raven felt the heat between her thighs, and tangling her fingers in his hair, pressed him closer. She arched and shuddered not from fear but from passion.

Heat unlike anything she had ever known or imagined was building inside her. She was still aware of the flicker of the fire and candlelight on her closed lids, of the soft brush of linen sheets against her back, of the faint, pleasant smell of woodsmoke. But these sensations were dim, while her being seemed focused on the liquefying touch of his tongue over her skin, the feathery brush of his fingers on her thighs. Over the hiss of rain and fire, she heard him murmur her name, heard her own soft, mindless response.

Her breath quickened, and her mouth grew hungry. Suddenly desperate, she drew his face back to hers. She wrapped her arms around him tightly as the pressure of the kiss pushed her head deep into the pillow. Brand lay across her, flesh to flesh, so that her breasts yielded to his chest. Raven could feel the light mat of his hair against her skin.

His hand lay on her stomach and drifted down as she moved under him. There was a flash of panic as he slid between her thighs, then her breath caught in a heady rush of pleasure. He was still patient, his fingers gentle and unhurried as they gradually increased her rhythm.

For Raven, there was no world beyond the firelit room, beyond the four-poster bed. His mouth took hers, his tongue probing deeply, then moving to her ear, her throat, her neck and back to her lips. All the while, his hands and fingers were taking her past all thought, past all reason.

Then he was on top of her, and she opened for him, ready to give, to receive. She was too steeped in wonder to comprehend his strict, unwavering control. She knew only that she wanted him and urged him to take her. There was a swift flash of pain, dulled by a pleasure too acute to be measured. She cried out, but the sound was muffled against his mouth, then all was lost on wave after wave of delight.

Chapter 11

With her head in the curve of Brand's shoulder, Raven watched the fire. Her hand lay over his heart. She could feel its quick, steady rhythm under her palm.

The room was quiet, and outside, the rain had slackened to a murmur. Raven knew she would remember this moment every time she lay listening to rain against windows. Brand's arm was under her, curled over her back with his hand loosely holding her arm. Since he had rolled from her and drawn her against his side, he had been silent. Raven thought he slept and was content to lie with him, watching the fire and listening to the rain. She shifted her head, wanting to look at him and found he wasn't asleep. She could see the sheen of his eyes as he stared at the ceiling. Raven lifted a hand to his cheek.

"I thought you were asleep."

Brand caught her hand and pressed it to his lips. "No, I..." Looking down at her, he broke off, then slowly brushed a tear from her lash with his thumb. "I hurt you."

"No." Raven shook her head. For a moment she buried her face in the curve of his neck, where she could feel his warmth, smell his scent. "Oh, no, you didn't hurt me. You made me feel wonderful. I feel...free." She looked up at him again and smiled. "Does that sound foolish?"

"No." Brand ran his fingers through the length of her hair, pushing it back when it would have hidden her face from him. Her skin was flushed. In her eyes he could see the reflected flames from the fire. "You're so beautiful."

She smiled again and kissed him. "I've always thought the same about you."

He laughed, drawing her closer. "Have you?"

She lay half across him, heated flesh to heated flesh. "Yes, I always thought you'd make a remarkably lovely girl, and I see by your sister's picture that I was right."

He lifted a brow. "Strange, I never realized the direction of your thoughts. Perhaps it's best I didn't."

Raven gave one of her low, rich chuckles and pressed her lips against the column of his throat. She loved the way his tones could become suddenly suavely British. "I'm sure you make a much better man."

"That's comforting," he said dryly as he began to stroke her back, "under the circumstances." His fingers lingered at her hip to caress.

"I'm sure I like you much better this way." Raven kissed the side of his throat again, working her way to his ear. Under her breast she felt the sudden jump and scramble of his heartbeat. "Brandon..." She sighed, nuzzling his ear. "You're so good to me, so kind, so gentle."

She heard him groan before he rolled over, reversing their positions. His eyes were heated and intense and very green, reminding her of the moment he had held her like this on the plane. Now again her pulse began to hammer, but not with fear.

"Love isn't always kind, Raven," he said roughly. "It isn't always gentle."

His mouth came down on hers crushingly, urgently, as all the restraints he had put on himself snapped. There was no patience in him now, only passion. Where before he had taken her up calmly, easily, now he took her plummeting at a desperate velocity. Her mouth felt bruised and tender from his, yet she learned hunger incited hunger. Raven wanted more, and still more, so she caught him closer.

Demanding, possessing, he took his hands over her. "So long," she heard him mutter. "I've wanted you for so long." Then his teeth found the sensitive area of her neck, and she heard nothing. She plunged toward the heat and the dark.

Brand felt her give and respond and demand. He was nearly wild with need. He wanted to touch all of her, taste all of her. He was as desperate as a starving man and as ruthless. Where before, responding to her innocence, he had been cautious, now he took what he had wanted for too many years. She was his as he had dreamed she would be: soft and yielding, then soft and hungry beneath him.

He could hear her moan, feel the bite of her fingernails in his shoulders as he took his mouth down the curve of her breast. The skin of her stomach was smooth and quivered under his tongue. He slipped a hand between her thighs, and she strained against him so that he knew she was as desperate as he. Yet he wouldn't take her, not yet. He felt an impossible greed. His tongue moved to follow the path of his hands. All the years he'd wanted her, all the frustrated passion, burst out, catching them both in the explosion. Not knowing the paths, Raven went where he led her and learned that desire was deeper, stronger, than anything she had known possible.

He was pulling her down—down until the heat was too intense to bear. But she wanted more. His hands were rough, bruising her skin. But she craved no gentleness. She was steeped in passion too deep for escape. She called out for him, desperately, mindlessly, for him to take her. She knew there couldn't be more; they'd gone past all the rules. Pleasure could not be sharper; passion could not be darker than it was at that moment.

Then he was inside her, and everything that had gone before paled against the color and the heat.

His mouth was buried at her neck. From far off he heard her gasps for breath merge with his own. They moved together like lightning, so that he could no longer think. There was only Raven. All passion intensified, concentrated, until he thought he would go mad from it. The pain of it shot through him, then flowed from him, leaving him weak.

They lay still, with Brand over her, his face buried in her hair. His breathing was ragged, and he gave no thought to his weight as he relaxed completely. Beneath him Raven shuddered again and again with the release of passion. She gripped his shoulders tightly, not wanting him to move, not wanting to relinquish the unity. If he had shown her the tenderness and compassion of loving the first time, now he had shown her darker secrets.

A log fell in the grate, scattering sparks against the screen. Brand lifted his head and looked down at her. His eyes were heavy, still smoldering, as they lowered to her swollen mouth. He placed a soft kiss on them, then, shifting his weight, prepared to rise.

"No, don't go." Raven took his arm, sitting up as he did.

"Only to bank the fire."

Bringing her knees to her chest, Raven watched as Brand stacked the fire for the night. The light danced over his skin as she stared, entranced. The ripple of muscles was surprising in one so lean. She saw them in his shoulders, his back, his thighs. The passion in the cool, easygoing man was just as surprising, but she knew the feel of it now, just as she knew the feel of the muscles. He turned and looked at her with the fire leaping at his back. They studied each other, both dazed by what had passed between them. Then he shook his head.

"My God, Raven, I want you again."

She held her arms out to him.

There was a brilliant ribbon of sunlight across Raven's eyes. It was a warm, red haze. She allowed her lids to open slowly before turning to Brand.

He slept still, his breathing deep and even. She had to suppress the urge to brush his hair away from his face because she didn't want to wake him. Not yet. For the first time in her life she woke to look at her lover's face. She felt a warm, settled satisfaction.

He *is* beautiful, she thought, remembering how he had been faintly distressed to hear her say so the night before. *And I love him.* Raven almost said the words aloud as she let herself think them. I've always loved him, right from the beginning, all through the years in between—and even more now that we're together. But no mistakes this time. She closed her eyes tight on the sudden fear that he could walk out of her life again. *No demands, no pressures.* We'll just be together; that's all I need.

She dropped her eyes to his mouth. It had been tender in the night, she remembered, then hungry, almost brutal. She hadn't realized how badly he had wanted her, or she him, until the barriers had shattered. *Five years, five empty years!* Raven pushed the thought away. There was no yesterday, no tomorrow; only the present.

Suddenly she smiled, thinking of the enormous breakfasts he habitually ate. She would usually stumble into the kitchen for coffee as he was cleaning off a plate. Cooking wasn't her best thing, she mused, but it would be fun to surprise him. His arm was tossed around her waist, holding her against him so that their bodies had warmed each other even in sleep. Carefully Raven slipped out from under it. Padding to the closet, she found a robe, then left Brand sleeping to go downstairs.

The kitchen was washed in sunlight. Raven went straight to the percolator. First things first, she decided. Strangely, she was wide-awake, there was none of the drowsy fogginess she habitually used coffee to chase away. She felt vital, full of energy, very much the way she felt when finishing a live concert, she realized as she scooped out coffee. Perhaps there was a parallel. Raven fit the lid on the pot, then plugged it in. She had always felt that performing for an audience was a bit like making love: sharing yourself, opening your emotions, pulling down the barriers. That's what she had done with Brand. The thought made her smile, and she was singing as she rummaged about for a frying pan.

Upstairs, Brand stirred, reached for her and found her gone. He opened his eyes to see that the bed beside him was empty. Quickly he pushed himself up and scanned the room. The fire was still burning. It had been late when he had added the last logs. The drapes were open to the full strength of the sun. It spilled across the bed and onto the floor. Raven's nightgown lay where it had fallen the night before.

Not a dream, he told himself, tugging a hand through his hair. They'd been together last night, again and again until every ounce of energy had been drained. Then they had slept, still holding each other, still clinging. His eyes drifted to the empty pillow beside him again. *But where—where the devil is she now?* Feeling a quick flutter of panic, he rose, tugged on his jeans and went to find her.

Before Brand reached the bottom of the stairs, her voice drifted to him.

Every morning when I wake,
I'll see your eyes.
And there'll only be the love we make,
No more good-byes.

He recognized the song as the one he had teased her about weeks before when they had sat in his car in the hills above Los Angeles. The knot in his stomach untied itself. He walked down the hall, listening to the husky, morning quality of her voice, then paused in the doorway to watch her.

Her movements suited the song she sang: cheerful, happy. The kitchen was filled with morning noises and scents. There was the popping rhythm of the percolator as the coffee bubbled on the burner, the hiss and sizzle of the fat sausage she had frying in a cast-iron skillet, the clatter of crockery as she searched for a platter. Her hair was streaming down her back, still tumbled from the night, while the short terry robe she wore rode high up on her thighs as she stretched to reach the top shelf of a cupboard.

Raven stopped singing for a moment to swear good-naturedly about her lack of height. After managing to get a grip on the platter, she lowered her heels back to the floor and turned. She gave a gasp when she spotted Brand, dropped the fork she held and just managed to save the platter from following it.

"Brandon!" Raven circled her throat with her hand a moment and took a deep breath. "You scared me! I didn't hear you come down."

Brand didn't answer her smile. He didn't move but only looked at her. "I love you, Raven."

Her eyes widened, and her lips trembled open, then shut again. The words, she reminded herself, mean so many different things. It was important not to take a simple statement and deepen its meaning. Raven kept her voice calm as she stooped to pick up the fork. "I love you, too, Brandon."

He frowned at the top of her head, then at her back as she turned away to the sink. She turned on the tap to rinse off the fork. "You sound like my sister. I've already two of those; I don't need another."

Raven took her time. She turned off the tap, composed her face into a smile, then turned. "I don't think of you as a brother, Brandon." The tension at the back of her neck made it difficult to move calmly back to the cupboard for cups and saucers. "It isn't easy for me to tell you how I feel. I needed your support, your compassion. You helped me last night more than I can say."

"Now you make me sound like a bloody doctor. I said I love you, Raven." There was a snap of anger in the words this time. When Raven turned back to him, her eyes were eloquent.

"Brandon, you don't have to feel obligated…" She broke off as his eyes flared. Storming into the room, he flicked off the gas under the smoking sausage, then yanked the percolator cord from the wall. Coffee continued to pop for a few moments, then subsided weakly.

"Don't tell me what I have to do!" he shouted. "I know what I have to do." He grabbed her by the shoulders and shook her. "I *have* to love you. It's not an obligation, it's a fact, it's a demand, it's a terror."

"Brandon…"

"Shut up," he commanded. He pulled her close, trapping the dishes she held between them before he kissed her. She tasted the desperation, the temper. "Don't tell me you love me in that calm, steady voice." Brand lifted his head only to change the angle of the kiss. His mouth was hard and insistent before it parted from hers. "I need more than that from you, Raven, much more than that." His eyes blazed green into hers. "I'll have more, damn it!"

"Brandon." She was breathless, dizzy, then laughing. This was no dream. "The cup's digging a permanent hole in my chest. Please, let me put the dishes down."

He said something fierce about the dishes, but she managed to pull away from him enough to put them on the counter. "Oh, Brandon!" Immediately Raven threw her arms around his neck. "You have more; you have everything. I was afraid—and a fool to be afraid—to tell you how much I love you." She placed her hands on his cheeks, holding his face away from her so that he could read what was in her eyes. "I love you, Brandon."

Quick and urgent, their lips came together. They clung still when he swept her up in his arms. "You'll have to do without your coffee for a while," he told her as she pressed a kiss to the curve of his neck. She only murmured an assent as he began to carry her down the hall.

"Too far," she whispered.

"Mmm?"

"The bedroom's much too far away."

Brand turned his head to grin at her. "Too far," he agreed, taking a sharp right into the music room. "Entirely too far." They sank together on a sofa. "How's this?" He slipped his hands beneath the robe to feel her skin.

"We've always worked well together here." Raven laughed into his eyes, running her fingers along the muscles of his shoulders. It was real, she thought triumphantly, kissing him again.

"The secret," Brand decided, then dug his teeth playfully into her neck, "is a strong melody."

"It's nothing without the proper lyric."

"Music doesn't always need words." He switched to the other side of her neck as his hand roamed to her breast.

"No," she agreed, finding that her own hands refused

to be still. They journeyed down his back and up again. "But harmony—two strong notes coming together and giving a bit to each other."

"Melding," he murmured. "I'm big on melding." He loosened the belt of her robe.

"Oh, Brandon!" she exclaimed suddenly, remembering. "Mrs. Pengalley…she'll be here soon."

"This should certainly clinch her opinion of show people," he decided as his mouth found her breast.

"Oh, no, Brandon, stop!" She laughed and moaned and struggled.

"Can't," he said reasonably, trailing his lips back up to her throat. "Savage lust," he explained and bit her ear. "Uncontrollable. Besides," he said as he kissed her, then moved to her other ear, "it's Sunday, her day off."

"It is?" Raven's mind was too clouded to recall trivial things like days of the week. "Savage lust?" she repeated as he pushed the robe from her shoulders. "Really?"

"Absolutely. Shall I show you?"

"Oh, yes," she whispered and brought his mouth back to hers. "Please do."

A long time later Raven sat on the hearth rug and watched Brand stir up the fire. She had reheated the coffee and brought it in along with the sausages. Brand had pulled a sweater on with his jeans, but she still wore the short, terry robe. Holding a coffee cup in both hands, she yawned and thought that she had never felt so relaxed. She felt like a cat sitting in her square of sunlight, watching Brand fix a log onto snapping flames. He turned to find her smiling at him.

"What are you thinking?" He stretched out on the floor beside her.

"How happy I am." She handed him his coffee, leaning over to kiss him as he took it. It all seemed so simple, so right.

"How happy?" he demanded. He smiled at her over the rim of the cup.

"Oh, somewhere between ecstatic and delirious, I think." She sought his hand with hers. Their fingers linked. "Bordering on rapturous."

"Just bordering on?" Brand asked with a sigh. "Well, we'll work on it." He shook his head, then kissed her hand. "Do you know you nearly drove me mad in this room yesterday?"

"Yesterday?" Raven tossed her hair back over her shoulder with a jerk of her head. "What are you talking about?"

"I don't suppose you'll ever realize just how arousing your voice is," he mused as he sipped his coffee and studied her face. "That might be part of the reason— that touch of innocence with a hell-smoked voice."

"I like that." Raven reached behind her to set down her empty cup. The movement loosened the tie of her robe, leaving it open to brush the curve of her breasts. "Do you want one of these sausages? They're probably awful."

Brand lifted his eyes from the smooth expanse of flesh that the shift of material had revealed. He shook his head again and laughed. "You make them sound irresistible."

"A starving man can't be picky," she pointed out. Raven plucked one with her fingers and handed it over. "They're probably greasy."

He lifted a brow at this but took a bite. "Aren't you going to have one?"

"No. I know better than to eat my own cooking." She handed him a napkin.

"We could go out to eat."

"Use your imagination," she suggested, resting her hands on her knees. "Pretend you've already eaten. It always works for me."

"My imagination isn't as good as yours." Brand finished off the sausage. "Maybe if you tell me what I've had."

"An enormous heap of scrambled eggs," she decided, narrowing her eyes. "Five or six, at least. You really should watch your cholesterol. And three pieces of toast with that dreadful marmalade you pile on."

"You haven't tried it," he reminded her.

"I imagined I did," she explained patiently. "You also had five slices of bacon." She put a bit of censure in her voice, and he grinned.

"I've a healthy morning appetite."

"I don't see how you could eat another bite after all that. Coffee?" Raven reached for the pot.

"No, I imagine I've had enough."

She laughed and leaning over, linked her arms around his neck. "Did I really drive you mad, Brandon?" She found the taste of her own power delicious and sweet.

"Yes." He rubbed her nose with his. "First it was all but impossible to simply be in the same room with you, wanting you as I did. Then that song." He gave a quiet laugh, then drew back to look at her. "Music doesn't always soothe the savage beast. And then that damn album jacket. I had to be furious, or I'd have thrown you down on the rug then and there."

He saw puzzlement, then comprehension, dawn in

her eyes. "Is that why you…" She stopped, and the smile grew slowly. Raven tilted her head and ran the tip of her tongue over her teeth. "I suppose that now that you've had your way with me, I won't drive you mad anymore."

"That's right." He kissed her lightly. "I can take you or leave you." Brand set down his empty cup, then ruffled her hair, amused by her wry expression. "It's noon," he said with a glance at the clock. "We'd best get to it if we're going to get any work done today. That novelty number we were toying with, the one for the second female lead—I'd an idea for that."

"Really?" Raven unhooked her hands from behind his neck. "What sort of idea?"

"We might bounce up the beat, a bit of early forties jive tempo, you know. It'd be a good contrast to the rest of the score."

"Hmmm, could be a good dance number." Raven slipped her hands under his sweater and ran them up his naked chest. She smiled gently at the look of surprise that flickered in his eyes. "We need a good dance number there."

"That's what I was thinking," Brand murmured. The move had surprised him, and the light touch of her fingers sent a dull thud of desire hammering in his stomach. He reached for her, but she rose and moved to the piano.

"Like this, then?" Raven played a few bars of the melody they had worked with, using the tempo he had suggested. "A little boogie-woogie?"

"Yes." He forced his attention to the bouncing, repetitive beat but found his blood beating with it. "That's the idea."

She looked back over her shoulder and smiled at him.

"Then all we need are the lyrics." She experimented a moment longer, then went to the coffeepot. "Cute and catchy." Raven drank, smiling down at Brand. "With a chorus."

"Any ideas?"

"Yes." She set down the cup. "I have some ideas." Raven sat down beside him, facing him, and thoughtfully brushed the hair back from his forehead. "If they're going to cast Carly, as it appears they're going to do, we need something to suit that baby-doll voice of hers. Her songs should be a direct foil for Lauren's." She pressed her lips lightly to his ear. "Of course, the chorus could carry the meat of it." Again she slipped a hand under his sweater, letting her fingertips toy with the soft mat of hair on his chest. She slid her eyes up to his. "What do you think?"

Brand took her arm and pulled her against him, but she turned her head so that the kiss only brushed her cheek. "Raven," he said after a laughing moan. But when she trailed her finger down to his stomach, she felt him suck in air. Again he moaned her name and crushed her against him.

Raven tilted her head back for the kiss. It was deep and desperate, but when he would have urged her down, she shifted so that her body covered his. She buried her mouth at his neck and felt the pulse hammering against her lips. Her hands were still under his sweater so that she was aware of the heating of his skin. He tugged at her robe, but she only pressed harder against him, lodging the fabric between them. She nipped at the cord of his neck.

"Raven." His voice was low and husky. "For God's sake, let me touch you."

"Am I driving you mad, Brandon?" she murmured, nearly delirious with her own power. Before he could answer, she brought her lips to his and took her tongue deep into his mouth. Slowly she hiked up his sweater, feeling the shudders of his skin as she worked it over his chest and shoulders. Even as she tossed it aside, Raven began journeying down his chest, using her lips and tongue to taste him.

It was a new sensation for her: the knowledge that he was as vulnerable to her as she was to him. There was harmony between them and the mutual need to make the music real and full. Before, he had guided her, but now she was ready to experiment with her own skill. She wanted to toy with tempos, to take the lead. She wanted to flow *pianissimo,* savoring each touch, each taste. Now it was her turn to teach him as he had taught her.

His skin was hot under her tongue. He was moving beneath her, but the first wave of desperation had passed into a drugged pleasure. Her fingers weren't shy but rather sought curiously, stroking over him to find what excited, what pleased. His taste was something she knew now she would starve without. She could feel his fingers in her hair tightening as his passion built. As she had the night before, she sensed his control, but now the challenge of breaking it excited her.

His stomach was taut and tightened further when she glided over it. She heard his breathing catch. Finding the snap to his jeans, she undid it, then began to tug them down over his hips. The rhythm was gathering speed.

Then her mouth was on his, ripping them both far beyond the gentle pace she had initiated. She was suddenly starving, trembling with the need. Pushing herself up, Raven let the robe fall from her shoulders. Her hair tumbled forward to drape her breasts.

"Touch me." Her eyes were heavy but locked in his. "Touch me now."

Brand's fingers tangled in her hair as they sought her flesh. When she would have swayed back down to him, he held her upright, wanting to watch the pleasure and passion on her face. Her eyes were blurred with it. The need built fast and was soon too great.

"Raven." There was desperate demand in his voice as he took her hips.

She let him guide her, then gave a sharp gasp of pleasure. Their bodies fused in a soaring rhythm, completely tuned to each other. Raven shuddered from the impact. Then, drained, she lowered herself until she lay prone on him. He brought his arms around her to hold her close as the two of them flowed from passion to contentment.

Tangled with him, fresh from loving in a room quiet and warm, Raven gave a long, contented sigh. "Brandon," she murmured, just wanting to hear the sound of his name.

"Hmm?" He stroked her hair, seemingly lost somewhere in a world between sleep and wakefulness.

"I never knew it could be like this."

"Neither did I."

Raven shifted until she could look at his face. "But you've been with so many women." She curled up at his side, preparing to rest her head in the curve of his shoulder.

Brand rose on his elbow, then tilted her face up to his. He studied her softly flushed cheeks, the swollen mouth and drowsy eyes. "I've never been in love with my lover before," he told her quietly.

For a moment there was silence. Then she smiled. "I'm glad. I suppose I've never been sure of that until now."

"Be sure of it." He kissed her, hard and quick and possessively.

She settled against him again but shivered, then laughed. "A few moments ago I'd have sworn I'd never be cold again."

Grinning, Brand reached for her robe. "I seriously doubt we'll get any work done unless you get dressed. In fact, I'd suggest unattractive clothes."

After tugging her arms through the sleeves, Raven put her hands on his shoulders. Her eyes were light and full of mischief. "Do I distract you, Brandon?"

"You might put it that way."

"I'll probably be tempted to try all the time, now that I know I can." Raven kissed him, then gave a quick shrug. "I won't be able to help myself."

"I'll hold you to that." Brand lifted a brow. "Would you like to start now?"

She gave his hair a sharp tug. "I don't think that's very flattering. I'm going to go see about those unattractive clothes."

"Later," he said, pulling her back when she started to rise.

Raven laughed again, amazed with what she saw in his eyes. "Brandon, really!"

"Later," he said again and pressed her back gently to the floor.

Chapter 12

Summer came to Cornwall in stages. Cool mornings turned to warm afternoons that had bees humming outside the front windows. The stinging chill of the nights mellowed. The first scent of honeysuckle teased the air. Then the roses, lush wild roses, began to bloom. And all through the weeks the countryside blossomed, Raven felt that she, too, was blooming. She was loved.

Throughout her life, if anyone had asked her what one thing she wanted most, Raven would have answered, "To be loved." She had starved for it as a child, had hungered as an adolescent when she had been shuffled from town to town, never given the opportunity to form lasting friendships and affections. It was this need, in part, that had made her so successful as a performer. Raven was willing to let the audience love her. She never felt herself beyond their reach when she stood in the spotlight. And they knew it. The love she had gained from her audiences had filled an enormous need. It had filled her but had not satisfied her as much, she discovered, as Brand's love.

As the weeks passed, she forgot the demands and responsibilities of the performer and became more and more in tune with the woman. She had always known herself; it had been important early that she grasp an identity. But for the first time in her life Raven focused on her womanhood. She explored it, discovered it, enjoyed it.

Brand was demanding as a lover, not only in the physical sense but in an emotional one as well. He wanted her body, her heart, her thoughts, with no reservations. His need for an absolute commitment was the only shadow in the summery passing of days. Raven found it impossible not to hold parts of herself in reserve. She'd been hurt and knew how devastating pain could be when you loved without guard. Her mother had broken her heart too many times to count, with always a promise of happiness after the severest blow. Raven had learned to cope with that, to guard against it to some extent.

She had loved Brand before, naively perhaps, but totally. When he had walked out of her life, Raven had thought she would never be whole again. For five years she had insulated herself against the men who had touched her life. They could be friends—loving friends—but never lovers. The wounds had healed, but the scar had been a constant reminder to be careful. She had promised herself that no man would ever hurt her as Brand Carstairs had. And Raven discovered the vow she had made still held true. He was the only man who would ever have the power to hurt her. That realization was enough to both exhilarate and frighten.

There was no doubt that he had awakened her physically. Her fears had been swept away by the tides of love. Raven found that in this aspect of their relationship she could indeed give herself to Brand unreservedly. Knowing she could arouse him strengthened her growing confidence as a woman. She learned her passions were as strong and sensitive as his. She had kept them restricted far too long. If Brand could heat her blood with a look, Raven was aware he was just as susceptible to her. There was nothing of the cool, British reserve in his lovemaking; she thought of him as all Irish then, stormy and passionate.

One morning he woke her at dawn by strewing the bed with wild rosebuds. The following evening he surprised her with iced champagne while she bathed in the ancient footed tub. At night he could be brutally passionate, waking and taking her with a desperate urgency that allowed no time for surprise, protest or response. At times he appeared deliriously happy; at others she would catch him studying her with an odd, searching expression.

Raven loved him, but she could not yet bring herself to trust him completely. They both knew it, and they both avoided speaking of it.

Seated next to Brand at the piano, Raven experimented with chords for the opening bars of a duet. "I really think a minor mode with a raised seventh." She frowned thoughtfully. "I imagine a lot of strings here, a big orchestration of violins and cellos." She played more, hearing the imagined arrangement rather than the

solitary piano. "What do you think?" Raven turned her
head to find Brand looking down at her.

"Go ahead," he suggested, drawing on a cigarette.
"Play the lot."

She began, only to have him interrupt during a
bridge. "No." He shook his head. "That part doesn't fit."

"That was your part," she reminded him with a grin.

"Genius is obliged to correct itself," he returned, and
Raven gave an unladylike snort. He looked down his
very straight British nose. "Had you a comment, then?"

"Who, me? I never interrupt genius."

"Wise," he said and turned back to spread his own
fingers over the keys. "Like this." Brand played the
same melody from the beginning, only altering a few
notes on the bridge section.

"Did you change something?"

"I realize your inferior ear might not detect the sub-
tlety," he began. She jammed her elbow into his ribs.
"Well said," he murmured, rubbing the spot. "Shall we
try again?"

"I love it when you're dignified, Brandon."

"Really?" He lifted an inquiring brow. "Now, where
was I?"

"You were about to demonstrate the first movement
from Tchaikovsky's Second Symphony."

"Ah." Nodding, Brand turned back to the keys. He
ran through the difficult movement with a fluid skill
that had Raven shaking her head.

"Show-off," she accused when he finished with a
flourish.

"You're just jealous."

With a sigh she lifted her shoulders. "Unfortunately,
you're right."

Brand laughed and put his hand palm to palm with hers. "I have the advantage in spread."

Raven studied her small, narrow-boned hand. "It's a good thing I didn't want to be a concert pianist."

"Beautiful hands," Brand told her, making one of his sudden and completely natural romantic gestures by lifting her fingers to his lips. "I'm quite helplessly in love with them."

"Brandon." Disarmed, Raven could only look at him. A tremble of warmth shot up her spine.

"They always smell of that lotion you have in the little white pot on the dresser."

"I didn't think you'd notice something like that." She shivered in response when his lips brushed the inside of her wrist.

"There's nothing about you I don't notice." He kissed her other wrist. "You like your bath too hot, and you leave your shoes in the most unexpected places. And you always keep time with your left foot." Brand looked back up at her, keeping one hand entwined with hers while he reached up with the other to brush the hair from her shoulder. "And when I touch you like this, your eyes go to smoke." He ran a fingertip gently over the point of her breast and watched her irises darken and cloud. Very slowly he leaned over and touched his lips to hers. Lazily he ran his finger back and forth until her nipple was taut and straining against the fabric of her blouse.

Her mouth was soft and opened willingly. Raven tilted her head back, inviting him to take more. Currents of pleasure were already racing along her skin. Brand drew her closer, one hand lingering at her breast.

"I can feel your bones melt," he murmured. His

mouth grew hungrier, his hand more insistent. "It drives me crazy." His fingers drifted from her breast to the top button of her blouse. Even as he loosened it, the phone shrilled from the table across the room. He swore, and Raven gave a laugh and hugged him.

"Never mind, love," she said on a deep breath. "I'll remind you where you left off this time, too." Slipping out of his arms, she crossed the room to answer. "Hello."

"Hello, I'd like to speak with Brandon Carstairs, please," a voice said.

Raven smiled at the musical lilt in the voice and wondered vaguely how one of Brand's fans had gotten access to his number. "Mr. Carstairs is quite busy at the moment." She grinned over at him and got both a grin and a nod of approval before he crossed to her. He began to distract her by kissing her neck.

"Would you ask him to call his mother when he's free?"

"I beg your pardon?" Raven stifled a giggle and tried to struggle out of Brand's arms.

"His mother, dear," the voice repeated. "Ask him to call his mother when he has a minute, won't you? He has the number."

"Oh, please, Mrs. Carstairs, wait! I'm sorry." Wide-eyed, she looked up at Brand. "Brandon's right here. Your mother," Raven said in a horrified whisper that had him grinning again. Still holding her firmly to his side, he accepted the receiver.

"Hullo, Mum." Brand kissed the top of Raven's head, then chuckled. "Yes, I was busy. I was kissing a beautiful woman I'm madly in love with." The color rising in Raven's cheeks had him laughing. "No, no, it's all right, love, I intend to get back to it. How are you? And the rest?"

Raven nudged herself free of Brand's arm. "I'll make some tea," she said quietly, then slipped from the room.

Mrs. Pengalley had left the kitchen spotlessly clean, and Raven spent some time puttering around it aimlessly while the kettle heated on the stove. She found herself suddenly hungry, then remembered that she and Brand had worked straight through lunch. She got out the bread, deciding to make buttered toast fingers to serve with the tea.

Afternoon tea was one of Brand's rituals, and Raven had grown fond of it. She enjoyed the late afternoon breaks in front of the fireplace with tea and biscuits or scones or buttered toast. They could be any two people then, Raven mused, two people sitting in front of a fireplace having unimportant conversations. The kettle sang out, and she moved to switch off the flame.

Raven went about the mechanical domestic tasks of brewing tea and buttering toast, but her thoughts kept drifting back to Brand. There had been such effortless affection in his voice when he had spoken to his mother, such relaxed love. And Raven had felt a swift flash of envy. It was something she had experienced throughout childhood and adolescence, but she hadn't expected to feel it again. Raven reminded herself she was twenty-five and no longer a child.

The chores soothed her. She loaded the tray and started back down the hall with her feelings more settled. When she heard Brand's voice, she hesitated, not wanting to interrupt his conversation. But the weight of the tray outbalanced her sense of propriety.

He was sunk into one of the chairs by the fire when

Raven entered. With a smile he gestured her over so that she crossed the room and set the tray on the table beside him. "I will, Mum, perhaps next month. Give everyone my love." He paused and smiled again, taking Raven's hand. "She's got big gray eyes, the same color as the dove Shawn kept in the coop on the roof. Yes, I'll tell her. Bye, Mum. I love you."

Hanging up, Brand glanced at the ladened tea tray, then up at Raven. "You've been busy."

She crouched down and began pouring. "I discovered I was starving." She watched with the usual shake of her head as he added milk to his tea. That was one English habit Raven knew she would never comprehend. She took her own plain.

"My mother says to tell you you've a lovely voice over the phone." Brand picked up a toast finger and bit into it.

"You didn't have to tell her you'd been kissing me," Raven mumbled, faintly embarrassed. Brand laughed, and she glared at him.

"Mum knows I have a habit of kissing women," he explained gravely. "She probably knows I've occasionally done a bit more than that, but we haven't discussed that particular aspect of my life for some time." He took another bite of toast, studying Raven's face. "She wants to meet you. If the score keeps going along at this pace, I thought we might drive up to London next month."

"I'm not used to families, Brandon," she said. Raven reached for her cup, but he placed his hand over hers, waiting until she looked back up at him.

"They're easy people, Raven. They're important to me. You're important to me. I want them to know you."

She felt her stomach tighten, and lowered her eyes.

"Raven." Brand gave a short, exasperated sigh. "When are you going to talk to me?"

She couldn't pretend not to understand him. She could only shake her head and avoid the subject a little while longer. The time when they would have to return to California and face reality would come soon enough. "Please, tell me about your family. It might help me get used to being confronted with all of them if I know a bit more than I've read in the gossip columns." Raven smiled. Her eyes asked him to smile back and not to probe. Not yet.

Brand struggled with a sense of frustration but gave in. He could give her a little more time. "I'm the oldest of five." He gestured toward the mantel. "Michael's the distinguished-looking one with the pretty blond wife. He's a solicitor." Brand smiled, remembering the pleasure it had given him to send his brother to a good university. He'd been the first Carstairs to receive that sort of education. "There was nothing distinguished about him at all as a boy," Brand remarked. "He liked to give anyone within reach a bloody nose."

"Sounds like a good lawyer," Raven observed dryly. "Please go on."

"Alison's next. She graduated from Oxford at the top of her class." He watched Raven glance up at the photo of the fragile, lovely blonde. "An amazing brain," Brand continued, smiling. "She does something incomprehensible with computers and has a particular fondness for rowdy rugby matches. That's where she met her husband."

Raven shook her head, trying to imagine the delicate-looking woman shouting at rugby games or programming sophisticated computers. "I suppose your other brother's a physicist."

"No, Shawn's a veterinarian." Affection slipped into Brand's voice.

"Your favorite?"

He tilted his head as he reached for more tea. "If one has a favorite among brothers and sisters, I suppose so. He's simply one of the nicest people I know. He's incapable of hurting anyone. As a boy he was the one who always found the bird with the broken wing or the dog with a sore paw. You know the type."

Raven didn't, but she murmured something and continued to sip at her tea. Brand's family was beginning to fascinate her. Somehow, she had thought that people raised in the same house under the same circumstances would be more the same. These people seemed remarkably diverse. "And your other sister?"

"Moray." He grinned. "She's in school yet, claims she's going into finance or drama. Or perhaps," he added, "anthropology. She's undecided."

"How old is she?"

"Eighteen. She thinks your records are smashing, by the way, and had them all the last time I was home."

"I believe I'll like her," Raven decided. She let her gaze sweep the mantel again. "Your parents must be very proud of all of you. What does your father do?"

"He's a carpenter." Brand wondered if she was aware of the wistful look in her eyes. "He still works six days a week, even though he knows money isn't a problem anymore. He has a great deal of pride." He paused a moment, stirring his tea, his eyes on Raven. "Mum still hangs sheets out on a line, even though I bought her a perfectly good dryer ten years ago. That's the sort of people they are."

"You're very lucky," Raven told him and rose to wander about the room.

"Yes, I know that." Brand watched her move around the room with her quick, nervous stride. "Though I doubt I thought a great deal about it while I was growing up. It's very easy to take it all for granted. It must have been very difficult for you."

Raven lifted her shoulders, then let them fall. "I survived." Walking to the window, she looked out on the cliffs and the sea. "Let's go for a walk, Brandon. It's so lovely out."

He rose and walked to her. Taking her by the shoulders, Brand turned her around to face him. "There's more to life than surviving, Raven."

"I survived intact," she told him. "Not everyone does."

"Raven, I know you call home twice a week, but you never tell me anything about it." He gave her a quick, caring shake. "Talk to me."

"Not about that, not now, not here." She slipped her arms around him and pressed her cheek to his chest. "I don't want anything to touch us here—nothing from the past, nothing from tomorrow. Oh, there's so much ugliness, Brandon, so many responsibilities. I want time. Is that so wrong?" She held him tighter, suddenly possessive. "Can't this be our fantasy, Brandon? That there isn't anybody but us? Just for a little while."

She heard him sigh as his lips brushed the crown of her head. "For a little while, Raven. But fantasies have to end, and I want the reality, too."

Raven lifted her face, then framed his with her

hands. "Like Joe in the script," she reflected and smiled. "He finds his reality in the end, doesn't he?"

"Yes." Brand bent to kiss her and found himself lingering over it longer than he had intended. "Proving dreams come true," he murmured.

"But I'm not a dream, Brandon." She took both of his hands in hers while her eyes smiled at him. "And you've already brought me to life."

"And without magic."

Raven lifted a brow. "That depends on your point of view," she countered. "I still feel the magic." Slowly she lifted his hand to the neckline of her blouse. "I think you were here when we left off."

"So I was." He loosened the next button, watching her face. "What about that walk?"

"Walk? In all that rain?" Raven glanced over to the sun-filled window. "No." Shaking her head, she looked back at Brand. "I think we'd better stay inside until it blows over."

He ran his finger down to the next button, smiling at her while he toyed with it. "You're probably right."

Chapter 13

Mrs. Pengalley made it a point to clean the music room first whenever Raven and Brand left her alone in the house. It was here they spent all their time working—if what show people did could be considered work. She had her own opinion on that. She gathered up the cups, as she always did, and sniffed them. Tea. Now and again she had sniffed wine and occasionally some bourbon, but she was forced to admit that Mr. Carstairs didn't seem to live up to the reputation of heavy drinking that show people had. Mrs. Pengalley was the smallest bit disappointed.

They lived quietly, too. She had been sure when Brand had notified her to expect him to be in residence for three months that he would have plans to entertain. Mrs. Pengalley knew what sort of entertainment show business people went in for. She had waited for the fancy cars to start arriving, the fancy people in their outrageous clothes. She had told Mr. Pengalley it was just a matter of time.

But no one had come, no one at all. There had been no disgraceful parties to clean up after. There had only been Mr. Carstairs and the young girl with the big gray eyes who sang as pretty as you please. But of course, Mrs. Pengalley reminded herself, she was in *that* business, too.

Mrs. Pengalley walked over to shake the wrinkles from the drapes at the side window. From there she could see Raven and Brand walking along the cliffs. Always in each other's pockets, she mused and sniffed to prevent herself from smiling at them. She snapped the drape back into place and began dusting off the furniture.

And how was a body supposed to give anything a proper dusting, she wanted to know, when they were always leaving their papers with the chicken scratchings on them all over everywhere? Picking up a piece of staff paper, Mrs. Pengalley scowled down at the lines and notes. She couldn't make head nor tail out of the notations; she scanned the words instead.

Loving you is no dream/I need you here to hold on to/Wanting you is everything/Come back to me.

She clucked her tongue and set the paper back down. Fine song, that one, she thought, resuming her dusting. Doesn't even rhyme.

Outside, the wind from the sea was strong, and Brand slipped his arm around Raven's shoulders. Turning her swiftly to face him, he bent her backward and gave her a long, lingering kiss. She gripped his shoulders for balance, then stared at him when his mouth lifted.

"What," she began and let out a shaky breath, "was that for?"

"For Mrs. Pengalley," he answered easily. "She's peeking out the music room window."

"Brandon, you're terrible." His mouth came down to hers again. Her halfhearted protest turned into total response. With a quiet sound of pleasure, Brand deepened the kiss and dragged her closer to him. Raven could feel the heat of the sun on her skin even as the sea breeze cooled it. The wind brought them the scent of honeysuckle and roses.

"That," he murmured as his mouth brushed over her cheeks, "was for me."

"Have any other friends?" Raven asked.

Laughing, Brand gave her a quick hug and released her. "I suppose we've given her enough to cluck her tongue over today."

"So that's what you want me for." Raven tossed her head. "Shock value."

"Among other things."

They wandered to the sea wall, for some moments looking out in comfortable silence. Raven liked the cliffs with their harsh faces and sheer, dizzying drop. She liked the constant, boiling noise of the sea, the screaming of the gulls.

The score was all but completed, with only a few minor loose ends and a bit of polishing to be done. Copies of completed numbers had been sent back to California. Raven knew they were drawing out a job that could be finished quickly. She had her own reasons for procrastinating, though she wasn't wholly certain of Brand's. She didn't want to break the spell.

Raven wasn't sure precisely what Brand wanted from

her because she hadn't permitted him to tell her yet. There were things, she knew, that had to be settled between them—things that could be avoided for the time being while they both simply let themselves be consumed by love. But the time would come when they would have to deal with the everyday business of living.

Would their work be a problem? That was one of the questions Raven refused to ask herself. Or if she asked it, she refused to answer. Commitments went with their profession, time-consuming commitments that made it difficult to establish any sort of a normal life. And there was so little privacy. Every detail of their relationship would be explored in the press. There would be pictures and stories, true and fabricated. The worst kind, Raven mused, were those with a bit of both. All of this, she realized, could be handled with hard work and determination if the love was strong enough. She had no doubt theirs was, but she had other doubts.

Would she ever be able to rid herself of the nagging fear that he might leave her again? The memory of the hurt kept her from giving herself to Brand completely. And her feelings of responsibility to her mother created yet another barrier. This was something she had always refused to share with anyone. She couldn't even bring herself to share it with the person she cared for most in the world. Years before, she had made a decision to control her own life, promising herself she would never depend too heavily on anything or anyone. Too often she had watched her mother relinquish control and lose.

If she could have found a way, Raven would have prolonged the summer. But more and more, the knowledge that the idyll was nearly at an end intruded into her thoughts. The prelude to fantasy was over. She hoped the fantasy would become a reality.

Brand watched Raven's face as she leaned her elbows on the rough stone wall and looked out to sea. There was a faraway look in her eyes that bothered him. He wanted to reach her, but their time alone together was slipping by rapidly. A cloud slid across the sun for a moment, and the light shifted and dimmed. He heard Raven sigh.

"What are you thinking?" he demanded, catching her flying hair in his hand.

"That of all the places I've ever been, this is the best." Raven tilted her head to smile up at him but didn't alter her position against the wall. "Julie and I took a break in Monaco once, and I was sure it was the most beautiful spot on earth. Now I know it's the second."

"I knew you'd love it if I could ever get you here," Brand mused, still toying with the ends of her hair. "I had some bad moments thinking you'd refuse. I'm not at all sure I could have come up with an alternate plan."

"Plan?" Raven's forehead puckered over the word. "I don't know what you mean. What plan?"

"To get you here, where we could be alone."

Raven straightened away from the wall but continued looking out to sea. "I thought we came here to write a score."

"Yes." Brand watched the flight of a bird as it swooped down over the waves. "The timing of that was rather handy."

"Handy?" Raven felt the knot start in her stomach. The clouds shifted over the sun again.

"I doubt you'd have agreed to work with me again if the project hadn't been so tempting," he said. Brand frowned up at a passing cloud. "You certainly wouldn't have agreed to live with me."

"So you dangled the score in front of my nose like a meaty bone?"

"Of course not. I wanted to work with you on the project the moment it was offered to me. It was all just a matter of timing, really."

"Timing and planning," she said softly. "Like a chess game. Julie's right; I've never been any good at strategy." Raven turned away, but Brand caught her arm before she could retreat.

"Raven?"

"How could you?" She whirled back to face him. Her eyes were dark and hot, her cheeks flushed with fury. Brand narrowed his eyes and studied her.

"How could I what?" he asked coolly, releasing her arm.

"How could you use the score to trick me into coming here?" She dragged at her hair as the wind blew it into her face.

"I'd have used anything to get you back," Brand said. "And I didn't trick you, Raven. I told you nothing but the truth."

"Part of the truth," she continued.

"Perhaps," he agreed. "We're both rather good at that, aren't we?" He didn't touch her, but the look he gave her became more direct. "Why are you angry? Because I love you or because I made you realize you love me?"

"Nobody *makes* me do anything!" She balled her hands into fists as she whirled away. "Oh, I detest being maneuvered. I run my own life, make my own decisions."

"I don't believe I've made any for you."

"No, you just led me gently along by the nose until I *chose* what was best for myself." Raven turned back again, and now her voice was low and vibrant with anger. "Why couldn't you have been honest with me?"

"You wouldn't have let me anywhere near you if I'd been completely honest. I had experience with you before, remember?"

Raven's eyes blazed. "Don't tell me what I would've done, Brandon. You're not inside my head."

"No, you've never let me in there." He pulled out a cigarette, cupped his hands around a match and lit it. Before speaking, he took a long, contemplative drag. "We'll say I wasn't in the mood to be taking chances, then. Will that suit you?"

His cool, careless tone fanned her fury. "You had no right!" she tossed at him. "You had no right to arrange my life this way. Who said I had to play by your rules, Brandon? When did you decide I was incapable of planning for myself?"

"If you'd like to be treated as a rational adult, perhaps you should behave as one," he suggested in a deceptively mild tone. "At the moment I'd say you're being remarkably childish. I didn't bring you here under false pretenses, Raven. There was a score to be written, and this was a quiet place to do it. It was also a place I felt you'd have the chance to get used to being with me again. I wanted you back."

"*You* felt. *You* wanted!" Raven tossed back her hair. "How incredibly selfish! What about *my* feelings? Do you think you can just pop in and out of my life at your convenience?"

"As I remember, I was pushed out."

"You left me!" The tears came from nowhere and

blinded her. "Nothing's ever hurt me like that before. Nothing!" Tears of hurt sprang to her eyes. "I'll be damned if you'll do it to me again. You went away without a word!"

"You mightn't have liked the words I wanted to say." Brand tossed the stub of his cigarette over the wall. "You weren't the only one who was hurt that night. How the hell else could I be rational unless I put some distance between us? I couldn't have given you the time you seemed to need if I'd stayed anywhere near you."

"Time?" Raven repeated as thoughts trembled and raced through her mind. "You gave me time?"

"You were a child when I left," he said shortly. "I'd hoped you'd be a woman when I came back."

"You had hoped…" Her voice trailed off into an astonished whisper. "Are you telling me you stayed away, giving me a chance to—to grow up?"

"I didn't see I had any choice." Brand dug his hands into his pockets as his brows came together.

"Didn't you?" She remembered her despair at his going, the emptiness of the years. "And of course, why should you have given me one? You simply took it upon yourself to decide for me."

"It wasn't a matter of deciding." He turned away from her, knowing he was losing his grip on his temper. "It was a matter of keeping sane. I simply couldn't stay near you and not have you."

"So you stayed away for five years, then suddenly reappeared, using my music as an excuse to lure me into bed. You didn't give a damn about the quality of *Fantasy.* You just used it—and the talent and sweat of the performers—for your own selfish ends."

"That," he said in a deadly calm voice, "is beyond contempt." Turning, he walked away. Within moments Raven heard the roar of an engine over the sound of the sea.

She stood, watching the car speed down the lane. If she had meant to deal a savage blow, she had succeeded. The shock of her own words burned in her throat. She shut her eyes tightly.

Even with her eyes closed, she could see clearly the look of fury on Brand's face before he had walked away. Raven ran a shaking hand through her hair. Her head was throbbing with the aftereffects of temper. Slowly she opened her eyes and stared out at the choppy green sea.

Everything we've had these past weeks was all part of some master plan, she thought. Even as she stood, the anger drained out of her, leaving only the weight of unhappiness.

She resented the fact that Brand had secretly placed a hand on the reins of her life, resented that he had offered her the biggest opportunity in her career as a step in drawing her to him. And yet… Raven shook her head in frustration. Confused and miserable, she turned to walk back to the house.

Mrs. Pengalley met her at the music room door. "There's a call for you, miss, from California." She had watched the argument from the window with a healthy curiosity. Now, however, the look in the gray eyes set her maternal instincts quivering. She repressed an urge to smooth down Raven's hair. "I'll make you some tea," she said.

Raven walked to the phone and lifted the receiver. "Yes, hello."

"Raven, it's Julie."

"Julie." Raven sank down in a chair. She blinked back fresh tears at the sound of the familiar voice. "Back from the isles of Greece?"

"I've been back for a couple weeks, Raven."

Of course. She should have known that. "Yes, all right. What's happened?"

"Karter contacted me because he wasn't able to reach you this morning. Some trouble on the line or something."

"Has she left again?" Raven's voice was dull.

"Apparently she left last night. She didn't go very far." Hearing the hesitation in Julie's voice, Raven felt the usual tired acceptance sharpen into apprehension.

"Julie?" Words dried up, and she waited.

"There was an accident, Raven. You'd better come home."

Raven closed her eyes. "Is she dead?"

"No, but it's not good, Raven. I hate having to tell you over the phone this way. The housekeeper said Brand wasn't there."

"No." Raven opened her eyes and looked vaguely around the room. "No, Brandon isn't here." She managed to snap herself back. "How bad, Julie? Is she in the hospital?"

Julie hesitated again, then spoke quietly. "She's not going to make it, Raven. I'm sorry. Karter says hours at best."

"Oh, God." Raven had lived with the fear all her life, yet it still came as a shock. She looked around the room again a little desperately, trying to orient herself.

"I know there's no good way to tell you this, Raven, but I wish I could find a better one."

"What?" She brought herself back again with an enormous effort. "No, I'm all right. I'll leave right away."

"Shall I meet you and Brand at the airport?"

The question drifted through Raven's mind. "No. No, I'll go straight to the hospital. Where is she?"

"St. Catherine's, intensive care."

"Tell Dr. Karter I'll be there as soon as I can. Julie…"

"Yes?"

"Stay with her."

"Of course I will. I'll be here."

Raven hung up and sat staring at the silent phone.

Mrs. Pengalley came back into the room carrying a cup of tea. She took one look at Raven's white face and set it aside. Without speaking, she went to the liquor cabinet and took out the brandy. After pouring out two fingers, she pressed the snifter on Raven.

"Here now, miss, you drink this." The Cornish burr was brisk.

Raven's eyes shifted to her. "What?"

"Drink up, there's a girl."

She obeyed as Mrs. Pengalley lifted the glass to her lips. Instantly Raven sucked in her breath at the unexpected strength of the liquor. She took another sip, then let out a shaky sigh.

"Thank you." She lifted her eyes to Mrs. Pengalley again. "That's better."

"Brandy has its uses," the housekeeper said righteously.

Raven rose, trying to put her thoughts in order. There were things to be done and no time to do them. "Mrs.

Pengalley, I have to go back to America right away. Could you pack some things for me while I call the airport?"

"Aye." She studied Raven shrewdly. "He's gone off to cool his heels, you know. They all do that. But he'll be back soon enough."

Realizing Mrs. Pengalley spoke of Brand, Raven dragged a hand through her hair. "I'm not altogether certain of that. If Brandon's not back by the time I have to go to the airport, would you ask Mr. Pengalley to drive me? I know it's an inconvenience, but it's terribly important."

"If that's what you want." Mrs. Pengalley sniffed. Young people, she thought, always flying off the handle. "I'll pack your things, then."

"Thank you." Raven glanced around the music room, then picked up the phone.

An hour later she hesitated at the foot of the stairs. Everything seemed to have happened at once. She willed Brand to return, but there was no sign of his car in the driveway. Raven struggled over writing a note but could think of nothing to say on paper that could make up for the words she had thrown at him. And how could she say in a few brief lines that her mother was dying and she had to go to her?

Yet there wasn't time to wait until he returned. She knew she couldn't risk it. Frantically she pulled a note pad from her purse. "Brandon," she wrote quickly, "I had to go. I'm needed at home. Please, forgive me. I love you, Raven."

Dashing back into the music room, she propped the note against the sheet of staff paper on top of the pile on the piano. Then, hurrying from the room, she grabbed her suitcases and ran outside. Mr. Pengalley was waiting in his serviceable sedan to drive her to the airport.

Chapter 14

Five days passed before Raven began thinking clearly again. Karter had been right about there only being a matter of hours. Raven had had to deal not only with grief but also with an unreasonable guilt that she hadn't been in time. The demand of details saved her from giving in to the urge to sink into self-pity and self-rebuke. She wondered once, during those first crushing hours, if that was why people tied so many traditions and complications to death: to keep from falling into total despair.

She was grateful that Karter handled the police himself in a way that ensured the details would be kept out of the papers.

After the first busy days there was nothing left but to accept that the woman she had loved and despised was gone. There was no more she could do. The disease had beaten them, just as surely as if it had been a cancer. Gradually she began to accept her mother's death as the result of a long, debilitating illness. She didn't cry, knowing she had already mourned, knowing it was time to put away the unhappiness. She had never had control of her mother's life; she needed the strength to maintain control of her own.

A dozen times during those days Raven phoned the house in Cornwall. There was never an answer. She could almost hear the hollow, echoing sounds of the ring through the empty rooms. More than once she considered simply getting on a plane and going back, but she always pushed the thought aside. He wouldn't be there waiting for her.

Where could he be? she wondered again and again. *Where would he have gone? He hasn't forgiven me.* And worse, she thought again and again, *he'll never forgive me.*

After hanging up the phone a last time, Raven looked at herself in her bedroom mirror. She was pale. The color that had drained from her face five days ago in Cornwall had never completely returned. There was too much of a helpless look about her. Raven shook her head and grabbed her blusher. Borrowed color, she decided, was better than none at all. She had to start somewhere.

Yes, she thought again, still holding the sable brush against her cheek. I've got to start somewhere. Turning away from the mirror, Raven again picked up the phone.

Thirty minutes later she came downstairs wearing a black silk dress. She had twisted her hair up and was setting a plain, stiff-brimmed black hat over it as she stepped into the hall.

"Raven?" Julie came out of the office. "Are you going out?"

"Yes, if I can find that little envelope bag and my car keys. I think they're inside it." She was already poking into the hall closet.

"Are you all right?"

Raven drew her head from the closet and met Julie's look. "I'm better," she answered, knowing Julie wouldn't be satisfied with a clichéd reply. "The lecture you gave me after the funeral, about not blaming myself? I'm trying to put it into practice."

"It wasn't a lecture," Julie countered. "It was simply a statement of facts. You did everything you could do to help your mother; you couldn't have done any more."

Raven sighed before she could stop herself. "I did everything I knew how to do, and I suppose that's the same thing." She shook off the mood as she shut the closet door. "I *am* better, Julie, and I'm going to be fine." She smiled, then, glimpsing a movement, looked beyond Julie's shoulder. Wayne stepped out of the office. "Hello, Wayne, I didn't know you were here."

He moved past Julie. "Well, I can definitely approve of that dress," he greeted her.

"And so you should," Raven returned dryly. "You charged me enough for it."

"Don't be a philistine, darling. Art has no price." He flicked a finger over the shoulder of the dress. "Where are you off to?"

"Alphonso's. I'm meeting Henderson for lunch."

Wayne touched Raven's cheek with a fingertip. "A bit heavy on the blush," he commented.

"I'm tired of looking pale. Don't fuss." She placed a hand on each of his cheeks, urging him to bend so that she could kiss him. "You've been a rock, Wayne.

I haven't told you how much I appreciate your being here the last few days."

"I needed to escape from the office."

"I adore you." She lowered her hands to meet his arms and squeezed briefly. "Now, stop worrying about me." Raven shot a look past his shoulder to Julie. "You, too. I'm meeting Henderson to talk over plans for a new tour."

"New tour?" Julie frowned. "Raven, you've been working nonstop for over six months. The album, the tour, the score." She paused. "After all of this you need a break."

"After all this the thing I need least is a break," Raven corrected. "I want to work."

"Then take a sabbatical," Julie insisted. "A few months back you were talking about finding a mountain cabin in Colorado, remember?"

"Yes." Raven smiled and shook her head. "I was going to write and be rustic, wasn't I? Get away from the glitter-glamour and into the woods." Raven grinned, recalling the conversation. "You said something about not being interested in anything more rustic than a margarita at poolside."

Julie lifted a thin, arched brow. "I've changed my mind. I'm going shopping for hiking boots."

Wayne's comment was a dubious *"hmmm."*

Raven smiled. "You're sweet," she said to Julie as she kissed her cheek. "But it isn't necessary. I need to do something that takes energy, physical energy. I'm going to talk to Henderson about a tour of Australia. My records do very well there."

"If you'd just talk to Brand…" Julie began, but Raven cut her off.

"I've tried to reach him; I can't." There was something final and flat in the statement. "Obviously he doesn't want to talk to me. I'm not at all sure I blame him."

"He's in love with you," Wayne said from behind her. Raven turned and met the look. "A few thousand people saw the sparks flying the night of your concert in New York."

"Yes, he loves me, and I love him. It doesn't seem to be enough, and I can't quite figure out why. No, please." She took his hand, pressing it between both of hers. "I have to get my mind off it all for a while. I feel as if I had been having a lovely picnic and got caught in a landslide. The bruises are still a bit sore. I could use some good news," she added, glancing from one of them to the other, "if the two of you are ever going to decide to tell me."

Raven watched as Wayne and Julie exchanged glances. She grinned, enjoying what she saw. "I've been noticing a few sparks myself. Isn't this a rather sudden situation?"

"Very," Wayne agreed, smiling at Julie over Raven's head. "It's only been going on for about six years."

"Six years!" Raven's brows shot up in amazement.

"I didn't choose to be one of a horde," Wayne said mildly, lighting one of his elegant cigarettes.

"And I always thought he was in love with you," Julie stated, letting her gaze drift from Raven to Wayne.

"With *me?*" Raven laughed spontaneously for the first time in days.

"I fail to see the humour in that," Wayne remarked from behind a nimbus of smoke. "I'm considered by many to be rather attractive."

"Oh, you are," she agreed, then giggled and kissed his cheek. "Madly so. But I can't believe anyone could think you were in love with me. You've always dated those rather alarmingly beautiful models with their sculpted faces and long legs."

"I don't think we need bring all that up at the moment," Wayne retorted.

"It's all right." Julie smiled sweetly and tucked her hair behind her ear. "I haven't any problem with Wayne's checkered past."

"When did all this happen, please?" Amused, Raven cut into their exchange. "I turn my back for a few weeks, and I find my two best friends making calf's eyes at each other."

"I've never made calf's eyes at anyone," Wayne remonstrated, horrified. "Smoldering glances, perhaps." He lifted his rakishly scarred brow.

"When?" Raven repeated.

"I looked up from my deck chair the first morning out on the cruise," Julie began, "and who do you suppose is sauntering toward me in a perfectly cut Mediterranean white suit?"

"Really?" Raven eyed Wayne dubiously. "I'm not certain whether I'm surprised or impressed."

"It seemed like a good opportunity," he explained, tapping his expensive ashes into a nearby dish, "if I could corner her before she charmed some shipping tycoon or handy sailor."

"I believe I charmed a shipping tycoon a few years ago," Julie remarked lazily. "And as to the sailor…"

"Nevertheless," Wayne went on, shooting her a glance. "I decided a cruise was a very good place to begin winning her over. It was," he remarked, "remarkably simple."

"Oh?" Julie's left brow arched. "Really?"

Wayne tapped out his cigarette, then moved over to gather her in his arms. "A piece of cake," he added carelessly. "Of course, women habitually find me irresistible."

"It would be safer if they stopped doing so. I might be tempted to wring their necks," Julie cooed, winding her arms around his neck.

"The woman's going to be a trial to live with." Wayne kissed her as though he'd decided to make the best of it.

"I can see you two are going to be perfectly miserable together. I'm so sorry." Walking over, Raven slipped an arm around each of them. "You will let me give you the wedding?" she began, then stopped. "That is, are you having a wedding?"

"Absolutely," Wayne told her. "We don't trust each other enough for anything less encumbering." He gave Julie a flashing grin that inexplicably made Raven want to weep.

Raven hugged them both again fiercely. "I needed to hear something like this right now. I'm going to leave you alone. I imagine you can entertain yourselves while I'm gone. Can I tell Henderson?" she asked. "Or is it a secret?"

"You can tell him," Julie said, watching as Raven adjusted her hat in the hall mirror. "We're planning on taking the plunge next week."

Raven's eyes darted up to Julie's in the mirror. "My, you two move fast, don't you?"

"When it's right, it's right."

Raven smiled in quick agreement. "Yes, I suppose

it is. There's probably champagne in the refrigerator, isn't there, Julie?" She turned away from the mirror. "We can have a celebration drink when I get back. I'll just be a couple of hours."

"Raven." Julie stopped her as she headed for the door. Raven looked curiously over her shoulder. "Your purse." Smiling, Julie retrieved it from a nearby table. "You won't forget to eat, will you?" she demanded as she placed it in Raven's hand.

"I won't forget to eat," Raven assured her, then dashed through the door.

Within the hour Raven was seated in the glassed-in terrace room of Alphonso's toying with a plate of scampi. There were at least a dozen people patronizing the restaurant whom she knew personally. A series of greetings had been exchanged before she had been able to tuck herself into a corner table.

The room was an elaborate jungle, with exotic plants and flowers growing everywhere. The sun shining through the glass and greenery gave the terrace a warmth and glow. The floor was a cool ceramic tile, and there was a constant trickle of water from a fountain at the far end of the room. Raven enjoyed the casual elegance, the wicker accessories and the pungent aromas of food and flowers that filled the place. Now, however, she gave little attention to the terrace room as she spoke with her agent.

Henderson was a big, burly man whom Raven had always thought resembled a logjammer rather than the smooth, savvy agent he was. He had a light red thatch of hair that curled thinly on top of his head and bright merry blue eyes that she knew could sharpen to a sword's point. There was a friendly smattering of freckles over his broad, flat-featured face.

He could smile and look genial and none too bright. It was one of his best weapons. Raven knew Henderson was as sharp as they came, and when necessary, he could be hard as nails. He was fond of her, not only because she made him so rich, but because she never resented having done so. He couldn't say the same about all of his clients.

Now Henderson allowed Raven to ramble on about ideas for a new tour, Australia, New Zealand, promotion for the new album that was already shooting up the charts a week after its release. He ate his veal steadily, washing it down with heavy red wine while Raven talked and sipped occasionally from her glass of white wine.

He noticed she made no mention of the *Fantasy* score or of her time in Cornwall. The last progress report he had received from her had indicated the project was all but completed. The conversations he had had with Jarett had been enthusiastic. Lauren Chase had approved each one of her numbers, and the choreography had begun. The score seemed to be falling into place without a hitch.

So Henderson had been surprised when Raven had returned alone so abruptly from Cornwall. He had expected her to phone him when the score was completed, then to take the week or two she had indicated she and Brand wanted to relax and do nothing. But here she was, back early and without Brand.

She chattered nervously, darting from one topic to another. Henderson didn't interrupt, only now and again making some noncommittal sounds as he attended to his meal. Raven talked nonstop for fifteen minutes, then began to wind down. Henderson waited, then took a long swallow of wine.

"Well, now," he said, patting his lips with a white linen napkin. "I don't imagine there should be any problem setting up an Australian tour." His voice suited his looks.

"Good." Raven pushed the scampi around on her plate. She realized she had talked herself out. Spearing a bit of shrimp, she ate absently.

"While it's being set up, you could take yourself a nice little vacation somewhere."

Raven's brows rose. "No, I thought you could book me on the talk-show circuit, dig up some guest shots here and there."

"Could do that, too," he said genially. "After you take a few weeks off."

"I want gigs, not a few weeks off." Her brows lowered suspiciously. "Have you been talking to Julie?"

He looked surprised. "No, about what?"

"Nothing." Raven shook her head, then smiled. "Gigs, Henderson."

"You've lost weight, you know," he pointed out and shoveled in some more veal. "It shows in your face. Eat."

Raven gave an exasperated sigh and applied herself to her lunch. "Why does everyone treat me like a dimwitted child?" she mumbled, swallowing shrimp. "I'm going to start being temperamental and hard to get along with until I get some star treatment." Henderson said something quick and rude between mouthfuls which she ignored. "What about Jerry Michaels?

Didn't I hear he was lining up a variety special for the fall? You could get me on that."

"Simplest thing in the world," Henderson agreed. "He'd be thrilled to have you."

"Well?"

"Well what?"

"Henderson." Resolutely, Raven pushed her plate aside. "Are you going to book me on the Jerry Michaels show?"

"No." He poured more wine into his glass. The sun shot through it, casting a red shadow on the tablecloth.

"Why?" Annoyance crept into Raven's tone.

"It's not for you." Henderson lifted a hand, palm up, as she began to argue. "I know who's producing the show, Raven. It's not for you."

She subsided a bit huffily, but she subsided. His instincts were the best in the field. "All right, forget the Michaels gig. What, then?"

"Want some dessert?"

"No, just coffee."

He signaled the waiter, then, after ordering blueberry cheesecake for himself and coffee for both of them, he settled back in his chair. "What about *Fantasy?*"

Raven twirled her wineglass between her fingers. "It's finished," she said flatly.

"And?"

"And?" she repeated, looking up. His merry blue eyes were narrowed. "It's finished," she said again. "Or essentially finished. I can't foresee any problem with the final details. Brandon or his agent will get in touch with you if there are, I'm sure."

"Jarett will probably need the two of you off and on

during the filming," Henderson said mildly. "I wouldn't consider myself finished with it for a while yet."

Raven frowned into the pale golden liquid in her glass. "Yes, you're right, of course. I hadn't thought about it. Well…" She shook her head and pushed the wine away. "I'll deal with that when the times comes."

"How'd it go?"

She looked at Henderson levelly, but her thoughts drifted. "We wrote some of the best music either one of us has ever done. That I'm sure of. We work remarkably well together. I was surprised."

"You didn't think you would?" Henderson eyed the blueberry cheesecake the waiter set in front of him.

"No, I didn't think we would. Thank you," this to the waiter before she looked at Henderson again. "But everything else apart, we did work well together."

"You'd worked well together before," he pointed out. "'Clouds and Rain.'" He saw her frown but continued smoothly. "Did you know sales on that have picked up again after your New York concert? You got yourself a lot of free press, too."

"Yes," Raven mumbled into her coffee. "I'm sure we did."

"I've had a lot of questions thrown at me during the last weeks," he continued blandly, even when her eyes lifted and narrowed. "From the inside," he said with a smile, "as well as the press. I was at a nice little soiree just last week. You and Brand were the main topic of conversation."

"As I said, we work well together." Raven set down her cup. "Brandon was right; we are good for each other artistically."

"And personally?" Henderson took a generous bite of cheesecake.

"Well." Raven lifted a brow. "You certainly get to the point."

"That's all right, you don't have to answer me." He swallowed the cake, then broke off another piece. "You can tell *him*."

"Who?"

"Brand," Henderson answered easily and added cream to his coffee. "He just walked in."

Raven whirled around in her chair. Instantly her eyes locked on Brand's. With the contact came a wild, swift surge of joy. Her first instinct was to spring from the table and run to him. Indeed, she had pushed the chair back, preparing to do so, when the expression on his face cut through her initial spring of delight. It was ice-cold fury. Raven sat where she was, watching as he weaved his way through the crowded restaurant toward her. There were casual greetings along the way which he ignored. Raven heard the room fall silent.

He reached her without speaking once or taking his eyes from her. Raven's desire to hold out a hand to him was also overcome. She thought he might strike it away. The look in his eyes had her blood beating uneasily. Henderson might not have been sitting two feet away.

"Let's go."

"Go?" Raven repeated dumbly.

"Now." Brand took her hand and yanked her to her feet. She might have winced at the unexpected pressure if she hadn't been so shocked by it.

"Brandon…"

"Now," he repeated. He began to walk away, dragging her behind him. Raven could feel the eyes following them. Shock, delight, anxiety all faded into temper.

"Let go of me!" she demanded in a harsh undertone. "What's the matter with you? You can't drag me around like this." She bumped into a lunching comedian, then skirted around him with a mumbled apology as Brand continued to stalk away with her hand in his. "Brandon, stop this! I will not be dragged out of a public restaurant."

He halted then and turned so that their faces were very close. "Would you prefer that I say what I have to say to you here and now?" His voice was clear and cool in the dead silence of the room. It was very easy to see the violence of temper just beneath the surface. Raven could feel it in the grip of his hand on hers. They were spotlighted again, she thought fleetingly, but hardly in the manner in which they had been in New York. She took a deep breath.

"No." Raven struggled for dignity and kept her voice lowered. "But there isn't any need to make a scene, Brandon."

"Oh, I'm in the mood for a scene, Raven," he tossed back in fluid British tones that carried well. "I'm in the mood for a bloody beaut of a scene."

Before she could comment, Brand turned away again and propelled her out of the restaurant. There was a Mercedes at the curb directly outside. He shoved her inside it, slamming the door behind her.

Raven straightened in the seat, whipping her head around as he opened the other door. "Oh, you're going to get one," she promised and ripped off her hat to throw it furiously into the back seat. "How *dare* you..."

"Shut up. I mean it." Brand turned to her as she

started to speak again. "Just shut up until we get where we're going, otherwise I might be tempted to strangle you here and be done with it."

He shot away from the curb, and Raven flopped back against her seat. I'll shut up, all right, she thought on wave after wave of anger. I'll shut up. It'll give me time to think through exactly what I have to say.

Chapter 15

By the time Brand stopped the car in front of the Bel-Air, Raven felt she had her speech well in order. As he climbed out of his side, she climbed out of hers, then turned to face him on the sidewalk. But before she could speak, he had her arm in a tight grip and was pulling her toward the entrance.

"I told you not to drag me."

"And I told you to shut up." He brushed past the doorman and into the lobby. Raven was forced into an undignified half-trot in order to keep up with his long-legged stride.

"I will *not* be spoken to like that," she fumed and gave her arm an unsuccessful jerk. "I will *not* be carted through a hotel lobby like a piece of baggage."

"I'm tired of playing it your way." Brand turned, grabbing both of her shoulders and dragging her against him. His fingers bit into her skin and shocked her into silence. "My game now, my rules."

His mouth came down hard on hers. It was a kiss of rage. His teeth scraped across her lips, forcing them open so that he could plunder and seek. He held her bruisingly close, as if daring her to struggle.

When Brand pulled away, he stared at her for a long silent moment, then swore quickly, fiercely. Turning he pulled her to the elevators.

Though she was no longer certain if it was fear or anger, Raven was trembling with emotion as they took the silent ride up. Brand could feel the throbbing pulse as he held her arm. He swore again, pungently, but she didn't glance at him. As the doors slid open, he pulled her into the hall and toward the penthouse.

There were no words exchanged between them as he slid the key into the lock. He released her arm as he pushed the door open. Without protest, Raven walked inside. She moved to the center of the room.

The suite was elegant, even lush, in a dignified, old-fashioned style with a small bricked fireplace and a good, thick carpet. Behind her the door slammed—a final sound—and she heard Brand toss the key with a faint metallic jingle onto a table. Raven drew a breath and turned around.

"Brandon…"

"No, I'll do the talking first." He crossed to her, his eyes locked on hers. "My rules, remember?"

"Yes." She lifted her chin. Her arm throbbed faintly where his fingers had dug into it. "I remember."

"First rule, no more bits and pieces. I won't have you closing parts of yourself off from me anymore." They were standing close. Now that the first dazed shock and surprise were passing, Raven noticed signs of strain and fatigue on his face. His words were spilling out so quickly, she couldn't interrupt. "You did the same thing to me five years ago, but then we weren't lovers. You were always holding out, never willing to trust."

"No." She shook her head, scrambling for some defense. "No, that's not true."

"Yes, it's true," he countered and took her by the shoulders again. "Did you tell me about your mother all those years ago? Or how you felt, what you were going through? Did you bring me into your life enough to let me help you, or at least comfort you?"

This was not what she had expected from him. Raven could only press her hand to her temple and shake her head again. "No, it wasn't something..."

"Wasn't something you wanted to share with me." He dropped her arms and stepped away from her. "Yes, I know." His voice was low and furious again as he pulled out a cigarette. He knew he had to do something with his hands or he'd hurt her again. He watched as she unconsciously nursed her arm where he had gripped her. "And this time, Raven, would you have told me anything about it if it hadn't been for the nightmare? If you hadn't been half asleep and frightened, would you have told me, trusted me?"

"I don't know." She made a small sound of confusion. "My mother had nothing to do with you."

Brand hurled the cigarette away before he lit it. "How can you say that to me? How can you stand there and say that to me?" He took a step toward her, then checked himself and stalked to the bar. "Damn you, Raven," he said under his breath. He poured bourbon and drank. "Maybe I should have stayed away," he managed in a calmer tone. "You'd already tossed me out of your life five years ago."

"*I* tossed you out?" This time her voice rose. "You walked out on me. You left me flat because I wouldn't be your lover." Raven walked over to the bar and leaned her palms on it. "You walked out of my house and out of my life, and the only word I had from you was what I read in the paper. It didn't take you long to find other women—several other women."

"I found as many as I could," Brand agreed and drank again. "As quickly as I could. I used women, booze, gambling—anything—to try to get you out of my system." He studied the dregs of liquor in his glass and added thoughtfully, "It didn't work." He set the glass down and looked at her again. "Which is why I knew I had to be patient with you."

Raven's eyes were still dark with hurt. "Don't talk to me about tossing you out."

"That's exactly what you did." Brand grabbed her wrist as she turned to swirl away from him. He held her still, the narrow, mahogany bar between them. "We were alone, remember? Julie was away for a few days."

Raven kept her eyes level. "I remember perfectly."

"Do you?" He arched a brow. Both his eyes and voice were cool again. "There might be a few things you don't remember. When I came to the house that night I was going to ask you to marry me."

Raven could feel every thought, every emotion, pour out of her body. She could only stare at him.

"Surprised?" Brand released her wrist and again reached in his pocket for a cigarette. "Apparently we have two differing perspectives on that night. I *loved* you." The words were an accusation that kept her speechless. "And God help me, all those weeks we were together I was faithful to you. I never touched another woman." He lit the cigarette, and as the end flared, Raven heard him say softly, "I nearly went mad."

"You never told me." Her voice was weak and shaken. Her eyes were huge gray orbs. "You never once said you loved me."

"You kept backing off," he retorted. "And I knew you were innocent and afraid, though I didn't know why." He gave her a long, steady look. "It would have made quite a lot of difference if I had, but you didn't trust me."

"Oh, Brandon."

"That night," he went on, "you were so warm, and the house was so quiet. I could feel how much you wanted me. It drove me crazy. Good God, I was trying to be gentle, patient, when the need for you was all but destroying me." He ran a tense hand through his hair. "And you were giving, melting, everywhere I touched you. And then—then you were struggling like some terrified child, pushing at me as if I'd tried to kill you, telling me not to touch you. You said you couldn't bear to have me touch you."

He looked back at her, but his eyes were no longer cool. "You're the only woman who's ever been able to hurt me like that."

"Brandon." Raven shut her eyes. "I was only twenty, and there were so many things…"

"Yes, I know now; I didn't know then." His tone was flat. "Though there really weren't so many changes this time around." Raven opened her eyes and started to speak, but he shook his head. "No, not yet. I've not finished. I stayed away to give you time, as I told you before. I didn't see any other way. I could hardly stay, kicking my heels in L.A., waiting for you to make up your mind. I didn't know how long I'd stay away, but during those five years I concentrated on my career. So did you."

Brand paused, spreading his long, elegant hands on the surface of the bar. "Looking back, I suppose that's all for the best. You needed to establish yourself, and I had a surge of productivity. When I started reading about you regularly in the gossip columns I knew it was time to come back." He watched her mouth fall open at that, and her eyes heat. "Get as mad as you damn well like when I've finished," he said shortly. "But don't interrupt."

Raven turned away to search for control. "All right, go on," she managed and faced him again.

"I came to the States without any real plan, except to see you. The solid idea fell into my lap by way of *Fantasy* when I was in New York. I used the score to get you back," he said simply and without apology. "When I stood up in that recording booth watching you again, I knew I'd have used anything, but the score did nicely." He pushed his empty glass aside with his fingertip. "I wasn't lying about wanting to work with you again for professional reasons or about feeling you were particularly right for *Fantasy*. But I would have if it had been necessary. So perhaps you weren't so far wrong about what you said on the cliffs that day." He moved from the bar to the window. "Of course, there was a bit more to it in my mind than merely getting you to bed."

Raven felt her throat burn. "Brandon." She swallowed and shut her eyes. "I've never been more ashamed of anything in my life than what I said to you. Anger is hardly an excuse, but I'd hoped—I'd hoped you'd forgive me."

Brand turned his head and studied her a moment. "Perhaps if you hadn't left, it would have been easier."

"I had to. I told you in the note…"

"What note?" His voice sharpened as he turned to face her.

"The note." Raven was uncertain whether to step forward or back. "I left it on the piano with the music."

"I didn't see any note. I didn't see anything but that you were gone." He let out a long breath. "I dumped all the music into a briefcase. I didn't notice a note."

"Julie called only a little while after you'd left to tell me about the accident."

His eyes shot back to hers again. "What accident?"

Raven stared at him.

"Your mother?" he said, reading it in her eyes.

"Yes. She'd had an accident. I had to get back right away."

He jammed his hands into his pockets. "Why didn't you wait for me?"

"I wanted to; I couldn't." Raven laced her fingers together to prevent her hands from fluttering. "Dr. Karter said it would only be a matter of hours. As it was…" She paused and turned away. "I was too late, anyway."

Brand felt the anger drain from him. "I'm sorry. I didn't know."

Raven didn't know why the simple, quiet statement should bring on the tears she hadn't shed before. They blinded her eyes and clogged her throat so that speech was impossible.

"I went a bit crazy when I got back to the house and found you'd packed and gone." Brand spoke wearily now. "I don't know exactly what I did at first; afterwards I got roaring drunk. The next morning I dumped all the music together, packed some things and took off for the States.

"I stopped off for a couple of days in New York, trying to sort things out. It seems I spend a great deal of time running after you. It's difficult on the pride. In New York I came up with a dozen very logical, very valid reasons why I should go back to England and forget you. But there was one very small, very basic point I couldn't argue aside." He looked at her again. Her back was to him, her head bent so that with her hair pulled up he could see the slender length of her neck. "I love you, Raven."

"Brandon." Raven turned her tear-drenched face toward him. She blinked at the prisms of light that blinded her, then shook her head quickly when she saw him make a move to come to her. "No, please don't. I won't be able to talk if you touch me." She drew in a deep breath, brushing the tears away with her fingertips. "I've been very wrong; I have to tell you."

He stood away from her, though impatience was beginning to simmer through him again. "I had my say," he agreed. "I suppose you should have yours."

"All those years ago," she began. "All those years ago there were things I couldn't say, things I couldn't even understand because I was so—dazzled by everything. My career, the fame, the money, the perpetual spotlight." The words came quickly, and her voice grew stronger with them. "Everything happened at once; there didn't seem to be any time to get used to it all. Suddenly I was in love with Brandon Carstairs." She laughed and brushed at fresh tears. "*The* Brandon Carstairs. You have to understand, one minute you were an image, a name on a record, and the next you were a man, and I loved you."

Raven moistened her lips, moving to stare from the window as Brand had. "And my mother—my mother was my responsibility, Brandon. I've felt that always, and it isn't something that can be changed overnight. You were the genuine knight on a charger. I couldn't— wouldn't talk to you about that part of my life. I was afraid, and I was never sure of you. You never told me you loved me, Brandon."

"I was terrified of you," he murmured, "of what I was feeling for you. You were the first." He shrugged. "But you were always pulling back from me. Always putting up No Trespassing signs whenever I started to get close."

"You always seemed to want so much." She hugged her arms. "Even this time, in Cornwall, when we were so close. It didn't seem to be enough. I always felt you were waiting for more."

"You still put up the signs, Raven." She turned, and his eyes locked on hers. "Your body isn't enough. That isn't what I waited five years for."

"Love should be enough," she tossed back, suddenly angry and confused.

"No." Brand shook his head, cutting her off. "It isn't enough. I want a great deal more than that." He waited a moment, watching the range of expressions on her face. "I want your trust, without conditions, without exceptions. I want a commitment, a total one. It's all or nothing this time, Raven."

She backed away. "You can't own me, Brandon."

A quick flash of fury shot into his eyes. "Damn it, I

don't want to own you, but I want you to belong to me. Don't you know there's a difference?"

Raven stared at him for a full minute. She dropped her arms, no longer cold. The tension that had begun to creep up the back of her neck vanished. "I didn't," she said softly. "I should have."

Slowly she crossed to him. She was vividly aware of every detail of his face: the dark, expressive brows drawn together now with thought, the blue-green eyes steady but with the spark of temper, the faint touch of mauve beneath them that told her he'd lost sleep. It came to her then that she loved him more as a woman than she had as a girl. A woman could love without fear, without restrictions. Raven lifted her fingertip to his cheek as if to smooth away the tension.

Then they were locked in each other's arms, mouth to mouth. His hands went to her hair, scattering pins until it tumbled free around them. He murmured something she had no need to understand, then plunged deep again into her mouth. Hurriedly, impatiently, they began to undress each other. No words were needed. They sought only touch, to give, to fulfill.

His fingers fumbled with the zipper of her dress, making him swear and her laugh breathlessly until he pulled her with him to the rug. Then, somehow, they were flesh to flesh. Raven could feel the shudders racing through him to match her own as they touched. His mouth was no more greedy than hers, his hands no less demanding. Their fire blazed clean and bright. Need erupted in them both so that she pulled him to her, desperate to have him, frantic to give.

Raw pleasure shot through her, rocking her again and again as she moved with him. His face was buried in her hair, his body damp to her touch. Air was forcing its way from her lungs in moans and gasps as they took each other higher and faster. Then the urgency passed, and a sweetness took its place.

Time lost all meaning as they lay together. Neither moved nor spoke. Tensions and angers, ecstasies and desperations, had all passed. All that was left was a soft contentment. She could feel his breath move lightly against her neck.

"Brandon," Raven murmured, letting her lips brush his skin.

"Hmm?"

"I think I still had something to say, but it's slipped my mind." She gave a low laugh.

Brand lifted his head and grinned. "Maybe it'll come back to you. Probably wasn't important."

"You're right, I'm sure." She smiled, touching his cheek. "It had something to do with loving you beyond sanity or some such thing and wanting more than anything in the world to belong to you. Nothing important."

Brand lowered his mouth to hers and nipped at her still tender lip. "You were distracted," he mused, seeking her breast with his fingertip.

Raven ran her hands down his back. "I was in a bit of a hurry."

"This time…" He began to taste her neck and shoulder. "This time we'll slow down the tempo. A bit more orchestration, don't you think?" His fingers slid gently and teasingly over the point of her breast.

"Yes, quite a bit more orchestration. Brandon…" Her words were lost on a sound of pleasure as his tongue found her ear. "Once more, with feeling," she whispered.

* * * * *

DUAL IMAGE

Chapter 1

Balancing a bag of groceries in one arm, Amanda let herself into the house. She radiated happiness. From outside came the sound of birds singing in the spring sunshine. The gold of her wedding ring caught the light. As a newlywed of three months, she was anxious to prepare a special, intimate dinner as a surprise for Cameron. Her demanding hours at the hospital and clinic often made it impossible for her to cook, and as a new bride she found pleasure in it. This afternoon, with two appointments unexpectedly canceled, she intended to fix something fancy, time-consuming and memorable. Something that went well with candlelight and wine.

As she entered the kitchen she was humming, a rare outward show of emotion for she was a reserved woman. With a satisfied smile, she drew a bottle of Cameron's favorite Bordeaux from the bag. As she studied the label, a smile lingered on her face while she remembered the first time they'd shared a bottle. He'd been so romantic, so attentive, so much what she'd needed at that point in her life.

A glance at her watch told her she had four full hours before her husband was expected home. Time enough to prepare an elaborate meal, light the candles and set out the crystal.

First, she decided, she was going upstairs to get out of her practical suit and shoes. There was a silk caftan upstairs, sheer, in misty shades of blue. Tonight, she wouldn't be a psychiatrist, but a woman, a woman very much in love.

The house was scrupulously neat and tastefully decorated. Such things came naturally to Amanda. As she walked toward the stairs, she glanced at a vase of Baccarat crystal and wished fleetingly she'd remembered fresh flowers. Perhaps she'd call the florist and have something extravagant delivered. Her hand trailed lightly over the polished banister as she started up. Her eyes, usually serious or intent, were dreamy. Carelessly, she pushed open the bedroom door.

Her smile froze. Utter shock replaced it. As she stood in the doorway, all color seemed to drain out of her cheeks. Her eyes grew huge before pain filled them. Out of her mouth came one anguished word.

"Cameron."

The couple in bed, locked in a passionate embrace, sprang apart. The man, smoothly handsome, his sleek hair disheveled, stared up in disbelief. The woman— feline, sultry, stunning—smiled very, very slowly. You could almost hear her purr.

"Vikki." Amanda looked at her sister with anguished eyes.

"You're home early." There was a hint, only a suspicion of a laugh in her sister's voice.

Cameron put a few more inches between himself and his sister-in-law. "Amanda, I…"

In one split second, Amanda's face contorted. With her eyes locked on the couple in bed, she reached in her jacket pocket and drew out a small, lethal revolver. The lovers stared at it in astonishment, and in silence. Coolly, she aimed and fired. A puff of confetti burst out.

"Ariel!"

Dr. Amanda Lane Jamison, better known as Ariel Kirkwood, turned to her harassed director as the couple in bed and members of the television crew dissolved into laughter.

"Sorry, Neal, I couldn't help myself. Amanda's *always* the victim," she said dramatically while her eyes danced. "Just think what it might do for the ratings if she lost her cool just once and murdered someone."

"Look, Ariel—"

"Or even just seriously injured them," she went on rapidly. "And who," she continued, flinging her hand toward the bed, "deserves it more than her spineless husband and scheming sister?"

At the hoots and applause of the crew, Ariel took a bow, then reluctantly turned over her weapon to her director when he held out his hand.

"You," he said with a long-suffering sigh, "are a certified loony, and have been since I've known you."

"I appreciate that, Neal."

"This time the tape's going to be running," he

warned and tried not to grin. "Let's see if we can shoot this scene before lunch."

Agreeably, Ariel went down to the first floor of the set. She stood patiently while her hair and makeup were touched up. Amanda was always perfection. Organized, meticulous, calm—all the things Ariel herself wasn't. She'd played the character for just over five years on the popular daytime soap opera *Our Lives, Our Loves*.

In those five years, Amanda had graduated with honors from college, had earned her degree in psychiatric medicine and had gone on to become a respected therapist. Her recent marriage to Cameron Jamison appeared to be made in heaven. But, of course, he was a weak opportunist who'd married her for her money and social position, while lusting after her sister—and half the female population of the fictional town of Trader's Bend.

Amanda was about to be confronted with the truth. The story line had been leading up to this revelation for six weeks, and the letters from viewers had poured in. Both they and Ariel thought it was about time Amanda found out about her louse of a husband.

Ariel liked Amanda, respected her integrity and poise. When the cameras rolled, Ariel *was* Amanda. While in her personal life she would much prefer a day at an amusement park to an evening at the ballet, she understood all the nuances of the woman she portrayed.

When this scene was aired, viewers would see a neat, slender woman with pale blond hair sleeked back into a sophisticated knot. The face was porcelain, stunning, with an icy kind of beauty that sent out signals of restrained sexuality. Class. Style.

Lake-blue eyes, high curved cheekbones added to the look of polished elegance. A perfectly shaped mouth tended toward serious smiles. Finely arched brows that were shades darker than the delicate blond of her hair accented luxurious lashes. A flawless beauty, perfectly composed—that was Amanda.

Ariel waited for her cue and wondered vaguely if she'd turned off her coffeepot that morning.

They ran through the scene again, from cue to cut, then a second time when it was discovered that Vikki's strapless bathing suit could be seen when she shifted in bed. Then came reaction shots—the camera zoomed in close on Amanda's pale, shocked face and held for several long, dramatic seconds.

"Lunch."

Response was immediate. The lovers bounded out of either side of the bed. In his bathing trunks, J. T. Brown, Ariel's on-screen husband, took her by the shoulders and gave her a long hard kiss. "Look, sweetie," he began, staying in character, "I'll explain about all this later. Trust me. I gotta call my agent."

"Wimp," Ariel called after him with a very un-Amandalike grin before she hooked her arm through that of Stella Powell, her series sister. "Pull something over that suit, Stella. I can't face the commissary food today."

Stella tossed back her tousled mass of auburn hair. "You buying?"

"Always sponging off your sister," Ariel mumbled. "Okay, I'll spring, but hurry up. I'm starving."

On her way to her dressing room, Ariel walked off the set, then through two more—the fifth floor of Doctors Hospital and the living room of the Lanes, Trader Bend's leading family. It was tempting to shed her costume and take down her hair, but it would only mean fooling with wardrobe and makeup after lunch. Instead, she just grabbed her purse, an outsize hobo bag that looked a bit incongruous with Amanda's elegant business suit. She was already thinking about a thick slice of baklava soaked in honey.

"Come on, Stella." Ariel stuck her head in the adjoining dressing room as Stella zipped up a pair of snug jeans. "My stomach's on overtime."

"It always is," her coworker returned as she pulled on a bulky sweatshirt. "Where to?"

"The Greek deli around the corner." More than ready, Ariel started down the hall in her characteristically long, swinging gait while Stella hurried to keep up. It wasn't that Ariel rushed from place to place, but simply that she wanted to see what was next.

"My diet," Stella began.

"Have a salad," Ariel told her without mercy. She turned her head to give Stella a quick up-and-down glance. "You know, if you weren't always wearing those skimpy outfits on camera, you wouldn't have to starve yourself."

Stella grinned as they came to the street door. "Jealous."

"Yeah. I'm always elegant and *always* proper. You have all the fun." Stepping outside, Ariel took a deep breath of New York. She loved it—had always loved it in a way usually reserved for tourists. Ariel had lived on the long thin island of Manhattan all of her life, and yet it remained an adventure to her. The sights, the smells, the sounds.

It was brisk for mid-April, and threatening to rain. The air was damp and smelled of exhaust. The streets and sidewalks were clogged with lunchtime traffic—

everyone hurrying, everyone with important business to attend to. A pedestrian swore and banged a fist on the hood of a cab that had clipped too close to the curb. A woman with spiked orange hair hustled by in black leather boots. Somone had written something uncomplimentary on a poster for a hot Broadway play. But Ariel saw a street vendor selling daffodils.

She bought two bunches and handed one to Stella.

"You can never pass up anything, can you?" Stella mumbled, but buried her face in the yellow blooms.

"Think of all I'd miss," Ariel countered. "Besides, it's spring."

Stella shivered and looked up at the leaden sky. "Sure."

"Eat." Ariel grabbed her arm and pulled her along. "You always get cranky when you miss meals."

The deli was packed with people and aromas. Spices and honey. Beer and oil. Always a creature of the senses, Ariel drew in the mingled scents before she worked her way to the counter. She had an uncanny way of getting where she was going through a throng without using her elbows or stepping on toes. While she moved, she watched and listened. She wouldn't want to miss a scent, or the texture of a voice, or the clashing colors of food. As she looked behind the glass-fronted counter, she could already taste the things there.

"Cottage cheese, a slice of pineapple and coffee— black," Stella said with a sigh. Ariel sent her a brief, pitying look.

"Greek salad, a hunk of that lamb on a hard roll and a slice of baklava. Coffee, cream and sugar."

"You're disgusting," Stella told her. "You never gain an ounce."

"I know." Ariel moved down the counter to the cashier. "It's a matter of mental control and clean living." Ignoring Stella's rude snort she paid the bill then made her way through the crowded deli toward an empty table. She and a bull of a man reached it simultaneously. Ariel simply held her tray and sent him a stunning smile. The man straightened his shoulders, sucked in his stomach and gave way.

"Thanks," Stella acknowledged and dismissed him at the same time, knowing if she didn't Ariel would invite him to join them and upset any chance of a private conversation. The woman, Stella thought, needed a keeper.

Ariel did all the things a woman alone should know better than to do. She talked to strangers, walked alone at night and answered her door without the security chain attached. It wasn't that she was daring or careless, but simply that she believed in the best of people. And somehow, in a bit more than twenty-five years of living, she'd never been disillusioned. Stella marveled at her, even while she worried about her.

"The gun was one of your best stunts all season," Stella remarked as she poked at her cottage cheese. "I thought Neal was going to scream."

"He needs to relax," Ariel said with her mouth full. "He's been on edge ever since he broke up with that dancer. How about you? Are you still seeing Cliff?"

"Yeah." Stella lifted her shoulder. "I don't know why, it's not going anywhere."

"Where do you want it to go?" Ariel countered. "If you have a goal in mind, just go for it."

With a half laugh, Stella began to eat. "Not everyone plunges through life like you, Ariel. It always amazes me that you've never been seriously involved."

"Simple." Ariel speared a fork into her salad then chewed slowly. "I've never met anyone who made my knees tremble. As soon as I do, that'll be it."

"Just like that?"

"Why not? Life isn't as complicated as most people make it." She added a dash of pepper to the lamb. "Are you in love with Cliff?"

Stell frowned—not because of the question, she was used to Ariel's directness. But because of the answer. "I don't know. Maybe."

"Then you're not," Ariel said easily. "Love's a very definite emotion. Sure you don't want any of this lamb?"

Stella didn't bother to answer the question. "If you've never been in love, how do you know?"

"I've never been to Turkey, but I'm sure it's there."

With a laugh, Stella picked up her coffee. "Damn, Ariel, you've always got an answer. Tell me about the script."

"Oh, God." Ariel put down her fork, and leaning her elbows on the table, folded her hands. "It's the best thing I've ever read. I want that part. I'm going to get that part," she added with something that was apart from confidence. It was simple fact. "I swear, I've been waiting for the character of Rae to come along. She's heartless," Ariel continued, resting her chin on her folded hands. "Complex, selfish, cold, insecure. A part like that..." She trailed off with a shake of her head. "And the story," she added on a long breath as her mind jumped from one aspect to the next. "It's nearly as cold and heartless as she is, but it gets to you."

"Booth DeWitt," Stella mused. "It's rumored that he based the character of Rae on his ex-wife."

"He didn't gloss it over either. If he's telling it

straight, she put him through hell. In any case," she
said, as she began to eat again, "it's the best piece of
work that's come my way. I'm going to read for it in a
couple of days."

"TV movie," Stella said thoughtfully. "Quality tele-
vision with DeWitt writing and Marshell producing.
You'd have our own producer at your feet if you got it.
Boy, what a boost for the ratings."

"He's already playing politics." With a small frown,
Ariel broke off a chunk of baklava. "He got me an invitation to a party tonight at Marshell's condo. DeWitt's
supposed to be there. From what I hear, he's got the last
say on casting."

"He's got a reputation for wanting to push his own
buttons," Stella agreed. "So why the frown?"

"Politics're like rain in April—you know it's got
to happen, but it's messy and annoying." Then she
shrugged the thought away as she did anything un-
avoidable. In the end, from what she knew of Booth
DeWitt, she'd earn the part on her own merit. If there
was one thing Ariel had an abundance of, it was confidence. She'd always needed it.

Unlike Amanda, the character she played on the
soap, Ariel hadn't grown up financially secure. There'd
been a great deal more love than money in her home.
She'd never regretted it, or the struggle to make ends
meet. She'd been sixteen when her mother had died and
her father had gone into a state of shock that had lasted
nearly a year. It had never occurred to her that she was
too young to take on the responsibilities of running a
home and raising two younger siblings. There'd been
no one else to do it. She'd sold powder and perfume in a
department store to pay her way through college, while

managing the family home and taking any bit part that came her way.

They'd been busy, difficult years, and perhaps that in itself had given her the surplus of energy and drive she had today. And the sense that whatever had to be done, could be done.

"Amanda."

Ariel glanced up to see a small, middle-aged woman carrying a take-out bag that smelled strongly of garlic. Because she was called by her character's name almost as often as she was by her own, she smiled and held out her hand. "Hello."

"I'm Dorra Wineberger and I wanted to tell you you're just as beautiful as you are on TV."

"Thank you, Dorra. You enjoy the show?"

"I wouldn't miss it, not one single episode." She beamed at Ariel then leaned closer. "You're wonderful, dear, and so kind and patient. I just feel someone ought to tell you that Cameron— He's not good for you. The best thing for you to do is send him packing before he gets his hands on your money. He's already pawned your diamond earrings. And this one…" Dorra folded her lips and glared at Stella. "Why you bother with this one, after all the trouble she's caused you… If it hadn't been for her, you and Griff would be married like you should be." She sent Stella an affronted glare. "I know you've got your eyes on your sister's husband, Vikki."

Stella struggled with a grin and, playing the role, tossed her head and slanted her eyes. "Men are interested in me," she drawled. "And why not?"

Dorra shook her head and turned back to Ariel. "Go back to Griff," she advised kindly. "He loves you, he always has."

Ariel returned the quick squeeze of her hand. "Thanks for caring."

Both women watched Dorra walk away before they turned back to each other. "Everyone loves Dr. Amanda," Vikki said with a grin. "She's practically sacred."

"And everyone loves to hate Vikki." With a chuckle, Ariel finished off her coffee. "You're so rotten."

"Yeah." Stella gave a contented sigh. "I know." She chewed her pineapple slowly, with a wistful look at Ariel's plate. "Anyway, it always strikes me as kind of weird when people get me confused with Vikki."

"It just means you're doing your job," Ariel corrected. "If you go into people's homes every day and don't draw emotion out of them, you better look for another line of work. Nuclear physics, log rolling. Speaking of work," she added with a glance at her watch.

"I know… Hey, are you going to eat the rest of that?"

Laughing, Ariel handed her the baklava as they rose.

It was well after nine when Ariel paid off the cab in front of P. B. Marshell's building on Madison Avenue. She wasn't concerned with being late because she wasn't aware of the time. She'd never missed a cue or a call in her life, but when it wasn't directly concerned with work, time was something to be enjoyed or ignored.

She overtipped the cabbie, stuffed her change in her bag without counting it, then walked through the light drizzle into the lobby. She decided it smelled like a funeral parlor. Too many flowers, too much polish. After giving her name at the security desk, she slipped into an elevator and pushed the penthouse button. It didn't occur to her to be nervous at the prospect of entering P. B. Marshell's domain. A party to Ariel was a party. She hoped he served champagne. She had a hankering for it.

The door was opened by a stiff-backed, stone-faced man in a dark suit who asked Ariel's name in a discreet British accent. When she smiled, he accepted her offered hand before he realized it. Ariel walked past the butler, leaving him with the impression of vitality and sex—a combination that left him disconcerted for several minutes. She lifted a glass of champagne from a tray, and spotting her agent, crossed the room to her.

Booth saw Ariel's entrance. For an instant, he was reminded of his ex-wife. The coloring, the bone structure. Then the impression was gone, and he was looking at a young woman with casually curling hair that flowed past her shoulders. It seemed misted with fine drops of rain. A stunning face, he decided. But the look of an ice goddess vanished the moment she laughed. Then there was energy and verve.

Unusual, he thought, as vaguely interested in her as he was in the drink he held. He let his eyes skim down her and decided she'd be slim under the casual pleated pants and boxy blouse. Then again, if she was, she would have exploited her figure rather than underplaying it. From what Booth knew of women, they accented whatever charms at their disposal and concealed the flaws. He'd come to accept this as a part of their innate dishonesty.

He gave Ariel one last glance as she rose on her toes to kiss the latest rage in an off-Broadway production. God, he hated these long, crowded pseudoparties.

"…If we cast the female lead."

Booth turned back to P. B. Marshell and lifted his glass. "Hmm?"

Too used to Booth's lapses of attention to be annoyed, Marshell backtracked. "We can get this into production and wrapped in time for the fall sweeps if we cast the female lead. That's virtually all that's holding us back now."

"I'm not worried about the fall sweeps," Booth returned dryly.

"The network is."

"Pat, we'll cast Rae when we find Rae."

Marshell frowned into his Scotch, then drank it. At two hundred and fifty pounds, he needed several glasses to feel any effect. "You've already turned down three top names."

"I turned down three actresses who weren't suitable," Booth corrected. He drank from his own glass as a man who knew liquor and maintained a cautious relationship with it. "I'll know Rae when I see her." His lips moved into a cool smile. "Who'd know better?"

A free, easy laugh had Marshell glancing across the room. For a moment his eyes narrowed in concentration. "Ariel Kirkwood," he told Booth, gesturing with his empty glass. "The network execs would like to push her your way."

"An actress." Booth studied Ariel again. He wouldn't have pegged her as such. Her entrance had caught his attention simply because it hadn't been an *entrance*. There was something completely unselfconscious about her that was rare in the profession. She'd been at the party long enough to have wangled an introduction to him and Marshell, yet she seemed content to stay across the room sipping champagne and flirting with an up-and-coming actor.

She stood easily, in a relaxed manner that wasn't a pose but would photograph beautifully. She made an unattractive face at the actor. The contrast of the ice-goddess looks and the freewheeling manner piqued his curiosity.

"Introduce me," Booth said simply and started across the room.

Ariel couldn't fault Marshell's taste. The condo was stylishly decorated in elegant golds and creams. The carpet was thick, the walls lacquered. She recognized the signed lithograph behind her. It was a room she knew Amanda would understand and appreciate. Ariel enjoyed visiting it. She'd never have lived there. She laughed up at Tony as he reminisced about the improvisation class they'd taken together a few years before.

"And you started using gutter language to make sure everyone was awake," she reminded him and tugged on the goatee he wore for his current part.

"It worked. What cause is it this week, Ariel?"

Her brows lifted as she sipped her champagne. "I don't have weekly causes."

"Biweekly," he corrected. "Friends of Seals, Save the Mongoose. Come on, what are you into now?"

She shook her head. "There's something that's taking up a lot of my time right now. I can't really talk about it."

Tony's grin faded. He knew that tone. "Important?"

"Vital."

"Well, Tony." Marshell clapped the young actor on the back. "Glad to see you could make it."

Though it was very subtly done, Tony came to attention. "It was nice that you were having this on a night when the theater's dark, Mr. Marshell. Do you know Ariel Kirkwood?" He laid a hand on her shoulder. "We go back a long way."

"I've heard good things about you." Marshell extended his hand.

"Thank you." Ariel left her hand in his a moment as she sorted her impressions. Successful—fond of food from the bulk of him—amiable when he chose to be. Shrewd. She liked the combination. "You make excellent films, Mr. Marshell."

"Thank you," he returned and paused, expecting her to do some campaigning. When she left it at that, he turned to Booth. "Booth DeWitt, Ariel Kirkwood and Tony Lazarus."

"I've seen your play," Booth told Tony. "You know your character very well." He shifted his gaze to Ariel. "Ms. Kirkwood."

Disconcerting eyes, she thought, so clear and direct a green in such a remote face. He gave off signals of aloofness, traces of bitterness, waves of intelligence. Obviously he didn't concern himself overmuch with trends or fashion. His hair was thick and dark and a bit long for the current style. Yet she thought it suited his face. She thought the face belonged to the nineteenth century. Lean and scholarly with a touch of ruggedness and a harshness in the mouth that kept it from being smooth.

His voice was deep and appealing, but he spoke with a clipped quality that indicated impatience. He had the eyes of an observer, she thought. And the air of a man who wouldn't tolerate interference or intimacies. She wasn't certain she'd like him, but she did know she admired his work.

"Mr. DeWitt." Her palm touched his. Strength—she'd expected that. It was in his build, long, rangy—and in his face. Distance—she'd expected that as well. "I enjoyed *The Final Bell*. It was my favorite film of last year."

He passed this off as he studied her face. She exuded sex, in her scent, in her looks—not flagrant or elusive, but light and free. "I don't believe I'm familiar with your work."

"Ariel plays Dr. Amanda Lane Jamison on *Our Lives, Our Loves*," Tony put in.

Good God, a soap opera, Booth thought. Ariel caught the faint disdain on his face. It was something else she'd expected. "Do you have a moral objection to entertainment, Mr. DeWitt?" she said easily as she sipped champagne. "Or are you just an artistic snob?" She smiled as she spoke, the quick, dashing smile that took any sting from the words.

Beside her, Tony cleared his throat. "Excuse me a minute," he said and exited stage left. Marshell mumbled something about freshening his drink.

When they were alone, Booth continued to study her face. She was laughing at him. He couldn't remember the last time anyone had had the courage, or the occasion, to do so. He wasn't certain if he was annoyed or intrigued. But at the moment he wasn't what he'd been for the past hour. Bored.

"I haven't any moral objections to soap operas, Ms. Kirkwood."

"Oh." She sipped her champagne. A sliver of sapphire on her finger winked in the light and seemed to reflect in her eyes. "A snob then. Well, everyone's entitled. Perhaps there's something else we can talk about.

How do you feel about the current administration's foreign policy?"

"Ambivalent," he murmured. "What sort of character do you play?"

"A sterling one." Her eyes continued to dance. "How do you feel about the space program?"

"I'm more concerned about the planet I'm on. How long have you been on the show?"

"Five years." She beamed a smile at someone across the room and raised her hand.

He looked at her again, carefully, and for the first time since he'd come into the party, he smiled. It did something attractive to his face, though it didn't make him quite as approachable as it indicated. "You don't want to talk about your work, do you?"

"Not particularly." Ariel returned his smile with her own open one. Something stirred faintly in him that he'd thought safely dormant. "Not with someone who considers it garbage. In a moment, you'd ask me if I'd ever considered doing any serious work, then I'd probably get nasty. My agent tells me I'm supposed to charm you."

Booth could feel the friendliness radiating from her and distrusted it. "Is that what you're doing?"

"I'm on my own time," Ariel returned. "Besides—" she finished off her champagne "—you aren't the type to be charmed."

"You're perceptive," Booth acknowledged. "Are you a good actress?"

"Yes, I am. It would hardly be worth doing something if you weren't good at it. What about sports?" She twirled her empty glass. "Do you think the Yankees stand a chance this year?"

"If they tighten up the infield." Not your usual type,

he decided. Any other actress up for a prime part in one of his scripts would've been flooding him with compliments and mentioning every job she'd ever had in front of the camera. "Ariel…" Booth plucked a fresh glass of champagne from a passing waiter and handed it to her. "The name suits you. A wise choice."

She felt a pull, a quick, definite pull, that seemed to come simply from the way he'd said her name. "I'll tell my mother you said so."

"It's not a stage name?"

"No. My mother was reading *The Tempest* when she went into labor. She was very superstitious. I could have been Prospero if I'd been a boy." With a little shudder, she sipped. "Well, Booth," she began, deciding she'd been formal long enough. "Shouldn't we just come out with the fact that we both know I'll be reading for the part of Rae in a couple of days? I intend to have it."

He nodded in acknowledgment. Though she was refreshingly direct, this was more what he'd expected. "Then I'll be frank enough to tell you that you're not the type I'm looking for."

She lifted a brow without any show of discomfort. "Oh? Why?"

"For one thing, you're too young."

She laughed—a free, breezy sound that seemed completely unaffected. He didn't trust that either. "I think my line is I can be older."

"Maybe. But Rae's a tough lady. Hard as a rock." He lifted his own drink but never took his eyes off her. "You've got too many soft points. They show in your face."

"Because this is me. And I've yet to play myself in

front of a camera." She paused a moment as the idea worked around in her head. "I don't think I'd care to."

"Is any actress ever herself?"

Her eyes came back to his. He was watching her again with that steady intenseness most would have found unnerving. Though the pull came again, Ariel accepted the look because it was part of him. "You don't care for us much as a breed, do you?"

"No." For some reason he didn't question, Booth felt compelled to test her. He lifted a strand of her hair. Soft—surprisingly soft. "You're a beautiful woman," he murmured.

Ariel tilted her head as she studied him. His eyes had lost nothing of their directness. She might have felt pleasure in the compliment if she hadn't recognized it as calculated. Instead she felt disappointment. "And?"

His brows drew together. "And?"

"That line usually leads to another. As a writer I'm sure you have several tucked away."

He let his fingers brush over her neck. She felt the strength in them, and the carelessness of the gesture. "Which one would you like?"

"I'd prefer one you meant," Ariel told him evenly. "But since I wouldn't get it, why don't we skip the whole thing? You know, your character, Phil, is narrow-minded, cool blooded and rude. I believe you portrayed yourself very well." She lifted her glass one last time and decided it was a shame that he thought so little of women, or perhaps of people in general. "Good night, Booth."

When she walked away, Booth stood looking after her for several moments before he started to laugh. At the time, it didn't occur to him that it was the first easy laugh he'd had in almost two years. It didn't even occur to him that he was laughing at himself.

No, she wasn't his Rae, he mused, but she was good. She was very, very good. He was going to remember Ariel Kirkwood.

Chapter 2

Booth stood by the wide expanse of window in Marshell's office and watched New York hustle by. From that height, he felt removed from it, and the rush and energy radiating up from the streets and sidewalks. He was satisfied to be separate. Connections equaled involvement.

None of the actresses they'd auditioned in the past two weeks came close to what he was after. He knew what he wanted for the part of Rae—who better?

When he'd first started the script it had been an impulse—therapy, he mused with a grim smile. Cheaper than a psychiatrist and a lot more satisfying. He'd never expected to do any more than finish it, purge his system and toss it in a drawer. That was before he'd realized it was the best work he'd ever done. Perhaps anger was the tenth Muse. In any case, he was first and foremost a writer. However painful it was to expose himself and his mistakes to the public, there was no tossing his finest work in a drawer. And since he was going to have it performed, he was going to have it performed well.

He'd thought it would be difficult to cast the part of Phil, the character who was essentially himself. And yet that had been surprisingly simple. The core of the story wasn't Phil, but Rae, a devastatingly accurate mirror of his ex-wife, Elizabeth Hunter. A superb actress, a gracious celebrity—a woman without a single genuine emotion.

Their marriage had started with a whirlwind and ended in disaster. Booth didn't consider himself blameless, though he placed most of the blame on his own gullibility. He'd believed in her image, fallen hard for the perfection of face and body. He could have forgiven the faults, the flaws soon discovered. But he could never, would never, forgive being used. And yet, Booth was still far from sure whether he blamed Liz for using him, or himself for allowing it to happen.

Either way, the tempestuous five-year marriage had given him grist for a clean, hard story that was going to be an elaborate television movie. And more, it had given him a firm distrust of women, particularly actresses. Two years before, when the break had finally come, he'd promised himself that he'd never become involved with another woman who could play roles that well. Honesty, if it truly existed, was what he'd look for when he was ready.

His thoughts came back to Ariel. Perhaps she was centered in his mind because of her surface resemblance to Liz, but he wasn't certain. There was no similarity in mannerisms, voice cadence or style of dress. And the biggest contrast seemed to be in personality. She hadn't put herself out to charm him or to hold his attention. And she'd done both. Perhaps she'd simply used a different angle on an old game.

While he hadn't trusted it, he'd enjoyed her lack of artifice. The breezy laugh, the unaffected gestures, the candid looks. It had been a long time since a woman had lingered in his mind. A pity, Booth mused, that she was unsuitable for the part. He could have used the distraction. Instinct told him that Ariel Kirkwood would be nothing if she wasn't a distraction.

"I'm still leaning toward this Julie Newman." Chuck Tyler, the director, tossed an eight-by-ten glossy on Marshell's desk. "A lot of camera presence and her first reading was very good."

With the photo in one hand, Marshell tipped back in his deep leather chair. The sun at his back streamed over both the glossy and the gold he wore on either hand. "An impressive list of credits, too."

"No." Booth didn't bother to turn around, but stood watching the traffic stream. For some odd reason he visualized himself on his boat in Long Island Sound, sailing out to sea. "She lacks the elegance. Too much vulnerability."

"She can act, Booth," Marshell said with a now familiar show of impatience.

"She's not the one."

Marshell automatically reached in his pocket for the cigars he'd given up a month before. He swore lightly under his breath. "And we're running out of time and options."

Booth gave an unconcerned shrug. Yes, he'd like to be sailing, stripped to the waist with the sun on his back and the water so blue it hurt the eyes. He'd like to be alone.

When the buzzer on his desk rang, Marshell heaved a sigh and leaned forward to answer. "Ms. Kirkwood's here for her reading, Mr. Marshell."

With a grunt, Marshell flipped open the portfolio Ariel's agent had sent him, then passed it to Chuck. "Send her in."

"Kirkwood," Chuck mused, frowning over Ariel's publicity shot. "Kirkwood... Oh, yeah, I saw her last summer in an off-Broadway production of *Streetcar*."

Vaguely interested, Booth looked over his shoulder. "Stella?"

"Blanche," Chuck corrected, skimming over her list of credits.

"Blanche DuBois?" Booth gave a short laugh as he turned completely around. "She's fifteen to twenty years too young for that part."

Chuck merely lifted his eyes. "She was good," he said simply. "Very good. And from what I'm told, she's very good on the soap. I don't have to tell you how many of our top stars started that way."

"No, you don't." Booth sat negligently on the arm of a chair. "But if she's stuck with the same part for five years, she's either not good enough for a major film or major theater, or she's completely without ambition. Because she's an actress, I'd have to go with the former."

"Keep sharpening your cynicism," Marshell said dryly. "It's good for you."

Booth's grin flashed—that rare one that came and went so quickly it left the onlooker dazzled and unsure why. Ariel caught a glimpse of it as she entered the room. It went a long way toward convincing her to change her initial opinion of him. It passed through her mind, almost as quickly as Booth's grin, that perhaps he had some redeeming personal qualities after all. She was always ready to believe it.

"Ms. Kirkwood." Marshell heaved his bulk from the chair and extended his hand.

"Mr. Marshell, nice to see you again." She took a brief scan of the room, her gaze lingering only fleetingly on Booth as he remained seated on the arm of the chair. "Your office is just as impressive as your home."

Booth waited while she was introduced to Chuck. She'd dressed very simply, he noticed. Deceptively so if you considered the bold scarves she'd twisted at the waist of the demure blue dress. Violets and emeralds and wild pinks. A daring combination, and stunningly effective. Her hair was loose again, giving her an air of youth and freedom he would never equate with the character she wanted to portray. Absently, he took out a cigarette and lit it.

"Booth." Ariel gave him an easy smile before her gaze flicked over the cigarette. "They'll kill you."

He took a drag and let out a lazy stream of smoke. "Eventually." She wore the same carelessly sexy scent he'd noticed the night of the party. Booth wondered why it was that it suited her while contrasting at the same time. She fascinated. It seemed to be something she did effortlessly. "I'm going to cue you," he continued and reached for a copy of the script. "We'll use the confrontation scene in the third act. You're familiar with it?"

All business, Ariel noted curiously. Does he ever relax? Does he ever choose to? Though she was rarely tense herself, she recognized tension in him and wondered why he was nervous. What nerves she felt herself were confined to a tiny roiling knot in the center of her stomach. She always acknowledged it and knew, if anything, it would help to push her through the reading.

"I'm familiar with it," she told him, accepting another copy of the script.

Booth took a last drag on his cigarette then put it out. "Do you want a lead-in?"

"No." Now her palms were damp. Good. Ariel knew better than to want to be relaxed when twinges of emotions would sharpen her skills. Taking deep, quiet breaths she flipped through the bound script until she found the right scene. It wasn't a simple one. It stabbed at the core of the character—selfish ambition and icy sex. She took a minute.

Booth watched her. She looked more like the guileless ingenue than the calculating leading lady, he mused and was almost sorry there wasn't a part for her in the film. Then she looked up and pinned him with a cold, bloodless smile that completely stunned him.

"You always were a fool, Phil, but a successful one and so rarely boring, it's hardly worth mentioning."

The tone, the mannerisms, even the expression was so accurate, he couldn't respond. For a moment, he completely lost Ariel in the character and the woman he'd fashioned her after. He felt a twist in his stomach, not of attraction or even admiration, but of anger—totally unexpected and vilely real. Booth didn't have to look at the script to remember the line.

"You're so transparent, Rae. It amazes me that you could deceive anyone into believing in you."

Ariel laughed, rather beautifully, so that all three men felt a chill race up their spine. "I make my living at deception. Everyone wants illusions, so did you. And that's what you got."

With a long, lazy stretch, she ran a hand through her hair, then let it fall, pale gold in the late-morning sunlight. It was one of Liz Hunter's patented gestures. "I acted my way out of that miserable backwater town in Missouri where I had the misfortune to be born, and I've acted my way right up to the top. You were a great help." She walked over to him with the small, cool smile still on her lips, in her eyes. With an eloquent gesture, she brushed her hand down his cheek. "And you were compensated. Very, very well."

Phil grabbed her wrist and tossed it aside. Ariel merely lifted a brow at the violence of the movement. "Sooner or later you're going to slip," he threatened.

She tilted her head and spoke very softly. "Darling, I never slip."

Slowly, Booth rose. The expression on his face might have had any woman trembling, would have had any woman making some defensive move. Ariel merely looked up at him with the same coldly amused expression. It was he who had to force himself to calm.

"Very good, Ariel Kirkwood." Booth tossed the script aside.

She grinned, because every instinct told her she'd won. With the long expelled breath, she could almost feel Rae drain out of her. "Thanks. It's a tremendous part," she added as her stomach unknotted. "Really a tremendous part."

"You've done your research," Marshell murmured from behind his desk. Because he knew Elizabeth Hunter, Ariel's five-minute read had left him uncomfortable and impressed. And he knew Booth. There was little doubt in his mind as to what Rae's creator was feeling. "You'll be available for a callback?"

"Of course."

"I saw your Blanche DuBois, Ms. Kirkwood," Chuck put in. "I was very impressed then, and now."

She flashed him an unaffected smile though she was aware Booth was still staring at her. If he was moved, she thought, then the reading had gone better than she could have hoped. "It was my biggest challenge, up until now." She wanted to get out, walk, breathe the air, savor the almost-victory while she could. "Well, thank you." She pushed her hair from shoulder as she scanned the three men again. "I'll look forward to hearing from you."

Ariel walked toward the elevator too frightened to believe she was right, too terrified to believe she was wrong. Up until that moment, she hadn't let herself dwell on just how much she wanted the part, and just what it could mean in her life.

She wasn't without ambition, but she had chosen acting and had continued with it for the love of it. And the challenge. Playing the part of Rae would hand her all three needs on a silver platter. As she stepped into the elevator, her palms were dry and her heart was pounding. She didn't hear Booth approach.

"I'd like to talk to you." He stepped in with her and punched the button for the lobby.

"Okay." A long sigh escaped as she leaned back against the side of the car. "God, I'm glad that's over. I'm starving. Nothing makes me hungrier than a reading."

He tried to relate the woman who was smiling at him with eyes warm and alive with the woman who had just exchanged lines with him. He couldn't. She was a better actress than he'd given her credit for, and therefore, more dangerous. "It was an excellent reading."

She eyed him curiously. "Why do I feel I've just been insulted?"

After the doors slid open Booth stood for a moment, then nodded. "I think I said before that you were perceptive."

Her slim heels clicked over the tile as she crossed the lobby with him. Booth noticed a few heads turn, both male and female, to look after her. She was either unaware or unconcerned. "Why are you on daytime TV?"

Ariel slanted him a look before she began to walk north. "Because it's a good part on a well-written, entertaining show. That's number one. Number two is that it's steady work. When actors are between jobs, they wait tables, wash cars, sell toasters and generally get depressed. While I might not mind the first three too much, I hate the fourth. Have you ever seen the show?"

"No."

"Then you shouldn't turn your nose up." She stopped by a sidewalk vendor and drew in the scent of hot pretzels. "Want one?"

"No," Booth said again and tucked his hands in his pockets. Sexuality, sensuality—both seemed to pour out of her as she stood next to a portable pretzel stand on a crowded sidewalk. He continued to watch her as she took the first generous bite.

"I could live off them," she told him with her mouth full and her eyes laughing. "Good nutrition's so admirable and so hard to live with. I like to ignore it for long stretches of time. Let's walk," she suggested. "I have to when I'm keyed up. What do you do?"

"When?"

"When you're keyed up," Ariel explained.

"Write." He matched her casually swinging pace while the bulk of pedestrian traffic bustled by them.

"And when you're not keyed up you write," Ariel added as she took another bite of her pretzel. "Have you always been so serious?"

"It's steady work," he countered and she laughed.

"Very quick. I didn't think I'd like you, but you've got a nice sense of cautious humor." Ariel stopped at another vendor and bought a bunch of spring violets. She closed her eyes and breathed deep. "Wonderful," she murmured. "I always think spring's the best until summer. Then I'm in love with the heat until fall. Then fall's the best until winter." Laughing, she looked over the blooms into his eyes. "And I also tend to ramble when I'm keyed up."

When she lowered the flowers, Booth took her wrist, not with the same violence as he had during the reading, but with the same intensity. "Who are you?" he demanded. "Who the hell are you?"

Her smile faded but she didn't draw away. "Ariel Kirkwood. I can be a lot of other people when there's a stage or a camera, but when it's over, that's who I am. That's all I am. Are you looking for complications?"

"I don't have to look for them—they're always there."

"Strange, I rarely run into any." She studied him, all frank eyes and creamy beauty. Booth didn't care for the stir it brought him. "Come with me," she invited, then took his hand before he'd thought to object.

"Where?"

She threw back her head and pointed up the magnificently sheer surface of the Empire State Building.

"To the top." Laughing, she pulled him inside. "All the way to the top."

Booth looked around impatiently as she bought tickets for the observation deck. "Why?"

"Does there always have to be a reason?" She slipped the violets into the twisted scarves at her waist, then tucked her arm through his. "I love things like this. Ellis Island, the Staten Island ferry, Central Park. What's the use of living in New York if you don't enjoy it? When's the last time you did this?" Her shoulder rested against his upper arm as they crowded into an elevator.

"I think I was ten." Even with the press of bodies and mingling scents he could smell her, wild and sweet.

"Oh." Ariel laughed up at him. "You grew up. Too bad."

Booth said nothing for a moment as he studied her. She seemed to always be laughing—at him or at some private joke she was content to keep to herself. Was she really that easy with herself and her life? Was anyone? Then he asked, "Don't we all?"

"Of course not. We all get older, but the rest is a personal choice." They herded off one elevator and onto another that would take them to the top.

This was a man she could enjoy, Ariel mused as she stood beside Booth. She could enjoy that serious, high-minded streak and the dry, almost reluctant humor. Still, there was the part in the film to think of. Ariel would have to be very careful to keep her feelings for one separate from her feelings for the other. But then, she'd never been a person who'd had any trouble separating the woman and the actress.

For now, the reading was over and the afternoon was free. Her mood was light, and there was a man with her who'd be fascinating to explore. The day could hardly offer anything more.

The souvenir stands were crowded with people—different countries, different voices. Ariel decided she'd buy something foolish on her way out. She caught Booth looking around him with his eyes slightly narrowed. An observer, she thought with a slight nod of approval. She was one herself, though perhaps on a different level. He'd dissect, analyze and file. She just enjoyed the show.

"Come on outside," she invited and took his hand in a characteristic gesture. "It's wonderful." Pushing open the heavy door, Ariel welcomed the first slap of wind with a laugh. With her hand still firmly gripping Booth's, she hurried to the wall to take in New York.

She never saw it as a toy board as many did from that height, but as something real enough to touch and smell from any distance. It never failed to excite and fascinate her. Ariel rarely asked more of anything or anyone. When she was here, she always believed she could accomplish whatever she needed to.

"I love heights." She leaned out as far as she could and felt the frantic current of air swirl around her. "Staggering heights. And wind. If I could, I'd come here every day. I'd never get tired of it."

Though it was normally an intimacy he would have shunned, Booth allowed his hand to stay in hers. Her skin was smooth and elegant; her face was flushed in the brisk air while her hair blew wildly. The eyes, he thought, the eyes were too alive, too full of everything. A woman like this would demand spectacular emotions from everyone she touched. The stir he felt wasn't as easily suppressed this time. Deliberately, he looked away from her and down.

"Why not the World Trade Center?" he asked and let his gaze skim over the island he lived on.

Ariel shook her head. "It doesn't have the same feeling as this, nothing does. Just like there's only one Eiffel Tower, one Grand Canyon and one Olivier." She didn't bother to brush her hair back from her face as she tilted toward him. "They're all spectacular and unique. What do you like, Booth?"

A family walked by laughing, the mother holding her skirt, the father carrying a toddler. He watched them pause nearby and look over the wall. "In what way?"

"In any way," Ariel told him. "If you could've spent today doing anything you wanted, what would you have done?"

"Gone sailing," he said, remembering that moment in Marshell's office. "I'd've been sailing on the sound."

Interest flickered in her eyes as it seemed every emotion or thought she had did. "You have a boat?"

"Yes. I don't have much time for it."

Don't take much time for it, she corrected silently. "A solitary pursuit. That's admirable." She turned, leaning back against the wall so that she could watch the people circle the deck. The wind plastered her dress against her, revealing the slenderness, the elegance of the woman. "I don't often like to be solitary," she murmured. "I need people, the contacts, the contrasts. I don't have to know them. I just like knowing they're there."

"Is that why you act?" They were face-to-face now, their bodies casually close—as if they were friends. It struck Booth as odd, but he had no desire to back away. "So you can have an audience?"

Her expression become thoughtful, but when she smiled, it was easy. "You're a very cynical man."

"That's the second time today that's been mentioned."

"It's all right. It probably comes in handy with your writing. Yes, I act for an audience," she continued. "I won't deny my own ego, but I think I act for myself first." She lifted her face so that the air could race over it. "It's a marvelous profession. How else can you be so many people? A princess, a tramp, a victim, a loser. You write to be read, but don't you first write to express yourself?"

"Yes." He felt something odd, almost unfamiliar—a loosening of muscles, an easing of thought. It took him a moment to realize he was relaxing, and only a moment longer to draw back. When you relaxed, you got burned. That much he was certain of. "But then writers have egos that nearly rival actors'."

Ariel made a sound that was somewhere between a sigh and an expulsion of air. "She really put you through the mill, didn't she?"

His eyes frosted, his voice chilled. "That's none of your business."

"You're wrong." Though she felt a twinge of regret when she sensed his withdrawal, Ariel went on. "If I'm going to play Rae, it's very much my business. Booth..." She laid a hand on his arm, wishing she understood him well enough to get past the wall of reserve, the waves of bitterness. "If you'd wanted to keep this part of your life private, you wouldn't have written it out."

"It's a story," he said flatly. "I don't put myself on display."

"In most cases, no," she agreed. "I've always felt a

certain sense of distance in your work, though it's always excellent. And for someone so successful, you kept a fairly low profile, even when you were married to Liz Hunter. But you've let something out in this script. It's too late to pull it back now."

"I've written a story about two people who are totally unsuited to each other, who used each other. The man is a bit of an idealist, and just gullible enough to fall for an exquisite face. Before the story ends, he learns that appearances mean little and that trust and loyalty are illusions. The woman is cold, ambitious and gifted, but she'll never be satisfied with her own talents. She's a vampire in the pure sense of the word, and she sucks him dry. There may be similarities between the story and actuality, but my life is still my life."

"No trespassing." Ariel turned to look back down into the city, the world she understood. "All right, the signs are posted." She listened to the sound of the wind, the sound of voices. Someone reeked of a drugstore cologne. An empty bag of potato chips skimmed and rustled along the concrete. "I'm not a very good businesswoman. I won't apologize for my lifestyle or my personality, but I will do my best to keep our conversations very professional."

She took a deep breath and turned back to him. Some of the warmth had left her eyes, and he felt a momentary regret. "I'm a good actress, an excellent craftsman. I've known since the first moment I picked up the script that I could play Rae. And I'm astute enough to know how well my reading went."

"No, you're not a fool." Even with the regret, Booth felt more comfortable on this level. He understood her now—an actress in search of that prime part. "I wouldn't have said you were what I was looking for—until this afternoon. No one's come even close to the core of that character before you."

She felt the tickling dryness down in her throat, the sudden lurch of her heart rate. "And?" she managed.

"And I want you to come back and read with Jack Rohrer. He's cast as Phil. If the chemistry's there, you've got the part."

Ariel took a deep breath. She leaned against the sturdy observation glass and tried to take it calmly. She'd told him she'd be professional. No good, she realized as the pleasure bubbled up inside her. It simply wasn't any use. With a shout of laughter, she threw her arms around his neck and clung. The touching was vital, the sharing essential.

Ariel Kirkwood—the skinny dreamer from West 185th Street—was going to star in a DeWitt script, a P. B. Marshell production opposite Jack Rohrer. Would life never stop amazing her? As she clung to Booth, Ariel dearly hoped it wouldn't.

His hands had come to her waist in reflex, but he left them there as her laughter warmed his ear. He found it odd that he was sharply reminded of two things—his young niece's boundless pleasure when he'd given her an elaborate dollhouse one Christmas, and the first time, as a man, he'd ever held a woman. The softness was there—that unique strength and give only a woman's body has. The childlike pleasure was there—with the innocence only the young possess.

He could have held her. It moved him to do so, just to hold something soft and sweet and without shadows. She fit so well against him. The curve of cheek against his, the alignment of bodies. She fit too well, so that he stood perfectly still and drew her no closer.

Something drifted through her pleasure and excitement. He smelt of soap—solid—as his body felt. There was nothing casual about him, nothing easy. He was all intensity and intellect. The strength drew her; his reserve drew her. He was a man who would be there to pick you up, however reluctantly, if you stumbled. Who would demand that you keep pace with him, and who would expect you to give him exactly the amount of room he wanted it when he wanted it. He was a man whom a woman who ran on her emotions and her senses would do well to avoid. She wished almost painfully that his arms would come around her, even while she knew they wouldn't.

Ariel drew away but kept their faces close so that she might have a hint of what it would be like to have that serious, unsmiling mouth lowered to hers. She was breathless, and her eyes made no secret of her attraction or her surprise in feeling it.

"I'm sorry," she said quietly. "Physical displays come naturally to me. I have a feeling you don't care for them."

Had there ever been a woman he'd wanted to kiss more than this one? Almost, almost, he could taste the mouth inches from his own. Nearly, very nearly, he could feel its texture against his own. When he spoke, his voice was indifferent, his eyes remote. "There's a time and a place."

Ariel let out a long breath and decided she'd set herself up for a backhanded slap. "You're a tough man, Booth DeWitt," she murmured.

"I'm a realist, Ariel." He took out a cigarette, cupping his lighter against the wind with hands that amazed him because they weren't steady.

"What a hard thing to be." Consciously, she relaxed—shoulder muscles, stomach muscles, hands. A moment's awareness didn't equal trouble. She'd felt it before; it was a blessing and a curse in a woman like herself. Ariel didn't understand indifference to people or to things. Everything you saw, touched, heard, triggered some emotion. "But then, you're stuck with it." More at ease, she smiled at him. "I'm going to enjoy working with you, Booth, though I know it's not going to be a picnic. I'm going to give your script my very best shot, and we'll both benefit."

He nodded as the smoke whipped up and away. "I don't accept anything less than the best."

"Fine, you won't be disappointed." It was in her nature to reach out and touch, to add something personal. But one slap was enough for one day.

"Good."

With a laugh, she shook her head. "You're attractive, Booth. I haven't the least idea why because I don't think you're a very nice person."

He blew out another stream of smoke and watched her lazily. "I'm not," he agreed.

"In any case, we'll give each other what's needed professionally."

Then because she rarely resisted impulses of any kind, she kissed his cheek before thrusting the violets at him and walking away. Booth stood in the wind on top of New York with a handful of spring flowers and stared after her.

Chapter 3

Booth had been on and around sets most of his professional life. There were eighteenth-century drawing rooms, twentieth-century bedrooms, bars and restaurants and department stores. Spaceships and log cabins. With props and backdrops and ingenuity, anything could be created.

When you came to the bottom line, one set was the same as another—technicians, lights, cameras, booms, miles of cable. It was an industry of illusion and image. What looked glamorous outside the business was ultimately only a job, and often a tedious and exacting one. Long hours, lengthy delays, lights that made a studio into a furnace, bitter coffee.

From the outset of his career, he'd never been content to be isolated with his typewriter and ideas. He'd insisted from his very first screenplay on being involved with the production end. He understood the practicality and the creativity of the right camera angle, the proper lighting. It appealed to the realistic part of him. Still, he had the ability to see the set and the people while blocking out the crowding equipment. To watch as an outsider, to see as a viewer. This appealed to the dreamer he'd always kept under strict control.

Booth wasn't sure what had motivated him to visit the set of *Our Lives, Our Loves.* He knew that the script he was currently working on had hit a snag, and that he wanted to see Ariel again. Perhaps it was the scent of violets that continued to drift to him as he tried to work. Twice he'd started to throw them away…but he hadn't. Part of him, deep, long repressed, needed such things, however much he disliked acknowledging it.

So he had come to see Ariel, telling himself he simply wanted to watch her work before he committed himself to choosing her for the part of Rae. It was logical, practical. It was something he'd tried very hard to resist.

Ariel sat at the kitchen table with her bare feet propped in a chair while Jack Shapiro, who played Griff Martin, Amanda's college sweetheart, mulled over a hand of solitaire. On another part of the soundstage, her television parents were discussing their offspring. After they'd finished, she and Jack would tape their scene.

"Black six on the red seven," she mumbled, earning herself a glare from Jack.

"Solitaire," he reminded her. "As in alone."

"It's an antisocial game."

"You think headphones are antisocial."

"They are." Smiling sweetly, she moved the six herself.

"Why don't you go call the Committee for the Salvation of Three-legged Land Mammals? They probably want you at their next luncheon."

The timing wasn't quite right, she decided, to ask him to contribute to the Homes for Kittens fund she was currently involved with. "Don't get snotty," she said mildly. "You're supposed to adore me."

"Should've had my head examined after you threw me over for Cameron."

"It's your own fault for not explaining what you were doing alone in that hotel room with Vikki."

Jack sniffed and turned over another card. "You should've trusted me. A man has his pride."

"Now I'm stuck in a disastrous marriage *and* I might be pregnant."

Glancing up, he grinned. "Great for the ratings. Did you see them posted this week? We're up a whole point."

She leaned her elbows on the table. "Wait until things start heating up between Amanda and Griff again." She put a black ten on the jack of diamonds. "Sizzle, spark, smolder."

He smacked her hand. "You're a great smolderer." Unable to resist, he leered. "I haven't kissed you in six months."

"Then when you get your chance, big guy, make it good. Amanda's no pushover." Rising, she strolled away for a last-minute check with makeup.

The hospital set had already been prepared for the brief but intense meeting between the former lovers, Amanda and Griff. Some subtle dark smudges were added under her eyes to give the appearance of a sleepless night. The rest of her makeup gave her a slight pallor.

By the time the cameras rolled, Amanda was in her

office, going through her patient files. She seemed very calm, very much in control. Her expression was totally serene. Abruptly, she slammed the drawer back in the cabinet and whirled around to pace. When the tape was edited, it would flash back to her discovery of her husband and sister. Amanda grabbed a china cup from her desk and hurled it against the wall. With the back of her hand to her mouth, she stared at the broken pieces. The knock at her office door had her balling her fists and making a visible struggle for control. Deliberately, she walked around her desk and sat down.

"Come in."

The camera focused on Jack as Dr. Griff Martin, rough-and-ready looks, rough-and-ready temper— Amanda's first and only lover before her marriage. Ariel knew what the director would edit in a reaction shot later, but now, with the tape running on Jack's entrance, she screwed up her face and stuck out her tongue. Jack gave her one of his character's patented lengthy looks designed to make the female heart flutter.

"Amanda, have you got a minute?"

When the lens was focused on her again, her face was properly composed with just a hint of strain beneath the serenity. "Of course, Griff." For a subtle sign of nerves, she gripped her hands together on the desktop.

"I've got a case of wife beating," he began in the clipped, almost surly tone of his character. Both Amanda and several million female viewers had found his diamond-in-the-rough style irresistible. "I need your help."

They went through the scene, laying the ground-work for a story line that would throw them together again and again over the next few weeks, building the sexual tension. When the camera was briefly at Jack's back he crossed his eyes at Ariel and bared his teeth. As she went back to her patient file, she made certain she walked over his foot. Neither of them lost the rhythm of the scene.

"You look tired." As Griff, Jack started to touch her shoulder, then stopped himself. Frustration radiated from his eyes. "Is everything all right?"

Amanda turned and gave him a soulful eye-locking look. Her mouth trembled open, then closed again. Slowly, she turned back to the file and shut the drawer quietly. "Everything's fine. I have a heavy workload right now. And I have a patient due in a few minutes."

"I'll get out of here then." He started for the door and paused. With his hand on the knob, he stared at her. "Mandy…"

Amanda kept her back to him. The camera came in close as she shut her eyes and fought for control. "I'll see your patient tomorrow, Griff." There was the faintest of tremors in her voice.

He waited five humming seconds. "Yeah, fine."

When she heard the door close, Amanda pressed her hands to her face.

"Cut."

"I'm going to get you for that," Jack said as he pushed the prop door open again. "I think you broke one of my toes."

Ariel fluttered her lashes at him. "You're such a baby."

"All right, children," the director said mildly. "Let's get the reaction shots."

Agreeably, Ariel moved behind Amanda's desk again. It was then she saw Booth. Surprise and pleasure showed on her face, though his expression wasn't welcoming. He was frowning at her, his arms crossed over a casual black sweater. He didn't return her smile, nor did she expect him to. Booth DeWitt wasn't a man who smiled often or easily. It only made her more determined to nudge him into it.

She'd thought about him—surprisingly often. At the moment, she had enough on her mind, both personally and professionally, yet she'd found herself wondering about Booth DeWitt and what went on inside that aloof exterior. She'd seen flashes of something warm, something approachable. For Ariel, it was enough to make her dig for more.

And there'd been that pull—the pull she remembered with perfect clarity. She wanted to feel it again, to enjoy it, to understand it.

She finished the taping and had an hour before she and Stella would play out their confrontation scene on the Lane living-room set. "Jerry, I found a kitten for your daughter," she told one of the technicians as she rose. "It's a little calico, I can bring it in on Friday."

"Been to the pound again," Jack said with a sigh. Ignoring him, Ariel stepped over some cable and walked to Booth.

"Hi, want some coffee?"

"All right."

"I keep a Mr. Coffee in my dressing room. The stuff at the commissary's poison." She led the way, not bothering to ask why he was there. Her door was open, as she usually left it. Walking in, she went directly to the coffeemaker. "You have to make do with powdered milk."

"Black's fine."

Her dressing room was chaos. Clothes, magazines, pamphlets were tossed over all available space. Her dressing table was littered with jars and bottles and framed photographs of the cast. It smelled of fresh flowers, makeup and dust.

On the wall was a calendar that read February though it was midway through April. An electric clock was unplugged and stuck on 7:05. Booth counted three and one-half pairs of shoes on the floor.

In the midst of it, Ariel stood in a raw-silk suit the color of apricots with her hair pale and glowing in a sophisticated knot. She smelled like a woman should at sunset—soft, with a hint of anticipation. As the coffee began to drip, she turned back to him.

"I'm glad to see you again."

The simplicity of the statement made Booth almost believe it. Cautiously, he kept half the room between them as he watched her. "The taping was interesting. You're very good, Ariel. You milked that five-minute scene for everything there was."

Again she had the impression more of criticism than flattery. "It's important in a soap. You're working in little capsules. Some people only tune in a couple times a week. Then there are those who turn it on as a whim. You hope to grab them."

"Your character." He eyed the suit, approving the subdued style. "I'd say she's a very controlled professional woman who's currently going through some personal crisis. There were a lot of sexual sparks bouncing around between her and the young doctor."

"Very good." With a smile, Ariel picked up two cups, mismatched. "That's neatly tied up. Want some M&M's? I keep a stash in my drawer."

"No. Do you always play around on set when you're not on camera?"

She stirred powdered milk into her coffee, added a generous spoon of sugar, then handed Booth his. "Jack and I have a running contest on who can make who blow their lines. Actually, it makes us sharper and lowers the tension level." Carelessly, she took magazines from a chair and left them stacked on the floor. "Sit down."

"How many pages of dialogue do you have to learn a week?"

"Varies," she said and sipped. "We run about eighty-five pages of script a day now that we've gone to an hour. Some days I might have twenty or thirty where my character's involved. But for the most part, I tape about three days a week—we don't do a lot of takes." Opening the drawer on her dressing table, she took a handful of candies and began to eat them one at a time. "I'm told it's the closest thing to live TV you can get."

Watching her, he drank. "You really enjoy it."

"Yes, I've been very comfortable with Amanda. Which is why I want to do other things as well. Ruts are monotonous places, but so easy to stay in."

He glanced around the room. "I can't imagine you in one."

Ariel laughed and sat on the edge of her dressing table. "A great compliment. You're frugal with them." Something in his aloof, cool expression made her smile. "Would you like to have dinner?" she asked on impulse.

For an instant surprise flickered over his face—the first time she'd seen it. "It's a bit early for dinner," he said mildly.

"I like the way you do that," she said with a nod.

"Conversations with you are never boring. If you're free tonight, I could pick you up at seven."

She was asking him for a date, he thought, very simply, very smoothly, in a manner more friendly than flirtatious. As he had often since the first time he'd met her, Booth wondered what made her tick. "All right, seven." Reaching in his pocket, he pulled out a note pad and scrawled on it. "Here's the address."

Taking it, Ariel scanned the words with a small sound of approval. "Mmm, you've got a great view of the park." She looked up and grinned in the way that always made him think she'd just enjoyed a little private joke. "I'm a sucker for views."

"I've gathered that already."

Booth walked over to set down his mug and stood close enough so that his legs brushed hers. She didn't back away but watched him with clear, curious eyes. There was something deadly in that face, she thought. Something any woman would recognize and a wary one would retreat from. Fascinated, she counted the beat of her own rapid pulse.

"I'll let you get back to work."

With the slightest move on his part, the contact was broken. Ariel stayed exactly where she was. "I'm glad you stopped by," she said, though she was no longer sure it was precisely the truth.

With a nod, he was gone. Ariel sat on the edge of her cluttered dressing table and wondered if for the first time in her life she'd bitten off more than she could chew.

Because the sun was setting and it was a huge red ball, Ariel paid off the cab two blocks from Booth's apartment building. She wanted some time to think about a phone call she'd received about Scott, her brother's child.

Poor little guy, she thought. So vulnerable, so grown-up. She wondered how much longer it would be before the courts decided his fate. Because she wanted him with her so badly, Ariel refused to believe anything else would happen. Her brother's son, so suddenly orphaned, so miserably unhappy with his maternal grandparents.

They didn't want him, she reflected. Not really. There was such a world of difference between love and duty. Once everything was arranged, she'd be able to give him the kind of easy, unfettered childhood she'd had—with the financial advantages she hadn't known.

She wouldn't think of the complications now. To think of them would make her start doubting the outcome, and she couldn't bear it. She and her lawyers were taking all the possible steps.

Because she wanted no publicity to touch her nephew, Ariel had kept the entire matter to herself—something she rarely did. Perhaps because she had no one to speak to about it, she worried. Every day she told herself Scott would be with her permanently before the end of summer. As long as she kept telling herself, she was able to believe it. Now it was evening, and there was no more she could do.

It was only a little past seven o'clock when she pushed the button of the elevator for Booth's floor in the sleek building on Park Avenue. She'd already set aside that one flash of nerves she felt about him and had decided to enjoy the evening. The idea that he'd been able to make her nervous at all was intriguing enough.

She liked men, the basic personality differences between them and women. Of her closest friends, many were men, in and out of the business. The key word remained *friends*—she was very cautious about lovers. She ran on emotion, and knowing it, had always been careful of physical relationships.

She was a romantic, unashamedly. Ariel had never doubted that there was one great love waiting for everyone. She had no intention of settling for less—with hearts and flowers and skyrockets included. When she found the right man, she'd know. Whether it was tomorrow or twenty years from tomorrow didn't matter, as long as she found him. In the meantime, she filled her life with work, her friends and her causes. Ariel Kirkwood simply didn't believe in boredom.

She approved of the quiet, carpeted hallway as she strolled down to Booth's apartment. It was wainscoted and elegant. But as she lifted her hand to press the button on his door, she felt that odd flutter of nerves again.

Inside, Booth was standing by the high wide window that looked out over Central Park. He was thinking of her, had been thinking of her for most of the day. And he didn't care for it.

Twice, he'd nearly called to cancel the dinner, telling himself he had work to do. Telling himself he didn't have the time or the inclination to spend an evening with an actress he hardly knew. But he hadn't canceled because he could still see the way her eyes warmed, the way her whole face moved when she smiled.

A professional trick. Liz had had a bagful of them, and unless his perception was very, very wrong, this woman was as skilled an actress as Liz Hunter. That's what he told himself, and yet… And yet he hadn't canceled.

When the buzzer rang, Booth looked over his shoulder at the closed door. It was simply an evening, he decided. A few hours out of the day in which he could study the woman being considered for a major part in an important film. He had little doubt that she would make a pitch for the part before the night was over. With a shrug, Booth walked to the door. That was the business, and she was entitled.

Then, when he opened the door, she smiled at him. He realized he wanted her with an intensity he hadn't felt in years. "Hi. You look nice," she said.

The struggle with desire only made him more remote, made his voice more scrupulously polite. "Come in."

Ariel walked through the door then studied the room with open curiosity. Neat. Her first impression was one of meticulous order. Style. Who could fault a gleaming mix of Chippendale and Hepplewhite? The colors were muted, easy on the eyes. The furniture was arranged in such a way as to give a sense of balance. She could smell neither dust nor polish. It was as though the room was perpetually clean and rarely lived in. Somehow, she didn't think it really suited that harsh, nineteenth-century face. No, there was too much formality here for a man who looked like Booth, for a man who moved like him.

Though she felt no sense of welcome, she could appreciate the rather stationary beauty and respect the organized taste.

"A very fastidious man," she murmured, then walked over to study his view of the city.

She wore a dress with yards of skirt and whirls of color. Booth wondered if that was why he suddenly felt life jump into the room. He preferred the quiet, the settled, even the isolated. Yet somehow, for the first time, he felt the appeal of having warmth in his home.

"I was right about this," Ariel said and put her hands into the deep pockets of her skirt. "It's lovely. Where do you work?"

"I have an office set up in another room."

"I'd probably have put my desk right here." Laughing, she turned to him so that the mix of colors in her dress seemed to vibrate. "Then again, I wouldn't get much work done." His eyes were very dark and very steady, his face so expressionless he might have been thinking of anything or nothing. "Do you stare at everyone that way?"

"I suppose I do. Would you like a drink?"

"Yes, some dry vermouth if you have it." She wandered over to a cherrywood breakfront and studied his collection of Waterford. No one chose something so lovely, or so capable of catching light and fire if they lacked warmth. Where was his, she wondered. Buried so deep that he'd forgotten it, or simply dormant from lack of use?

Booth paused beside her and offered a glass. "You like crystal?"

"I like beautiful things."

What woman didn't? he thought brittlely. A Russian lynx, a pear-shaped diamond. Yes, women liked beautiful things, particularly when someone else was providing them. He'd already done more than his share of that.

"I watched your show today," Booth began, deciding to give her the opening for her pitch and see what she did with it. "You come across very well as the competent psychiatrist."

"I like Amanda." Ariel sipped her vermouth. "She's a very stable woman with little hints of vulnerability and passion. I like seeing how subtle I can make them without hiding them completely. What did you think of the show?"

"A mass of complication and intrigue. I was surprised that the bulk of the plots didn't concern fatal diseases and bed hopping."

"You're out of step." She smiled over the rim. "Of course, every soap has some of those elements, but we've done a lot of expanding. Murder, politics, social issues, even science fiction. We do quite a bit of location shooting now in the race for ratings." She drank again. This time it was an opal, milky blue, that gleamed on her hand. "Last year we shot in Greece and Venice. I've never eaten so much in my life. Griff and Amanda had a lovers' rendezvous in Venice that was sabotaged. You must've noticed Stella—she plays my sister Vikki."

"The barracuda." Booth nodded. "I recognized the type."

"Oh, Vikki's that all right. Plotting, scheming, being generally nasty. Stella has a marvelous time with her. Vikki's had a dozen affairs, broken up three marriages, destroyed a senator's career. Just last month she pawned our mother's emerald brooch to pay off gambling debts." With a sigh, Ariel drank again. "She has all the fun."

Booth's grin flashed, lingering in his eyes as they met Ariel's. "Are you talking about Stella or Vikki?"

"Both, I suppose. I wondered if I'd be able to do that."

"What?"

"Make you smile. You don't very often, you know."

"No?"

"No." She felt the tug again, sharp and very physical. Indulging herself, she let her gaze lower briefly to his mouth and enjoyed the sensation it brought to her own. "I guess you're too busy picking up parts of people and filing them away."

Finishing off his drink, he set the glass aside. "Is that what I do?"

"Always. It's natural, I suppose, in your line of work, but I decided I was going to pull one out of you before the evening was over." He was still watching her, and though the smile was only a hint now, it was still lurking. It suited him, she thought, that trace of amusement—a cautious, even reluctant amusement. And again, she felt the tug of attraction. With her brows slightly drawn together, she stepped closer. It wasn't something she could or would walk away from.

"Aren't you curious?" she asked quietly, then went on when he didn't answer. "The thing is, I'm not certain I can go through the evening wondering what it would be like."

She put one hand on his shoulder and leaned forward just until their lips touched. There was no pressure, no demand on either side, and yet she felt that slightest of contacts through her whole system. There was a twinge deep inside her, a soft rushing sound in her ears. The mouth against hers was warmer than she'd expected and its taste more potent. Their bodies weren't touching, and the kiss remained a mere meeting of lips. Ariel felt herself open and was mildly surprised. Then, she felt her knees tremble and was stunned.

Slowly, she backed up, unaware that her eyes were wide with shock. Desire had ripped through him at the taste of her mouth, but Booth knew how to conceal his emotions. He wanted her—in the part of Rae and in his bed. To his thinking it wouldn't be long before she offered him one to ensure the other. He'd been much younger when Liz had lured him into bed for a part. He was older now and knew the game. And somehow, he felt Ariel would be more honest in her playing.

"Well…" Ariel let out a long breath while her mind raced. She wished she had five minutes alone to think this through. Somehow she'd always expected she'd fall in love in the blink of an eye, but she wasn't idealistic enough to believe it would be handed back to her. She needed to work out her next move. "And now that the pressure's off—" she set her glass aside "—why don't we go eat?"

Before she could step away, Booth took her arm. If they were going to play out the scene, he wanted to do it then and there. "What do you want?"

There was none of the quiet warmth in his voice that she'd felt in the kiss. Ariel looked into his eyes and saw nothing but a reflection of herself. An unwise man to love, she thought. And, of course, she should have expected that was what would happen to her when the time came. "To go to dinner," she told him.

"I've given you the opportunity to mention the part, you haven't. Why?"

"That's business. This isn't."

He gave a quick laugh. "In this business, it's all business," he countered. "You want to play Rae."

"I wouldn't have read for it if I didn't want it. And once I finish the next reading I'll have it." It frustrated her that she couldn't read him. "Booth, why don't you tell me what you're getting at? It'd be easier for both of us."

He inclined his head, and with his hand on her arm drew her an inch closer. "Just how much are you willing to do for it?"

His meaning was like a slap in the face. Outrage didn't come, but a piercing hurt that made her face pale and her eyes darken. "I'm willing to give the very best performance I'm capable of." Jerking out of his hold, she started for the door.

"Ariel…" He hadn't expected to call her back, but the look in her eyes had made him feel foul. When she didn't pause, he was going across the room before he could stop himself. "Ariel." Taking her arm again, he turned her around.

The hurt radiating from her was so sharp and real he couldn't convince himself not to believe it. The strength of the need to draw her against him was almost painful. "I'll apologize for that."

She stared at him, wishing it was in her to tell him to go to hell. "I'll accept it," she said instead, "since I'm sure you don't make a habit of apologizing for anything. She took a few pieces out of you, didn't she?"

His hand dropped away from her arm. "I don't discuss my private life."

"Maybe that's part of the problem. Is it women in general, or just actresses you detest?"

His eyes narrowed so that she could only see a glint of the anger. It wasn't necessary to see what you could feel. "Don't push me."

"I doubt anyone could." Though she felt the anger was a promising sign, Ariel didn't feel capable of dealing with it, or her own feelings at the moment. "It's a pity," she continued as she turned for the door again. "When whatever's frozen inside you thaws, I think you'll be a remarkable man. In the meantime, I'll stay out of your way." She opened the door, then turned back. "About the part, Booth, please deal with my agent." Quietly, she closed the door behind her.

Chapter 4

"No, Scott, if you eat any more cotton candy your teeth're going to fall right out. And then—" Ariel hauled her nephew up for one fierce hug "—you'd be stuck with stuff like smashed bananas and strained spinach."

"Popcorn," he demanded, grinning at her.

"Bottomless pit." She nuzzled into his neck and let the love flow over her.

Sunday was precious, not only because of the sunshine and balmy spring temperatures, not only because there were hours and hours of leisure time left to her, but because she had the afternoon to spend with the most important person in her life.

He even smells like his father, Ariel thought and wondered if it were possible to inherit a scent. Still holding him, with his sturdy legs wrapped around her waist, she studied his face.

Essentially, it was like looking in a mirror. There'd only been ten months between Ariel and her brother, Jeremy, and they'd often been taken for twins. Scott had pale curling hair, clear blue eyes and a face that promised to be lean and rather elegant once it had fined down from childhood. At the moment, it was sticky with pink spun sugar. Ariel kissed him firmly and tasted the sweetness.

"Yum-yum," she murmured, kissing him again when he giggled.

"What about your teeth?"

Arching a brow, she shifted his weight to a more comfortable position. "It doesn't count when it's sec-ondhand."

He gave her a crooked smile that promised to be a heartbreaker in another decade. "How come?"

"It's scientific," Ariel claimed. "Probably the sugar evaporates after being exposed to air and skin."

"You're making that up," he told her with great ap-proval.

Struggling with a smile, she tossed her long smooth braid behind her back. "Who me?"

"You're the best at making up."

"That's my job," she answered primly. "Let's go look at the bears."

"They better have big ones," Scott stated as he wrig-gled down. "*Great* big ones."

"I hear they're enormous," she told him. "Maybe even big enough to climb right out of the cages."

"Yeah?" His eyes lit up at the idea. Ariel could al-most see him writing out the scenario in his mind. The escape, the panic and screams of the crowd and his ulti-mate heroism in driving the giant, drooling bears back behind the bars. Then, of course, his humbleness in accepting the gratitude of the zookeepers. "Let's go!"

Ariel allowed herself to be dragged along at Scott's dashing pace, winding through the stream of people who'd come to spend their day at the Bronx Zoo. This she could give him, she thought. The fun, the preciousness of childhood. It was such a short time, so concentrated. So many years were passed as an adult—with obligations, responsibilities, worries, timetables. She wanted to give him the freedom, to show him what boundaries you could leap over and the ones you had to respect. Most of all, she wanted to give him love.

She loved and wanted him, not only for the memories he brought back of her brother, but for himself— his uniqueness and odd stability. Though she was a woman who ran her life on a staggered routine that wasn't a routine at all, who enjoyed coming and going on the impulse of the moment, she'd always needed stability—someone to care for, to nurture, to give her back some portion of the emotion she spent. There was nothing like a child, with its innocence and lack of restrictions, to give and take of love. Even now, while he raced and laughed and pointed, caught up in the day and the animals, Scott was feeding her.

If Ariel had believed Scott was happy living with his grandparents, she could have accepted it. But she knew that they were smothering all the specialness that radiated from him.

They weren't unkind people, she mused, but simply set in their thinking. A child was to be formed along certain lines, and that was that. A child was a duty, a solemn one. While she understood the duty, it was joy that came first. They would raise him to be responsible, polite and well-read. And they'd forget the wonder of it.

Perhaps it would have been easier if Scott's grandparents hadn't disapproved of Ariel's brother so strongly or if Scott hadn't been conceived in youthful defiance and passion…and out of wedlock. Marriage and Scott's birth hadn't eased over the strain in the relationship, nor had the tragic and sudden accident that had taken her brother and young sister-in-law. Scott's grandparents would look at the boy and be reminded that their daughter had married against their wishes and was dead. Ariel looked at him and saw life at its best.

He needs me, she thought, and ruffled his hair as he stood staring wide-eyed at a lumbering bear. Even when her heart wasn't involved, she'd never been able to resist a need. With Scott, her heart had been lost the first time she'd seen him—red and scrawny behind a hospital glass wall.

And she understood that she needed him. To have someone receive her love was vital. She thought of Booth.

He needed her, too, she thought, as a small secret smile touched her lips. Though he didn't know it. A man like that needed the ease that love could bring to his life, and the laughter. And she wanted to give it to him.

Why? Leaning against the barrier, Ariel shook her head. She had no solid reason, and that was enough to convince her it was right. When you could dissect something and find all the answers, you could find all the wrong ones. She trusted instincts and emotions much more than she trusted the intellect. She loved—quickly, unwisely and completely. When she thought about it,

Ariel decided she should never have expected it to be otherwise.

If she told him now, he'd think she was lying or insane. She could hardly blame him. It wouldn't be easy to win the confidence of a man as wary or as cynical as Booth DeWitt. With a smile, Ariel nibbled on some of Scott's popcorn. Challenges kept the excitement in life, after all. Whether Booth realized it or not, she was about to add some excitement to his.

"Why're you laughing, Ariel?"

She grinned down at Scott, then scooped him up. He laughed as he always did at her quick, physical shows of affection. "Because I'm happy. Aren't you? It's a happy day."

"I'm always happy with you." His arms went tight around her neck. "Can't I stay with you? Can't I live at your house—all the time?"

She buried her face in the curve of his shoulder—a tender place—knowing she couldn't tell him how hard she was trying to give him that. "We have today," she said instead. "All day."

Holding him, she could smell the scent of his soap and shampoo, the scent of roasted popcorn, the hot, pungent scent of the sun. With another laugh, she set her nephew down. Today, she told herself, that was what she'd show him.

"Let's go see the snakes. I like to watch them slither."

Booth couldn't understand why she kept crowding his mind. He should have been able to push Ariel into a corner of his brain and keep her there while he worked. Instead, she kept filling it.

He could have accepted it if he'd been able to keep

her in her slot—the actress he was all but certain would play his Rae. He could have rationalized his obsession if it had remained a professional one. But Booth kept seeing her as she'd been on top of New York, with her hair blowing frantically and her eyes filled with the wonder of it. That woman had nothing in common with the character of Rae.

And he could see her as she'd looked in his apartment. Vital, fresh—with energy and integrity shimmering from her. He could remember her hurt when he'd been deliberately cruel, and his own guilt—a sensation he'd sworn he'd never feel again. He hardly knew her, and yet she was drawing things out of him he'd promised himself he wouldn't feel again. He was perceptive enough to know she was a woman who could draw out more. For that reason, he'd decided to keep a safe, professional distance between them.

Still, as Booth watched Ariel talk with Jack Rohrer before the reading, he couldn't keep the established lines firmly in place. Was it because she was beautiful and he had always been susceptible to beauty? Was it because she was just unique enough to catch the attention and hold it?

As a writer he couldn't suppress his fascination with the unusual. But he got something from her—some feeling of absolute stability despite the fact that she dressed somewhere between a Gypsy and a teenager. He'd already asked her who she was and had been far from satisfied with her answer. Perhaps, just perhaps he should find out for himself.

"They look good together," Marshell murmured.

The sound Booth made might have been agreement or disinterest, but he didn't take his eyes from Ariel.

If he hadn't remembered her first reading so well, he'd have sworn he was making a mistake even considering her for the part. Her smile was much too open, her gestures too fluid. You could look at her and feel the warmth. He found it disconcerting to realize she made him nervous.

Desire. Yes, he felt desire. Booth weighed and measured it. Strong, hard and very nearly urgent—and that with only a look. Of course, she was a woman a man had to want. He wasn't worried about the desire, or even his interest, but about the niggling sensation that something was being slipped out of him without his knowledge and against his will.

Pulling out a cigarette, he watched her through the blue-tinted smoke. It might be worth his while, both as a man and as a writer, to see how many faces she could wear, and how easily she wore them. He sat on the edge of Marshell's desk.

"Let's get started."

At the brief, quiet order, Ariel turned her head and met Booth's gaze. *He's different today,* she thought, but couldn't quite pigeonhole the reason. He still looked at her with that intrusive, serious stare that bordered on the brooding. The distance was still there; she was sensitive enough to recognize the wall he kept erected between himself and the rest of the world. But there was something…

Ariel smiled at him. When he didn't respond, she picked up her copy of the script. She was going to give the best damn reading of her career. For herself and— for some odd reason—for Booth.

"All right, I'd like you to start at the top of the scene where they've come home from the party." Absently

Booth tapped his cigarette in a gold-etched ashtray. Behind him, Marshell nibbled on a stomach mint. "Do you want to read it over first?"

Ariel glanced up from the script. *He still thinks I'm going to blow it,* she realized, and was grateful for the hard knot in her stomach. "It isn't necessary," she told him, then turned to Jack.

For the second time, Booth witnessed the transformation. How was it that even her eyes seemed to go paler, icier when she spoke as Rae? He could feel the old sexual pull and intellecutal abhorrence his ex-wife had always brought to him. With the cigarette smoldering between his fingertips, Booth listened to Rae's scorn and Phil's anger—and remembered all too clearly.

A vampire. He'd called her that and accurately. Bloodless, heartless, alluring. Ariel slipped into the character as if it were a second skin. Booth knew he should admire her for it, even be grateful that she'd made his search for the right actress end. But her chameleon skill annoyed him.

The chemistry was right. Ariel and Jack hurled their lines at each other while the anger and sexual sparks flew. There wasn't any escaping it and no logical reason to try. Without knowing why, Booth was certain that giving Ariel the part was good professional judgment and a serious personal error. He'd just have to deal with the latter as he went.

"That'll do."

The moment Booth cut the scene, Ariel threw her head back and let out breathless laughter. The release—the sudden absence of tension—was tremendous. It would always be that way, she realized, with a part as tough and as cold as this one.

"Oh God, she's so utterly hateful, so completely self-consumed." Eyes alight, face flushed, she whirled to Booth. "You despise her, and yet she pulls you in. Even when you see the knife she's going to slide under your ribs, it's hard to step away."

"Yes." Watching the scene had disturbed him more than he'd expected. Rising, Booth left his hands in his pockets. "I want you for the part. We'll contact your agent and negotiate the details."

She sighed, but the smile lingered around her mouth. "I can see I've overwhelmed you," Ariel said dryly. "But the bottom line is the part. You won't regret it. Mr. Marshell, Jack, it'll be a pleasure working with you."

"Ariel…" Marshell rose and accepted her offered hand. It had been a long time since he'd watched a scene that had left him as shaken as this one. "Unless I miss my guess—and I never do—you're going to hit it big with this."

She flashed him a grin and felt like flying. "I don't suppose I'll complain. Thank you."

Booth had her elbow before she could turn around, and before he'd realized he intended to touch her. He wanted to vent fury on something, someone, but reasoned it away. "I'll walk you out."

Feeling the tension in his fingers, she had to resist the urge to soothe it. This wasn't a man who'd appreciate stroking. "All right."

They followed the same route they'd taken the week before, but this time in silence. Ariel sensed he needed it. When they came to the street door, she waited for him to say whatever he intended to say.

"Are you free?" he asked her.

A bit puzzled, she tilted her head.

"For an early dinner," he elaborated. "I feel I owe you a meal."

"Well." She brushed the hair back from her face. His invitation, such as it was, pleased her—something she took no trouble to hide. "Technically that's the other way around. Why do you want to have dinner with me?"

Just looking at her—the laughing eyes, the generous mouth—pulled him in two directions. Get closer before you lose it. Back off before it's too late. "I'm not completely sure."

"Good enough." She took his hand and lifted her free one for a cab. "Do you like grilled pork chops?"

"Yes."

She laughed over her shoulder before pulling him into the cab. "An excellent start." After giving the driver an address in Greenwich Village, she settled back. "I think the next move is to have a conversation without a word, one single word, that has to do with business. We might just make it in each other's company for more than an hour."

"All right." Booth nodded. He'd made the decision to get to know her and get to know her he would. "But we'll steer away from politics, too."

"Deal."

"How long have you lived in New York?"

"I was born here. A native." She grinned and crossed her legs. "You're not. I read somewhere that you're from Philadelphia and very top-drawer. Lots of influential relatives." She didn't even glance around when the cab skidded and swerved. "Are you happy in New York?"

He'd never thought about equating it with happiness, but now that he did, the answer came easily. "Yes.

I need the demands and the movement for long periods of time."

"And then you need to go away," she finished. "And be alone—on your boat."

Before he could be uncomfortable with her accuracy, he'd accepted it. "That's right. I relax when I'm sailing and I like to relax alone."

"I paint," she told him. "Terrible paintings." With a laugh, she rolled her eyes. "But it helps me work the kinks out when I get them. I keep threatening people with an original Kirkwood as a Christmas present, but I haven't the heart to do it."

"I'd like to see one," he murmured.

"The problem seems to be that I splatter my mood on the canvas. Here we are." Ariel hopped out of the cab and stood on the curb.

Booth glanced around at the tiny storefronts. "Where're we going?"

"To the market." In her easy manner, she hooked her arm through his. "I don't have any pork chops at home."

He looked down at her. "Home?"

"Most of the time I'd rather cook than eat out. And tonight I'm too wired to deal with a restaurant. I have to be busy."

"Wired?" After studying her profile, Booth shook his head. His hair was dark in the lowering sun, and the movement sent it settling carelessly around his face. A contrast, Ariel mused, to the rather formal exterior. "I'd have said you look remarkably calm."

"Uh-uh. But I'm trying to save the full explosion until after my agent calls and tells me everything's carved in granite. Don't worry—" she smiled up at him "—I'm a fair cook."

If a man judged only by that porcelain face, he'd never have believed she'd know one end of the stove from the other. But Booth knew about surfaces. Maybe, just maybe, there'd be a surprise under hers. Despite all the warnings he'd given himself, he smiled. "Only fair?"

Her eyes lit in appreciation. "I hate to brag, but actually, I'm terrific." She steered him into a small, cluttered market that smelled heavily of garlic and pepper, and began a haphazard selection for the evening meal. "How're the avocados today, Mr. Stanislowski?"

"The best." The grocer looked over her head to study Booth out of the corner of his eye. "Only the best for you, Ariel."

"I'll have two then, but you pick them out." She poked at a head of romaine. "How did Monica do on her history quiz?"

"Ninety-two percent." His chest swelled a bit under his apron, but he continued to speculate on the dark, brooding man who'd come in with Ariel.

"Terrific. I need four really nice center-cut chops." While he selected them, she studied the mushrooms, well aware that he was bursting with curiosity over Booth. "You know, Mr. Stanislowski, Monica would love a kitten."

As he started to weigh the meat, the grocer sent her an exasperated glance. "Now, Ariel…"

"She's certainly old enough to care for one on her own," Ariel continued and pinched a tomato. "It'd be company for her, and a responsibility. And she did get ninety-two on that quiz." Looking over, she sent him a dashing, irresistible smile. He flushed and shifted his feet.

"Maybe if you were to bring one by, we could think about it."

"I will." Still smiling, she reached for her wallet. "How much do I owe you?"

"That was smoothly done," Booth murmured when they stepped outside. "And it's the second time I've heard you palming off a kitten. Did your cat have a litter?"

"No, I just happen to know about a number of homeless kittens." She tilted her face toward him. "If you're interested…"

"No." The answer was firm and brief as he took the bag from her.

Ariel merely smiled and decided she could work on him later. Now, she breathed in the scent of spices and baking from the open doorways. Some children raced along the sidewalk, laughing. A few old men sat out on the stoops to gossip. After the dinner hour, Ariel knew other members of the family would come out to talk and exchange news and enjoy the spring weather. Through a screened window she heard some muted snatches of Beethoven's Ninth, and farther down the pulse of top forty rock.

Two years before, Ariel had moved to the Village for the neighborhood feel, and had never been disappointed. She could sit outside and listen to the elderly reminisce, watch the children play, hear about the latest teenage heartthrob or the newest baby. It had been exactly what she'd needed when her family had gone its separate ways.

"Hi, Mr. Miller, Mr. Zimmerman."

The two old men who sat on the steps of the converted brownstone eyed Booth before they looked at

Ariel. "Don't think you should give that Cameron another chance," Mr. Miller told her.

"Boot him out." Mr. Zimmerman gave a wheeze that might have been a chuckle. "Get yourself a man with backbone."

"Is that an offer?" She kissed his cheek before climbing the rest of the steps.

"I'll have a dance at the block party," he called after her.

Ariel winked over her shoulder. "Mr. Zimmerman, you can have as many as you want." As they started up the inside steps, Ariel began to fish in her bag for her keys. "I'm crazy about him," she told Booth. "He's a retired music instructor and still teaches a few kids on the side. He sits on the stoop so he can watch the women go by." She located the keys attached to a large, plastic, grinning sun. "He's a leg man."

Automatically, Booth glanced over his shoulder. "He told you?"

"You just have to watch the direction his eyes take when a skirt passes."

"Yours included?"

Her eyes danced. "I fit into the category of niece. He thinks I should be married and raising large quantities of babies."

She fit a single key into a single lock, something Booth thought almost unprecedented for New York, then pushed open the door. He'd been expecting the unusual. And he wasn't disappointed.

The focal point of the living room was a long oversize hammock swinging from brass ceiling hooks. One end of it was piled with pillows and beside it was a washstand holding one thick candle, three-quarters

burned down. There was color—he'd known there'd
be an abundance of it—and a style that was undefinable.

The sofa was a long, curved French antique uphol-
stered with faded rose brocade, while a long wicker
trunk served as a coffee table. As in Ariel's dressing
room, the entire area was cluttered with books, papers
and scents. He caught the fragrance of candle wax, potpourri and fresh flowers. Bunches of spring blossoms
were spilling from a collection of vases that ran from
dime-store pottery to Meissen.

There was an umbrella stand in the shape of a stork
that was filled with ostrich and peacock feathers. A pair
of boxing gloves hung in the corner behind the door.

"I guess you'd class as a featherweight," Booth
mused.

Ariel followed his gaze and smiled. "They were my
brother's. He boxed in high school. Want a drink?" Before he could answer, she took the bag from him, then
headed down a hallway.

"A little Scotch and water." When he turned, his
attention and his senses were struck by a wall of paintings. They were hers, of course. Who else would paint
with that kind of kinetic energy, verve and disregard
for rules? There were splotches of color, lines of it,
zigzags. Moving closer, Booth decided that while he
wouldn't call them terrible, he wasn't quite sure what
he'd call them. Vivid, eccentric, disturbing. Certainly
they weren't paintings to relax by. They showed both
flair and heedlessness, and whether she'd intended them
to or not they suited the room to perfection.

As he continued to study the paintings, three cats
came into the room. Two were hardly more than kittens, coal black and amber eyed. They dashed around

his legs once before they made a beeline for the kitchen. The other was a huge tiger who managed to walk with stiff dignity on three legs. Booth could hear Ariel laugh and say something to the two cats who had found her. The tiger watched Booth with quiet patience.

"Scotch and water." Ariel came back in, barefoot, carrying two glasses.

Booth accepted the glass, then gestured with it. "Those must be some kinks you work out."

Ariel glanced toward her paintings. "Looks like it, doesn't it? Saves money on a therapist—though I shouldn't say that since I play the role of one."

"You've quite a place here."

"I learned I thrive on confusion." Laughing up at him, she sipped. "You've met Butch, I see." She bent and slid one hand over the tiger's back. He arched, letting out a grumble of a purr. "Keats and Shelley were the rude ones. They're having their dinner."

"I see." Booth glanced down to see Butch rub against Ariel's leg before he waddled over to the sofa and leaped onto a cushion. "Don't you find it difficult tending three cats in a city apartment while dealing with a demanding profession?"

She only smiled. "No. I'm going to start the grill."

Booth lifted a brow. "Where?"

"Why, on the terrace." Ariel walked over and slid open a door. Outside was a postage-stamp balcony more along the lines of a window ledge. On it she'd crammed pots of geraniums and a tiny charcoal grill.

"The terrace," Booth murmured over her shoulder. Only an incurable optimist or a hopeless dreamer would have termed it so. He found himself grateful she had. Laughing, he leaned against the doorjamb.

After straightening from the grill, Ariel stared at him. The sound of his laughter whispered along her skin and eased her mind. "Well, well. That's very nice. Do you know that's the first time since I've met you that you've laughed and meant it?"

Booth shrugged and sipped at his Scotch. "I suppose I'm out of practice."

"We'll soon fix that," Ariel said. She smiled, holding her hand out, palm up. "Got a match?"

Booth reached in his pocket, but something—perhaps the humor in her eyes—changed his mind. Stepping forward, he took her shoulders and lowered his mouth to hers.

He'd caught her off guard. Ariel hadn't expected him to do anything on impulse, and he'd given no sign of his intention. Before she had time to prepare, the power of the kiss whipped through her, touching the emotions, the senses, then taking over.

It wasn't a mere touching of lips this time, but a hard, thorough demand that had her wrapped in his arms and trapped against the side of the door. She reached up to take his face in her hands as she gave, unquestioningly, what he sought from her.

There was no gradual smoldering, no experimentation, but a leap of flame so intense and quick it seemed they were already lovers. She felt the instant intimacy and understood it. Her heart was already his, she couldn't deny him her body.

He felt the need churn and was relieved. It had been long, too long, since he'd more than indifferently wanted a woman. There was nothing indifferent about the passion he felt now. It was hard and clear, like the wind that buffeted him when he sailed. It spelled freedom. Drawing her closer, Booth absorbed it.

He could smell her—that warm, teasing fragrance that seemed to pulse out of her skin. How often had that scent come to him when he'd only thought of her? He remembered her taste. Alluring, giving and again warm. And the feel of her body—slender, soft, with still more warmth. It was that that touched every aspect of her, that promised to fill him. He needed it, though he'd gone for years without knowing it. Perhaps he needed her.

And it was that that had him pulling back when he wanted more and more of what she had an abundance of.

Her eyes opened slowly when her mouth was free. Ariel looked directly, unblinkingly at him. This time she saw more than a reflection of self. She saw longings and caution and a glimpse of emotion that stirred her.

"I've wanted you to do that," she murmured.

Booth forced himself to level, forced himself to think past the senses she sent swimming. "I haven't got anything for you."

That hurt, but Ariel knew love wasn't painless. "I think you're wrong. But then, I have a tendency to rush into things. You don't." She took a deep breath and a step back. "Why don't you light this and I'll go make a salad?" Without waiting for his answer she turned and walked into the kitchen.

Steady, she ordered herself. She knew she had to be steady to deal with Booth and the feelings he brought to her. He wasn't a man who would accept a flood of emotion all at once, or the demands that went with it. If she wanted him in her life, she'd have to tread carefully, and at his pace.

He wasn't nearly as hard and cool as he tried to be,

Ariel mused. With a half smile, she began to wash the fresh vegetables. She could tell from his laugh, and from those flickers of amusement in his eyes. And, of course, she was certain she couldn't have fallen in love with a man without a sense of humor. It pleased her to be able to draw it out of him. The more they were together, the easier it was. She wondered if he knew. Humming, she began to slice an avocado.

Booth watched her from the doorway. A smile lingered on her lips, and her eyes held that light he was growing too used to. She used the kitchen knife with the careless confidence of one who was accustomed to domestic chores. In one easy movement she tossed her hair behind her back.

Why should such a simple scene hold so much appeal for him, he wondered. Just looking at her standing at the sink, her hands full, the water running, he could feel himself relaxing. What was it about her that made him want to put his feet up and his head back? At that moment, he could see himself going to her to wrap his arms around her waist and nuzzle. He must be going mad.

She knew he was there. Her senses were keen, and sharper still where Booth was involved. Keeping her back to him, she continued preparing the salad. "Have any trouble lighting it?"

He lifted a brow. "No."

"Well, it doesn't take long to heat up. Hungry?"

"A bit." He crossed the room to her. He wouldn't touch her, but he'd get just a little closer.

Smiling, she held up a thin slice of avocado, offering him a bite. Ariel could see the wariness in his eyes as he allowed her to feed him. "I'm never a bit hungry," she told him, finishing off the slice herself. "I'm always starving."

He'd told himself he wouldn't touch her, yet he found that the back of his hand was sliding over the side of her face. "Your skin," he murmured. "It's beautiful. It looks like porcelain, feels like satin." His gaze skimmed over her face, over her mouth before it locked on hers. "I should never have touched you."

Her heart was pounding. Gentleness. That was unexpected and would undermine her completely. "Why?"

"It leads to more." His fingers ran slowly down the length of her hair before he dropped his hands. "I haven't any more. You want something from me," he murmured.

Her breath trembled out. She'd never realized what a strain it was to hold in your emotions. She'd never tried. "Yes, I do. For now, just some companionship at dinner. That should be easy."

When she started to turn back to the sink, Booth stopped her. "Nothing about this is going to be easy. If I continue to see you, like this, I'm going to take you to bed."

It would be easy, so easy, just to go into his arms. But he'd never accept the generosity, and she'd never survive the emptiness. "Booth, I'm a grown woman. If I go to bed with you, it's my choice."

He nodded. "Perhaps. I just want to make sure I have one." He turned and left her alone in the room.

Ariel took a deep breath. She wasn't going to have it, she decided. No, not any of it. He'd simply have to learn how to cope without the moodiness and tension. Lifting the platter of chops, she went back into the living room.

"Lighten up, DeWitt," she ordered and caught a

glimpse of surprise on his face as she went to the grill. "I have to deal with melodrama and misery in every episode. I don't let it into my personal life. Fix yourself another drink, sit down and relax." Ariel set the chops on the grill, added some freshly ground pepper, then walked to the stereo. She switched on jazz, bluesy and mellow.

When she turned around he was still standing, looking at her. "I mean it," she told him. "I have a firm policy about worrying about what complications might come up. They're going to happen if you think about it or if you don't. So why waste your time?"

"Is it that easy for you?"

"Not always. Sometimes I have to work at it."

Thoughtfully, he drew out a cigarette. "We won't be good together," he said after he'd lit it. "I don't want anyone in my life."

"Anyone?" She shook her head. "You're too intelligent to believe a person can live without anyone. Don't you need friendship, companionship, love?"

Blowing out a stream of smoke, he tried to ignore the twinge the question brought him. He'd spent more than two years convincing himself he didn't. Why should he just now, so suddenly, realize the fruitlessness of it? "Each one of those things requires something in return that I no longer want to give."

"Want to give." Her gaze was thoughtful, her mouth unsmiling. "At least you're honest in your phrasing. The more I'm around you, the more I realize you never lie to anyone—but yourself."

"You haven't been around me enough to know who or what I am." He crushed out his cigarette and thrust his hands in his pockets. "And you're much better off that way."

"I or you?" she countered, then shook her head when he didn't answer. "You're letting her make a victim out of you," Ariel murmured. "I'm surprised."

His eyes narrowed; the green frosted. "Don't open closets unless you know what's inside, Ariel."

"Too safe." She preferred the simple anger she felt from him now. With a half laugh, she crossed to him and put her hands on his upper arms. "There's no fun in life without risks. I can't function without fun." Her fingers squeezed, gently. "Look, I enjoy being with you. Is that all right?"

"I'm not sure." She was pulling him in again, with the lightest of touches. "I'm not sure it is for either of us."

"Do yourself a favor," she suggested. "Don't worry about it for a few days and see what happens." Rising on her toes, she brushed his mouth in a gesture that was both friendly and intimate. "Why don't you fix that drink?" she added, grinning. "Because I'm burning the chops."

Chapter 5

"No, Griff, I won't discuss my marriage." Amanda picked up a delft-blue watering can and meticulously tended the plants in her office window. The sun, a product of the sweltering stage lights, poured through the glass.

"Amanda, you can't keep secrets in small towns. It's already common knowledge that you and Cameron aren't living together any longer."

Beneath the trim, tailored jacket, her shoulders stiffened. "Common knowledge or not, it's my business." Keeping her back to him, she examined a bloom on an African violet.

"You're losing weight, there are shadows under your eyes. Damn it, Mandy, I can't stand to see you this way."

She waited a beat, then turned slowly. "I'm fine. I'm capable of handling what needs to be handled."

Griff gave a short laugh. "Who'd know that better than I do?"

Something flared in her eyes, but her voice was cool and final. "I'm busy, Griff."

"Let me help you," he said with sudden, characteristic passion. "It's all I've ever wanted to do."

"Help?" Her voice chilled as she set down the can. "I don't need any help. Do you think I should confide in you, trust you after what you did to me?" As she tilted her head, the tiny sapphires in her ears glinted. She shifted on her mark. "The only difference between you and Cameron is that I let you tear up my life. I won't make the same mistake again."

Fury burst from him as he grabbed her arm. "You never asked me what Vikki was doing in my room. Not then, and not in all these months. You bounced back quick, Mandy, and ended up with another man's ring on your finger."

"It's still there," she said quietly. "So you'd better take your hands off me."

"Do you think that's going to stop me now that I know you don't love him?" Passion, rage, desire—all emanated from his eyes, his voice, his body. "I can look at you and see it," he went on before she could deny it. "I know what's inside you like no one else does. So handle it." He dragged his hands through her hair and dislodged pins. The camera dollied closer. "And handle this."

Pulling her against him, Griff crushed her mouth with his. She nearly tore away. Nearly. For a heartbeat, she was still. Amanda lifted her hands to his shoulders to push away, but clung instead. A soft, muffled moan escaped as passion flared. For a moment, they were locked together as they'd once been. Then, he dragged her away, keeping his hands tight on her arms. Desire and anger sparked between them. His tangible, hers restrained.

"You're not going to back away from me this time," he told her. "I'll wait, but I won't wait long. You come to me, Mandy. That's where you belong."

Releasing her, Griff stormed out of the office. Amanda lifted an unsteady hand to her lips and stared at the closed door.

"Cut."

Ariel marched around the prop wall of her office. "You ate those onions on purpose."

Jack tugged on her disheveled hair. "Just for you, sweetie."

"Swine."

"God, I love it when you call me names." Dramatically, Jack gathered her in his arms and bent her backward in an exaggerated dip. "Let me take you to bed and show you the true meaning of passion."

"Not until you chew a roll of breath mints, fella." Giving him a firm push, Ariel freed herself, then turned to her director. The furnace of stage lights had already been dimmed. "Neal, if that's it for today, I've got an appointment across town."

"Take off. See you at seven on Monday."

In the dressing room, Ariel stripped Amanda's elegant facade away and replaced it with slim cotton pants and a billowy, tailored man's shirt. After slipping on flat shoes she left the studio and went outside. There was a small group of fans waiting, hoping that someone recognizable would appear. They clustered around Amanda, autograph books in hand, as they chattered about the show and tossed questions.

"Are you going to go back with Griff?"

Ariel looked over at the sparkling-eyed teenager and grinned. "I don't know...he's awfully hard to resist."

"He's super! I mean, his eyes are just so *green*." She tucked her gum into the corner of her mouth and sighed. "I'd die if he looked at me the way he looks at you."

Ariel thought of another pair of green eyes and nearly sighed herself. "We'll have to wait to see what develops, won't we? I'm glad you like the show." Easing away from the crowd, she hailed a cab. The minute she gave the address, she slumped back against the seat.

She wasn't sure why she felt so tired. She supposed it was the prospect of the meeting that made her so bone weary. True, she hadn't been sleeping as well as was her habit, but she'd gone through wakeful phases before without any strain.

Booth. If Booth were the only thing on her mind, she could have dealt with it well enough. She hoped she would. But there was Scott.

The idea of confronting his grandparents didn't frighten her, but it did weary her. Ariel had spoken with them before. There was no reason to believe this session would be any different.

She remembered the way Scott had beamed and glowed at the zoo. Such a simple thing. Such a vital thing. The way he'd clung to her—it tore at her heart. If there were just some other way...

Closing her eyes, she sighed. She didn't believe there would be another way, not even with all her natural optimism. In the end, they'd come to a complicated, painful custody suit with Scott caught in the middle.

What was best? What was right? Ariel wanted someone to tell her, to advise and comfort her. But for the first time in her life she felt it impossible to confide in anyone. The more private she kept this affair, the less chance there was of Scott being hurt by it. She would just have to follow her instincts, and hope.

With her mind on a dozen other things, Ariel paid the cabbie and walked into the sleek steel building that housed her lawyer's offices. On the way from the lobby to the thirtieth floor, she gathered all her confidence together. This would be perhaps the last time she'd have the opportunity to speak with Scott's grandparents on an informal basis. She needed to give it her best shot.

The little tremor in her stomach wasn't so different from stage fright. Comfortable with it, Ariel walked into Bigby, Liebowitz and Feirson.

"Good afternoon, Ms. Kirkwood." The receptionist beamed a smile at Ariel and wondered if she could get away with a similar outfit. Not slim enough, she decided wistfully. Instead of looking dashing, she'd just look frumpy. "Mr. Bigby's expecting you."

"Hello, Marlene. How's the puppy working out?"

"Oh, he's so smart. My husband couldn't believe that a mutt could learn so many tricks. I really want to thank you for arranging it for me."

"I'm glad he's got a good home." She caught herself lacing her fingers together—a rare outward sign of tension. Deliberately Ariel dropped her hands to her sides as the receptionist rang through.

"Ms. Kirkwood's here, Mr. Bigby. Yes, sir." She rose as she replaced the receiver. "I'll take you back. If you have time before you leave, Ms. Kirkwood, my sister'd love your autograph. She never misses your show."

"I'd be happy to." Ariel's fingers groped for each other and she restrained them. *Save the nerves for later,* she told herself, *when you can afford them*. For once, she'd apply some of Amanda's steady calm to her personal life.

"Well, Ariel." The spindly, bearded man behind the massive desk rose as she entered. The room carried a vague scent of peppermint and polish. "Right on time."

"I never miss a cue." Ariel crossed the plush carpet with both hands extended. "You look good, Charlie."

"I feel good since you talked me into giving up smoking. Six months," he said with a grin. "Three days and—" he checked his watch "—four and a half hours."

She squeezed his hands. "Keep counting."

"We've got about fifteen minutes before the Andersons are due. Want some coffee?"

"Oh, yeah." On the words, Ariel sunk into a creamy leather chair.

Bigby pushed his intercom. "Would you bring some coffee back, Marlene? So…" He set down the receiver and folded his neat, ringless hands. "How're you holding up?"

"I'm a wreck, Charlie." She stretched out her legs and ordered herself to relax. First the toes, then the ankles, then all the way up. "You're practically the only one I can talk to about this. I'm not used to holding things in."

"If things go well you won't have to much longer."

She sent him a level look. "What chance do we have?"

"A fair one."

With a small sigh, Ariel shook her head. "Not good enough."

After a brief knock, Marlene entered with the coffee tray. "Cream and sugar, Ms. Kirkwood?"

"Yes, thank you." Ariel accepted the cup then immediately rose and began to pace. Maybe if she could turn some of the nerves to energy she wouldn't burst. Maybe. "Charlie, Scott needs me."

And you need him, he thought as he watched her. "Ariel, you're a responsible member of your community with a good reputation. You have a steady job with an excellent income, though it can and will be argued that it's not necessarily stable. You put your brother through college and have some sort of an involvement with every charity known to man." He saw her smile at that and was pleased. "You're young, but not a child. The Andersons are both in their midsixties. That should have some bearing on the outcome, and you'll have the emotion on your side."

"God, I hate to think of there being sides," she murmured. "There're sides in arguments, in wars. This can't be a war, Charlie. He's just a child."

"As difficult as it is, you're going to have to think practically about this."

With a nod, she sipped uninterestedly at her coffee. Practical. "But I'm single, and I'm an actress."

"There're pros and cons. This last-ditch meeting was your idea," he continued. "I don't like to see you get churned up this way."

"I have to try just once more before we find ourselves in court. The idea that Scotty might have to testify…"

"Just an easy talk with the judge in chambers, Ariel. It's not traumatic, I promise you."

"Not to you, maybe not to him, but to me…" She whirled around, her eyes dark with passion. "I'd give it up, Charlie. I swear I'd give it up this minute if I could believe he'd be happy with them. But when he looks at me…" Breaking off, she shook her head. Both hands were clenched on the coffee cup and she concentrated on relaxing them. "I know I'm being emotional about this, but it's the only way I've ever been able to judge what was right and what was wrong. If I look at it practically, I know they'll feed him and shelter him and educate him. But nurturing…" She turned to stare out of the window. "I keep coming back to the nurturing. Am I doing the best for him, Charlie? I just want to be sure."

For a moment, he sat fondling the gold pen on his desk. She asked hard questions. In the law, it wasn't a matter of best, but of justice. The two weren't always synonymous. "Ariel, you know the boy. At the risk of sounding very unlawyerlike, I say you have to do what your heart tells you."

Smiling, she turned back. "You say the right things. That's all I've ever been able to do." For a moment, she hesitated, then plunged. Since she was here for advice, she'd go all the way with it. "Charlie, if I told you I'd fallen in love with a man who thinks relationships are to be avoided at all costs and actresses are the least trustworthy individuals on the planet, what would you say?"

"I'd say it was typical of you. How long do you figure it'll take you to change his mind?"

Laughing, she dragged a hand through her hair. "Always the right thing," she said again.

"Sit down and drink your coffee, Ariel," he advised. "You're the one who says if something's meant to happen, it happens."

"When have I ever said anything so trite?" she demanded but did as he said. "All right, Charlie." She heaved a long sigh. "Do you want to give me the lecture on what I should expect and what I shouldn't say?"

"For what good it'll do." He toyed with the edge of

Ariel's file. "You'll meet the Andersons' lawyer, Basil Ford. He's very painstaking and very conservative. I've dealt with him before."

"Did you win?"

Bigby grinned at her as he leaned back in his chair. "I'd say we're about even. Since this is a voluntary, informal meeting, there won't be that much for either Ford or me to do. But if he asks you a question you shouldn't answer, I'll take care of it." Meticulously, Bigby settled the English bone-china cup back in its saucer. "Otherwise, say what you want, but don't elaborate more than necessary. Above all, don't lose your temper or your grip. If you want to yell or cry, wait until they've gone."

"You've gotten to know me very well," she murmured. "All right, I'll be calm and lucid." When the buzzer sounded on his desk, Ariel balled her hands into fists.

"Yes, Marlene, bring them in. And we'll need more coffee." He looked across at Ariel, measuring the strain in her eyes against the strength. "It's a discussion," he reminded her. "It's doubtful anything will be decided here today."

She nodded and concentrated on relaxing her hands.

When the door opened, Bigby rose, all joviality. "Basil, good to see you." He stretched his hand out to meet that of the erect, gray-suited man with thinning hair. "Mr. and Ms. Anderson, please have a seat. We'll have coffee in a moment. Basil Ford, Ariel Kirkwood."

Ariel nearly let out a tense giggle at the cocktail introduction. "Hello, Mr. Ford." She found his handshake firm and his gaze formidable.

"Ms. Kirkwood." He sat smoothly with his briefcase by his side.

"Hello, Mr. Anderson, Ms. Anderson."

Ariel received a nod from the woman and a brief formal handshake from her husband. Attractive people. Solid people. She'd always felt that from them—along with their rigidity. Both stood straight, a product of their military training. Anderson had retired from active service as a full colonel ten years before, and in her youth, his wife had been an Army nurse.

They'd met during the war, had served together and married. You could sense their closeness—the intimacy of thoughts and values. Perhaps, Ariel mused, that was why they had trouble seeing anyone else's viewpoint.

Together, the Andersons sat on a cushy two-seater sofa. Both were conservatively dressed: her iron-gray hair was skimmed back and his snowy white was cropped close. Feeling the waves of their disapproval, Ariel bit back a sigh. Instinct and experience told her she'd never get through to them on an emotional level.

While coffee was served, Bigby steered the conversation into generalities. The Andersons answered politely and ignored Ariel as much as possible. Because they spoke around her, she took care not to ask them any direct questions. She'd antagonize them soon enough.

She recognized the signal when Bigby sat behind his desk and folded his hands on the surface.

"I believe we can all agree that we have one mutual concern," he began. "Scott's welfare."

"That's why we're here," Ford said easily.

Bigby skimmed his gaze over Ford and concentrated on the Andersons. "Since that's the case, an informal meeting like this where we can exchange points of view and options should be to everyone's benefit."

"Naturally, my clients' main concern is their grandchild's well-being." Ford spoke in his beautiful orator's voice before he sipped his coffee. "Ms. Kirkwood's interest is understood, of course. As to the matter of custody, there's no question as to the rights and capability of Mr. and Ms. Anderson."

"Nor of Ms. Kirkwood's," Bigby put in mildly. "But it isn't rights and capabilities we're discussing today. It's the child himself. I'd like to make it clear that, at this point, we're not questioning your intentions or your ability to raise the child." He spoke to the Andersons again, skillfully bypassing his colleague. "The issue is what's best for Scott as an individual."

"My grandson," Anderson began in his deep, raspy voice, "belongs where he is. He's well fed, well dressed and well disciplined. His upbringing will have a sense of order. He'll be sent to the best schools available."

"What about well loved?" Ariel blurted out before she could stop herself. "What money can't buy..." Leaning forward she focused her attention on Scott's grandmother. "Will he be well loved?"

"An abstract question, Ms. Kirkwood," Ford put in briskly. "If we could—"

"No, it isn't," Ariel interrupted, sparing him a glance before she turned back to the Andersons. "There's nothing more solid than love. Nothing more easily given or withheld. Will you hold him at night if he's frightened of shadows? Will you understand how important it is to pretend that he's protecting you? Will you always listen when he needs to talk?"

"He won't be coddled if that's what you mean." Anderson set down his coffee and rested a hand on one knee. "A child's values are molded early. These fantasies—that you encourage—aren't healthy. I have no intention of allowing my grandson to live in a dream-world."

"A dreamworld." Ariel stared at him and saw a solid rock wall of resistance. "Mr. Anderson, Scott has a beautiful imagination. He's full of life, and visions."

"Visions." Anderson's lips thinned. "Visions will do nothing but make him look for what isn't there, expect what he can't have. The boy needs a firm basis in re-ality. In what *is*. You make your living from pretend-ing, Ms. Kirkwood. My grandson won't live his life in a storybook."

"There're twenty-four hours in every day, Mr. An-derson. Isn't there enough reality in that so we can put a small portion of time aside for wishing? All children need to believe in wishes, especially Scott after so much has been taken away from him. Please…" Her gaze shifted to the stiff-backed woman on the sofa. "You've known grief. Scott lost the two people in the world who meant love and security and normality. All of those things have to be given back to him."

"By you?" Ms. Anderson sat very still, her eyes re-mained very level. In them Ariel saw remnants of pain. "My daughter's child will be raised by me."

"Ms. Kirkwood." Ford interrupted smoothly, then crossed his legs. "To touch on more practical matters, I'm aware that you currently have a key role in a— Day-time drama, I believe is the word. This equals a regu-lar job with a steady income. But to be down-to-earth for a moment, it's habitual for these things to change. How would you support a child if your income was in-terrupted?"

"My income won't be interrupted." Bigby caught her eye, so with an effort Ariel held on to her temper. "I'm under contract. I'm also signed to do a film with P. B. Marshell." Noticing the flicker of speculation, Ariel blessed fate for throwing the part her way.

"That's very impressive," Ford told her. "However, I'm sure you'd be the first to admit that your profession is renowned for its ups and downs."

"If we're talking financial stablity, Mr. Ford, I assure you that I'm capable of giving Scott all the material requirements necessary. If my career should take a downswing, I'd simply supplement it. I've experience in both the retail and the restaurant business." A half smile teased her mouth as she thought of her days selling perfume and powder, and waiting tables. Oh, yes, *experience* was the right word. "But I can't believe any of us would put a bank statement first when we're discussing a child." It was said calmly, with only a hint of disdain.

"I'm sure we all agree that the child's monetary well-being is of primary importance," Bigby put in. The subtle tone of his voice was his warning to Ariel. "There's no question that both the Andersons and my client are capable of providing Scott with food, shelter, education, etc."

"There's also the matter of marital status." Ford stroked a long finger down the side of his nose. "As a single woman, a single professional woman, Ms. Kirkwood, just how much time would you be able to spare for Scott?"

"Whatever he needs," Ariel said simply. "I recognize my priorities, Mr. Ford."

"Perhaps." He nodded, resting a hand on the arm of his chair. "And perhaps you haven't thought this through completely. Having never raised a child, you might not be fully aware of the time involved. You have an active social life, Ms. Kirkwood."

His words and tone were mild, his meaning clear. Any other time, in any other place, she would have been amused. "Not as active as it reads in print, Mr. Ford."

Again, he nodded. "You're also a young woman, attractive. I'm sure it's reasonable to assume that marriage is highly likely at some time in the future. Have you considered how a potential husband might feel about the responsibility of raising someone else's child?"

"No." Her fingers laced together. "If I loved a man enough to marry him, he'd accept Scott as part of me, of my life. Otherwise, he wouldn't be the kind of man I'd love."

"If you had to make a choice—"

"Basil." Bigby held up a hand, and though he smiled, his eyes were hard. "We shouldn't get bogged down in this sort of speculation. No one expects us to solve this custody issue here today. What we want is to get a clear picture of everyone's feelings. What your clients and mine want for Scott."

"His well-being," Anderson said tersely.

"His happiness," Ariel murmured. "I want to believe they're the same thing."

"You're no different from your brother." Anderson's voice was sharp and low, like the final snap of a whip. "Happiness. He preached happiness at all costs to my daughter until she tossed aside all her responsibilities, her education, her values. Pregnant at eighteen, married to a penniless student who put more effort into flying a kite than keeping a decent job."

Ariel's mouth trembled open as the pain struck. No, she wouldn't waste her breath defending her brother.

He needed no defense. "They loved each other," she said instead.

"Loved each other." Color rose in Anderson's cheeks, the first and only sign of emotion Ariel had seen from him. "Can you honestly believe that's enough?"

"Yes. They were happy together. They had a beautiful child together. They had dreams together." Ariel swallowed as the urge to weep pounded at her. "Some people never have that much."

"Barbara would still be alive if we'd kept her away from him."

Ariel looked over at the older woman and saw more than pain now. The strong, bony hands shook slightly, the voice broke. It was a combination of grief and fury that Ariel recognized and understood. "Jeremy's gone, too, Ms. Anderson," she said quietly. "But Scott's here."

"He killed my daughter." The woman's eyes glowed against a skin gone abruptly pale.

"Oh, no." Ariel reached out, shocked by the words, drawn by the pain. "Ms. Anderson, Jeremy adored Barbara. He'd never have done anything to hurt her."

"He took her up in that plane. Barbara had no business being up in one of those small planes. She wouldn't have been if he hadn't taken her."

"Ms. Anderson, I know how you feel—"

She jerked away from Ariel's offer of comfort, her breath suddenly coming fast and shallow. "Don't you tell me you know how I feel. She was my only child. My only child." Rising, she sent Ariel an icy stare that shimmered with tears. "I won't discuss Barbara with you, or Barbara's son." She walked from the office in quick, controlled steps that were silent on the carpet.

"I won't have you upsetting my wife." Mr. Anderson stood, erect and unyielding. "We've known nothing but misery since the first time we heard the name Kirkwood."

Though her knees had begun to shake, Ariel rose to face him. "Scott's name is Kirkwood, Mr. Anderson."

Without a word, he turned and strode out of the room.

"My clients are understandably emotional on this issue." Ford's voice was so calm Ariel barely heard it. With the slightest nod of agreement, she wandered to stare out the window.

She didn't register the subdued conversation the attorneys carried on behind her. Instead, she concentrated on the flow of traffic she could see but not quite hear from thirty floors below. She wanted to be down there, surrounded by cars and buses and people.

Strange how she'd nearly convinced herself she was resigned to her brother's death. Now, the helpless anger washed over her again until she could have screamed with it. Screamed just one word. *Why?*

"Ariel." Bigby put a hand on her shoulder and repeated her name before Ariel turned her head. Ford and his clients had left. "Come sit down."

She lifted a hand to his. "No, I'm all right."

"Like hell you are."

With a half laugh, she rested her forehead against the glass. "I will be in a minute. Why is it, Charlie, I never believe how hard or how ugly things can be until they happen? And even then— Even then I can't quite understand it."

"Because you look for the best. It's a beautiful talent of yours."

"Or an escape mechanism," she murmured.

"Don't start coming down on yourself, Ariel." His voice was sharper then he'd intended, but he had the satisfaction of seeing her shoulders straighten. "Another of your talents is being able to pull in other people's emotions. Don't do it with the Andersons."

Letting out a long sigh, she continued to stare down to the street. "They're hurting. I wish there was a way we could share the grief instead of hurling it at one other. But there's nothing I can do about them," she whispered and closed her eyes briefly, tightly. "Charlie, Scott doesn't belong with them. He's all I care about. Not once, not one single time did either of them call him by name. He was always the boy, or my grandchild, never Scott. It's as though they can't give him his own identity, maybe because it's too close to Jeremy's." For an extra moment she rested her palms against the window ledge. "I only want what's right for Scott—even if it's not me."

"It's going to go to court, Ariel, and it's going to be very, very hard on you."

"You've explained all that before. It doesn't matter."

"I can't give you any guarantees on the outcome."

She moistened her lips and turned to face him. "I understand that, too. I have to believe that whatever happens will be what's best for Scott. If I lose, I was meant to lose."

"At the risk of being completely unprofessional—" he touched the tips of her hair "—what about what's best for you?"

With a smile, she cupped his face in her hand and kissed his cheek. "I'm a survivor, Charlie, and a whole hell of a lot tougher than I look. Let's worry about Scott."

He was capable of worrying about more than one

thing at a time, and she was still pale, her eyes still a bit too bright. "Let me buy you a drink."

Ariel rubbed her knuckles against his beard. "I'm fine," she said definitely. "And you're busy." Turning, she picked up her purse. Her stomach was quivering. All she wanted to do was to get out in the air and clear her head. "I just need to walk for a bit," she said half to herself. "After I think it all the way through again I'll feel better."

At the door she paused and looked back. Bigby was still standing by the window, a frown of concern on his face. "Can you tell me we have a chance of winning?"

"Yes, I can tell you that. I wish I could tell you more."

Shaking her head, Ariel pulled open the door. "It's enough. It has to be enough."

Chapter 6

Booth considered taking everything he'd written that day and ditching it. That's what sensible people did with garbage. Leaning back in his chair, he scowled at the half-typed sheet staring back at him, and at the stack of completed pages beside his machine. Then again, tomorrow it might not seem quite so much like garbage and he could salvage something.

He couldn't remember the last time he'd hit a wall like this in his work. It was like carving words into granite—slow, laborious, and the finished product was never perfectly clear and sharp. You got sweaty, your muscles and eyes ached, and you barely made a dent. He'd given the script ten hours that day, and perhaps half of that with his full concentration. It was out of character. It was frustrating.

It was Ariel.

What the hell was he going to do about it? Booth ran his hands over his face with a weariness that came from lack of production rather than lack of energy. There'd never been a woman he couldn't block out of his mind for long periods of time—even Liz at the height of their disastrous marriage. But this woman… With a sound of annoyance, Booth pushed away from the typewriter. This woman was breaking all the rules. His rules—the ones he'd formed for personal survival.

The worst of it was he just wanted to be with her. Just to see her smile, hear her laugh, listen to her talk about something that didn't have to make sense.

And the hardest of it was the desire. It shifted and rippled continually under the surface of his thoughts. He had the blessing-curse of a writer's imagination. No effort was needed for Booth to feel the way her skin would heat under his hands, the way her mouth would give and take. And it took no effort to project mentally how she could foul up his life.

Because they'd be working together, he could only avoid her so much. Making love with her was inevitable—so inevitable he knew he'd have to weigh the consequences. But for now, with his rooms quiet around him and thoughts of Ariel crowding his mind, Booth couldn't think beyond having her. Prices always had to be paid…. Who would know that better than he?

Glancing down at his work, Booth admitted that he was already paying. His writing was suffering because he couldn't control his concentration. His pace, usually smooth, was erratic and choppy. What he was producing lacked the polish so integral to his style.

Too often, he caught himself staring into space—something writers do habitually. But it wasn't his characters who worked in his mind. Too often, he found himself awake before dawn after a restless night. But it wasn't his plot that kept him from sleep.

It was Ariel.

He thought of her too much, too exclusively for comfort. And he was a man who hoarded his comfort. His work was always, had always been, of paramount importance to him. He intended it to continue to be. Yet he was allowing someone to interfere, intrude.

Allowing? Booth shook his head as he lit a cigarette. He was a man of words, of shades of meanings, and knew that wasn't the proper one. He hadn't allowed Ariel into his mind—she'd invaded it.

The smoke seared his throat. Too many cigarettes, he admitted as he took another drag. Too many long days and nights. He was pushing it—and there were moments, a few scattered moments when he took the time to wonder why.

Ambition wasn't the issue. Not if ambition equaled the quest for glory and money. Glory had never concerned him, and money had never been a prime motivation. Success perhaps, in that he had always sought then insisted on quality when anything was associated with his name. But it was more a matter of obsession—that was what his writing had been since he'd first put pen to paper.

When a man had one obsession, it was easy to have two. Booth stared at the half-typed page and thought of Ariel.

The doorbell rang twice before he roused himself to answer it. If his work had been flowing at all, he would have ignored it completely. Interruptions, he thought ruefully as he left the littered desk behind, sometimes had their advantages.

"Hi." Ariel smiled at him and kept her hands in her pockets. It was the only way she could keep them from lacing together. "I know I should've called, but I was walking and took the chance that you wouldn't be frantically writing some monumental scene." *You're babbling,* she warned herself and clenched both hands.

"I haven't written a monumental scene in hours." He studied her a moment, perceptive enough to know that beneath the smile and animated voice there was trouble. A week before, perhaps even days before, he'd have made an excuse and shut her out. "Come in."

"I must've caught you at a good time," Ariel commented as she crossed the threshold. "Otherwise you'd've growled at me. Were you working?"

"No, I'd stopped." She looked ready to burst, he mused. The casualness, the glib remarks didn't mask the outpouring of emotion. It showed in her eyes, in her movements. A quick glance showed him that her hands were fists in her pockets. Tension? One didn't associate the word with her. He wanted to touch her, to soothe, and had to remind himself that he didn't need anyone else's problems. "Want a drink?"

"No— Yes," she amended. Perhaps it would calm her more than the two-hour walk had done. "Whatever's handy. It's a beautiful day." Ariel paced to the window and found herself reminded too much of standing in Bigby's office. She turned her back on the view. "Warm. Flowers are everywhere. Have you been out?"

"No." He handed her a dry vermouth without offering her a chair. In this mood he knew she'd never sit still.

"Oh, you shouldn't miss it. Perfect days're rare." She drank, then waited for her muscles to loosen. "I was going to walk through the park, then found myself here."

He waited a moment as she stared down into her glass. "Why?"

Slowly, Ariel lifted her eyes to his. "I needed to be with someone—it turned out to be you. Do you mind?"

He should have. God knows he wanted to. "No." Without thinking, Booth took a step closer—physically, emotionally. "Do you want to tell me about it?"

"Yes." The word came out on a sigh. "But I can't." Turning away, she set down her glass. She wasn't going to level. Why had she been so sure she would? "Booth, it isn't often I can't handle things or find myself so scared that running away looks like the best out. When it happens, I need someone."

He was touching her hair before he could stop himself, was turning her to face him before he'd weighed the pros and cons. And he was holding her before either of them could be surprised by the simplicity of it.

Ariel clung as relief flowed over her. He was strong—strong enough to accept her strength and understand the moments of weakness. She needed that very basic human support, without question, without demands. His chest was hard and firm against her. Over her back his hands ran gently. He said nothing. For the first time in hours, Ariel felt her balance return. Kindness gave her hope; she was a woman who'd always been able to survive on that alone.

What's troubling her, Booth wondered. He could feel the panic in the way her hands gripped him. Even when he felt her begin to relax he remembered that first frantic grip. Her work, he thought. Or something more personal? Either way, it had nothing to do with him. And yet... While she was soft and vulnerable in his arms he felt it had everything to do with him.

He should step back. His lips brushed through her hair as he breathed in her fragrance. It was never safe to lower the wall. His lips skimmed along her temple.

"I want to help you." The words ran through his mind and spilled out before he was aware of them.

Ariel's arms tightened around him. That phrase meant more, infinitely more, than I love you. Without knowing it, he'd just given her everything she needed. "You have." She tilted her head back so that she could see his face. "You are."

Lifting a hand, she ran her fingers over the long firm bones in his face, over the taut skin roughened by a day's growth of beard. Love was something that moved in her too strongly to be ignored. She needed to share it, if not verbally, then by touch.

Softly, slowly, she closed the distance and brushed his lips with hers. Her lids lowered, but through her lashes she watched his eyes as he watched hers. The intensity in his never altered. Ariel knew he was absorbing her mood, and testing it.

It was he who shifted the angle, without increasing the pressure. Easily he toyed with her mouth, nipping into the softness of her bottom lip, tracing the shape with just the tip of his tongue until the flutter in her stomach spread to her chest. He needed to draw in the sensation of her as a woman, as an individual. He wanted to know her physically; he needed to understand the subtleties of her mind. As she felt her body give, her mind yield, Ariel wondered how it was he didn't hear the love shouting out of her.

He was struck by the emotion that raced from her. He'd never held a woman capable of such feeling, or one who, by possessing it, demanded it in return. It wasn't a simple matter of response. Even as his senses began to swim, Booth understood that. He wanted to give to her. And though he wanted, he knew he couldn't. Risks were for the foolish, and he couldn't afford to play the fool a second time.

Compassion, however, touched off compassion. If nothing else, he could give her a few hours' relief from whatever plagued her mind. He ran his hands up her arms for the sheer pleasure of it. "How nice a day is it?" he asked.

Ariel smiled. Her fingers were still on his face, her lips only inches from his. "It's spectacular."

"Let's go out." Booth paused only long enough to take her hand before he headed for the door.

"Thank you." Ariel touched her head briefly to his shoulder in one more simple show of affection he wasn't accustomed to. It warmed him—and cautioned him.

"What for?"

"For not asking questions." Ariel stepped into the elevator, leaned back against the wall and sighed.

"I generally stay out of other people's business."

"Do you?" She opened her eyes and the smile lingered. "I don't. I'm an inveterate meddler—most of us are. We all like to get inside other people. You just do it more subtly than most."

Booth shrugged as the elevator reached lobby level. "It's not personal."

Ariel laughed as she stepped out. Swinging her purse

over her shoulder, she moved in her habitual quick step. "Oh, yes, it is."

He stopped a moment and met the humor in her eyes. "Yes," he admitted. "It is. But then, as a writer I can observe, dissect, steal other people's thoughts and feelings without having to get involved enough to advise or comfort or even sympathize."

"You're too hard on yourself, Booth," Ariel murmured. "Much too hard."

His brow quirked in puzzlement. Of all the things he'd ever been accused of, that wasn't one of them. "I'm a realist."

"On one level. On another you're a dreamer. All writers are dreamers on some level—the same way all actors are children on one. It has nothing to do with how clever you are, how practical, how smart. It goes with the job." She stepped out into the warmth and the sun. "I like being a child, and you like being a dreamer. You just don't like to admit it."

Annoyance. He should've felt annoyance but felt pleasure instead. As long as he could remember, no one else had ever understood him. As long as he could remember, he'd never cared. "You've convinced yourself you know me very well."

"No, but I've made a few scratches in the surface." She sent him a saucy look. "And you've a very tough surface."

"And yours is very thin." Unexpectedly he cupped her face in his hand for a thorough study. His fingers were firm, as if he expected resistance and would ignore it. "Or seems to be." How could he be sure, he wondered. How could one person ever be sure of another?

Ariel was too used to being examined, and already

too used to Booth to be disconcerted. "There's little underneath that doesn't show through."

"Perhaps that's why you're a good actress," he mused. "You absorb the character easily. How much is you, and how much is the role?"

He was far from ready to trust, she realized when he dropped his hand. "I can't answer that. Maybe when the film's over, you'll be able to."

He inclined his head in acknowledgment. It was a good answer—perhaps the best answer. "You wanted to walk in the park."

Ariel tucked her arm companionably through his. "Yeah. I'll buy you an ice cream."

Booth turned his head as they walked. "What flavor?"

"Anything but vanilla," Ariel said expansively. "There's nothing remotely vanilla about today."

She was right, Booth decided. It was a spectacular day. The grass was green, the flowers vivid and pungent. He could smell the park smells. Peanuts and pigeons. Enthusiastic joggers pumped by in colorful sweatbands and running shorts, streaks of sweat down their backs.

Spring would soon give way to early summer. The trees were full, the leaves a hardy shade rather than the tender hue they'd been only weeks before. Shade spread in invitation while the sun baked the benches and paths. He knew Ariel would choose the sun. And he wondered, as he strolled along beside her, why he'd gone so long without seeking it himself.

As Ariel bit into an ice cream confection coated with chocolate and nuts, she thought of Scott. But this time, the apprehension was gone. She'd only needed to lean on someone for a moment, draw on someone else's emotional strength, to have her faith return. Her head was clear again, her nerves gone. With a laugh, she turned into Booth's arms and kissed him hard.

"Ice cream does that to me." She was still laughing as she dropped onto a swing. "And sunshine." She leaned way back and kicked her feet to give herself momentum. The tips of her hair nearly skimmed the ground. It was pale, exquisitely pale in the slanting sun. As it fell back, it left her face unframed and stunning. Her skin was flushed with color as she pushed off again and let herself glide.

"You seem to be an expert." Booth leaned against the frame of the swing as her legs flashed by him.

"Absolutely. Want to join me?"

"I'll just watch."

"It's one of your best things." Ariel threw out her legs again for more height and enjoyed the thrill that swept through her stomach. "When's the last time you were on one of these?"

A memory surged through his mind—of himself at five or six and his primly uniformed, round-faced nanny. She'd pushed him on a swing while he'd squealed and demanded to go higher. At the time he hadn't believed there was any more to life than that rushing pendulum ride. Abruptly, he appreciated Ariel's claim that she enjoyed being a child.

"A hundred years ago," he murmured.

"Too long." Skimming her feet on the ground, she slowed the swing. "Get on with me." She blew the hair out of her eyes and grinned at his blank expression. "You can stand, one foot on either side of me. It's sturdy enough—if you are," she added with just enough of a challenge in the tone to earn a scowl.

"Practicing your psychiatry?"

Her grin only widened. "Is it working?"

She was laughing at him again, and knowing it, Booth took the bait. "Apparently." He stepped behind her to grab the chain with his hands. "How high do you want to go?"

Ariel tipped back her head to give him an upside-down smile. "As high as I can."

"No crying uncle," Booth warned as he began to push her.

"Ha." Ariel tossed back her hair and shifted her grip. "Fat chance, DeWitt."

She felt him jump nimbly onto the swing as they began to fly, then threw her body into it until the rhythm steadied. The sky tilted over her, blue and dusted with clouds. The ground swayed, brown and green. She rested her head against a firm, muscled thigh and let the sensations carry her.

Grass. She could smell it, sun drenched and trampled, mixed with the dusty scent of dry earth. Children's laughter, cooing pigeons, traffic—Ariel could hear each separate sound individually and as a mixture.

The air tasted of spring—sweet, light. An image of a watermelon ran through her mind. Yes, that was what she thought of as the breeze fluttered over her cheeks. But overall, most of all, it was Booth who played with her senses. It was him she felt firmly against her back, his quiet breathing she heard beneath all the other sounds. She could smell him—salt and soap and tobacco. She had only to shift the angle of her head to see his strong, capable hands around the chain of the child's swing. Ariel closed her eyes and absorbed it all. It was like coming home. Content, she slid her hands higher on the chain so that they brushed his. The contact, warm flesh to warm flesh, was enough.

He'd forgotten what it was like to do something for no reason. And by forgetting it, Booth had forgotten the purity of pleasure. He felt it now, without the intellectual justifications he so often restricted himself with. Because he understood that freedom brought vulnerability, he'd doled it out to himself miserly. Only on those rare occasions when he was completely alone, away from responsibilities and his work, had he allowed his heart and mind to drift. Now, it happened so spontaneously he hardly realized it. Bypassing the dangers of relaxation, Booth enjoyed the ride.

"Higher!" Ariel demanded on a breathless laugh as she leaned into the arch. "Much higher!"

"Much higher and you'll land on your nose."

Her sound of pleasure rippled over the air. "Not me. I land on my feet. Higher, Booth!"

When she turned her head up to laugh into his face, he lost himself in her. Beauty—it was there, but not the cool, distant beauty he saw on camera. Looking at her now, he saw nothing of his Rae, nothing of her Amanda. There was only Ariel. For the first time in longer than he cared to remember, he felt a twinge of hope. It scared the hell out of him.

"Faster!" she shouted, not giving him any time to dwell on what was happening inside him. Her laughter was infectious, as was her enthusiasm. They soared together until his arms ached. When the swing began to slow, she leaped from it and left him wobbling.

"Oh, that was wonderful." Still laughing, Ariel

turned in a circle, arms wide. "Now I'm starving. Absolutely starving."

"You just had ice cream." Booth leaped off the swing to find himself breathless and his blood pumping.

"Not good enough." Ariel whirled around to him and linked her hands behind his head. "I need a hot dog—really need a hot dog with everything."

"A hot dog." Because it seemed so natural, he bent to kiss her. Her mouth was warm, the lips curved. "Do you know what they put in those things?"

"No. And I don't want to. I want to stuff myself with whatever nasty stuff it has in it and feel wonderful."

Booth ran his hands down her sides. "You do feel wonderful."

Her smile changed, softened. "That's about the nicest thing you've ever said to me. Kiss me again, right here, while I'm still flying."

Booth drew her closer as his lips tasted hers. Fleetingly he wondered why the gentle kiss moved him equally as much as the passion had yet somehow differently. He wanted her. And along with her body he wanted that energy, that verve, the joie de vivre. He wanted to explore and measure it, and to test it for its genuineness. Booth was still far from sure that anyone in the world he knew could be quite so real. And yet, he was beginning to want to believe it.

Drawing her away he watched her lashes flutter up, her lips curve. But he remembered that sense of panic he'd felt from her when he'd first opened his door. If her emotions were as vibrant as they seemed, she wouldn't be limited to joy and vivacity.

"A hot dog," he repeated and speculated on how

much he would learn of her and how long it would take. "It's your stomach, but I'll spring for it."

"I knew you could be a sport, Booth." She slipped her arm around his waist as they walked. "I just might have two."

"Masochistic tendencies run in your family?"

"No, just gluttony. Tell me about yours."

"I don't have masochistic tendencies."

"Your family," she corrected, chuckling. "They must be very proud of you."

His brow lifted while a ghost of a smile played around his mouth. "That depends on your point of view. I was supposed to follow family tradition and go into law. Throughout most of my twenties I was the black sheep."

"Is that so?" Tilting her head, she studied him with fresh interest. "I can't imagine it. I've always had a fondness for black sheep."

"I would've made book on it," Booth said dryly. "But one might say I've been accepted back into the fold in the past few years."

"It was the Pulitzer that did it."

"The Oscar didn't hurt," Booth admitted, seeing the humor in something he'd barely noticed before. "But the Pulitzer had more clout with the DeWitts of Philadelphia."

Ariel scented the hot dog stand and guided him toward it. "You'll be adding an Emmy to the list next year."

He pulled out his wallet as Ariel leaned over the stand and breathed deeply. "You're very confident."

"It's the best way to be. Are you having one?"

The scent was too good to resist. When had he eaten

last? What had he eaten? Booth shrugged the thoughts way. "I suppose."

Ariel grinned and held up two fingers to the concessionaire. When hers was in its bun she began to go through the condiments one at a time. "You know, Booth—" she piled on relish "—*The Rebellion* was brilliant, clean, hard-hitting, exquisite characterizations, but it wasn't as entertaining as your *Misty Tuesday.*"

Booth watched her take the first hefty bite. "My purpose in writing isn't always to entertain."

"No, I understand that." Ariel chewed thoughtfully, then accepted the soda Booth offered her. "It's just my personal preference. That's why I'm in the profession. I want to be entertained, and I need to entertain."

He added a conservative line of mustard to his hot dog. "That's why you've been satisfied with daytime drama."

She shot him a look as they began to walk again. "Don't get snide. Quality entertainment's the core of it. If I was handy juggling plates and riding a unicycle, that's what I'd do."

After the first bite, Booth realized the hot dog was the best thing he'd eaten in a week, perhaps in months. "You have a tremendous talent," he told her, but didn't notice the surprised lift of her brow at the ease of the compliment. "It's difficult for me to understand why you aren't doing major films or theater. A series, even a weekly series is dragging, backbreaking work. Being a major character in a show that airs five days a week has to be exhausting, impossible and frustrating."

"Exactly why I do it." She licked mustard from her thumb. "I was raised right here in Manhattan. The pace's in my blood. Have you ever considered why L.A. and New York are on opposite ends of the continent?"

"A lucky geographical accident."

"Fate," Ariel corrected. "Both might be towns where show business is of top importance, but no two cities could have more opposing paces. I'd go crazy in California—mellow isn't my speed. I like doing the soap because it's a daily challenge, it keeps me sharp. And when there's the time and the opportunity, I like doing things like *Streetcar*. But…" She finished off her hot dog with a sigh. "Doing the same play night after night becomes too easy, and you get too comfortable."

He drank down cola—a flavor he'd nearly forgotten. "You've been playing the same character for five years."

"Not the same thing." She crunched an ice cube and enjoyed the shock of cold. "Soaps're full of surprises. You never know what kind of angle they're going to throw at you to pump up ratings or lead in a fresh story line." She scooted around a middle-aged matron walking a poodle. "Right now Amanda's facing a crumbling marriage and a personal betrayal, the possibility of an abortion and a rekindling of an old affair. Not dull stuff. And though it's top secret, I'll tell you she's going to work with the police on a profile of the Trader's Bend Ripper."

"The what?"

"As in Son of Jack the Ripper," she said mildly. "Her former lover Griff's the number-one suspect."

"Doesn't it ever bother you that so much melodrama goes on in a small town with four or five connecting families?"

She stopped to look at him. "Do you know your Coleridge?"

"Passably."

"'The willing suspension of disbelief.'" Ariel crumbled her napkin, then tossed both it and her empty cup into a trash can. "It's all that's necessary to get along in this world. Believe it might happen, it could happen. Plausibility's all that's necessary. As a writer, you should know that."

"Perhaps I should. I've always leaned more toward reality."

"If it works for you." The lift of her shoulders seemed to indicate that all was accepted. "But sometimes it's easier to believe in coincidence, or magic or simple luck. Straight reality without any detours is a very hard road."

"I've had a few detours," he murmured. It occurred to him that Ariel Kirkwood had already led him off the paved road he'd adhered to for years. Booth began to wonder just where her twisting direction would lead them. Lost in thought, he didn't notice that they were in front of his building until she stopped. His work was waiting, his privacy, his solitude. He wanted none of it.

"Come up with me."

The request was simple, the meaning clear. And her need was huge. Shaking her head, Ariel touched the hair that had fallen over his forehead. "No, it's best that I don't."

He took her hand before she could drop it back to her side. "Why? I want you, you want me."

If it were only so simple, she thought as the desire to love him grew and grew. But she knew, instinctively, that it wouldn't be simple, not for either of them once begun. For him there was too much distrust, for her too many vulnerabilities.

"Yes, I want you." Ariel saw the change in his eyes

and knew it would be much more difficult to walk away than to go with him. "And if I came upstairs, we'd make love. Neither of us is ready for that, Booth, not with each other."

"If it's a game you're playing to make me want you more, it's hardly necessary."

She drew her hand from his and stood on her own. "I like to play games," she said quietly. "And I'm very good at most of them. Not this kind."

Pulling out a cigarette, he lit it with a snap of his lighter. "I've no patience for the wine and candlelight routine, Ariel."

He saw the humor light in her eyes and could have cursed her. "How lucky that I don't have a need for them." Putting her hands on his shoulders, she leaned forward and kissed him. "Think of me," she requested and turned quickly to walk away.

As he stared after her, Booth knew he'd think of little else.

Chapter 7

It was going to be hard work, with long days, short nights and constant demands on both the body and the mind. Ariel was going to love every minute of it.

The producers of the soap were cooperating fully with Marshell; the network strategy was to everyone's advantage. The word, the big word, was always *ratings*. But it was Ariel who had to squeeze in the time for both projects, and Ariel who had to learn hundreds of pages of script as Amanda and as Rae.

Under different circumstances they might have simply written around her for a few weeks on *Our Lives, Our Loves,* but with Amanda and Griff's relationship heating up and the Ripper on the prowl, it wasn't possible. Amanda had a key role in too many vital scenes. So instead, Ariel had to shoot a backbreaking number of those scenes in a short period of time. This would give her three straight weeks to concentrate exclusively on the film. If that project ran behind schedule, she'd have to compensate by dividing her time and energies between Amanda and Rae.

The idea of eighteen-hour days and 5:00 a.m. calls couldn't dull her enthusiasm. The pace, merciless as it was, was almost natural to her in any case. And it helped keep her mind off the custody trial, which was set for the following month.

And there was Booth. Even the idea of working with him excited her. The daily contact would be stimulating. The professional competition and cooperation would keep her sharp. The preproduction stages had shown her that Booth would be as intimately involved with the film as any member of the cast and crew—and that he had unquestioned authority.

Throughout the sometimes hysterical meetings, he'd remained calm and had said little. But when he spoke, he was rarely questioned. It wasn't a matter of arrogance or overbearing, as Ariel saw it. Booth DeWitt simply didn't comment unless he knew he was right.

Perhaps, if it was meant to be, they'd move closer to each other as the film progressed. Emotion. It was what she wanted to give him, and what she needed from him. Time. She knew it was a major factor in whatever happened between them. Trust. This above all was needed—and this, above all, was missing.

There were times during the preproduction stages of the filming that Ariel felt Booth watching her too objectively, and distancing himself from her too successfully.

Ariel found herself at an impasse. The more skillfully she played Rae, the more firmly Booth stepped back from her. She understood it, and was helpless to change it.

The set was elegant, the lighting low and seductive. Across a small rococo table, Rae and Phil shared lobster bisque and champagne. Ariel's costume was clinging midnight silk. Diamonds and sapphires winked at her ears and throat. An armed guard in the studio attested to the fact that paste wasn't used on a Marshell production.

The intimate late-night supper was actually taking place at 8:00 a.m. in the presence of a full crew. Sipping lukewarm ginger ale from a tulip glass, Ariel gave a husky laugh and leaned closer to Jack.

She knew what was needed here—sex, raw and primitive under a thin sheen of sophistication. It would have to leap onto the screen with a gesture, a look, a smile, rather than through dialogue. She was playing a role within a role. Rae was her character, and Rae was never without a mask. Tonight, she would project a warmth, a soft femininity that was no more than a facade. It was Ariel's job to show both this, and the skill with which Rae played the part. If the actress Ariel portrayed wasn't clever, the impact on the character of Phil would waver. The connection between the two was vital. They fed each other, and by doing so, the entire story.

Rae wanted Phil, and the viewer had to know that she wanted him physically nearly as much as she wanted the connections he could bring her professionally. To win him, she had to be what he wanted. Ambition and skill were a deadly combination when added to beauty. Rae had all three and the capacity to use them. It was Ariel's job to show the duality of her nature, but to show it subtly.

The scene would end in the bedroom; that portion of the film would be shot at a different time. Now, the tension and the sexuality had to be heightened to a point where both Phil and the audience were completely seduced.

"Cut!"

Chuck ran a hand over the back of his neck and lapsed into silence. Both the actors and crew recognized the gesture from their director and remained silent and alert. The scene wasn't pleasing him, and he was working out why. Keyed up, Ariel didn't allow the tension to drain out of her. She needed the nerves to maintain the image of Rae. The sight of the ginger ale and the scent of the food in front of her made her stomach roll uneasily. They were already on the fourth take. Objectively, she watched her glass being refilled, her plate replaced. When this was over, she thought, she'd never even look at a glass of ginger ale again.

"Disgusting, isn't it?"

Glancing over, Ariel saw Jack Rohrer grimace at her. She locked Rae in a compartment of her brain before she grinned at him. "I've never wanted a cup of coffee and a bagel so much in my life."

"Please." He leaned back from the table. "Don't mention real food."

"More feline," Chuck said abruptly and focused on Ariel. "That's how I see Rae—a sleek black cat with manicured claws."

Ariel smiled at the image. Yes, that was Rae.

"When you say the line, 'One night won't be enough, you make me greedy,' you should practically purr it."

Ariel nodded while she flexed her hands. Yes, Rae would purr that line, while she calculated every angle.

Ariel had a mental image of a cat—glossy, seductive and just this side of evil.

Just before the clapper was struck for the next take, Ariel caught Booth's eye. He was frowning at her while he stood off camera. Though his hands were casually in his pockets and his expression was still and calm, she sensed the wall of tension around him. Unable to break it down, she used it and the eye contact to pull herself back into character.

As the scene unfolded, she forgot the flat, warm taste of the ginger ale, forgot the intrusion of cameras and crew. Her attention was completely focused on the man across from her, who was no longer a fellow actor but an intended victim. She smiled at something he said, a smile Booth recognized too well. Seductive as black lace, cold as ice. There wasn't a man alive who'd be immune to it.

When she reached the line Chuck had focused on, Ariel paused a beat, dipping her fingertip into Jack's glass, then slowly touched the dampened skin to her mouth, then his. The seductive ad lib had the temperature on the set soaring. Even while he mentally approved the gesture and Ariel's intuition, Booth felt his stomach muscles tighten.

She knew her character, he mused, almost as well as he did himself. So well, it was always an effort to separate them in his mind. This attraction that plagued him—at whom was it directed? That surge of jealousy he felt unexpectedly when the woman on set melted into another man's arms—for whom did he really feel it? He'd entwined reality and fiction so tightly in this script, then had chosen an actress skilled enough to blur those lines. Now, he found himself trapped between fiction and fact. Was the woman he wanted the shadow or the light?

"Cut! Cut and print! Fantastic." Grinning from ear to ear, Chuck walked over and kissed both Ariel and Jack. "We're lucky the camera didn't overload on that scene."

Jack flashed a white-toothed smile. "You're lucky I didn't. You're damn good." Jack laid a hand on Ariel's shoulder. "So damn good I'm going to have a cup of coffee and call my wife."

"Ten minutes," Chuck announced. "Set up for reaction shots. Booth, what'd you think?"

"Excellent." With his eyes on Ariel, Booth walked toward them. There was nothing of the cat about her now. If anything, she looked a bit weary. He found that while the knot in his stomach had loosened, he had to fight the urge to stroke her cheek. Booth was more accustomed to the first sensation. "You look like you could use some coffee yourself."

"Yeah." Again, Ariel forced herself to lock Rae's personality away. She wanted nothing more than to relax completely, but knew she could only allow herself a few degrees. "You buying?"

Nodding, he led her off set where a catering table was already set up with coffee, doughnuts and Danishes. Ariel's stomach revolted at the thought of food, but she took the steaming Styrofoam cup in both hands.

"This schedule's difficult," Booth commented.

"Mmm." She shrugged that off and let the coffee wash away the aftertaste of ginger ale. "No, the schedule's no tighter than the soap's—lighter in some ways. The scene was difficult."

He lifted a brow. "Why?"

The scent of the coffee was real and solid. Ariel

could almost forget the spongy food she'd had to nibble on for the past two hours. "Because Phil's smart and cautious—not an easy man to seduce or to fool. Rae has to do both, and she's in a hurry." She glanced over the rim of her cup. "But then, you know that."

"Yes." He took her wrist before she could drink again. "You look tired."

"Only between takes." She smiled, touched by the reluctant concern. "Don't worry about me, Booth. Frantic's my natural pace."

"There's something else."

She thought of Scott. It's not supposed to show, she reminded herself. The minute you walk into the studio, it's not supposed to show. "You're perceptive," she murmured. "A writer's first tool."

"You're stalling."

Ariel shook her head. If she thought about it now, too deeply, her control would begin to slip. "It's something I have to deal with. It won't interfere with my work."

He took her chin firmly into his hand. "Does anything?"

For the first time, Ariel felt a threat of pure anger run through her. "Don't confuse me with a role, Booth—or another woman." She pushed his hand away, then turning her back on him, walked back onto the set.

The temper pleased him, perhaps because it was easier to trust negative emotions. Leaning back against the wall, Booth made a decision. He was going to have her—tonight. It would ease a portion of the tension in him and alleviate the wondering. Then both of them, in their own way, would have to deal with the consequences.

Ariel found the anger was an advantage. Rae, she

mused, was a woman who had anger simmering just below the surface at all times. It added to the discontent, and the ambition. Instead of trying to rid herself of it—something she wasn't certain she could do in any case—Ariel used it to add more depth to an already complicated character. As long as she clung to Rae's mercurial, demanding personality, she didn't feel her own weariness or frustrations.

True, her senses were keen enough so that she knew exactly where Booth was and where his attention was focused even when she was in the middle of a scene. That was something to be dealt with later. The more he pushed at her—mentally, emotionally—the more she was determined to give a stellar performance.

By six and wrap time, Ariel discovered that Rae had drained her. Her body ached from the hours of standing under the lights. Her mind reeled from the repetition of lines, the drawing and releasing of emotions. It was only the first week of filming, and already she felt the strain of the marathon.

Nobody said it'd be easy, Ariel reminded herself as she slipped into her dressing room to change into her street clothes. And it wouldn't be nearly so important if it were. The trouble was, she was beginning to equate her success in the part with her success in her relationship with Booth. If she could pull one off, she could do the same with the other.

Shaking her head, Ariel stripped out of her costume, shedding Rae as eagerly as she did the silk. An idea like that, she reminded herself, had a very large trapdoor. Rae was a part to be acted, no matter how entangled it was with reality. Booth was real life—her life. No matter how willing she was to take risks or accept a challenge, that was something she couldn't afford to forget.

Gratefully, Ariel creamed off her stage makeup and let her skin breathe. She sat, propping her feet on her dressing table so that the short kimono she wore skimmed her thighs. Taking her time, letting herself come down, she undid the sleek knot the hairdresser had arranged and let her hair fall free. With a contented sigh, Ariel tipped her head back, shut her eyes and fell into a half doze.

That was how Booth found her.

The room was cluttered in her usual fashion so that she seemed to be a single island of calm. The air was assaulted with scents—powder, face cream, the same potpourri just hinting of lilac that she kept at home. The lights around her mirror were glaring. Her breathing was soft and even.

As he shut the door behind him, Booth let his gaze run up the long slender length of her legs, exposed from toe to thigh. The kimono was loosely, almost carelessly knotted, so that it gaped intriguingly down the center of her body nearly to the waist. Her hair fell behind the chair, mussed from her own hands so that the curve of neck and shoulder made an elegant contrast.

Her face seemed a bit pale without the color needed for the camera…fragile. Without it, the faintest of shadows could be seen under her eyes.

Booth wanted almost painfully to possess her, just as she was at that moment. With hardly a thought as to what he was doing, he turned the lock on the door. He sat on the arm of a chair, lit a cigarette and waited.

Ariel woke slowly. She tended to sleep quickly and wake gradually. Even before she'd drifted from that twilight world to consciousness, she knew she was refreshed. The nap had been no more than ten minutes. Any longer and she'd have been groggy, any shorter, tense. With a sigh, she started to stretch. Then she sensed she wasn't alone. Curious, she turned her head and looked at Booth.

"Hello."

He saw no remnants of the anger in her eyes, nor was there any coolness, that sign of resentment, in her voice. Even the weariness he'd sensed in her briefly had vanished. "You didn't sleep long." His cigarette had burned down nearly to the filter without his noticing. He crushed it out. "Though I don't know anyone who could've slept at all in that position."

"For a ten-minute session, I can sleep anywhere." She pointed her toes, tensing all her muscles, then released them. "I had to recharge."

"A decent meal would help."

Ariel put a hand to her stomach. "It wouldn't hurt."

"You barely touched anything at lunch."

It didn't surprise her that he'd noticed, only that he'd commented on it. "Normally I'd have gorged myself. Eating lobster bisque at dawn threw my whole system out of whack. A bagel's more my style. Or a bowl of Krispie Krinkies."

"Of what?"

"Eight essential vitamins," she said with a half grin. Reluctantly, she slid her feet to the floor. The gap in her robe shifted, and absently she tugged at the lapels. "We are wrapped for the day, aren't we? There isn't a problem?"

"We wrapped," he agreed. "And there's a problem."

The brush she'd lifted paused halfway to her hair. "What kind?"

"Personal." He rose and took the brush from her hand. "Every day this week I've watched you, listened to you, smelled you. And every day this week, I've wanted you." He took the brush through her hair in one long, smooth stroke while in the lighted mirror, his eyes met hers. When she didn't move, he drew the brush down again, cupping the curve of her shoulder with his free hand. "You asked me to think of you. I have."

Too close to the surface, Ariel warned herself. Her emotions were always too close to the surface. There was nothing she could do about it. "Every day this week," she began in a voice that was already husky, "you've watched me and listened to me be someone else. You might be wanting someone else."

His eyes remained on hers as he lowered his mouth to her ear. "I'm not watching anyone else now."

Her heart lurched. Ariel would have sworn she felt the jerk of movement inside her breast. "Tomorrow—"

"The hell with tomorrow." Booth let the brush drop as he drew her to her feet. "And yesterday." His gaze was intense, a hot, hot green that had her throat going dry. She'd wondered what it would be like if he allowed any emotion freedom. This was his passion, and it was going to sweep her away.

If she hadn't loved him... But, of course, she did. All caution whipped away as her mouth met his. There was a time for thinking, and a time for feeling. There was a time for withholding, and a time for giving freely. There was a time for reason, and a time for romance.

All that Ariel had, all that she felt, thought, wished, went into the touch of mouth to mouth. And as her body followed her heart, she wrapped herself around him and offered unconditionally. She felt the floor tilt and the air freeze before she became lost in her own longings. Her lips parted, inviting; her tongue touched, arousing. Her breath fluttered, answering.

She was firm, as he was, yet softer. Feeling the hard length of man against her, she became completely, utterly feminine. The pleasure was liquid, passing through her as warmed wine. As his grip tightened, she melted further until she was as pliant as any man's fantasy. But she was very real.

He'd never known another woman like her, so utterly free with emotions that flowed and crested until he was drowning in them. Passion had been expected and was there, but… More, infinitely more, was a range of feeling so intense, so sweet, it was irresistible.

As he'd watched her on the set, he'd wanted her. When he'd come into the room to see her sleeping, desire had assaulted him. Now, with her yielding, vibrating with emotions he could hardly name, Booth needed her as he'd never needed anyone. And had never wanted to.

Too late. The thought ran through his mind that it was too late for her—too late for him. Then his hands were buried in her hair, his thoughts a kaleidoscope of sensations.

She smelled faintly of lemon from the cream she'd used on her face, while her hair carried the familiar fragrance of light sexuality. The thin material of her kimono swished as his hands parted it to find her. And she was softer than a dream, but so small he had a moment's fear that he would hurt her. Then her body arched, pressing against his hand so that it was her

strength that aroused him. With a sound that was more
of surrender than triumph, he buried his face against
her throat.

Even while her mind was floating, Ariel knew she
had to feel the texture of his flesh against hers. Slowly,
her hands ran up his sides, drawing up his sweater. She
followed the movement, over his shoulders, until there
was nothing barring her exploration—and nothing to
stop her sensitized skin from meeting his.

When he drew her down she went willingly. As her
back rested against the littered sofa, she cupped her
hands behind his head and brought his mouth back to
hers. The taste of his passion rippled through her and
lit the next spark.

Not so passive now, not so pliant, she moved under
him, sending off twinges of excitement to pulse through
both of them. The sudden aggression of her lips was
welcome. The kiss went on and on, deeper, moister,
while two pairs of hands began to test and appreciate.

He could feel the frantic beat of her heart under his
palm. When he pressed his lips against her breast, he
felt her shudder. The outrageous desire to absorb her
ran through him as he began to draw in her variety of
tastes, now with his lips, now with the tip of his tongue.
Sometimes, some places, it was hot, others sweet, but
always it was Ariel.

The lights glared into the room, reflecting from the
mirror as he began a thorough, intense journey over her.
The curve of her shoulder held fascinations he'd never
known before. The skin at the inside of her wrist was
so delicate he almost thought he could hear the blood
run through the veins. Everywhere he touched, he felt

her pulse. She was so giving. That alone was enough to make his head swim.

And as he touched, tasted, took, so did she. If he became more demanding, she responded in kind, keeping pace with him. Or perhaps it was he who kept pace with her. She stroked with those long, elegant fingers so that he knew what it was to be on the verge of madness, and within sight of heaven.

She wanted nothing more than what she could find in him. Touches of tenderness that moved her. Flares of fires that tormented her. His hair brushed over her skin and that alone excited her. Flesh grew damp with passion and the struggle to control—the struggle to prolong. Ariel learned that pleasure alone was a shallow thing; but pleasure, when combined with love, was all.

Together, they understood that there could be no more waiting. The final barriers of clothing were tugged impatiently away. She opened for him. Madness and heaven became one.

Ariel felt as though she could run for miles. Her body was alive with so many sensations. Her mind leaped with them. She lay beneath Booth, tingling with an awareness that radiated down to her toes and fingertips. With her eyes closed, her body still aligned with his, she counted his heartbeats as they thudded against her. In that private, liquid world they'd gone to, Booth hadn't been calm, he hadn't been detached. Letting her lashes flutter up, she smiled. His hand was laced with hers. She wondered if he were aware of it. He'd wanted her. Just her.

Contentment. Was that what he was feeling? Booth lay sated, drained, aware only of Ariel's warm, slim form beneath him. As far as he could remember, he'd never experienced anything remotely like this. Total relaxation…a complete lack of tension. He didn't even have the energy to dissect the feeling, and instead enjoyed it. With a sound of pure pleasure, he turned his face in to her throat. He felt as well as heard her gurgle of laughter.

"Funny?" he murmured.

Ariel ran her hands up the length of his back, then down again to his waist. "I feel good. So good." Her fingertips skimmed over his hips. "So do you."

Shifting slightly, Booth raised himself on one elbow so that he could look at her. Her eyes were laughing. With a fingertip he traced the spot just below her jaw where he'd discovered delectable, sensitive skin. "I still don't know what I'm doing with you."

She brushed the hair from his forehead and watched it fall back again. "Do you always have to have an intellectual reason?"

He frowned, but his fingers spread over her face as if he were blind and memorizing it. "I always have."

She wanted to sigh but smiled instead. Taking his face in her hands, Ariel brought him down for a hard kiss. "I defy the intellect."

That made him laugh, and because he was off balance, she was able to roll him over. With her body slanted across his, she stretched and nuzzled into his shoulder. Booth felt the crinkle of paper and the rumple of cloth beneath him. "What am I lying on?"

"Mmm. This and that."

Arching, he pulled a crumpled pamphlet from under his left hip. "Anyone ever mention that you're sloppy?"

"From time to time."

Absently, Booth glanced at the pamphlet about the plight of baby seals before he dropped it to the floor. He tugged at another paper stuck to his right shoulder. A halfway house for battered wives. Curiosity piqued, he twisted a bit and found another. ASPCA literature.

"Ariel, what is all this?"

She gave his shoulder a last nibble before she rested her cheek on it. He held several wrinkled leaflets. "I suppose you might call it my hobby."

"Hobby?" He put his free hand under her chin to lift it. "Which one?"

"All of them."

"All?" Booth looked at the leaflets in his hand again and wondered how many others were squashed beneath him. "You mean you're actively involved in all these organizations?"

"Yeah. More or less."

"Ariel, no one person would have the time."

"Oh, no." She shifted, folding her arms across his chest for support. "That's a cop-out. You make time." She tilted her head toward the papers he held. "Those baby seals, do you know what's done to them, how it's done?"

"Yes, but—"

"And those abused women. Most of them come into that shelter without any self-esteem, without any emotional or financial support. Then there's—"

"Wait a minute." He let the papers slide to the floor so he could take her shoulders. How slim they were, he realized abruptly. And how easily she could make him forget just how delicately she was formed. "I understand all that, but how can you be involved in all these causes, run your life and pursue your career?"

She smiled. "There're twenty-four hours in every day. I don't like to waste any of them."

Seeing that she was perfectly serious, Booth shook his head. "You're a remarkable woman."

"No." Ariel bent her head and kissed his chin. It dipped slightly in the center—not quite a cleft. "I just have a lot of energy. I need to put it somewhere."

"You could put all of it into furthering your career," he pointed out. "You'd be top box office within six months. There'd be no question of your success."

"Maybe. But I wouldn't be happy with it."

"Why?"

It was back; she felt it. The doubts, the distrust. With a sigh, Ariel sat up. In silence, she picked up her kimono and pulled it on. How quickly warmth could turn to chill. "Because I need more."

Dissatisfied, Booth took her arm. "More what?"

"More everything!" she said with a sudden passion that stunned him. "I need to know I've done my best, and not just in one area of my life. Do you really think I'm so limited?"

The fire in her eyes intrigued him. "I believe what I said indicated your lack of limitations."

"Professionally," she snapped. "I'm a person first. I need to know I touched someone, helped somehow." She dragged both hands through her hair in frustration. "I need to know I cared. Success isn't just a little gold statue for my trophy case, Booth." Whirling, she yanked open the door of her closet and pulled out her street clothes.

As Booth sat up, the papers beneath him rustled. "You're angry."

"Yes, yes, yes!" With her back to him, Ariel wrig-gled into her briefs. In the mirror, Booth could see the reflected temper on her face.

"Why?"

"Your favorite question." Ariel flung the kimono to the floor, then dragged a short-sleeved sweatshirt over her head. "Well, I'll give you the answer, and you're not going to like it. You still equate me with her." She flung the words at him; as they hit, he too began to dress. "Still," she continued, "even after what just happened between us, you still measure me by her."

"Maybe." He rose and drew his sweater over his head. "Maybe I do."

Ariel stared at him a moment, then stepped into her jeans. "It hurts."

Booth stood very still as the two words sliced into him. He hadn't expected them—their simplicity, their honesty. He hadn't expected his own reaction to them. "I'm sorry," he murmured.

Stepping closer, he touched her arm and waited for her to look up at him. The hurt was in her eyes, and he knew it was the second time he'd put it there. "I've never been a particularly fair man, Ariel."

"No," she agreed. "But it's hard for me to believe that someone so intelligent could be so narrow-minded."

He waited for his own anger to rise, and when it didn't, shook his head. "Maybe it's simplest to say you weren't in my plans."

"I think that's clear." Turning away, she began to brush her hair methodically. Hurt pulsed from her still, laced with anger. It never occurred to her to rely on pride and conceal them both. "I told you before that I tend to rush into things. I also understand that not everyone keeps the same pace. But I'd think by this time you'd see that I'm not the character you created—or the woman who inspired her."

"Ariel." She stiffened when he took her shoulders. He could see her fingers flex on the brush handle. "Ariel," he said again and lowered his brow to the top of her head. Why did he want so much what he'd cut himself off from? "I'll hurt you again," he said quietly. "I'm bound to hurt you if I continue to see you."

Her body relaxed on a sigh. Why was she fighting the inevitable? "Yes, I know."

"And knowing that, knowing what you could do to my own life, I don't want to stop seeing you."

She reached up to cover the hand on her shoulder with her own. "But you don't know why."

"No, I don't know why."

Ariel turned in his arms and held him. For a moment they stood close, her head on his shoulder, his hands at her waist. "Buy me dinner," she requested, then tipped back her head and smiled at him. "I'm starving. I want to be with you. Those are two definite facts. We'll just take the rest as it comes."

He'd been right to call her remarkable, Booth thought. He pressed his lips to her brow. "All right. What would you like to eat?"

"Pizza with mushrooms," she answered immediately. "And a cheap bottle of Chianti."

"Pizza."

"A huge one—with mushrooms."

With a half laugh he tightened his hold. He was no longer sure he could let go. "It sounds like a good start."

Chapter 8

At 7:00 a.m., Ariel sat in a makeup chair, with a huge white drop cloth covering her costume, going over her lines while a short, fussy-handed man with thinning hair slanted blusher over her cheekbones. She could hear, but paid no attention to, the buzz of activity around her. Someone shouted for gel for the lights. A coil of cable was dropped to the floor with a thud. Ariel continued to read.

The upcoming scene was a difficult one, with something perilously close to a soliloquy in the middle. If she didn't get the rhythm just right, the pitch perfect, the entire mood would be spoiled.

And her own mood wasn't helping her concentration.

She'd had another lovely Sunday with Scott, which had ended with a tense and tearful departure. Though she'd long ago resigned herself to the fact that she was a creature of emotional highs and lows, Ariel couldn't rid herself of the despondency or the nagging sense of guilt.

Scott had clung to her, with great, silent tears running down his cheeks, when she'd returned him to the Andersons' home in Larchmont. It was the first time in all the months since his parents' death that he'd created a scene at the end of their weekly visit. The Andersons had met his tears with grim, tight-lipped impatience while both had cast accusing glares at Ariel.

After she'd soothed him, Ariel had wondered all during the lengthy train ride home if she'd unconsciously brought on the scene. By wanting him so badly, was she encouraging him to want her? Did she spoil him? Was she overcompensating because of her love for his father and her pain in the loss?

She'd spent a sleepless night over it, and the questions had built and pressed on her. But there'd been no firm answers in the morning. Within a few weeks, she'd have to live with the decision of a judge who would see Scott as a minor rather than as a little boy who liked to play pretend games. Could a judge, however experienced, however fair, see the heart of a child? It was one more question that kept her awake at night.

Now, Ariel knew she had to put her personal business aside. Her part in the film was more than a job; it was a responsibility. Both the cast and the crew depended on her to do her best. Her name on the contract guaranteed she would give all her skill. And, she reminded herself as she rubbed an aching temple, worrying wasn't going to help Scott.

"My dear, if you continue to fidget, you'll spoil what I've already done."

Bringing herself back, Ariel smiled at the makeup man. "Sorry, Harry. Am I beautiful?"

"Almost exquisite." He pursed his lips as he touched up her brows. The natural arch, he thought with professional admiration, needed very little assistance from him. "For this scene, you should look like Dresden. Just a little more here...." Ariel sat obediently while he smoothed more color into her lips. "And I'll have to insist that there be no more frowning. You'll spoil my work."

Surprised, Ariel met his eyes. She'd been sure she'd had her expression, if not her thoughts, under control. Foolish, she decided, then reminded herself that problems were to be left on the other side of the studio door. That was the first rule of showmanship.

"No more frowns," she promised. "I can't be responsible for spoiling a masterpiece."

"Well, nothing changes. Still cramming before zero hour."

"Stella!" Ariel glanced up and broke into the first true smile of the day. "What're you doing here?"

"Taking a busman's holiday." Stella dropped into the chair beside Ariel, pulling up her legs, then folding them under her. "I used your name—and some charm," she added with a sweep of her lashes, "to get in. You don't mind if I watch the morning's shooting, do you?"

"Of course not. How're things at Trader's Bend?"

"Heating up, love, heating up." With a wicked smile, Stella tossed her thick mane of hair behind her shoulder. "Now that Cameron's trying to blackmail Vikki over her gambling debts, and the Ripper's claimed his third victim, *and* Amanda and Griff are starting to simmer, they can't keep up with the mail or the phone calls.

Rumor is *Tube* wants to do a two-part spread on the cast. That's big time."

Ariel's brow quirked. "Cover story?"

"That's what I hear through the grapevine. Hey, I got stopped in the market the other day. A woman named Ethel Bitterman gave me a lecture on moral standing and family loyalty over the cucumbers."

Laughing, Ariel drew off her protective drape to reveal a frothy, raspberry-colored sundress. This was what she'd needed, she realized. That sense of camaraderie and family. "I've missed you, Stella."

"Me, too. But tell me...." Stella's gaze skimmed up the dress that, while demure and feminine, reeked of sex. "How does it feel to be playing the bad girl for a change?"

Ariel's eyes lit up. "It's wonderful, but it's tough. It's the toughest part I've ever played."

Stella smiled and buffed her nails on her sleeve. "You always claimed I had all the fun."

"I might've been right," Ariel countered. "And I may've oversimplified. But I don't remember ever working harder than this."

Stella rested her chin on her hand. "Why?"

"I guess because Rae's always playing a part. It's like trying to get inside a half dozen personalities and make them one person."

"And you're eating it up," Stella observed.

"I guess I am." With a quick laugh she settled back. "Yeah, I am. One day I'll feel absolutely drained, and the next so wired..." She shrugged and set her script aside. If she didn't know her lines by now, she never would. "In any case, I know if I have a choice, when this is over, I'd like to do a comedy. A Judy Holliday type. Something full of fun and wackiness."

"What about Jack Rohrer?" Stella dug in her purse and found a dietary lemon drop. "What's he like to work with?"

"I like him." Ariel smiled ruefully. "But he doesn't make it a picnic. He's a perfectionist—like everyone else on this film."

"And the illustrious Booth DeWitt?"

"Watches everything," Ariel murmured.

"Including you." Moving only her eyes, Stella changed the focus of her attention. "At least he has been for the past ten minutes."

Ariel didn't have to turn her head. She already knew. In her mind's eye she could see him, standing a bit apart from the grips and gaffers as they checked the lighting and the set. He'd remove himself from the activity so as not to interfere with the flow, but his presence would be felt by everyone. And that presence alone would make everyone just tense enough to be sharp.

She knew he'd be watching her, half-wary, half-accepting. More than anything else, she wanted to merge the two into trust. And trust into love.

Booth watched her laugh at something Stella said. He watched the animated hand movements, the slight tilt of her head that meant she was avidly interested. Then again, Ariel rarely did anything that wasn't done avidly. Whatever had been clouding her mood when she'd come in earlier had been smoothed over. As he remembered the trouble in her eyes, Booth wondered what problem plagued her and why, when she seemed so willing to share everything, she was unwilling to share that.

Lighting a cigarette, Booth told himself he should be

grateful she kept it to herself. Why should he want to be involved? He knew very well that one of the quickest ways to become vulnerable to someone else was to become concerned with their problems.

Beside him a stagehand thoroughly sprayed an elegant arrangement of fresh flowers. The lighting director called for a final check on the candlepower. A mike boom was lowered into place. Booth wondered what Ariel had done over the weekend.

He'd wanted to spend it with her, but she'd put him off and he hadn't insisted. He wouldn't box her in, because by doing so he set limits on himself. That was a trap he wouldn't fall into. But he remembered the utter peace he'd felt lying with her in her dressing room after passion was spent.

He couldn't say she was a calming influence—too much energy crackled from her. Yet she had a talent for soothing the tension from his mind.

He wanted to talk to her again. He wanted to touch her again. He wanted to make love with her again. And he wanted to escape from his own needs.

"Places!" The assistant director called out as he paced the set, rechecking the blocking.

Booth leaned back against the wall, his thumbs hooked absently in his pockets. It never occurred to him, as it often had to Ariel, how seldom he sat.

They would shoot a section of an extensive scene that morning. The other parts would be filmed later on the lawns of a Long Island estate. The elegant lawn party they'd shoot on location was to be Rae's first full-scale attempt at entertaining since marrying Phil. And afterward, indoors and in private, would come their first full-scale argument.

She looked like something made of spun-sugar icing. Her words were as vicious as snake venom. And all the while, with the fury and the poison oozing from her, she hadn't a hair out of place. The fragile color in her cheeks never fluctuated. It was Ariel's job to keep the character cold-blooded, and the words smoldering.

She knew it was all in the eyes. Rae's gestures were a facade. Her smile was a lie. Both the ice and the fire had to come from the eyes. The scene had to be underplayed, understated from her end. It was a constant strain to keep her own emotions from bubbling out. If *she* were to fight with words, she'd shout them, hurl them—and fling off the ones tossed back at her. Rae drawled them, almost lazily. And Ariel ached.

This was Booth's life, she thought. Or a mirror image of what had been his life. This was his pain, his mistakes, his misery. She was caught up in it. If she hurt, how did he feel watching?

Rae gave Phil a bored look as he grabbed both her arms.

"I won't have it," he raged at her, eyes blazing while hers remained cool as a lake.

"Won't have it?" Rae repeated, transmitting utter disdain with the tone, with the movement of an eyebrow. "What is it you won't have?"

"I will not have you raying the pole." Jack closed his eyes and made a gargling sound.

"Raying the pole?" Ariel repeated. "Having a little trouble with your tongue?"

She felt the tension snap as the scene was cut, but wasn't certain if she was grateful or not. She wanted this one over.

"Playing the role," Jack enunciated carefully. "I will

not have you *playing* the *role*. I got it." He held up both hands, mocking himself and his flubbed line.

"Fine, as long as you understand that I can and will ray the pole whenever I choose."

He grinned at Ariel. "Smart mouth."

She patted his cheek. "Aw, yours'll wise up, Jack. Give yourself a chance."

"Places. Take it from the entrance."

For the third time that morning, Ariel swung through the French doors with her skirts billowing behind her.

They moved through the scene again, immersing themselves in the characters even with the starts and stops and changes of camera angles.

To end the scene, Rae was to laugh, take the glass of Scotch from Phil's hand, sip, then toss the contents into his face. Caught up in character, Ariel took the glass, tasted the warm, weak tea, then with an icy smile, poured the contents over the elegant floral arrangement. Without missing a beat in the change of staging, Jack ripped the glass out of her hand and hurled it across the room.

"Cut!"

Snapping back, Ariel stared at her director. "Oh, God, Chuck, I don't know where that came from. I'm sorry." With a hand pressed to her brow, she looked down at the now drenched mixture of fragile hothouse blooms.

"No, no. Damn!" Laughing, he gave her a bear hug. "That was perfect. Better than perfect. I wish I'd thought of it myself." He laughed again and squeezed Ariel until she thought her bones might crack. "She'd have done that. She *would* have done just that." With his arm slung around Ariel's shoulder, Chuck turned to Booth. "Booth?"

"Yes." Without moving, Booth indicated a nod. "Leave it as it stands." He pinned Ariel with cool, green eyes. He should have written it that way, he realized. Throwing a drink in Phil's face was too obvious for Rae. Even too human. "You seem to know her better than I do now."

She let out an uneven breath, giving Chuck's hand a squeeze before she walked toward Booth. "Is that a compliment?"

"An observation. They're setting up for the close-ups," he murmured, then brought his attention back to her. "I won't give you carte blanche, Ariel, but I'm willing to feed you quite a bit of rope in your characterization. And obviously so is Chuck. You understand Rae."

She could have been amused or annoyed. As always when she had a choice, Ariel chose amusement. "Booth, if I were playing a mushroom, I'd understand that mushroom. It's my job."

He smiled because she made it easy. "I believe you would."

"Didn't you catch the commercial where I played the ripe, juicy plum?"

"Must've been out of town."

"It was a classic. Over and above my shower scene for Fresh Wave shampoo—though, of course, sensuality was the basis in both spots."

"I want to come home with you tonight," he said quietly. "I want to stay with you tonight."

"Oh." When would she get used to the simple ways he had of saying monumental things?

"And when we're alone," Booth murmured as he

watched the pulse in her throat begin to flutter, "I want to take off your clothes, little by little, so that I can touch every inch of you. Then I want to watch your face while we make love."

"Ariel, let's get these close-ups!"

"What?" A bit dazed, she mumbled the word while she continued to stare at Booth. Already she could feel his hands on her, taste his breath as it mixed with her own.

"They can have your face—for now," Booth told her, more aroused by her reaction to his words than he would have thought possible. "Tonight, it's mine."

"Ariel!"

Flung back to the present, she turned to go back to the set. With a look that was amused and puzzled, she glanced back over her shoulder. "You're not predictable, Booth."

"Is that a compliment?" he countered.

She grinned. "My very best one."

Hour after hour, line after line, scene after scene, the morning progressed. Though the film was naturally shot out of sequence, Ariel could feel it beginning to jell. Because it was television, the pace was fast. Her pace. Because it was DeWitt and Marshell, the expectations were high. As were hers.

You sweltered under the lights; changed moods, costumes; were powdered, dusted and glossed. Again and again. You sat and waited during scene changes or equipment malfunctions. And somewhere between the tension and the tedium was your vocation.

Ariel understood all that, and she wanted all of that. She never lost the basic pleasure in performing, even after ten retakes of a scene where Rae rode an exercise bike while discussing a new script with her agent.

Muscles aching, she eased herself off the bike and dabbed at the sweat, which didn't have to be simulated, on her face.

"Poor baby." Stella grinned as a stagehand offered Ariel a towel. "Just remember, Ariel, we never work you this hard on *Our Lives*."

"Rae *would* have to be a fitness fanatic," she muttered, stretching her shoulders. "Body conscious. I'm conscious now." With a little moan, Ariel bent to ease a cramp in her leg. "Conscious of every muscle in my body that hasn't been used in five years."

"It's a wrap." Chuck gave her a companionable slap on the flank as he passed. "Go soak in a hot tub."

Ariel barely suppressed a less kind suggestion. She slung the towel over her shoulder, gripped both damp ends and stuck out her tongue.

"You never did have any respect for directors," Stella commented. "Come on, kid, I'll keep you company while you change. Then I've got a hot date."

"Oh, really?"

"Yeah. My new dentist. I went in for a checkup and ended up having a discussion on dental hygiene over linguine."

"Good God." Not bothering to hide a grin, Ariel pushed open her dressing-room door. "He works fast."

"Uh-uh, I do." With a laugh that held both pleasure and nerves, Stella walked into the room. "Oh, Ariel, he's so sweet—so serious about his work. And…" Stella broke off and dropped onto Ariel's cluttered sofa. "I remember something you said a few weeks ago about love—it being a definite emotion or something." She lifted her hands as if to wave away the exact phrase and grip the essence. "Anyway, I haven't come down to earth since I sat in that tilt-back chair and looked up into those baby-blue eyes of his."

"That's nice." For the moment Ariel forgot her sore muscles and the line of sweat dripping down her back. "That's really nice, Stella."

Stella searched for another lemon drop and found her supply depleted. Knowing Ariel, she walked to the dressing table, pulled open a drawer and succumbed to the stash of candy-coated chocolate. "I heard somewhere that people in love can spot other people in love." She slanted her friend a look as Ariel stripped out of her leotard. "To test a theory, my guess is that you've fallen for Booth DeWitt."

"Right the first time." Ariel pulled on the baggy sweatpants and shirt she'd worn to the studio.

With a frown, Stella crunched candy between her teeth. "You always liked the tough roles."

"I seem to lean toward them."

"How's he feel about you?"

"I don't know." Gratefully, Ariel creamed off the last of her makeup. With a flourish, she dumped one more part of Rae into the waste can. "I don't think he does, either."

"Ariel…" Reluctance to give advice warred with affection and loyalty. "Do you know what you're doing?"

"No," she answered immediately, both brows lifting. "Why would I want to?"

Stella laughed as she headed for the door. "Stupid question. By the way—" she stopped with her hand on the knob "—I just thought I'd mention that you were brilliant today. I've worked with you week after week for five years, and today you blew me away. When this thing hits the screen, you're going to take off so fast even you won't be able to keep up."

Astonished, pleased and, perhaps for the first time, a bit frightened, Ariel sat on the edge of her dressing table. "Thanks—I think."

"Don't mention it." Slipping into the character of Vikki, Stella blew Ariel a cool kiss. "See you in a couple of weeks, big sister."

For several moments after the door shut, Ariel sat in silence. Did she, when push came to shove, want to take off and take off fast? She remembered that P. B. Marshell had said something similiar to her after her second reading for the part, but Ariel had seen that more as an overall view of the project itself. She knew Stella, and understood that the praise from her had been directed personally and individually. For the first time the ripple effect of the role of Rae struck her fully. However much a cliché it sounded, it could make her a star.

Wearing her baggy sweats, one hip leaning on her jumbled dressing table, Ariel explored the idea.

Money—she shrugged that away. Her upbringing had taught her to view money for what it was, a means to an end. In any case, her financial status for the past three years had been more than adequate for both her needs and her taste.

Fame. She grinned at that. No, she couldn't claim she was immune to fame. It still brought her a thrill to sign her name in an autograph book or talk to a fan. That was something she hoped would never change. But fame had degrees, and with each rise in height, the payment for it became greater. The more fans, the less privacy. That was something she'd have to think about carefully.

Artistic freedom. It was that, Ariel admitted on a deep breath, that was the clincher. To be able to *choose* a part rather than be chosen. Glory and a big bank account were nothing in comparison. If Rae could bring her that...

With a shake of her head, she rose. Daydreaming about the future couldn't change anything. For now, her career, and her life, would simply have to go a day at a time. Still, she was a woman who liked to expect everything. Ariel would much rather be disappointed than pessimistic. She was grinning when she opened the door and nearly collided with Booth.

"You look happy," he commented as he took her arms to balance her.

"I am happy." Ariel kissed him hard and firm on the mouth. "It's been a good day."

The kiss, casual as it was, shot straight through him. "You should be exhausted."

"No, you should be exhausted after running the New York Marathon. How do you feel about a giant hamburger and a glutton's portion of fries?"

He'd had a quiet restaurant in mind—something French and dimly lit. After a glance at her sweat suit and glowing face, Booth shook his head. "Sounds perfect. It's your turn to buy."

Ariel tucked her arm through his. "You got it. Do you like banana milk shakes?"

His expression stated his opinion clearly. "I don't believe I've ever had one."

"You're going to love it," Ariel promised.

It wasn't as bad as he'd imagined—and the hamburger had been hefty and satisfying. Dusk was settling over the city when they returned to Ariel's apartment.

The moment she opened the door, the kittens dashed for her feet.

"Good grief, you'd think they hadn't been fed in a week." Bending, she scooped up both of them and nuzzled. "Did you miss me, you little pigs, or just your evening meal?"

Before Booth realized what she was up to, Ariel had thrust both kittens into his arms. "Hang on to them for me, will you?" she said easily. "I have to feed Butch, too." She sauntered toward the kitchen, with the three-legged Butch waddling behind. Booth was left with two mewing kittens and no choice but to follow. One—Keats or Shelley—climbed onto his shoulder as he went after Ariel.

"I'm surprised you don't have a litter of puppies, as well." He lifted a brow as the kitten sniffed at his ear.

Ariel laughed as the kitten batted playfully at Booth's hair. "I would if the landlord wasn't so strict. But I'm working on him. Meanwhile—" she set out three generous bowls of food "—it's chow time."

Chuckling, she took the kitten from Booth's shoulder while the other leaped to the floor. Within seconds all three cats were thoroughly involved. "See?" She brushed a few traces of cat hair from his shirt. "They're no trouble at all, hardly any expense and wonderful companions, especially for someone who works most often at home."

Booth gave her a steady look, cupped her face in his hands, then grinned despite himself. "No."

"No what?"

"No, I don't want a cat."

"Well, you can't have one of mine," she said amiably. "Besides, you look more like the dog type."

"Oh, really?" He slipped his arms around her waist.

"Mmm. A nice cocker spaniel that would sleep by your fire at night."

"I don't have a fireplace."

"You should have. But until you take care of that, the puppy could curl right up on a little braided rug by the window."

He caught her bottom lip between his teeth and nipped lightly. "No."

"No one should live alone, Booth. It's depressing."

He could feel her response in the quickening of her heartbeat, the quiet shudder of breath. "I'm used to living alone. I like it that way."

She liked the feel of his roughened cheek against hers. "You must've had a pet when you were a child," Ariel murmured.

Booth remembered the golden Labrador with the lolling tongue that he'd adored—and that he hadn't thought of in years. Oh, no, he thought as he felt himself begin to weaken. She wasn't going to get to him on this. "As a child, I had the time and the temperament for a pet." Slowly, he slipped his hands under her sweatshirt and up her back. "Now I prefer other ways of spending my free time."

But she'd laid the groundwork, Ariel thought with a small smile. Advance and retreat was the secret of a successful campaign. "I have to shower," she told him, drawing back far enough to smile again. "I'm still sticky from that last scene."

"I enjoyed watching it. You've fascinating thigh muscles, Ariel."

Amused, she lifted both brows. "I have *aching* thigh muscles. And I'll tell you something, if I were to ride a bike for the three or four miles I did today, it wouldn't be anchored to the floor."

"No." He gathered her hair in his hand to draw her head back. "You wouldn't be content to stay in the same place." He touched his mouth teasingly to hers, retreating when she would have deepened the touch to a kiss. "I'll wash your back."

Thrills raced up her spine as if he already were. "Hmm, what a nice idea. I suppose I should warn you," she continued as they walked out of the kitchen, "I like the water in my shower hot—very hot."

When they stepped into the bathroom, he slipped his hands under the baggy sweatshirt. She was slim and warm beneath. "Don't you think I can take it?"

"I figure you're pretty tough." Eyes laughing up at him, Ariel began to unbutton his shirt. "For a screenwriter."

In one surprising move, Booth whipped the sweatshirt over her head and bit down on her shoulder. "I'd say you're pretty soft." He ran his hands down her rib cage, then banded her waist. "For an actress."

"Touché," Ariel murmured breathlessly as he tugged loose the drawstring of her pants.

"I like to feel you," he said, stroking his hands over her as she continued to undress him. "Though there isn't much of you. An elegant little body. Long boned, hipless." His hands journeyed down her back, and farther. "Very smooth."

By the time they were both naked, Ariel was shivering. But not from cold. Drawing away, she turned the taps. Water rushed from the showerhead, striking porcelain and steaming toward the ceiling. Stepping in,

Ariel closed her eyes to let her body soak up the heat and the sensuality.

That was one of the things that continued to fascinate him about her—her capacity for experiencing. Nothing was ever ordinary to her, Booth decided as he stepped behind her and drew the curtain closed. She wouldn't know the meaning of boredom. Everything she did or thought was unique, and being unique, exciting.

As the water coursed over them both, he wrapped his arms around her and drew her back against his chest. This was affection, he realized, the sort he'd felt very rarely in his life. Yet he felt it for her.

Ariel lifted her face to the spray. So many sensations buffeted her at that moment, she couldn't keep up. So she stopped trying. It was enough to be close, to be held. And to love. Perhaps some people needed more—security, words, promises. Perhaps one day, she would, too. But now, just for now, she had all she wanted. Turning, she caught Booth close and fastened her mouth to his.

Passion flared in her quickly this time, as if it had been waiting for hours, days. Maybe years. It built so fast that the kiss alone had her gasping for air and fretting for more. Without being aware of it, she stood on her toes so that the curve of their bodies would be aligned. With desperate fingers, she combed through his hair and gripped, as if he might try to break away. But his arms were tight around her, and his mouth was as seeking as hers.

Reeling toward the crest, Ariel clung, and Ariel offered.

God, he'd never known anyone so giving. As he drank in all the flavors of her mouth, Booth wondered if it were possible for a woman to be so confident, so comfortable with herself that she could be this generous. Without any hesitation, her body was there for him. Her mind was tuned to him. Instinctively, Booth knew she thought more of his needs, his pleasures, than her own. And by doing so, she touched off a long dormant tenderness.

"Ariel..." Murmuring her name, he ran kisses over her face, which the water made incredibly soft, incredibly sweet. "You make me want things I'd forgotten— and almost believe in them again."

"Don't think." She rubbed her lips over his to soothe, to entice. "This time don't think at all."

But he would, Booth told himself. Or he'd take her too quickly, and perhaps too roughly. This time, he'd give her back a portion of what she'd already given him. Cupping the soap in his hand, he ran it over her back. He thought he heard her purr like one of her cats. It made him smile.

Her senses began to sharpen. She could hear the hiss of the spray as it struck tile, and feel the steam as it billowed in puffy clouds. Soapy hands slid over her—slick, soft, sensitive. His flesh was wet and warm where her mouth pressed. Through half-closed eyes she could see the lather cling to her, then him, before it was sluiced away.

His hand moved once between their slippery bodies to find her—stunningly—so that she cried out in surprise and rippling pleasure. Then it journeyed elsewhere while his lips traced hot and damp over her shoulder. The tang of citrus from the soap made her head reel.

"Do they still ache?" Booth asked her as his fingers kneaded the backs of her thighs.

"What?" Floating, Ariel leaned against him, her

arms curved over his back, her hands firm on his shoulders. Water struck her back in soft, hissing spurts, then seemed to slither away. "No, no, nothing aches now."

With a laugh, Booth dipped his tongue into her ear and felt her shiver. "Your hair goes to gold when it's wet."

She smelled the shampoo, felt its cool touch on her scalp before he began to massage. Nothing, Ariel thought, had ever aroused her more.

Slowly, lingeringly, he washed her hair while the frothy bubbles of shampoo ran down his arms. The scent was familiar to him now, that fresh, inviting fragrance that caught at him every time he was near her. He enjoyed the intimacy of having the scent spill over him and cling—to her skin, to his. Shifting his weight, he moved them both under the gush of the shower so that water and lather raced down their bodies and away.

And while they stood, hot and wet and entangled, he slipped into her. It seemed natural, as if he'd been her lover for years. It was thrilling, as though he'd never touched her before.

He felt Ariel's nails dig into his shoulders, heard her moan of surrender and demand. He took her there, with more care than he'd ever shown a woman. And he felt a rush of freedom.

Chapter 9

Ariel rode a roller coaster for two weeks. Her time with Booth seemed like a ride with dips and curves and speed and surprises. Of course, she'd always loved them—the faster and wilder the better.

She'd been right when she'd told Booth he was unpredictable. Neither was he a simple man to deal with. Ariel decided she wanted it no other way.

There were times he was incredibly tender, showing her flashes of romance and affection that she'd never expected from him. A box of wildflowers delivered before an early studio call. A rainy-day picnic in his apartment with champagne in paper cups while thunder raged.

Then there were the times he pulled away, drew into himself so intensely that she couldn't reach him. And when she knew, instinctively, not to try.

The anger and impatience in him were ingrained.

Perhaps it was that, contrasting with the glimpses of humor and gentleness, that had caused her to lose her heart. It was the whole man she loved, no matter how difficult. And it was the whole man she wanted to belong to. This man—brooding, angry, reluctantly sweet—was the man she'd been waiting for.

As the film progressed, their relationship grew closer, despite Booth's occasional stretches of isolation. Closer, yes, but without the simplicity she looked for. For love, in Ariel's mind, was a simple thing.

If he was resisting love, so much the better, Ariel told herself. When he accepted it—she wouldn't allow herself to doubt he would—it would be that much stronger. For she needed absolute love, the unconditional giving of heart and mind. She could wait a little longer to have it all.

If she had one regret, it was that she wasn't free to confide in him about Scott. The closer the trial came, the more she felt the need to talk to Booth about it, seek comfort, gain reassurance. Though it was tempting, Ariel never even considered it. This problem was hers, and hers alone. As Scott was hers to protect and defend.

When she thought of the future, it was still in sections. Booth, Scott, her career. She needed her own brand of absolute faith to believe that they'd all come together in the end.

After a long, hectic morning, Ariel considered the lengthy delay anticipated because of equipment breakdown a reward. It was the first time in weeks she'd be able to watch *Our Lives, Our Loves,* and catch up on Amanda's life with the people of Trader's Bend.

"You're not really going to watch television for the

next hour," Booth protested as Ariel pulled him down the corridor.

"Yes, I am. It's like visiting home." She shook the bag of pretzels in her hand. "And I've got provisions."

"When they get the soundboard fixed, you're going to have a hell of an afternoon ahead of you." He kneaded her shoulder as they walked. Though it didn't often show, he'd seen brief glimpses of strain in her eyes, isolated moments when she looked a bit lost. "You'd be better off putting your feet up and catching a nap."

"I never nap." When she pushed open her dressing room door, she upended a stack of magazines. Hardly sparing them a glance, she walked over to the small portable television set in the corner.

"I seem to recall coming in here one day and finding you with your feet up on the table and your eyes closed."

"That's different." She fiddled with a dial until she was satisfied with the color. "That was recharging. I'm not ready for recharging, Booth." Eyes wide and excited, she whirled around. "It's really going well, isn't it? I can feel it. Even after all these weeks, the edge is still on. That's a sure sign we're doing something special."

"I was a bit leery about doing a film for television." He took a few pamphlets from the sofa and dropped them onto a table. "Not anymore. Yes, it's going to be very special." He held out a hand to her. "You're very special."

As always, the subtle unexpected statement went straight to her heart. Ariel took the offered hand and brought it to her lips. "I'm going to enjoy watching you accept that Emmy."

He lifted a brow. "And what about yours?"

"Maybe," she said and laughed. "Just maybe." The

lead-in music for the soap distracted her. "Ah, here we go. Back to Trader's Bend." Dropping onto the sofa, she pulled Booth with her. After ripping open the bag of pretzels, Ariel became totally absorbed.

She didn't watch as an actress or as a critic, but as a viewer. Relaxing her mind, she let herself become caught up in the connecting plot lines and problems. Even when she saw herself on the screen, she didn't look for flaws or perfection. She didn't consider she was looking at Ariel, but at Amanda.

"Don't tell me what I want," Amanda told Griff in a low, vibrating voice. "You have no business offering me unsolicited advice on my life, much less coming into my house uninvited."

"Now, you look." Griff took her arm when she would have turned away. "You're pushing yourself right to the edge. I can see it."

"I'm doing my job," she corrected coolly. "Why don't you concentrate on yours and leave me alone?"

"Leaving you alone's the last thing I'm going to do." As the camera zoomed in, the viewer was witness to his struggle for control. When Griff continued, his voice was calmer but edged with his familiar passion. "Damn it, Mandy, you're almost as close to this Ripper thing as the cops. You know better than to stay in this house by yourself. If you won't let me help you, at least go stay with your parents for a while."

"With my parents." Her composure began to crack as she dragged a hand through her hair. "Stay with my parents, while Vikki's there? Just how much do you think I can take?"

"All right, all right." Frustrated, he tried to draw her

against him, only to have her jerk away. "Mandy, please, I'm worried about you."

"Don't be. And if you really want to help, leave me alone. I need to go over the psychiatric profile before I meet with Lieutenant Reiffler in the morning."

Fisted hands were shoved in his pockets. "Okay, look, I'll sleep down here on the couch. I swear I won't touch you. I just can't leave you out here alone."

"I don't want you here!" she shouted, losing her tenuous grip on control. "I don't want anyone, can't you understand that? Can't you understand that I need to be alone?"

He stared at her while she fought back tears, shoulders heaving. "I love you, Mandy," he said so quietly it could barely be heard. But his eyes had already said it.

As the camera zoomed in on her, a single tear spilled out and rolled down Amanda's cheek. "No," she whispered, turning away. But Griff's arms came around her, drawing her back against him.

"Yes, you know I do. There's never been anyone for me but you. It killed me when you left me, Mandy. I need you in my life. I need what we'd planned to have together. We've got a second chance. All we have to do is take it."

Staring into nowhere, Amanda pressed a hand to her stomach where she knew Cameron's baby was sleeping—a baby Griff would never accept, and one she had to. "No, there aren't any second chances, Griff. Please leave me alone."

"We belong together," he murmured, burying his face in her hair. "Oh, God, Mandy, we've always belonged together."

For his sake, for her own, she had to make him leave.

Pain flashed into her eyes before she controlled her expression. "You're wrong," she said flatly. "That was yesterday. Today I don't want you to touch me."

"I can't crawl anymore." Ripping himself away from her, Griff headed for the door. "I won't crawl anymore."

As the door slammed behind him, Amanda slumped down on the couch. Curling on her side, she buried her face in a pillow and wept. The camera panned slowly to the window to show a shadowy silhouette behind the closed curtains.

"Well, well," Booth murmured at the commercial break. "The lady has her problems."

"And then some." Ariel stretched and leaned back against the cushions. "That's the thing about soaps—one problem gets resolved and three more crop up."

"So, is she going to give Griff a break and take him back?"

Ariel grinned at the casualness of the question. He really wants to know, she mused, pleased. "Tune in tomorrow."

His eyes narrowed. "You know the story line."

"My lips are sealed," she said primly.

"Really?" Booth caught her chin in his hand. "Let's see." He pressed his to them firmly, and though hers curved, they remained shut. Challenged, he shifted closer and his fingers spread over her jawline, lightly stroking. With the barest of touches, he traced the shape of her mouth, wetting her lips, using no pressure. When he nibbled at one corner, then the other, he felt the telltale melting of her bones, heard the quiet sigh. Effortlessly, his tongue slipped between her lips to tease hers.

"Cheat," Ariel managed.

"Yeah." God, she made him feel so good. He'd almost stopped wondering how long it would last. The end, what he considered the inevitable end to what they brought each other, was becoming more blurred every day. "I've never believed in playing fair."

"No?" Her sudden aggression caught him off balance. Before he knew it, Booth was on his back, with her body pressed into his. "In that case, no holds barred."

The greedy kiss left him stunned, so that by the time he'd gripped some control again, she'd unbuttoned his shirt for her seeking hands. "Ariel…" Half-amused, half-protesting, he took her wrist, but her free hand skimmed down the center of his body to spread over his stomach.

Amusement, protests, reason, slipped away.

"I never get enough of you." He gripped her hair, destroying the sleek knot the hairdresser had tended so carefully hours before.

"I plan to see that you don't." With quick, open mouthed kisses she moved over his shoulder, drawing away the shirt as she went.

She took him over hills and into valleys with such speed and fury he could only follow. For as long as he could remember, Booth had led in every aspect of his life—not trusting enough to let another guide. But now he could barely keep pace with her. The energy, the verve he'd so long admired in her was in complete control. As he was swept along, Booth wondered why it was suddenly so easy to break yet another rule. Then, as she had once requested, he didn't think at all.

Feelings. Ariel drew them in as they radiated from him. This was what she'd been so patiently, so desperately waiting for. Emotions were finally overtaking him.

As they merged with her own, she felt the bond, the link, and nearly wept with the wonder of it.

He loves me, she thought. Maybe he doesn't know it yet, maybe he won't for days and weeks to come. But it's there. The urge to weep altered to an urge to laugh. And it was with laughter and with joy that she took him into her.

Winded, Booth lay still while Ariel curled like a cat on his chest. "Was all that just to keep me from learning the story line?"

Her chuckle was muffled against his skin. "There're no lengths I won't go to to protect security." She snuggled against him. "No sacrifice too great."

"With that in mind, I think I'll ask about the identity of the Ripper—tonight." Drawing her up, he examined her. The silk blouse she'd been wearing was unbuttoned and trailing over one shoulder. The thin slacks lay in a heap on the floor. Her hair was a provocative tangle. "You're going to catch hell from wardrobe and makeup."

"It was worth it." Straightening her blouse, Ariel began to do up the buttons. "I'll tell them I took a nap."

With a laugh, he sat up and tugged on her tumbled hair. "There's no mistaking what you've been up to. Your eyes always give you away."

"Do they?" Carefully, she stepped into her slacks. "I wonder." Absently smoothing out the creases, she turned to him. "You haven't seen it in all these weeks." As she watched, his brows drew together. "You're a perceptive man, and I've never had a strong talent or a strong desire to hide my feelings." She smiled as he continued to frown at her. "I love you."

His face, his body—Ariel thought even his mind—went very still. He said nothing. "Booth, you don't have to look as though I've just pulled a gun on you." Stepping closer, she touched the back of her hand to his cheek. "Taking love's easy—giving it's a bit harder, for some people anyway. Please, take it as it's offered. It's free."

He wasn't at all certain what he was feeling—only that he'd never felt anything like it before. The very novelty made him wary. "It's not wise to give things away, Ariel, especially to someone who isn't ready for them."

"And holding on to something when it needs to be given's even more foolish. Booth, can't you trust me even now, just enough to accept my feelings?"

"I don't know," he murmured. As he rose, conflicting emotions, conflicting desires tore at him. He wanted to distance himself as quickly and as completely as possible. He wanted to hold her and never let go. Panic, he felt the stab of it. Pleasure, the sweetness of it.

"They're there whether you can or can't. I've never been good at controlling my emotions, Booth. I'm not sorry for it."

Before he could speak there was a brisk knock on the door. "Ariel, you're needed on the set in fifteen minutes."

"Thank you."

He had to think, Booth told himself. Be logical…. Be careful. "I'll send the hairdresser in."

"Okay." She smiled, and it almost reached her eyes. When he'd gone, Ariel stared at her reflection in the mirror. The lights around it were dull and dark. "So who expected it'd be easy?" she asked herself.

In just under fifteen minutes, Ariel walked back toward the set. She looked every bit as cool and as sleek as she had when she'd walked off over an hour before.

Despite Booth's reaction, which she'd half expected, she felt lighter, easier, after telling Booth of her feelings. It was, after all, merely stating aloud what was, sharing what couldn't be changed. As a general rule, Ariel considered concealments a waste of time, and consequences a by-product of living. Her gait was free and easy as she crossed the studio.

She knew something was happening before she saw the thicket of people or heard the excited voices. Tension in the air. She felt it and thought instantly of Booth. But it wasn't Booth she saw when she passed the false wall of the living-room set.

Elizabeth Hunter.

Elegance. Ice. Smooth, smooth femininity. Outrageous beauty. Ariel saw her laugh lightly and lift a slender cigarette to her lips. She posed effortlessly, as if the cameras were on and focused on her. Her hair shimmered, pale, frosty. Her skin was so exquisite it might have been carved from marble.

On the screen, she was larger than life, desirable, unattainable. Ariel saw little difference in the flesh. There couldn't be a man alive who wouldn't dream of peeling off that layer of frost and finding something molten and wild inside. If she were truly like Rae, Ariel thought, that man—any man—would be disappointed. Curious, she walked closer.

"Pat, how could I stay away?" Liz lifted one graceful hand and touched Marshell's check. A fantasy of diamonds and sapphires winked on her ring finger. "After all, one might say I have a…vested interest in this film." The provocative pout—a Hunter trademark—touched her mouth. "Don't tell me you're going to chase me away."

"Of course not, Liz." Marshell looked uncomfortable and resigned. "None of us knew you were in town."

"I just wrapped the Simmeon film in Greece." She drew on the slender cigarette again and carelessly flicked ashes on the floor. "I flew right in." She shot a look over Marshell's shoulder. Not hostile, not grim, but simply predatory. It was then Ariel saw Booth.

He stood slightly apart from the circle of people around Liz, as if he again sought distance without wholly removing himself. He met the look his ex-wife sent him without a flicker of expression. Even if Ariel had chosen to intrude, she doubted if she could have gauged his thoughts.

"I wasn't allowed to read the screenplay." Liz continued to talk to Marshell though her eyes remained on Booth. "But little dribbles leaked through to me. I must say, I'm fascinated. And a bit miffed that you didn't ask me to do the film."

Marshell's eyes hardened, but he stuck with diplomacy. "You were unavailable, Liz."

"And inappropriate," Booth added mildly.

"Ah, Booth, always the clever last word." Liz blew smoke in his direction and smiled.

It was a smile Ariel recognized. She'd seen it on the screen in countless Hunter movies. She'd mimicked it herself as Rae. It was the smile a witch wore before she cut the wings off a bat. Without realizing it, Ariel moved forward in direct defense of Booth. Liz's gaze shifted and locked.

It wasn't a pleasant survey. Again, not hostile but simply and essentially cold. Ariel studied Liz in turn and absorbed impressions. She was left with a sensation of emptiness. And what she felt was pity.

"Well…" Liz held out her cigarette for disposal. A small woman with a wrinkled face plucked it from her fingers. "It's easy to deduce that this is Rae."

"No." Unconsciously, Ariel smiled with the same cold glitter as Liz. "I'm Ariel Kirkwood. Rae's a character."

"Indeed." The haughty lift of brow had been used in a dozen scenes. "I always try to absorb the character I portray."

"And it works brilliantly for you," Ariel acknowledged with complete sincerity. "I limit that to when the lights are on, Miss Hunter."

Only the barest flicker in her eyes betrayed annoyance. "Would I have seen you do anything else, dear?"

There was no mistaking the patronizing tone. Again, Ariel felt a flash of sympathy. "Possibly."

He didn't like seeing them together. No, Booth thought violently, by God, he didn't. It had given him a wave of sheer pleasure to see Liz again and feel nothing. Absolutely nothing. No anger, no frustration. Not even disgust. The lack of feeling had been like a balm. Until Ariel had come on set.

Face-to-face, they could have been sisters. The resemblance was heightened by the fact that Ariel's hair, makeup and wardrobe were styled to Liz's taste. He saw too many similarities. And as he looked closer, too many contrasts. Booth wasn't sure which annoyed him more.

No matter how she was dressed, warmth flowed from Ariel. The inner softness edged through. He could feel the emotion from her even three feet away. And he saw…pity? Yes, it was pity in her eyes. Directed at Liz. Booth lit a cigarette with a jerk of his wrist. God, he'd rid himself of one and was being reeled in by another. Standing there, he could feel the quicksand sucking at his legs. Was there any closer analogy for love?

"Let's get started," he ordered briefly. Liz shot him another look.

"Don't let me hold things up. I'll stay out of the way." She glided to the edge of the set, sat in a director's chair and crossed her legs. A burly man, the small woman and what was hardly more than a boy settled behind her.

The audience had Ariel's adrenaline pumping. The scene they were to shoot was the same one she'd auditioned with. More than any other, Ariel felt it encapsulated Rae's personality, her motives, her essence. She didn't think Liz Hunter would enjoy it, but…Ariel felt she'd be able to gauge just how successful her performance was by Liz's reaction to it.

With a faintly bored expression on her face, Liz sat back and watched the scene unfold. The dialogue was not precisely a verbatim account of what had occurred between her and Booth years before, but she recognized the tenor. Damn him, she thought with a flicker of anger that showed nowhere on her sculpted face. Damn him for his memory and his talent. So this was his revenge.

While she hoped the film fell flat, she was too shrewd to believe it would. She could shrug that off. Liz was clever enough, experienced enough to make the film work for her rather than against her. With the right angle, she could get miles and miles of publicity from Booth's work. That balanced things…to a point.

She was a woman of few emotions, but the most finely tuned of these was jealousy. It was this that ate at her as she sat, silent, watching. Ariel Kirkwood, she thought as one rose-tipped nail began to tap on the arm of the chair. Liz was vain enough to consider herself more beautiful, but there was no denying the difference in age. Years were something that haunted her.

And talent. Her teeth scraped against each other because she wanted to scream. Her own skill, the accolades and awards she'd received for it were never enough. Especially when she was faced with a beautiful, younger woman of equal ability. Damn them both. Her finger began to tap harder, staccato. The young man put a soothing hand on her shoulder and was shrugged away.

Liz could taste the envy that edged toward fury. The part should have been hers, she thought as her lips tightened. If she had played Rae, she'd have added a dozen dimensions to the part—such as it was. She had more talent in the palm of her hand than this Ariel Kirkwood had in her whole body. More beauty, more fame, more sexuality. Her head began to pound as she watched Ariel skillfully weave sex and ice into the scene.

Then her eyes met Booth's, and she nearly choked on an oath. He was laughing at her, Liz realized. Laughing, though his mouth was sober and his expression calm. He'd pay for that, she told herself as her lids lowered fractionally. For that and for everything else. She'd see that he and this no-talent actress from nowhere both paid.

Booth knew his ex-wife well enough to know what was going on in her mind. It should have pleased him; perhaps it would have only a few weeks before. Now, it did little more than slightly disgust him.

Shifting his gaze from her, he focused his attention on Ariel. Of all the scenes in the screenplay, this was the hardest for him. He'd crystallized himself too well as Phil in these few sharp, hard lines. And his Rae was too real here. Ariel made her too real, he thought as he wished for a cigarette. In this short, seven-minute scene, which would take much, much longer to complete, it was almost impossible to separate Ariel from Rae—and Rae from Liz.

Ariel had said she loved him. Fighting discomfort that was laced with panic, Booth watched her. Was it possible? Once before he'd believed a woman who'd whispered those words to him. But Ariel...there was no one and nothing quite like Ariel.

Did he love her? Once before he'd believed himself in love. But whatever emotion it had been, it hadn't been love. And it had been smeared with a fascination for great beauty, great talent, cool, cool sex. No, he didn't understand love—if it existed in the way he believed Ariel thought of it. No, he didn't understand it, and he told himself he didn't want it. What he wanted was his privacy, his peace.

And while he stood there, watching his own scene being painstakingly reproduced on film, he had neither.

"Cut. Cut and print." Chuck ran a hand along the back of his neck to ease the tension. "Hell of a job." Letting out a long breath, he walked toward Ariel and Jack. "Hell of a job, both of you. We'll wrap for today. Nothing's going to top that."

Relieved, Ariel let her stomach relax, muscle by muscle. She glanced over idly at the sound of quiet applause.

Liz rose gracefully from her chair. "Marvelous job." She gave Jack her dazzling, practiced smile before she turned to Ariel. "You have potential, dear," Liz told her. "I'm sure this part will open a few doors for you."

Ariel recognized the swipe and took it on the chin.

"Thank you, Liz." Deliberately, she drew the pins from her hair and let it fall free. She wanted badly to shed Rae. "It's a challenging part."

"You did your best with it." Smiling, Liz touched her lightly on the shoulder.

I must've been on the money, Ariel thought and grinned. *I must've been right on the money.*

Liz wanted to rip the thick, tumbled hair out by the roots. She turned to Marshell. "Pat, I'd love to have dinner. We've a lot to catch up on." She slipped her arm through his and patted his hand. "My treat, darling."

Mentally swearing, Marshell acquiesced. The best way to get her out without a scene was simply to get her out. "My pleasure, Liz. Chuck, I'll want a look at the dailies first thing in the morning."

"Oh, by the way." Liz paused beside Booth. "I really don't think this little film will do much harm to your career, darling." With an icy laugh she skimmed a finger down his shirt. "And I must say, I'm rather flattered, all in all. No hard feelings, Booth."

He looked down at the beautiful, heartless smile. "No feelings, Liz. No feelings at all."

Her fingers tightened briefly on Marshell's arm before she swept away. "Oh, Pat, I must tell you about this marvelous young actor I met in Athens...."

"Exit stage left," Jack murmured, then shrugged when Ariel raised a brow at him. "Must still be functioning as Phil. But let me tell you, that's one lady I wouldn't turn my back on."

"She's rather sad," Ariel said half to herself.

Jack gave a snort of laughter. "She's a tarantula." With another snort he cupped a hand on Ariel's shoulder. "Let me tell you something, kid. I've been in the business a lot of years, worked with lots of actresses. You're first class. And that just gripped her cookies."

"And that's sad," Ariel repeated.

"Better put a layer of something over that compassion, babe," he warned. "You'll get burned." Giving her shoulder a last squeeze, he walked off the set.

Gratefully, Ariel dropped into a chair. The lights were off now, the temperature cooling. Most of the stagehands were gone, except for three who huddled in a corner discussing a poker game. Tipping her head back, she waited as Booth approached.

"That was a tough one," she commented. "How do you feel?"

"I'm fine. You?"

"A little drained. I've only a few scenes left, none of them on this scale. Next week, I'll be back to Amanda."

"How do you feel about that?"

"The people on the soap are like family. I miss them."

"Children leave home," he reminded her.

"I know. So will I when the time's right."

"We both know you won't be signing another contract with the soap." He drew out a cigarette, lighting it automatically, drawing in smoke without tasting it. "Whether you're ready to admit it or not."

Feeling his tension, she tensed in turn. "You're mixing us again," she said quietly. "Just how much longer is it going to take you to see me for who I am, without the shadows?"

"I know who you are," Booth corrected. "I'm not sure what to do about it."

She rose. Maybe it was the lingering strain from the scene, or perhaps her sadness from watching Liz Hunter suffer in her own way. "I'll tell you what you don't want," she said with an edge to her voice he hadn't heard before. "You don't want me to love you. You don't want the responsibility of my emotions or of your own."

He could deal with this, Booth thought as he took another drag. A fight was something he could handle effortlessly. "Maybe I don't. I told you what I thought right up front."

"So you did." With a half laugh, she turned away. "Funny that you're the one who's always preaching change at me, and you're the one so unable to do so yourself. Let me tell you something, Booth." She whirled back, vibrantly glowing Ariel. "My feelings are mine. You can't dictate them to me. The only thing it's possible for you to do is dictate to yourself."

"It isn't a matter of dictating." He found he didn't want the cigarette after all. It tasted foul. Booth left it smoldering, half-crushed, in an ashtray. "It's a matter of not being able to give you what you want."

"I haven't asked you for anything."

"You don't have to ask." He was angry, really angry, without being aware when he'd crossed the line. "You've pulled at me from the start—pulled at things I want left alone. I made a commitment once, I'll be damned if I'll do it again. I don't want to change my lifestyle. I don't want—"

"To risk failure again," Ariel finished.

His eyes blazed at her, but his voice was very, very calm. "You're going to have to learn to watch your step, Ariel. Fragile bones are easily broken."

"And they mend." Abruptly, she was too weary to argue, too weary to think. "You'll have to work out your own solution, Booth. The same as I'll work out mine.

I'm not sorry I love you, or that I've told you. But I am sorry that you can't accept a gift."

When he'd watched her walk away, Booth slipped his hands in his pockets and stared at the darkened set. No, he couldn't accept it. Yet he felt as though he'd just tossed away something he'd searched for all of his life.

Chapter 10

The water was a bit choppy. Small whitecaps bounced up, were swallowed, then bounced back again. Directly overhead the sky was a hard diamond blue, but to the east, dark clouds were boiling and building. There was the threat of rain in the wind that blew in from the Atlantic. Booth estimated he had two hours before the storm caught up with him—an hour before he'd be forced to tack to shore to avoid it.

And on shore the heat would be staggering, the humidity thick enough to slice. On the water, the breeze smelled of summer and salt and storms. He could taste it as it whipped by him and billowed his sail. Exhilaration—he knew it for the sensation that could clear the mind and chill the skin. Holding lightly to the rigging, he let the wind take him.

Booth wore nothing but cutoffs and deck shoes. He

hadn't bothered to shave for two days. His eyes had grown accustomed to squinting against the sun reflecting off the water, and his hands to the feel of rough rope against the palm. Both were harsh, both were challenging.

Exhilaration? This time it hadn't come with the force he'd expected. For days he'd sailed as long as the sun and the weather allowed. He'd worked at night until his mind was drained.

Escape? Was that a better word for what he'd come for? Perhaps, Booth mused as he sailed over the choppy water. Lifting a beer to his lips he let the taste race over his tongue. Perhaps he was escaping, but he was no longer needed on the set, and he had finally had to admit that he couldn't work in the city. He needed a few days away from the filming, from the pressure to produce, from his own standards of perfection.

That was all a lie.

None of those things had driven him out of Manhattan and onto Long Island. He'd needed to get away from Ariel—from what Ariel was doing to him. And perhaps most of all from his feelings for her. Yet the miles didn't erase her from his thoughts. It took no effort to think of her, and every effort not to. Though she haunted him, Booth was certain he'd been right to come away. If thinking of her ate at him, seeing her, touching her would have driven him mad.

He didn't want her love, he told himself savagely. He couldn't—wouldn't—be responsible for the range of emotions Ariel was capable of. Booth took another long pull from the beer can, then scowled at the water. He wasn't capable of loving her in return. He didn't possess those kinds of feelings. Whatever emotions he had were directed exclusively toward his work. He'd promised himself that. Inside, in the compartment that held the brighter feelings one person had for another, he was empty. He was void.

He ached for her—body, mind, soul.

Damn her, he thought as he jerked at the rigging. Damn her for pulling at him, for crowding him…for asking nothing of him. If she'd asked, demanded, pleaded, he could have refused. It was so simple to say no to an obligation. All she did was give until he was so full of her, he was losing himself.

He'd work, Booth told himself as he began to tack methodically back toward shore. The boat bucked beneath him as the wind kicked up. Adjusting the sails, he concentrated on the pure physicality of the task. Use your muscles, your back, not your brain. Don't think, he warned himself, until it's time to write again.

He'd bury himself in work for the rest of the afternoon. He'd pour himself into his writing through the evening, late into the night, until his mind was too jumbled to think of anything—anyone. He'd stay away from her physically until he could stay away from her mentally. Then he'd go back to New York and pick up his life as he'd left it. Before Ariel.

Thunder rumbled ominously as he docked the boat.

Ariel watched the lightning snake across the sky and burst. The night sky was like a dark mirror abruptly cracked then made whole again. Still no rain. The heat storm had been threatening all evening, building up in the east and traveling toward Manhattan. She'd looked forward to it. Wearing a long shirt and nothing else, she stood at the window to watch it come.

Earlier, her neighbors had been sitting on their stoops, fanning and sweating and complaining of the heat. She didn't mind it. Before the night was over the rain would wash away the stickiness. But at the moment, though her thin shirt was clinging damply to her back and thighs, she enjoyed the enervating quality of the heat, and the violence in the sky.

The storm was coming from the east, she thought again. Perhaps Booth was already watching the rain she still anticipated. She wondered if he was working, oblivious to the booming thunder. Or if, like her, he stood and watched the fury in the sky. She wondered when he'd come back—to her.

He would, Ariel affirmed staunchly. She only hoped he'd come back with an easy mind. She'd thrown him a curve. With a half smile, Ariel felt the first rippling breeze pass through the screen and over her skin. She wasn't sorry, though his reaction had hurt, then angered her. That was over. Perhaps, for a moment, she'd forgotten that to Booth love wasn't the open-ended gift it was to her. He'd see the restrictions, the risks, the pains.

The pains, she thought, resting her palms on the windowsill. Why was she always so surprised to find out she could hurt just as intensely as she could be happy? She wanted him, physically, but he was miles from her reach, emotionally, but he'd distanced himself from her feelings.

She hadn't been surprised when Booth had absented himself from the last few days of shooting. All the key scenes had been done. Nor was she surprised when Marshell had mentioned idly that Booth had gone to his secluded Long Island home to write and to sail. She missed him, she felt the emptiness; but Ariel was too independent to mourn the loss of him for a few days. He needed his solitude. A part of her understood that, enough to keep her from misery.

Hadn't she herself painted almost through the night after Liz Hunter had visited the set?

Ariel glanced around at the frantic canvas slashed with cobalt and scarlets. It wasn't a painting she'd keep in the living room for long. Too angry, too disturbing. As soon as she'd fully coped with those feelings, she'd stick the canvas in a closet.

Everyone had his or her own means of dealing with the darker emotions. Booth's was to draw into himself; hers was to let them lash out. Either way, any way, the resolution would come. She had only to hang on a little while longer.

And so she told herself when she thought of Scott. The hearing would begin at the end of the week. That, too, would be resolved, but Ariel refused to look at any more than one solution. Scott had to come to her. The doubts she'd once harbored about her right to claim him, his need to be with her, were gone. As time went on, he became more and more unhappy with the Andersons. His visits were punctuated by desperate hugs, and more and more by pleas that he be allowed to stay with her.

It wasn't a matter of abuse or neglect. It was a simple matter of love, unconditional love that came naturally from her, and didn't come at all from his grandparents. Whatever hardships she and Scott were facing now would be a thing of the past before long. It was a time to concentrate on whens instead of nows. That was how she got through the slowly moving days between the filming and the hearing. Without Booth.

Ariel closed her eyes as the rain began to gush out of the sky. Oh God, if only the night were over.

The rain was just tapering off as Booth pushed away from his computer. He'd gotten more accomplished than he'd anticipated, but the juices were drying up. He knew better than to push himself when he got to this point. In another hour he'd try again perhaps, or maybe not for a day or two. But it would come back, and the story would flow again.

No, he couldn't write anything now, but it was still this side of midnight and he was restless. The storm had cleared the air, making him wish he were on the water again, under the burgeoning moonlight. He should eat. As he rubbed the stiffness from his neck, he remembered he hadn't bothered with dinner. A meal and an early night.

As he walked through the house into the kitchen, silence drummed around him. Strange, he'd never noticed just how thick silence could be, just how empty a house could be when it had only one occupant. And stranger still, how only a few months before he'd have appreciated both, even expected both. Again, before Ariel. His life seemed to have come down to two stages. Before Ariel and after Ariel. It wasn't an easy admission for a man to make.

Booth pulled a tray of cold cuts out of the refrigerator without any real interest. Mechanically, he fixed a sandwich, found a ripe peach and poured a glass of milk. The solitary meal had never seemed less appealing—so much so he considered tipping the entire mess down the sink.

Shaking off the feeling, he carried it into his bedroom and set the plate on the dresser. What he needed was some noise, he decided. Something to occupy his mind without straining the brain. Booth switched on the television, then flipped the channel selector without any particular goal in mind.

Normally he would have bypassed the late-night talk show in favor of an old movie. When Liz's laughter flowed out at him, he paused. He might still have passed it by, but his curiosity was piqued. Thinking it might be an interesting diversion, Booth picked up his plate, set it on the bedside table and stretched out.

He'd been on the show himself a number of times. Though he wasn't overly fond of the format or the exposure, he knew the game well enough to understand the need to reach the public through the form. The show was popular, slickly run, and the host knew his trade. With boyish charm he could draw the unexpected out of celebrities and keep the audience from turning the channel or just flicking off the switch.

"Of course I was terribly excited to film on location in Greece, Bob." Liz leaned just a bit closer to her host while her ice-blue gown glistened coolly in the lights. "And working with Ross Simmeon was a tremendous experience."

"Didn't I hear you and Simmeon had a feud going?" Robert MacAllister tossed off the question with a grin. It said, come on, relax, you can tell me. It was a well-practiced weapon.

"A feud?" Liz fluttered her lashes ingenuously. She was much too sharp to be caught in that trap. She crossed her legs so that the gown shimmered over her body. "Why, no. I can't imagine where anyone would get that idea."

"It must have something to do with the three days you refused to come on set." With a little deprecating shrug, MacAllister leaned back in his chair. "A disagreement over the number of lines in a key scene."

"That's nonsense." *Damn Simmeon and all the rumormongers.* "I'd had too much sun. My physician put me on medication for a couple of days and recommended a rest." She glittered a smile right back at him. "Of course there were a few tense moments, as there will be on any major film, but I'd work with Ross tomorrow...." or the devil himself, her tone seemed to say. "If the right script came along."

"So, what're you up to now, Liz? You've had an unbroken string of successes. It must be getting tough to find just the right property."

"It's always hard to put together the right touch of magic." She gestured gracefully so that the ring on her hand caught the light and glittered. "The right script, the right director, the right leading man. I've been so lucky—particularly since *To Meet at Midnight.*"

Booth set his half-eaten sandwich aside and nearly laughed. *He'd* written it for her and had made her a major star. Top box office. Luck had had nothing to do with it.

"Your Oscar-winning performance," Bob acknowledged. "And of course a brilliant screenplay." He sent her an off-center smile. "You'd agree with that?"

It was the opening she'd been waiting for. And maneuvering toward. "Oh, yes. Booth DeWitt is possibly—no, assuredly the finest screenwriter of the eighties. Regardless of our, well, personal problems, we've always respected each other professionally."

"I know all about personal problems," Bob said ruefully and got the laugh. His three marriages had been well publicized. And so had his alimony figures. "How do you feel about his latest work?"

"Oh." Liz smiled and let one hand flutter to her throat before it fell into her lap. "I don't suppose the content's much of a secret, is it?"

Again the expected laugh, a bit more restrained.

"I'm sure Booth's script is wonderful, they all are. If it's, ah, one-sided," she said carefully, "it's only natural. From what I'm told it's common for a writer to reflect some parts of his personal life...and in his own way," she added. "As a matter of fact, I visited the set just last week. Pat Marshell's producing, you know, and Chuck Tyler's directing."

"But..." Bob prompted, noting her obvious reluctance.

"As I said, it's so difficult to find that right brand of magic." She tossed out the first seeds with a smile. "And Booth's never done anything for the small screen before. A difficult transition for anyone."

"Jack Rohrer's starring." Obligingly, Bob fed her the next line.

"Yes, excellent casting there. I thought Jack was absolutely brilliant in *Of Two Minds*. That was a script he could really sink his teeth into."

"But this one..."

"Well, I happen to be a big Jack Rohrer fan," Liz said, apparently sidestepping the question. "I doubt there's any part he can't find some meat on."

"And his costar?" Bob folded his hands on his desk. Liz was out for the jugular, he decided. It wouldn't hurt his ratings.

"The female lead's a lovely girl. I can't quite think of

her name, but I believe she has a part on a soap opera. Booth often likes to experiment rather than to go with experienced actors."

"As he did with you."

Her eyes narrowed fractionally. She didn't quite like that tone, or that direction. "You could put it that way." The haughtiness in her voice indicated otherwise. "But really, when one has the production rate this project has, one should shoot for the best talent available. Naturally, that's a personal opinion. I've always thought actors should pay their dues—God knows, I paid mine—rather than be cast in a major production because of a…shall we say personal whim?"

"Do you think Booth DeWitt has a personal whim going with Ariel Kirkwood? That's her name, isn't it?"

"Why, yes, I think it is. As to the other, I could hardly say." She smiled again, charmingly. "Especially on the air, Bob."

"Her physical resemblance to you is striking."

"Really?" Liz's eyes frosted. "I much prefer being one of a kind, though of course it's flattering to have someone attempt to emulate me. Naturally, I wish the girl the best of luck."

"That's gracious of you, Liz, particularly since the plot line's rumored to be less than kind to the character that some say mirrors you."

"Those that know me will pay little attention to a slanted view, Bob. All in all, I'll be fascinated to see the finished product." The statement was laced with boredom, almost as if she'd yawned. "That is, of course, if it's ever actually aired."

"Ever aired? You see some problem there?"

"Nothing I can talk about," she said with obvious

reluctance. "But you and I know how many things can happen between filming and airing, Bob."

"No plans to sue, huh, Liz?"

She laughed, but it came off hollow. "That would give the film entirely too much importance."

Bob mugged at the camera. "Well, with that we'll take a little break here. When we come back, James R. Lemont will be joining us to tell us about his new book, *Hollywood Secrets*. We know about those, too, don't we, Liz?" After his wink, the screen switched to the first commercial.

Leaning back against the pillows, his meal forgotten, Booth drew on his cigarette and sent the smoke to the ceiling. He was angry. He could feel it in the hard knot in his stomach. The swipes she'd taken at the film hadn't even been subtle, he reflected. Oh, perhaps she'd fool a certain percentage of people, but no one remotely connected with the business, and no one with any perception. She'd done her best to toss a few poison darts and had ended up, in Booth's opinion, by making a fool of herself.

But he was angry. And the anger, he discovered, came from the slices she'd taken at Ariel. Quite deliberate, quite calculated, and unfortunately for Liz, quite obvious. She was a cat, and normally a clever one. Jealousy was essentially the only thing that could make her lose that edge.

Naturally she'd be jealous of Ariel, Booth mused. Of anyone young, beautiful and talented. Add that to the bile she'd have to swallow over the film itself, and Liz would be as close to rage as her limited range of emotions would allow. And this was her way of paying back.

Rising, Booth slammed off the set before he paced

the room. She'd bring up the film—and Ariel—in every interview she gave, at every party she attended, in the hope to sabotage both. Of course, she wouldn't do any appreciable damage, but knowing that didn't ease his temper. No one had the right to take potshots at Ariel, and the fact that they were being taken through him, because of him, made it worse.

He could, if he chose, book himself on the circuit to promote the film and to counter Liz's campaign. That would only add fuel to the fire. He knew the best way to make the storm Liz was trying to brew fizzle was to keep silent. Frustrated, he walked to the window. He could hear the water from there. Just barely. He wondered if Ariel had watched the late-night talk show. And how she was dealing with it.

Stretched out in the hammock, plumped by pillows, with a bowl of fresh popcorn resting on her stomach, Ariel listened to Liz Hunter. Her brow lifted once as a reference was made to herself. Ariel crunched on popcorn and smiled as Robert MacAllister reminded Liz that *the girl's* name was Ariel Kirkwood.

Poor Liz, she thought. She was only making it worse for herself. Perhaps because Ariel had been inside Rae's skin for so many weeks, she noticed small things. The tapping of a fingertip on the arm of the chair, the brief tightening of the lips, the flash in the eyes that was a bit of anger, a bit of desperation. The more Liz talked, the shakier her support became.

She'd have been much better off if she'd said nothing, Ariel mused. A no-comment, a shrug of that haughty shoulder. Miscalculation, Ariel thought with a sigh. A foolish one.

I can't hurt her. Ariel shifted her gaze from the screen to the ceiling. No one can take her talent away from her. A pity she doesn't realize that. It's Booth she really wants to hurt, Ariel decided. She'd want to make him pay for using Rae to strip off a few masks. Yet didn't Liz realize he was just as bitterly honest with his own character?

Ariel glanced back at the television screen as Liz's face dominated the screen. There was a line of dissatisfaction between her brows, very faint. Ariel wondered if she were the only one who noticed it, because she was so intimately involved. I know you, Ariel told the image on the screen, I know you inside and out. And that made her swallow hard. It was just a little scary.

Ariel lay back, tuning out the sound of the set and tuning back into the rain. It was nearly over, only a patter now against the windowpane. Booth had probably seen it, she decided. And if he hadn't caught the show, he'd know of the content very soon. He'd be angry. Ariel could almost see his hard-eyed, grim-mouthed reaction. She herself had been fighting an edge of temper that threatened to dominate her other feelings.

Anger was useless; she wished she could tell him. He had to know that he'd opened the door for this when he'd written the script. She'd opened it a bit further when she'd taken the part. She hoped, when he'd calmed, that he'd see Liz Hunter had done the film more good than harm.

When the phone rang, Ariel leaned over. Years of experience kept her balanced rather than tumbling out of the hammock and onto the floor. Swinging a bit dangerously, she gripped the phone and hauled it up to her. "Hello."

"That witch."

With a half laugh, Ariel lay back on the pillows. "Hi, Stella."

"Did you catch the MacAllister show?"

"Yeah, I've got it on."

"Listen, Ariel, she's making a joke out of herself. Anyone with two brain cells will see that."

"Then why're you angry?"

She could hear Stella take a deep breath. "I've been sitting here listening to that woman talk, wishing you the *best* of luck." Stella muttered something under her breath, then began to talk so fast the words tumbled into each other. "The best of luck my foot. She'd like to see you drop off the face of the earth. She'd like to stick a knife in you."

"A nail file, maybe."

"How can you joke about it?" Stella demanded.

Because if I don't I might just start screaming. "How can you take it so seriously?" Ariel said instead.

"Listen, Ariel…" Stella's voice was barely controlled. "I know that kind of woman. I've been playing the type for the past five years. There's nothing she wouldn't do, nothing, if she thought she could get to you. Damn it, you trust everyone."

"Some less than others." Though the concern and the loyalty touched her, she laughed. "Stella, I'm not a complete fool."

"You're not a fool at all," Stella shot back, outraged. "But you're naive. You actually believe the kid who stops you on the street asking for a donation is really collecting for a foundling home."

"He might be," Ariel mumbled. "Besides, what does that have to do with—"

"Everything!" Stella cut her off with something close to a roar. "I care about you. I worry about you every time I think about you walking blithely down the street without a thought to the crazies in the world."

"Come on, Stella, if I thought about it too much I'd never go out at all."

"Well think about this: Liz Hunter's a powerful, vindictive woman who'd like to ruin you. You watch your back, Ariel."

Who'd know that better than I? Ariel thought with a quick shudder. *I've been playing her character for weeks.* "If I promise, will you stop worrying?"

"No." Slightly mollified, Stella sighed. "Promise anyway."

"You got it. Are you calm now?"

Stella made a quiet sound in her throat. "I don't understand why you're not angry."

"Why should I be when you're doing it for me—and so well?"

Stella heaved a long breath. "Good night, Ariel."

"Night, Stella… Thanks."

Ariel replaced the receiver and swung gently to and fro in the hammock. As she stared up at the ceiling, she marveled over how fortunate she was. Friendship was a precious thing. To have someone ready to leap to your defense, claws bared, was a comforting sensation. She had friends like that, and a job that paid her well for doing what she would gleefully have done for nothing. She had the unquestioning love of a little boy, and God willing, would have him to care for within a few weeks. She had so much.

As Ariel lay back, struggling to count her blessings, she thought of Booth. And ached for him.

Two days later, Ariel received a surprise visit. It was her first free day since resuming her role of Amanda. She was spending it doing something she rarely started, and more rarely finished. Housecleaning.

In tattered shorts and a halter, she sat on her windowsill two stories up, and leaning out, washed the outside of her windows. The volume on her radio was turned up so that the sinuous violins of *Scheherazade* all but shook the panes. Occasionally someone from the neighborhood would shout up at her. Ariel would stop working—something that took no effort at all—and shout back down.

The important thing was to keep busy, to keep occupied. If she gave herself more than a brief moment of spare time, time to think, she might go mad. The next day marked the beginning of the custody hearing. And a full two weeks since she'd last seen Booth. Ariel polished window glass until it shone.

She felt something like an itch between her shoulder blades, like a fingertip on the back of the neck. Twisting her head, she looked down and saw Booth on the sidewalk below. Relief came in waves. Even if she'd tried, even if she'd thought to try, she couldn't have stopped the smile that illuminated her whole face.

"Hi."

Looking up at her, he felt a need so great it buckled his knees. "What the hell are you doing?"

"Washing the windows."

"You could break your neck."

"No, I'm anchored." One of the kittens brushed

against her ankles so that she jolted and braced herself with her knees. "Are you coming up?"

"Yeah." Without another word, he disappeared from view.

As he climbed the stairs Booth reminded himself of his promise. He wasn't going to touch her—not once. He would say what he'd come to say, do what he'd come to do, then leave. He wouldn't touch her and start that endless cycle of longings and desires and dreams all over again. Over the past two weeks he'd purged himself of her.

As he reached the landing he nearly believed it. Then she opened the door.

She still held a damp rag in one hand. She wore no makeup; the flush of color in her cheeks came from pleasure and exertion. Her hair was scooped back and tied with a bit of yarn. The scent of ammonia was strong.

His fingers itched for just one touch, just one. Booth curled them into his palms and stuck them in his pockets.

"It's good to see you." Ariel leaned against the door and studied him. People didn't change in two weeks, she reminded herself as she compared every angle and plane in his face with the memory she'd been carrying with her. He looked the same, a bit browner perhaps from the sun, but the same. Love washed over her.

"You've been sailing."

"Yes, quite a bit."

"It's good for you. I can see it." She stepped back, knowing from the tense way he was standing that he wouldn't accept her hand if she offered. "Come in."

He stepped into chaos. When Ariel cleaned, it was

from the bottom up and nothing was safe. Drawers had been turned out, tables cleared off. Furniture and windows gleamed. There wasn't a clear place to stand, much less sit.

"Sorry," she said as she followed his survey. "I'm a bit behind on my spring cleaning." The pressure in her chest was increasing with every second they stood beside each other, and miles apart. "Want a drink?"

"No, nothing. I'll make this quick because you're busy." He'd make it quick because it hurt, physically, painfully, not to touch what he still wanted…and to still want what he'd convinced himself he couldn't have. "I'm assuming you saw the MacAllister show the other night."

"That's old news," Ariel countered. She sat on the hammock, legs dangling free, fingers locked tightly.

With his hands still in his pockets, Booth rocked back on his heels. "How'd you feel about it?"

With a shrug, Ariel crossed her ankles. "She took a couple stabs at the film, but—"

"She took a couple stabs at *you*," he corrected. His voice had tightened, his eyes narrowed.

Gauging his mood, Ariel decided to play it light. She smiled. "I'm not bleeding."

Booth frowned at her a moment, then judged she was a great deal less concerned than he. That was something he had to change. "She hasn't stopped there, Ariel." He walked closer, the better to study her face, the better to perhaps catch the drift of her scent. "She had quite a little session with the producer of your show, then with a few network executives."

"With my producer?" Puzzled, she tilted her head and tried to reason it out. "Why?"

"She wants them to fire you—or, ah, to let your contract lapse."

Stunned, she said nothing. But her face went pale. The rag slipped silently from her hand to the floor.

"She'd agree to do a series of guest spots for the show, if you were no longer on it. Your producer politely turned her down. So she went upstairs."

Ariel swallowed the panic. All she could think, all that drummed in her mind was, *not now, not during the hearing.* She needed the stability of that contract for Scott. "And?"

He hadn't expected this white-lipped, wide-eyed reaction. A woman with her temperament should have been angry, angry enough to rage, throw things, explode. He could even have understood amusement, a burst of laughter, a shake of the head and a shrug. She was confident enough for that. He'd thought she was. What he saw in her eyes was basic fear.

"Ariel, just how important do you think you are to the show?"

She found she had to swallow before she could form the first word. "Amanda's a popular character. I get the lion's share of mail, a lot of it addressed to Amanda rather than me. In my last contract, my scale was upgraded with the minimum amount of negotiation." She swallowed again and gripped her hands together. That was all very logical, all very practical. She wanted to scream. "Anyone can be replaced. On a soap, that's the number-one rule. Are they going to let me go?"

"No." Frowning at her, he stepped closer. "I'm surprised you'd think they would. You're already their biggest reason for the ratings lead. And with the film due in the fall, the show's bound to cash in on it. In a strictly practical way of thinking, you—day after day—are worth a great deal more to the network than Liz in a one-shot deal." When Ariel let out a long breath he had to fight the urge to take her into his arms. "Does the show mean that much to you?"

"Yes, it means that much to me."

"Why?"

"It's my show," she said simply. "My character." As the panic faded, the anger seeped in. "If I leave it, it'll be because it's what I want, or because I'm not good enough anymore." Giving in to rage she plucked up a little yellow vase from the table beside her and flung it and the baby's breath it held at the wall. Glass shattered, flowers spilled. "I've given five years of my life to that show." As her breathing calmed again, she stared at the shards of vase and broken blooms. "It's important to me," she continued, looking back up at Booth. "At the moment, for a lot of reasons, it's essential." Ariel gripped the side of the hammock and struggled to relax. "How did you hear about this?"

"From Pat. There's been quite a meeting of the minds as concerns you. We decided you should hear about this latest move privately."

"I appreciate it." The anger was fading. Relief made her light-headed. "Well, I'm sorry she feels so pressured that she'd try to do me out of a job, but I imagine she'll back off now."

"You're smarter than that."

"There's nothing she can do to me, not really. And every time she tries, she only makes it worse for herself." Slowly, deliberately, she relaxed her hands. "Every interview she gives is free publicity for the film."

"If there's any way she can hurt you, she will. I should've thought of that before I cast you as Rae."

Smiling, Ariel lifted her hands to his arms. "Are you worried about me? I'd like you to be…just a little."

He should have backed off right then. But he needed, badly needed to absorb that contact. Just her hands on his arms. If he were careful, very careful, it might be enough. "Whatever trouble she causes you I'm responsible for."

"That's a remarkably ridiculous statement—arrogant, egotistical." She grinned. "And exactly like you. I've missed you, Booth. I've missed everything about you."

She was drawing him closer, but more, she was drawing him in. Even as her hand reached for his face, he was lowering his mouth to hers. And the first taste was enough to make him forget every promise he'd made during this absence.

Ariel moaned as her lips met his. It seemed she'd been waiting for years to feel that melting thrill again. More. The greed flashed through her. She pulled him down so that the hammock swayed under their combined weight.

There was no gentleness in either of them now. Impatience shimmered. Without words they told each other to hurry—hurry and touch me; it's been too long. And as clothes were tugged away and flesh met flesh, they both took hungrily from the other.

The movement of the hammock was like the sea, and he felt the freedom. There was freedom simply in being near her again. And from freedom sprang the madness. He couldn't stop his hands from racing over her. He couldn't prevent his mouth from trying to devour every inch. He was starving for her and no longer cared that he had vowed to abstain. Her skin flowed warm and soft under his hands. Her mouth was hot and silky. The generosity he could never quite measure simply poured from her.

She'd stopped thinking the moment he'd kissed her again. Ariel didn't need the intellect now, only the senses. She could taste the salt on his skin as they clung together in the moist heat of the afternoon; the dark male flavor along his throat enticed her back, again and again. There was a fury of desire in him, more than she'd ever known in him before. It made her skin tremble to be wanted with such savagery.

But with the trembling came a mirroring desire in herself. The top of the hammock scraped against her back as his body pressed against hers. For one isolated moment, she thought she could feel the individual strands, then that sensation faded into another.

His hands were in her hair, holding her head back so that he could plunder her mouth. She heard his breath shudder, and saw, as her lashes fluttered up, that he was watching her. Always watching.

His eyes stayed open and on hers when he plunged into her. He wanted to see her, needed to know that her need for him was as great as his for her. And he could see it—in the trembling mouth. His name came from there in a breathy whisper. In the stunned pleasure in her eyes. He could bring her that. He could bring her that, Booth thought as he buried his face in her hair. He wanted to bring her everything.

"Ariel…" In the last sane corner of his mind he knew they were both near the edge. He took her face in his hands and crushed his mouth to hers so that they crested, swallowing each other's cry of pleasure.

The movement of the hammock eased, soothing now, like a cradle. They were wrapped together, facing, with her head in the curve of his shoulder. Their bodies were damp from the heat in the air, and from the heat within. A length of her hair fell over her and onto his chest.

"I thought of you," Booth murmured. His eyes were closed. His heartbeat was slowing, but the arms around her didn't loosen. "I could never stop thinking about you."

Ariel's eyes were open, and she smiled. She'd needed no other words but those. "Sleep with me awhile." Turning her head she kissed his shoulder before settling again. "Just for a little while."

For days and nights she'd thought only of tomorrows. The time had come again to think only of now. Long after he slept, she lay awake, feeling the hammock move gently.

Chapter 11

Ariel sat on a small wooden bench outside the courtroom. It was a busy hallway with people coming and going, but no one paid much attention to a solitary woman in a cream-colored suit who stared straight ahead.

The first day of the hearing was over, and she felt a curious mixture of relief and tension. It had begun; there was no going back. A door opened down the hall, and a flood of people poured out. She'd never felt more alone in her life.

Bigby had outlined it for her. There'd been no surprises. Despite the legal jargon, the first day had dealt basically with establishing the groundwork. Still, to Ariel's mind the preliminary questions had been terribly cut-and-dried. But the wheels had begun to turn, and now that they had, maybe the pace would pick up.

Just let it be over with quickly, she thought and closed her eyes briefly. *Just let it be done.* The tension came from the thought of tomorrow. The relief came from the absolute certainty that she was doing the right thing.

Bigby came out of the courtroom with his slim briefcase in his hand. With his other, he reached out to her. "Let me buy you a drink."

Ariel smiled, linking her hand with his as she rose. "Deal. But make it coffee."

"You did well in there today."

"I didn't do much of anything."

He started to speak, then changed his mind. Maybe it was best not to point out how much she'd done by simply being. Her freshness, the concern in her eyes, the tone of her voice—all of that had been a vital contrast to the stiff backs and stone faces of the Andersons. A judge in a custody suit, a good one, was influenced by more than facts and figures.

"Just keep doing it," he advised, then gave her hand a squeeze as they walked down the hall. Neither of them noticed the dark-suited man in horn rims who followed. "Tell me how the rest of your life's going," he requested. In his unobtrusive way, Bigby guided her through the doors as he guided her thoughts. "It isn't every day I represent a rising celebrity."

She laughed even as the first wave of heat rose off the sidewalk and struck her. New York in midsummer was hot and humid and sweaty. "Is that what I am?"

"Your picture was in *Tube*—and your name was brought up on the MacAllister show." He grinned as she arched a brow. "I'm impressed."

"Read *Tube,* do you, Charlie?" He was trying to keep her calm, she realized. And he was doing it expertly.

She slid a companionable arm through his. "I have to admit, the publicity isn't going to hurt the soap, the film or me."

"In that order?"

Ariel smiled and shrugged. "Depends on my mood." No, she wasn't without ambition. The *Tube* spread had given her a great deal of self-satisfaction. "It's been a long time between shampoo commercials, and I won't be sorry if I don't have to stand, lathered up, for three hours again anytime soon."

They entered a coffee shop where the temperature dropped by twenty-five degrees. Ariel gave a quick shiver and a sigh of relief. "So professionally, everything's rolling along?" Charlie asked.

"No complaints." Ariel slipped into the little vinyl booth and pushed off her shoes. "They're casting for *Chapter Two* next week. I haven't done live theater in too long."

Bigby clucked his tongue as he picked up a menu. The man in the dark suit took the booth behind them, settling with his back to Ariel's. "You don't sit still, do you?"

"Not any longer than I can help it. I have good feelings about the custody suit, maybe because I'm on a professional roll. It's all going to work out, Charlie. I'm going to have Scott with me, and Booth's film's going to be a smash."

He eyed her over his glasses, then grinned. "The power of positive thinking."

"If it works." She leaned her elbows on the table, then rested her chin on her fists. "All my life I've been moving toward certain goals, without really understanding that I was setting them for myself. They're almost within reach."

Bigby glanced up at the waitress before he turned back to Ariel. "How about some pie with the coffee?"

"You twisted my arm. Blueberry." She touched the tip of her tongue to her lip because she could almost taste it.

"Two of each," Bigby told the waitress. "Speaking of Booth DeWitt…" he went on.

"Were we?"

He caught the gleam of amusement in Ariel's eye. "I think you mentioned him to me a few weeks ago. A man who didn't think much of relationships or actresses?"

"You've quite a memory—and very sharp deductive skills."

"It was easy enough to put two and two together, particularly after Liz Hunter's performance on the Mac-Allister show the other night."

"Performance?" Ariel repeated with a half smile.

"An actor can usually see through another, I'd think. A lawyer's got a lot of actor in him." He paused and folded his hands on the chipped Formica much as he did on his desk. "She put DeWitt through the wringer a couple of years ago."

"They damaged each other. You know, sometimes I think people can be attracted to the specific persons who are the worst for them."

"Is that from personal experience?"

Her eyes became very sober, her mouth very soft. "Booth is right for me. In a lot of ways he'll make my life difficult, but he's right for me."

"What makes you so sure?"

"I'm in love with him." When the pie was brought

over, Ariel ignored the coffee and concentrated on it. "Bless you, Charlie," she said after the first bite.

He lifted a brow at the sliver of pie she was in raptures over. "You're easily impressed."

"Cynic. Eat it."

He picked up a fork and polished it absently with a paper napkin. "At the risk of putting my foot in it, De-Witt isn't the type of man I'd've matched you with."

Ariel swallowed the next mouthful. "Oh?"

"He's very intense, serious-minded. His scripts have certainly indicated that. And you're…"

"Flaky?" she suggested, breaking off the next piece of pie.

"No." Bigby opened one of the little plastic containers of cream that were heaped in a bowl on the table. "You're anything but that. But you're full of life—the joy of it. It's not that you don't face the hard side when it comes up, but you don't look for it. It seems to me DeWitt does."

"Maybe—maybe he expects it. If you expect it and it happens, you aren't as staggered by it. For some people, it's a defensive move." A small frown creased her brow before she smoothed it away. "I think Booth and I can learn a lot from each other."

"And what does Booth think—or am I out of line?"

"You're not out of line, Charlie," she said absently as she remembered how grim Booth had been when he'd come to her door, how intensely he'd made love to her. He'd relaxed, degree by slow degree. Then he'd slept, with his arms tightly around her, as if he'd just needed to hold on. To her, she'd wondered, or to the peace? Perhaps it didn't matter. "It's hard for Booth," she murmured. "He wanted to be left alone, wanted his life to go on a certain way. I've interfered with that. He needs more time, more space."

"And what do you need?"

She looked over and saw her answer hadn't pleased him. *He's thinking of me,* Ariel realized, touched. Reaching over, she laid a hand on his. "I love him, Charlie. That's enough, for now. I do know it's not enough for always, but people can't put a control switch on emotions. I can't," she corrected.

"Does that mean he can?"

"To a certain extent." Ariel opened her mouth again, then shook her head. "No, I don't want to change him, even in that way. Not change. I need the balance he brings me, and I need to be able to lighten some of those shadows he carries around. It's the same with Scott, in a way. I need the stability he brings to my life—the way Scott, maybe children in general, can center it. Basically, I have an outrageous need to be needed."

"Have you told Booth about Scott? About the custody hearing?"

"No." Ariel stirred sugar into her coffee but didn't drink it. "It doesn't seem fair to saddle him with a problem that was already in full swing when we met. Instinct tells me to handle it myself, then when it's resolved, to tell Booth in my own way."

"He might not like it," Bigby pointed out. "The one thing Ford brought up in our last meeting that I have to agree with is that some men can't or won't be responsible for another man's child."

Ariel shook her head. "I don't believe that of Booth. But if it's true, it's something I'll have to deal with."

"If you did have to make a choice?"

She said nothing at first, as she dealt with the ache

even the possibility brought her. "When you make a choice between two people you love," Ariel said quietly, "you choose the one who needs you the most." She lifted her eyes again. "Scott's only a child, Charlie."

He leaned across to pat her hand. "I just wanted to hear you say it. To be completely unprofessional again," he said with a grin, "there isn't a man in the world who'd turn down either you or Scott."

"That's why I'm crazy about you." She paused a moment, then touched her fork to her tongue. "Charlie, would you think I was really a hedonist if I ordered another piece of this pie?"

"Yes."

"Good." Ariel lifted a hand and gestured for the waitress. "Once in a while I just have to be decadent."

Amanda's life was a pressure cooker. As she went over the pacing of her lines one last time, Ariel decided she was grateful for the tension. It helped her deal with reality just a little better. She'd spent the morning in court, and the following day she was scheduled to take the stand. That was one part she couldn't rehearse for. But the good feeling she'd experienced the first day of the hearing hadn't faded, nor had her optimism. It was poor Amanda, Ariel mused, who'd continue to have problems that would never completely be resolved. That was life in a soap opera.

The rest of the cast had yet to return from the lunch break. Ariel sat alone in the studio—lounged, that is, on the rumpled bed she would rise from when Amanda was awakened by the sound of breaking glass. Alone and defenseless, she'd face the Trader's Bend Ripper.

She'd have only her wits and professional skill to protect her from a psychotic killer.

Already in costume, a plain nightshirt in periwinkle-blue, she continued to murmur her lines out loud while doing a few lazy leg lifts. She'd had some vague twinges of guilt about the second piece of blueberry pie.

"Well, well, so this is the lightning pace of daytime television."

Immersed in the gripping scene between Amanda and a psychopath, Ariel dropped the script and gasped. The pages fluttered back down to her stomach while her hand flew to her throat. "Good God, Booth. I hope you're up on your CPR, because my heart just stopped."

"I'll get it started again." Placing a hand on either side of her head, he leaned down and kissed her—softly, slowly, thoroughly. As surprised by the texture of the kiss as she'd been by his sudden appearance, Ariel lay still and absorbed. She knew only that something was different; but with her mind spinning and her blood pumping she couldn't grab on to it.

He knew. As he eased down to sit on the bed and prolonged the kiss, Booth understood precisely what was different. He loved her. He'd awakened alone in his own bed that morning, reaching for her. He'd read something foolish in the paper and had automatically thought how she'd have laughed. He'd seen a young girl with a balloon giggling as she'd dragged her mother toward the park. And he'd thought of Ariel.

And thinking of her, he'd seen that the sky was beautiful and blue, that the city was frantic and full of surprises, that life was a joy. How foolish he'd been to resist her, and all she offered.

She was his second chance.... No, if he were honest,

he'd admit that Ariel was his first chance at real happiness—complete happiness. He was no longer going to allow memories of ugliness to bar him from that, or from her.

"How's your heart rate?" he murmured.

Ariel let out a long breath, let her eyes open slowly. "You can cancel the ambulance."

He glanced at the tumbled bed, then down her very sedate, very appealing costume. "Were you having a nap?"

"I," she countered primly, "was working. The rest of the cast is at lunch, I wasn't due in till one." She pushed at the hair that fell dark and disordered over his brow. No tension, she thought immediately, and smiled. "What're you doing here? You're usually knee-deep in brilliant phrases this time of day."

"I wanted to see you."

"That's nice." Sitting up, she threw her arms around his neck. "That's very nice."

It would take so little, Booth mused as he held her close. What would her reaction be when he told her that he'd stopped resisting, and that nothing had ever made him happier than having her in his life? Tonight, he thought, nuzzling into her neck. Tonight when they were alone, when there was no one to disturb them, he'd tell her. And he'd ask her.

"Can you stay awhile?" Ariel didn't know why she felt so wonderful, nor did she want to explore the reasons.

"I'll stay until you wrap, then I'm going to steal you and take you home with me."

She laughed, and as she shifted her weight, the script crumpled beneath her.

"Your lines," Booth warned.

"I know them. This—" she flung back her head so that her eyes glittered "—is a climactic scene full of danger and drama."

He looked back at the bed. "And sex?"

"No!" Shoving him away she scrambled onto her knees. "Amanda's tossing and turning in bed, her dreams were disturbed. Fade out—soft focus—she's wandering through a mist, lost, alone. She hears footsteps behind her. Close-up. Fear. And then…" While her voice took on a dramatic pitch, she tossed her hair behind her back. "Up ahead, she sees a figure in the fog." Ariel lifted a hand as if to brush away a curtain of mist. "Should she run toward it—away from it? The footsteps behind her come faster, her breathing quickens. A sliver of moonlight—pale, eerie—cuts through. It's Griff up ahead holding out a hand to her, calling her name in an echoing, disembodied voice. He loves her, she wants to go to him. But the footsteps are closing in. And as she begins to run, there's the sharp, cruel glimmer of a knife."

Ariel grabbed both of his shoulders then did a mock faint into his lap. Booth grinned. A quick tug of her hair had her eyes opening. "And then?"

"The man wants more." Scrambling up again, Ariel pushed the script aside. "The scream's caught in her throat, and before she can free it, there's a crash, a splinter of glass. Amanda jerks up in bed, her face glistening with sweat, her breath heaving." When she demonstrated, Booth wondered if she knew just how clever she was. "Did she dream it, or did she really hear it? Frightened, but impatient with herself, she gets out of bed."

Swinging her feet to the floor, Ariel got out of bed,

frowning at the door as Amanda would do, absently pushing back her hair and reaching for the low light beside the bed. "Perhaps it was the wind," she continued. "Perhaps it was the dream, but she knows she'll never get back to sleep unless she takes a look. Music builds—lots of bass—as she opens the bedroom door. Cut to commercial."

"Come on, Ariel." Exasperated, he grabbed her hand and pulled her back toward the bed.

Obligingly she circled his neck with her arms as she stood in front of him. "Now you'll learn the best way to keep that shine on your no-wax floor."

He pinched her, hard. "It's the Ripper."

"Maybe," she said with a flutter of her lashes. "Maybe not."

"It's the Ripper," he said decisively. "And our intrepid Amanda goes downstairs. How does she get out of being victim number five?"

"Six," Ariel corrected. "The saying goes, that's for me to know and you to find out." With a jerk of his wrist, he'd whipped her around so that she tumbled into his lap, laughing. "Go ahead, torture me, do your worst. I'll never talk." Linking her hands around his neck, she looked up at him and smiled. And she was so beautiful, so full of life at its best that she took his breath away.

"I love you, Ariel."

He felt the fingers at his neck go limp, saw the smile fade, her eyes widen. Inside, Ariel felt as though someone had just cut off the flow of blood from her heart. "That's a tough way to find out a plotline," she managed after a moment. She would have sat up if she'd had the strength to resist the gentle pressure of his hand on her shoulder.

"I love you, Ariel," he repeated, forgetting all his plans for telling her with finesse and with intimacy. "I think I always have. I know I always will." He cupped her face in his hand as her eyes filled. "You're everything I've ever wanted and was afraid to hope for. Stay with me." He touched his lips to hers and felt the tremor. "Marry me."

When he would have drawn back, she clutched at his shirt. Burying her face in his shoulder she took a deep breath. "Be sure," she whispered. "Booth, be absolutely sure because I'll never give you a moment's peace. I'll never let you get away. Before you ask me again, remember that. I don't believe in mutual disagreements or irreconcilable differences. With me, it's forever, Booth. It's for always."

He forced her head back. In his eyes she saw the fire and the passion. And the love. "You're damn right." Her breathless laugh was muffled against his mouth. "I want to get married quickly." He punctuated the words with another kiss. "And quietly. Just how soon can they shoot around Amanda so we can have more than a weekend honeymoon?"

Ariel hadn't known anyone could outpace her. Now, her thoughts jumbled as she struggled to keep up. Marriage—he was already talking of marriage and honeymoons. "Well, I, let's see… After Griff saves Amanda from the Ripper, she loses the baby and goes into a coma. The hospital scenes could be—"

"Aha." With a self-satisfied smile, Booth kissed her nose. "So Griff saves her from the Ripper, which removes him from the list of suspects."

Ariel's eyes narrowed. "You rat."

"Just be glad I'm not a spy for another network. You're a pushover."

"I'll show you a pushover," Ariel claimed, and over-balanced him so that he landed on his back. He loved her. The thought brought on such giddiness, she collapsed against him, laughing. Before he could retaliate, they heard someone rushing up the stairs.

"Ariel! Ariel, you'd better take a look at—" Stella skidded to a halt when she saw Ariel and Booth laughing and half lying on the bed. She whipped the paper she held behind her back and swore under her breath. "Whoops!" With the aid of an embarrassed smile she called on all her skill to keep either of them from noticing that she felt slightly ill inside and desperately worried. "Well, I'd've knocked if you'd bothered to close the door." She gestured with her free hand toward the false wall. "Suppose I go out and come in again?" *Right after I burn this paper,* she thought grimly, and grinning, backed up.

"Don't go." Ariel struggled all the way up, but kept one hand tucked into Booth's. "I'm about to bestow a singularly great honor on you." She squeezed Booth's fingers. "My sister, however rotten, should be the first to know."

"By all means."

"Stella…" Ariel stopped because she caught a glimpse of something in her friend's eyes. A glimpse was enough. "What is it?"

"Nothing. I remembered I have to talk to Neal about something, that's all. Look, I'd better catch him before he—"

But Ariel was already rising from the bed. "What was it you wanted me to see, Stella?"

"Oh, nothing." There was a warning, a deliberate one, in her eyes. "It can wait."

Unsmiling, Ariel held out her hand, palm up.

Stella's fingers curled tighter around the paper. "Ariel, it's not a good time. I think you'd better—"

"I think I'd better see it now."

"Damn it." With a glance over Ariel's shoulder at Booth, Stella passed her the paper.

Celebrity Explorer, Ariel noted with a slight flicker of annoyance. As tabloids went it was bottom of the barrel. Half-amused, she glanced over the exploitive headlines. "Really, Stella, if this is the best you can do for lunchtime reading, I'm disillusioned." Absently, she turned it over and scanned under the fold. From behind her Booth saw the tension shoot into her body.

SOAP OPERA QUEEN'S DESPERATE BATTLE
FOR LOVE CHILD

Below the bold print headline was a grainy picture of Ariel sitting on the grass in Central Park with Scott's face caught in her hands. In one part of her mind she remembered that frozen moment from their last Sunday afternoon. As she stared at it, appalled, sickened, she didn't hear Booth rise and come to her.

Something slammed into his stomach—not a hammer but a fist that thrust then ground deep. Even the poor quality of the photo didn't disguise the stunning resemblance between Ariel and the child that laughed into her face. There was no mistaking the tie of blood. As the headline shouted out at him, Booth wanted to murder.

"Just what the hell is this?"

Shaken, Ariel looked up. Scott was not to see it, she thought over and over. This was not to touch him. How? How had it leaked? The Andersons? No, she rejected that thought instantly. They wanted publicity less than she did.

The picture…who'd taken it? Someone had followed her, she decided. Someone had followed her and found out about Scott, the custody hearing. Then they'd twisted it into an ugly headline and an exploitive article. But who…?

Liz Hunter. Ariel's fingers tightened on the newspaper. Of course, it had to be. There were few women who knew better than Ariel what that type of person was capable of. Liz hadn't been able to get to her professionally, so she'd taken the next step.

"Ariel, I asked you what the hell this is."

Ariel focused on Booth abruptly. *Oh God,* she thought, *now I have to work my way through the ugliness before I can explain.* Already, she saw the anger, the distrust. "I'd like to talk to you privately," she said calmly enough. "Down in my dressing room."

As Ariel turned to go, Stella reached out, then dropped her hand helplessly back to her side. "Ariel, I'm sorry."

She only shook her head. "No, it's all right. We'll talk later."

As they wound their way through the studio, down the corridors, she tried to think logically. All she could see was that nasty headline and grainy picture. When she walked into the dressing room she went directly to the coffeepot, needing to do something with her hands. She heard the door close and the lock click.

"This isn't the way I wanted to handle this, Booth."

She pulled in a deep breath as she fumbled with the coffee. "I didn't expect any publicity...I've been so careful."

"Yes, careful." He jammed his hands into his pockets.

She pressed her lips together as the tone of his voice pricked along her skin. "I know you must have questions. If I..."

"Yes, I have questions." He snatched the paper from her dressing table. He, too, needed to occupy his hands. "Are you involved in a custody suit?"

"Yes."

He felt the grinding in his stomach again. "So much for trust."

"No, Booth." She whirled around, then stopped as a hundred conflicting emotions, a hundred opposing answers hammered at her. Would this be the time of choice? Would she have to choose after all, when she almost had everything she needed? "Please, let me explain. Let me think how to explain."

"You're involved in a custody suit." He remembered those brief flashes of strain he'd seen in her from time to time. He wanted to tear the paper to shreds. "You have this child, and you didn't tell me. What does that say about trust?"

Confused, she dragged a hand through her hair. "Booth, I was already deeply involved in this before we even met. I couldn't drag you into it."

Bitterness seeped into him. Booth hated to taste it... again. "Oh, I see. You were already involved, so it was none of my business. It appears that you have two separate standards for your trust, Ariel. The one for yourself, and the one for everyone else."

"That's not true," she began, then fumbled to a halt. Was it? "I don't mean for it to be." Her voice began to shake, then her hands. "Booth, I've been frightened. Part of the fear was that something would leak out. The most important thing to me was that none of this touch Scott."

He waited, trying to be impassive as she brushed away the first tear. "That's the boy's name?"

"Yes. He's only four years old."

He turned away because the grief on her face was destroying him. "And his father?"

"His father's name was Jeremy. He's dead."

Booth didn't ask if she'd loved him. He didn't have to. She'd loved another man, he thought. Had borne another man's child. Could he deal with that, accept it? Resting his palms on her dressing table he let the emotion run through him. Yes, he thought so. It didn't change her, or him. And yet…and yet she hadn't told him. It was that that brought the change.

"Who has the boy now?" he asked stiffly.

"His grandparents. He's not…he's not happy with them. He needs me, Booth, and I need him. I need both of you. Please…" Her voice lowered to a whisper. "Don't ask me to choose. I love you. I love you so much but he's just a little boy."

"Choose?" Booth flicked on his lighter, then tossed it onto her cluttered dressing table as he took the first drag from his cigarette. "Damn it, Ariel, just how insensitive do you think I am?"

She waited until she could control the throb of her heart at the base of her throat. "Would you take both of us?"

Booth blew out smoke. Fury was just below the surface. "You kept it from me. That's the issue now. I could hardly turn away from a child that's part of you."

She reached for him. "Booth—"

"You kept it from me," he repeated, watching her hand drop away. "Why?"

"Please understand, if I kept it from you it was only because I wanted to protect him. He's had a difficult time already, and I was afraid that if I talked about the hearing to anyone, anyone at all, there was a risk of something like that." She gestured to the paper, then turned away.

"There's nothing you don't know about my life, Ariel. I can't help but resent that there was something so vital to yours that you kept from me. All this time, almost from the first minute, you've asked me to trust you. Now that I've given that to you, I find you haven't trusted me."

"I put Scott first. He needed someone to put him first."

"I might be able to understand that, if you could explain to me why you ever gave him up."

"Gave him up?" Ariel stared, but tears blurred her vision. "I don't know what you mean."

"I thought I knew you!" Booth exploded. "I believed that, and believing it fell in love with you when I'd sworn I'd never get emotionally involved again. How could you give up your child? How could you have a child and say nothing to me?"

"Give up my child?" she repeated dumbly. "But no, no! It's nothing like that."

"Damn it, Ariel, you've let someone else raise your child. And now that you want him back, now that you're involved in something as serious as a custody battle, you do it alone. How could you love me, how could you preach trust at me and say nothing?"

"I was afraid to tell you or anyone. You don't understand how it might affect Scott if he knew—"

"Or how it might affect you?" He swung his arm toward the discarded paper.

Ariel sucked in her breath and barely controlled a raging denial. Perhaps she'd deserved that. "My concern was for Scott," she said evenly. "A custody suit would hardly damage my reputation. Any more than an illegitimate child would—though he's not my child. Jeremy was my brother."

It was Booth's turn to stare. Nothing made sense. Underlying his confusion was the thought that tears didn't belong in Ariel's eyes. Her eyes were for laughter. "The boy's your nephew?"

"Jeremy and his wife died late last winter." She couldn't go to him now; she could see he wasn't ready. And neither was she. "His grandparents, the Andersons, were appointed guardians. He's not happy with them."

Not her child, Booth thought again, but her brother's child. He waited to gauge his own reaction and found he was still hurt, still angry. Whether the boy was her son or not hadn't been the issue. She'd blocked that part of her life from him.

"I think," Booth said slowly, "that you'd better start at the beginning."

Ariel opened her mouth, but before she could speak, someone pounded on her door. "Phone for you, Ariel, in Neal's office. Urgent."

Banking back frustration, she left the room, heading for Neal's office. So much to explain, she thought. To

Booth and to herself. She rubbed her temple with two fingers as she picked up the phone. "Hello."

"Ms. Kirkwood."

"Yes, this is Ariel Kirkwood." Her frown deepened. "Mr. Anderson?"

"Scott's missing."

Chapter 12

She said nothing. Only seconds passed, but a hundred thoughts raced through her mind, tumbling over each other one at a time so that none was clear. Every nerve in her stomach froze. Vaguely she felt the ache in her hand where she gripped the receiver.

"Ms. Kirkwood, I said that Scott is missing."

"Missing?" she repeated in a whisper. The word itself brought up too many visions. Terrifying ones. She wanted to panic, but forced herself, by digging her nails into her palm, to talk, and to listen carefully. But even the whisper she forced out shook. "How long?"

"Apparently since around eleven o'clock. My wife thought he was next door, playing with a neighbor's child. When she called him home for lunch, she learned he'd never been there."

Eleven... With a sick kind of dread Ariel looked

at her watch. It was nearly two. Three hours. Where could a small boy go in three hours? Anywhere. It was an eternity. "You've called the police?"

"Of course." His voice was brisk but through it ran a thread of fear Ariel was too dazed to hear. "The neighborhood's been searched, people questioned. Everything possible's being done."

Everything possible? What did that mean? She repeated the phrase over in her mind, but it still didn't make sense. "Yes, of course." She heard her own words come hollowly through the rushing noise in her head. "I'll be there right away."

"No, the police suggest that you go home and stay there, in case Scott contacts you."

Home, she thought. They wanted her to go home and do nothing while Scott was missing. "I want to come. I could be there in thirty minutes." The whisper shattered into a desperate plea. "I could help look for him. I could—"

"Ms. Kirkwood," Anderson cut her off, then breathed deeply before he continued. "Scott's an intelligent boy. He knows where you live, he knows your phone number. At a time like this it's best to admit that it's you he wants to be with. If he— If it's possible for him to contact anyone, it would be you. Please, go home. If he's found here, I'll call you immediately."

The single phrase ran through her mind three times. *If it's possible for him to contact anyone...*

"All right. I'll go home. I'll wait there." Dazed, she stared at the phone, not even aware that she'd replaced the receiver herself. Marveling that she could walk at all, she moved to the door.

Of course she could walk, Ariel told herself as she

pressed a hand to the wall for support. She could function—she had to function. Scott was going to want her when he was found. He'd be full of stories and adventures—especially if he had the chance to ride in a police car. He'd want to tell her about all of it. The phone would probably be ringing when she opened her front door. He'd probably just been daydreaming and wandered a few blocks away, that was all. They'd be calling, so she should get home quickly. Her legs felt like rubber and would hardly move at all.

Booth was brooding at the picture of Ariel and Scott when he heard the door open. He turned, the paper still in his hand, but the questions that had been pressing at him faded the moment he saw her. Her skin was like parchment. He'd never seen her eyes look vacant, nor had he expected to.

"Ariel…" He was crossing to her before he'd finished speaking her name. "What is it?"

"Booth." She put her hand on his chest. Warm, solid. She could feel the beat of his heart. No, none of it was a dream. Or a nightmare. "Scott's missing. They don't know where he is. He's missing."

He took a firm hold on her shoulders. "How long, Ariel?"

"Three hours." The first wave of fear rammed through the shock. "Oh God, no one's seen him in three hours. Nobody knows where he is!"

He only tightened his hold on her shoulders when her body began to shake. "The police?"

"Yes, yes, they're looking." Her fingers curled, digging at his shirt. "They don't want me to come, they want me to go home and wait in case he…Booth."

"I'll take you home." He brushed the hair away from

her face. His touch, his voice, was meant to soothe. "We'll go home and wait for the call. They're going to find him, Ariel. Little boys wander off all the time."

"Yes." She grabbed on to that, and to his hand. Of course that was true. Didn't she have to watch him like a hawk when they went to the park or the zoo? "Scott daydreams a lot. He could've just walked farther than he should. They're going to call me...I should be home."

"I'm going to take you." Booth kept hold of her as she took a disoriented study of the room. "You change, and I'll let them know you can't tape this afternoon."

"Change?" Puzzled she looked down and saw she still wore Amanda's nightshirt. "All right, I'll hurry. They could call any minute."

She tried to hurry, but her fingers kept fumbling with the most basic task. She needed her jeans, but her mind seemed to fade in and out as she pulled them on. Then her fingers slid over the snap. She tried to think logically but the pounding at the side of her head made it impossible. Holding off the nausea helped. It gave her something tangible to concentrate on while she fought with the laces of her shoes.

Booth was back within moments. When she turned to look at him he could feel her panic. "Ready?"

"Yes." She nodded and walked out with him, one foot in front of the other, while images of Scott, lost, frightened, streamed through her head. Or worse, much worse—Scott getting into a car with a stranger, a stranger whose face was only a shadow. She wanted to scream. She climbed into a cab.

Booth took her icy hand in his. "Ariel, it isn't like you to anticipate the worst. Think." He put his other hand over hers and tried to warm it. "There're a hundred harmless reasons for his being out of touch for a few hours. He might've found a dog, or chased a ball. He might've found some fascinating rock and taken it to a secret place to study it."

"Yes." She tried to picture those things. It would be typical of Scott. The image of the car and the stranger kept intruding. He had no basic fear of people, something she'd always admired in him. Now it filled her with fear. Turning her face in to Booth's shoulder she tried to convince herself that the phone would be ringing when she opened the front door.

When the cab stopped, she jerked upright and scrambled for the handle. She was dashing up the steps before Booth had paid the driver.

Silence. It greeted her like an accusation. Ariel stared at the phone and willed it to ring. When she looked at her watch, she saw it had been less than thirty minutes since Anderson's call. Not enough time, she told herself as she began to pace. *Too much time.* Too much time for a little boy to be alone.

Do something! The words ran through her mind as she struggled to find something solid to grip on to. She'd always been able to do something in any situation. There were answers, and if not answers, choices. But to wait. To have no answer, no choice but to wait… She heard the door close and turned. Her hands lifted, then fell helplessly.

"Booth. Oh God, I don't know what to do. There must be something—anything."

Without a word he crossed to her, wrapped his arms around her and let her cling to him. Strange that it would have taken this—something so frightening for her—to make him realize she needed him every bit as much as he needed her. Whatever doubts he'd had, and whatever anger had lingered that she'd kept part of her life from him, dropped away. Love was simpler than he'd ever imagined.

"Sit down, Ariel." As he spoke, he eased her toward a chair. "I'm going to fix you a drink."

"No, I—"

"Sit down," he repeated with a firmness he knew she needed. "I'll make coffee, or I'll see about getting you a sedative."

"I don't need a sedative."

He nodded, rewarded by the sharp, quick answer. If she was angry, just a little angry, she wouldn't fall apart. "Then I'll make coffee."

The moment he went into the kitchen she was up again. Sitting was impossible, calm out of the question. She should never have agreed to come back and wait, Ariel told herself. She should have insisted on going out and looking for Scott herself. It was useless here—she was useless here. But if he called and she wasn't there to answer… Oh, God. She pressed her hands to her face and tried not to crumble. What time was it?

This time when she looked at her watch she felt the first hysterical sob build.

"Ariel." Booth carried two cups of coffee, hot and strong. He watched as she shuddered, swallowing sobs, but the tears ran freely.

"Booth, where could he be? He's hardly more than a baby. He doesn't have any fear of strangers. It's my fault because—"

"Stop." He said the word softly, but it had the effect of cutting off the rapidly tumbling words. He held out the cup, waiting for her to take it in both hands. It shook, nearly spilling the coffee over the rim. As it depleted, she sat again. "Tell me about him."

For a moment she stared at the coffee, as if she had no idea what it was or how she'd come to be holding it. "He's four…almost five. He wants a wagon, a yellow one, for his birthday. He likes to pretend." Lifting the cup, she swallowed coffee, and as it scalded her mouth, she calmed a bit. "Scott has a wonderful imagination. You can give him a cardboard box and he'll see a spaceship, a submarine, an Egyptian tomb. Really see it, do you know what I mean?"

"Yes." He laid a hand on hers as he sat beside her.

"When Jeremy and Barbara died, he was so lost. They were beautiful together, the three of them. So happy."

Her eyes were drawn to the boxing gloves that hung behind the door. Jeremy's gloves. They'd be Scott's one day. Something ripped inside her stomach. Ariel began to talk faster. "He's a lot like his father, the same charm and curiosity. The Andersons, Barbara's parents, never approved of Jeremy. They didn't want Barbara to marry him, and rarely saw her after she did. After… after the accident, they were appointed Scott's guardians. I wanted him, but it seemed natural that he go with them. A house, a yard, a family. But…" Breaking off, she cast a desperate look at the phone.

"But?" Booth prompted.

"They just aren't capable of understanding the kind of person Scott is. He'll pretend he's an archeologist and dig a hole in their yard."

"That might annoy anyone," Booth said and drew a wan smile from her.

"But he wouldn't dig up the yard if he had a sand

dump and someone told him it could be a desert. Instead, he's punished for his imagination rather than having it redirected."

"So you decided to fight for him."

"Yes." Ariel moistened her lips. Had she waited too long? "Even if that were all, I might not have started proceedings. They don't love him." Her eyes shimmered as she looked up again. "They just feel responsible for him. I can't bear thinking he could grow up without all the love he should have."

Where is he, where is he, where is he?

"He won't." Booth drew her against him to kiss the tears at the corners of her eyes. "After you get custody, we'll see that he doesn't."

Cautiously, she pulled back, though her fingers were still tight on his shoulders. "We?"

Booth lifted a brow. "Is Scott part of your life?"

"Yes, he—"

"Then he's part of mine."

Her mouth trembled open twice before she could speak. "No questions?"

"I've wasted a lot of time with questions. Sometimes there's no need for them." He pressed her fingers to his lips. "I love you."

"Booth, I'm so afraid." Her head dropped against him. The dam burst.

He let her weep, those harsh sobs that were edged with grief and fear. He let her hold on and pull out whatever strength she could find in him. He lived by words, but knew when clever phrases were of no use. So in silence, Booth held her.

Crying would help, he thought, smoothing her hair. It would allow her to give in to fear without putting a name on it. While she was vulnerable to tears, it was he who willed the phone to ring. And he was denied.

The passion exhausted her. Ariel lay against Booth, light-headed, disoriented, only aware of that hollow ache inside that meant something vital was wrong. Her mind groped for the reason. *Scott.* He was missing. The phone hadn't rung. He was still missing.

"Time," she murmured, staring over his shoulder at the phone through eyes that were swollen and abused by tears. "What time is it now?"

"It's nearly four," he answered, hating to tell her, hating the convulsive jerk he felt because her body was pressed so close to his. There were a dozen things he could say to offer comfort. All useless. "I'll make more coffee."

At the knock on the door, she looked around listlessly. She wanted no company now. Ignoring the knock, she turned her back to the door. It was the phone that was important. "I'll get the coffee." Forcing herself to move, she rose. "I don't want to see anyone, please."

"I'll send them away." Booth walked to the door, already prepared to position himself in front of it to shield her. When he opened it, he saw a young woman wearing a bandanna and paint-smeared overalls. Then he saw the boy.

"Excuse me. This little boy was wandering a couple blocks from here. He gave this address. I wonder if—"

"Who are you?" Scott demanded of Booth. "This is Ariel's house."

"I'm Booth. Ariel's been waiting for you, Scott."

Scott grinned, showing small white teeth. Baby teeth, Booth realized. *He's hardly more than a baby.* "I would've been here sooner, but I got a little lost. Bobbi was painting her porch and said she'd walk me over."

Booth laid a hand on Scott's head and felt the softness of hair—like Ariel's. "We're very grateful to you, Miss…"

"Freeman, Bobbi Freeman." She grinned and jerked her head toward Scott. "No trouble. He might've lost his way a bit, but he sure knows what he wants. It seems to be Ariel and a peanut butter sandwich. Well, hey, I've got to get back to my porch. See you later, Scott."

"Bye, Bobbi." He yawned hugely. "Is Ariel home now?"

"I'll get her." Leaving Scott to climb onto the hammock, Booth walked toward the kitchen. He stopped Ariel in the doorway then took the two cups from her hands. "There's someone here to see you."

She shut her eyes. "Oh, please, Booth. Not now."

"I don't think he'll take no for an answer."

Something in his tone had her opening her eyes again, had her heart drumming against her ribs. Skirting passed him, she hurried into the living room. A small blond boy swung happily in her hammock with two kittens in his lap. "Oh, God, Scott!"

His arms were already reaching for her as she dashed across the room and yanked him against her. Warmth. She could feel the warmth of his small body and moaned from the joy of it. His rumpled hair brushed against her face. She could smell the faintest memory of soap from his morning wash, mixed with the sweat of the day and the gumdrops he was forever secreting in his pockets. Weeping, laughing, she sank to the floor holding him.

"Scott, oh, Scott. You're not hurt?" The quick fear

struck at her again and she pulled him away to examine his face, his hands, his arms. "Are you hurt anywhere?"

"Uh-uh." A bit miffed at the question, Scott squirmed. "I didn't see Butch yet. Where's Butch?"

"How did you get here?" Ariel grabbed him again and gave in to the need to kiss his face—the rounded cheeks, the straight little nose, the small mouth. "Scott, where've you been?"

"On the train." His whole face lit. "I rode on the train all by myself. For a surprise."

"You…" Incredulous, Ariel stared at him. "You came from your grandparents', all alone?"

"I saved up my money." With no little pride he reached in his pocket and pulled out what he had left— a few pennies, two quarters and some gumdrops. "I walked to the station, but it took lots longer than a cab does. It isn't as far in a cab," he decided with a small boy's logic. "And I paid for the ticket all by myself— just like you showed me. I'm hungry, Ariel."

"In a minute." Appalled at the idea of his traveling alone and defenseless, she took both his arms. "You walked all the way to the train station, then rode the train here?"

"And I only got a little bit lost once, when Bobbi helped me. And I was hardly scared at all." His lip trembled. Screwing up his face, he buried it against her. "I wasn't."

All the things that might have happened to him flashed hideously through her mind. Ariel tightened her hold and thanked God. "Of course you weren't," she murmured, struggling to hold on to her emotions until she'd both schooled and scolded. "You're so brave, and so smart to remember the way. But Scott—" she tilted his face to hers "—it was wrong for you to come here all alone."

"But I wanted to see you."

"I know, and I always want to see you." Again she kissed him, just to feel the warmth of his cheek. "But you left without telling your grandparents, and they're so worried. And I've been worried," she added, brushing the hair from his temple. "You have to promise you won't ever do it again."

"I don't want to do it again." With his mouth trembling again, he rubbed his fists against his eyes. "It took a long time and I got hungry, and then I got lost and my legs were so tired. But I wasn't scared."

"It's all right now, baby." Still holding him, she rose. "We'll fix you something to eat, then you can rest in the hammock. Okay?"

Scott sniffled, snuggling closer. "Can I have peanut butter?"

"Absolutely." Booth came back into the room and watched as both heads turned toward him. He might be her own child, he thought, wonderingly. Surprised, he felt a yearning to hold the boy himself. "I just saw a peanut butter sandwich in the kitchen. I think it's yours."

"Okay!" Scott scrambled out of Ariel's arms and bounced away.

Getting unsteadily to her feet, Ariel pressed the heel of her hand to her brow. "I could skin him alive. Oh, Booth," she whispered as she felt his arms go around her. "Isn't he wonderful?"

By dusk, Scott was asleep, with a tattered stuffed dog that had been his father's gripped in one hand. The three-legged Butch kept guard on the pillow beside him. Ariel sat on the sofa next to Booth and faced

Scott's grandfather. Coffee grew cold on the table between them. As always, Mr. Anderson sat erect; his clothes were impeccable. But there was a weariness in his eyes Ariel had never seen before.

"Anything might've happened to the boy on a jaunt like that."

"I know." Ariel slipped her hand into Booth's, grateful for the support. "I've made him promise he won't ever do anything like it again. You and your wife must've been sick with worry. I'm sorry, Mr. Anderson. I feel partially to blame because I've let Scott buy the train tickets before."

He shook his head, not speaking for a moment. "An intrepid boy," he managed at length. "Sharp enough to know which train to take, when to get off." His eyes focused on Ariel's again. "He wanted badly to be with you."

Normally the statement would have warmed her. Now, it tightened the already sensitive muscles of her stomach. "Yes. Children often don't understand the consequences of their actions, Mr. Anderson. Scott only thought about coming, not about the hours of panic in between or about the dangers. He was tired and frightened when he got here. I hope you won't punish him too severely."

Anderson took a deep breath and rested a hand on either thigh. "I realized something today, Ms. Kirkwood. I resent that boy."

"Oh, no, Mr. Anderson—"

"Please, let me finish. I resent him, and I don't like knowing that about myself." His voice was clipped, unapologetic and, Ariel realized, old. Not so much in years, she thought, but in attitude. "And more, I've realized that his presence in the house is a constant strain on my wife. He's a reminder of something we lost. I'm not going to justify my feelings to you," he added briskly. "The boy is my grandchild, and therefore, I'm responsible for him. However, I'm an old man, and not inclined to change. I don't want the boy, and you do." He rose while Ariel could only stare at him. "I'll notify my attorney of my feelings on the matter."

"Mr. Anderson." Shaken, Ariel rose. "You know I want Scott, but—"

"I don't, Ms. Kirkwood." With his shoulders straight, Anderson gave her a level look. "It's as basic as that."

And as sad. "I'm sorry" was all she could say.

With a nod only, he left.

"How," Ariel began after a stretch of silence, "could anyone feel that way about a child?"

"About the child?" Booth countered. "Or about themselves?"

She turned to him, puzzled only for a moment. "Yes, that's it, isn't it?"

"I'm an expert on the subject. The difference is—" he drew her down to him again, circling her with his arm so that her head rested against his shoulder "—someone pushed her way into my life and made me see it."

"Is that what I did?" She laughed, riding the next curve on the roller coaster the day had been. Scott was sleeping on her bed, with kittens curled at his feet. He could stay there now. No more tearful goodbyes. "Pushed my way into your life?"

"You can be very tenacious." He gave her hair a sharp tug then captured her mouth as she gasped. "Thank God."

"Should I warn you that once I push my way in, I won't ever get out?"

"No." He shifted so that she could sit across his lap, and he could watch her face. "Let me find out for myself."

"It won't be easy for you, you know."

"What?"

"Dealing with me if you decide to marry me."

His brow rose, and unable to resist, she traced it with a fingertip. "If?"

"I'm giving you your last chance for escape." Half-serious, Ariel pressed her palm to his cheek. "I do most things on impulse—eating, spending, sleeping. I much prefer living in chaos to living in order. The fact is I can't function in order at all. I'll get you involved, one way or the other, in any number of organizations."

"That one remains to be seen," Booth muttered.

Ariel only smiled. "I haven't scared you off yet?"

"No." He kissed her, and as the shadows in the room lengthened, neither of them noticed. "And you won't. I can also be tenacious."

"Remember, you'll be taking on a four-year-old child. An active one."

"You've a poor opinion of my stamina."

"Oh, no." This time when she laughed, it held a husky quality. "I'll drive you crazy with my disorganization."

"As long as you stay out of my office," he countered, "you can turn everything else into a building lot."

She tightened her arms around his neck and clung for a moment. He meant it, she told herself, giddy. He meant it all. She had Booth, and Scott. And with them, her life was taking the next turning point. She could hardly wait to find what waited around the corner.

"I'll spoil Scott," she murmured into Booth's neck. "And the rest of our children."

He drew her back slowly, a half smile on his mouth. "How many is implied by *the rest?*"

Her laughter was free and breezy. "Pick a number."

* * * * *

New York Times bestselling author

SUSAN MALLERY

invites readers back to her beloved series set in Fool's Gold featuring three newcomers who find love when they are least expecting it...

Available now wherever books are sold!

"Susan Mallery is one of my favorites."
—#1 *New York Times* bestselling author Debbie Macomber

New York Times **bestselling author**

RaeAnne Thayne

Lucy Drake and Brendan Caine have only one thing in common...

"Hope's Crossing is a charming series that inspires hope and the belief miracles are possible."
—DEBBIE MACOMBER,
#1 New York Times bestselling author

NEW YORK TIMES BESTSELLING AUTHOR

RaeAnne Thayne

Wild Iris Ridge

And it's likely to tear them apart. Because it was Brendan's late wife, Jessie—and Lucy's best friend—who'd brought them together in the first place. And since Jessie's passing, Brendan's been distracted by his two little ones...and the memory of an explosive kiss with Lucy years before his marriage. Still, he'll steer clear of her. She's always been trouble with a capital *T*.

Lucy couldn't wait to shed her small-town roots for the big city. But now that she's back in Hope's Crossing to take care of the Queen Anne home her late aunt has left her, she figures seeing Brendan Caine again is no big deal. After all, she'd managed to resist the handsome fire chief once before, but clearly the embers of their attraction are still smoldering....

Available now wherever books are sold!

Be sure to connect with us at:

Harlequin.com/Newsletters
Facebook.com/HarlequinBooks
Twitter.com/HarlequinBooks

HARLEQUIN® HQN™
www.Harlequin.com

PHRAT859

REQUEST YOUR FREE BOOKS!

2 FREE NOVELS
FROM THE ROMANCE COLLECTION
PLUS 2 FREE GIFTS!

YES! Please send me 2 FREE novels from the Romance Collection and my 2 FREE gifts (gifts are worth about $10). After receiving them, if I don't wish to receive any more books, I can return the shipping statement marked "cancel." If I don't cancel, I will receive 4 brand-new novels every month and be billed just $6.24 per book in the U.S. or $6.74 per book in Canada. That's a savings of at least 22% off the cover price. It's quite a bargain! Shipping and handling is just 50¢ per book in the U.S. and 75¢ per book in Canada.* I understand that accepting the 2 free books and gifts places me under no obligation to buy anything. I can always return a shipment and cancel at any time. Even if I never buy another book, the two free books and gifts are mine to keep forever.

194/394 MDN F4XY

Name _____ (PLEASE PRINT) _____

Address _____ Apt. # _____

City _____ State/Prov. _____ Zip/Postal Code _____

Signature (if under 18, a parent or guardian must sign)

Mail to the **Harlequin® Reader Service:**
IN U.S.A.: P.O. Box 1867, Buffalo, NY 14240-1867
IN CANADA: P.O. Box 609, Fort Erie, Ontario L2A 5X3

Want to try two free books from another line?
Call 1-800-873-8635 or visit www.ReaderService.com.

* Terms and prices subject to change without notice. Prices do not include applicable taxes. Sales tax applicable in N.Y. Canadian residents will be charged applicable taxes. Offer not valid in Quebec. This offer is limited to one order per household. Not valid for current subscribers to the Romance Collection or the Romance/Suspense Collection. All orders subject to credit approval. Credit or debit balances in a customer's account(s) may be offset by any other outstanding balance owed by or to the customer. Please allow 4 to 6 weeks for delivery. Offer available while quantities last.

Your Privacy—The Harlequin® Reader Service is committed to protecting your privacy. Our Privacy Policy is available online at www.ReaderService.com or upon request from the Harlequin Reader Service.

We make a portion of our mailing list available to reputable third parties that offer products we believe may interest you. If you prefer that we not exchange your name with third parties, or if you wish to clarify or modify your communication preferences, please visit us at www.ReaderService.com/consumerchoice or write to us at Harlequin Reader Service Preference Service, P.O. Box 9062, Buffalo, NY 14269. Include your complete name and address.

ROM13R

NORA ROBERTS

28594	O'HURLEY'S RETURN	__	$7.99 U.S.	__	$9.99 CAN.
28592	O'HURLEY BORN	__	$7.99 U.S.	__	$9.99 CAN.
28590	SWEET RAINS	__	$7.99 U.S.	__	$9.99 CAN.
28588	NIGHT TALES:				
	NIGHT SHIELD & NIGHT MOVES	__	$7.99 U.S.	__	$9.99 CAN.
28587	NIGHT TALES:				
	NIGHTSHADE & NIGHT SMOKE	__	$7.99 U.S.	__	$9.99 CAN.
28586	NIGHT TALES:				
	NIGHT SHIFT & NIGHT SHADOW	__	$7.99 U.S.	__	$9.99 CAN.
28578	THE LAW OF LOVE	__	$7.99 U.S.	__	$8.99 CAN.
28172	WHISPERED PROMISES	__	$7.99 U.S.	__	$8.99 CAN.
28171	FOREVER	__	$7.99 U.S.	__	$9.99 CAN.
28170	REFLECTIONS & DREAMS	__	$7.99 U.S.	__	$8.99 CAN.
28169	HAPPY ENDINGS	__	$7.99 U.S.	__	$9.99 CAN.
28168	CHANGE OF HEART	__	$7.99 U.S.	__	$9.99 CAN.
28167	CHARMED & ENCHANTED	__	$7.99 U.S.	__	$9.99 CAN.
28166	PLAYING FOR KEEPS	__	$7.99 U.S.	__	$8.99 CAN.
28165	CAPTIVATED & ENTRANCED	__	$7.99 U.S.	__	$9.99 CAN.
28164	FIRST IMPRESSIONS	__	$7.99 U.S.	__	$9.99 CAN.
28162	A DAY AWAY	__	$7.99 U.S.	__	$9.99 CAN.
28161	MYSTERIOUS	__	$7.99 U.S.	__	$9.99 CAN.
28160	THE MacGREGOR GROOMS	__	$7.99 U.S.	__	$9.99 CAN.
28159	THE MacGREGOR BRIDES	__	$7.99 U.S.	__	$9.99 CAN.
28158	ROBERT & CYBIL	__	$7.99 U.S.	__	$9.99 CAN.
28156	DANIEL & IAN	__	$7.99 U.S.	__	$9.99 CAN.
28154	GABRIELLA & ALEXANDER	__	$7.99 U.S.	__	$9.99 CAN.
28150	IRISH HEARTS	__	$7.99 U.S.	__	$9.99 CAN.
28133	THE MacGREGORS: SERENA & CAINE	__	$7.99 U.S.	__	$9.99 CAN.

(limited quantities available)

TOTAL AMOUNT	$ _____
POSTAGE & HANDLING	$ _____
($1.00 FOR 1 BOOK, 50¢ for each additional)	
APPLICABLE TAXES*	$ _____
TOTAL PAYABLE	$ _____

(check or money order—please do not send cash)

To order, complete this form and send it, along with a check or money order for the total above, payable to Harlequin Books, to: **In the U.S.:** 3010 Walden Avenue, P.O. Box 9077, Buffalo, NY 14269-9077; **In Canada:** P.O. Box 636, Fort Erie, Ontario, L2A 5X3.

Name: _____

Address: _____ City: _____

State/Prov.: _____ Zip/Postal Code: _____

Account Number (if applicable): _____

075 CSAS

*New York residents remit applicable sales taxes.
*Canadian residents remit applicable GST and provincial taxes.

Silhouette®
Where love comes alive™

Visit Silhouette Books at www.Harlequin.com

PSNR0714BL